STORM BAY

Jessica Blair grew up in Middlesbrough, trained as a teacher and now lives at Ampleforth College on the edge of the North York Moors. Married, with three grown-up daughters and a son, she now devotes her time to writing. She is the author of many novels, including two set in Whitby: *The Red Shawl* and *A Distant Harbour*.

JESSICA BLAIR

Storm Bay

HarperCollins*Publishers*

HarperCollins*Publishers*
77–85 Fulham Palace Road,
Hammersmith, London W6 8JB

This paperback edition 1996

1 3 5 7 9 8 6 4 2

First published in Great Britain by
Judy Piatkus (Publishers) Ltd 1995

Copyright © Bill Spence 1995

The Author asserts the moral right to
be identified as the author of this work

ISBN 0 00 649661 X

Set in Linotron Sabon by
Rowland Phototypesetting Ltd,
Bury St Edmunds, Suffolk

Printed in Great Britain by
HarperCollinsManufacturing Glasgow

For
Joan
Anne, Geraldine, Judith and Duncan
with grateful thanks for
much happiness

If you wake at midnight, and hear a horse's feet,
Don't go drawing back the blind, or looking in the
   street,
Them that ask no questions isn't told a lie,
Watch the wall my darling, while the Gentlemen go by!

Five and twenty ponies,
Trotting through the dark —
Brandy for the Parson,
'Baccy for the Clerk;
Laces for a lady, letters for a spy,
And watch the wall, my darling, while the Gentlemen
   go by!

'A Smuggler's Song' by Rudyard Kipling

Chapter One

'Stop loitering, Jay! Night'll soon be on us and there's mist rolling in from the sea.' Concern rang in Emma's reprimand as she turned and saw her sixteen-year-old brother squat once again to examine something in the heather.

Irritated by a wisp of auburn hair, she pushed it into place under her hood. She shivered, and grasping her cloak with her long fingers drew it more closely to her. She hoped the autumn mists of 1762 weren't going to be as frequent as last year.

'Coming,' called Jay half reluctantly. He had just spotted an adder and wanted to take a closer look, but he knew Emma was right. The moor was no place to be caught in the dark especially if a sea roak closed in as it could do on this part of the Yorkshire coast, south of Whitby. He wasn't going to take the blame for getting them all lost. He straightened and ran after his sisters. 'Thee shouldn't have stayed so long,' he panted as he caught them up.

Annoyed by his criticism, Emma cast him a sharp glance but made no counter-remark. She understood the boyishness still left in him though in the last year he had moved rapidly towards adulthood and now shared more time with his father. Jay was growing fast and stood as tall as Amy, his other sister. He was filling out and bore the Dugdale characteristics of high cheekbones, square jaw and arched eyebrows.

'Jay's right,' agreed eighteen-year-old Amy, then couldn't resist the temptation to admonish her elder sister. 'When thee and Cousin Meg get yapping, thee doesn't know what time it is.'

Emma tightened her lips and quickened her pace. A frown marred the pretty features of her usually calm face. Although her sister and brother were old enough to look after themselves, she, at two years older than Amy, felt responsible for their safety.

Amy hummed quietly to herself as if she hadn't a care in the world. Emma sometimes envied the happy-go-lucky, relaxed attitude with which her sister always seemed to face life. Good humour was just as much a part of Emma but she had a serious side which came from being the eldest child.

Both with the Dugdale dimples, they were very much alike, though Emma was the taller by two inches, but it was their eyes and hair which differentiated them. Emma's auburn hair, inherited from her mother, was the envy of everyone, especially when the light made it glisten with a copper sheen. Amy's, a dusky black, tumbled to her shoulders like dark waves breaking on a seashore. Emma's deep brown eyes sparkled with life but could take on a penetrating seriousness when faced with problems, whereas Amy's blue eyes reflected the happy-go-lucky nature which sang in her heart.

Emma chided herself for staying late, but she always enjoyed visiting her aunt and uncle and time just flew when she was with Meg. When attending a small Academy for Young Ladies in Whitby, Emma had stayed with her relations and the two girls had become more like sisters; in fact, she felt closer to Meg than she did to Amy. Emma had found pleasure in experiencing a different way of life to that which she led on the farm though she was happy enough at home; the family was close-knit with loving parents, and she appreciated the hard work her father put in as a tenant farmer to give them a comfortable life.

John and Grace Dugdale had seized the opportunity fifteen years ago when a considerate landlord had offered them the tenancy of Beck Farm which nestled close to a stream in a small valley cutting into the North Yorkshire moorland plateau. The land in the valley was good and the moors offered grazing for sheep. John figured, with hard work to get the farm running as he wished, he could derive a comfortable living from it. An enlightened couple, John and Grace saw that it would also give them the opportunity to send their girls to the Academy and Jay to the Reverend Borrisow, who supplemented his meagre income with tuition. Accordingly they arranged for their offspring to stay with John's brother, Robert, and his family during the school terms.

Emma had settled immediately and was delighted with the opportunity to spend more time with her cousin and taste life in the home of one of Whitby's leading merchants.

Robert did not like farming and saw opportunity in the growing port of Whitby. Although isolated on the bleak Yorkshire coast by the harsh hinterland of moors, with little in the way of reasonable tracks across them, Whitby developed as an important port with its own ships, built beside the River Esk, plying its trade to all known corners of the world. Robert had seized his chance, and with astute judgement and a nimble brain soon became a successful merchant. He had married Matilda, only child of a flourishing trader who also owned two merchantmen plying their trade with Europe. When her father died Robert was able to amalgamate the two businesses to become one of the leading exporters and importers in the town. Now his sons, Simon at twenty-three and George at twenty, were helping to expand the business even further.

The lowering sun set the purple sea of heather ablaze, stretching to the horizon in the shimmering light, but Emma had no eyes for it. She was keeping a wary watch on the mist which hugged the cliff tops but a mile distant and was threatening to move inland.

After the climb out of Whitby, the five-mile walk home to Beck Farm was hard going on the rough tracks which threaded the moors. Though darkness might catch them before they reached home, Emma was certain she would have no trouble finding the last mile or so of trackway, but if the mist rolled in it could be a different matter. Mist brought with it a strange sense of disorientation.

Jay grumbled at her for urging him on, but Amy, though disgruntled at Emma for staying so long, kept her own counsel and matched her sister stride for stride.

Distant clouds hastened the dusk before the sun touched the horizon. The sparkle went from the landscape, leaving a seemingly lifeless terrain. No sheep bleated, no curlew broke the silence with its plaintive cry. At these heights there was usually a breeze, no matter how slight, but this evening even that was missing.

The mist swirled as if stirred by some unseen hand. It twisted and turned, wraithlike, sending clammy fronds gliding across the heather. Its movement quickened as it spread further inland and in a matter of moments it was waist high.

Emma shivered. She knew the moors, but darkness and mist gave them a new perspective, one which she usually avoided. Today she had been careless. While enjoying the company of her cousin she forgot the time and now was paying for her thoughtlessness. If the mist rose further they could be in trouble. In a darkened, mist-enshrouded land-scape, holes and gullies set traps for the unwary.

'Listen!' Amy stopped. She pushed her hood from her head. Her dark hair, which had been neatly tied back when she left home, tumbled in disarray to her shoulders. She inclined her head as if straining to catch a sound.

Her sister and brother looked questioningly at her.

'What is it?' asked Emma. She too slipped her hood back and pushed her hair behind her ears. She could hear nothing but knew that Amy was blessed with an acute sense of hearing and picked up sounds long before anyone else.

Unnerved by the strange look which had come to her face, Jay tugged at her sleeve.

4

She shook him off without altering her rigid stance. 'Shhh! There it is again.'

Emma concentrated to try to pick up the sound but without success.

Amy nodded. 'A galloping horse.'

A moment later Emma and Jay heard it. The drumming hooves penetrated the shroud of mist.

'There's something odd . . .' Emma kept her voice low, and her voice was uncertain as she tried to identify what it was.

Instead of the usual thrumming of a galloping horse, the beat was subdued, eerie. It came dully through the dank air which drifted ever more thickly around the three figures isolated on the moor.

'Look!' Jay's exclamation made his sisters jump. They glanced at him to see his eyes widen with fright and his outstretched arm shaking as it pointed across the moor.

They followed his gaze. A chill gripped Emma though her heart was pounding. Her terrified mind tried to make sense of what she was seeing. She must try to keep a grip on her feelings for the sake of the others.

'I'm off!' Jay's cry startled her.

She turned quickly and grabbed him as he started to move. 'No!' she yelled, knowing that to run blindly on the moors could prove fatal.

She held him and was aware of Amy coming closer, stiff with fright. Only an utmost effort of will made her stand her ground. The desire to run was intense but even if it had been wise to do so she doubted if her legs would have obeyed for they felt like paper.

All three of them stared at the apparition which moved across the moor through the swirling mist.

'Marten's Ghost!' Jay's voice was so petrified it scarcely passed his lips.

His sisters, transfixed, did not answer.

The fog rose silently, momentarily obscuring the white horse with its rider dressed in a white hooded cloak, then moved just as quickly to reveal that the apparition was no figment of their imagination. Man and animal moved as one, progressing swiftly across the moor.

Emma's body tensed, her mind telling her that no human dare ride at such speed in this fog. Besides, a real horse, at full gallop, did not make such a sound as that drifting across the moor.

The mist rose and closed around them like a shroud. The ghost had gone, veiled from their sight. Emma shivered. She was consumed by fear but fought the panic which threatened to overwhelm her. She must keep a level head for all their sakes. Though she felt chilled to the bone her hands were wet with sweat. Her neck was taut and her breathing came fast, trying to relieve the constriction in her chest.

'We must go before Marten's Ghost returns,' she urged.

All three knew the story of Marten whose ghost was supposed to haunt the moor, but none of them had ever seen it before.

Ten years previously Jonas Marten had lived in a cottage on Deadman's Howe, an isolated place which stood about a mile off the main trackway between Whitby and the inland market town of Pickering. Returning home after a late night drinking with acquaintances in Whitby, he became lost in the fog. He wasn't missed for several days and then a half-hearted search revealed nothing. Jonas Marten had disappeared off the face of the earth and no one gave him a second thought. Six months later a farmer, gathering sheep off the moor, stumbled across the remains of Jonas and his horse in a gully some distance off the trackway. It appeared he had lost his way, the horse had tumbled into the gully, breaking its leg, and had fallen on top of him. Now, it was said, he still rode the moor trying to find his way home. The superstition was that anyone who saw him ride back towards Whitby would die.

'Hold hands so no one gets lost,' Emma ordered firmly. 'We must get home before it returns.'

She felt Jay trembling as she took his hand, and Amy's was as cold as ice. No longer was she the easy-going girl of a few minutes ago, but was heartily glad that Emma was with them. Amy looked sideways at her and saw that, though worry lined her face, there was a reassuring determination to keep calm and protect her younger sister and brother.

'We'll be all right.' Emma struggled to sound reassuring. 'Be careful where thee walk.' She curbed the urge to hurry and made a determined effort to hold on to her sense of direction which could easily desert her.

Their progress was slow as the mist and the fading light combined to obliterate the narrow trackway.

'I wish we could gan faster,' moaned Jay. 'Ghost'll be back and then . . .'

'Hush!' snapped Emma, not wanting to hear the consequences attached to Marten's return.

'Hear anything, Amy?' he asked.

'No.' A tremor came to her voice as she added, 'Don't want to.'

They stumbled over some clumps of heather.

'Stop!' cried Emma. 'We're off the track. Stand still.' She knew that there were treacherous patches of bog among the heather and one false step could plunge them into a life-sucking morass. 'I'll find the track. Don't move.' She edged carefully backwards and in a few steps had lost sight of Amy and Jay as the fog seemed determined to separate them. A few more and she thought she had found the track. She inched sideways and then back again and felt certain she was right. 'I've found it,' she called reassuringly. 'Come slowly backwards. I'll keep calling.'

Within a few minutes the three were united, finding relief in each other's presence.

'This way,' said Emma, and neither of the others questioned her for they had both lost their sense of direction and now placed implicit faith in their sister's judgement.

But they had not taken a step when they heard a sound

behind them. With hearts beating fast they turned and froze in horror to see the form looming out of the mist. The urge to run was strong but their limbs seemed fastened to the ground with a binding which could not be broken.

The form began to take shape as it moved slowly towards them. A horse and rider. Jonas Marten . . . they were doomed! Fear gripped them. Tears began to trickle down Amy's cheeks. She did not want to die out here on the lonely moor. If only she had heard it coming! But she had been so preoccupied with listening to Emma's calls that she had not had ears for anything else. Jay wanted to shout for his father but no sound came as he stood frozen in dread of their fate. Emma tried hard to control her own feeling of impending doom for she knew she must show strength for them all in facing the unknown.

The mist swirled and parted, drifting away from the figure and allowing the truth to be revealed. Relief swept over all three. This was no ghost.

'Joe! Joe Wade!' Emma's voice was tight with relief. Liberated from fear, she did not know whether to laugh or cry. Beside her, Amy could do nothing but sob with the joy of seeing the familiar face of someone she thought of as more than a friend, though she kept this to herself. Jay gulped back the fright which had taken hold of him.

They all drew comfort from the presence of this tall broadshouldered man. There seemed to be power enough in his body to combat any ghostly apparition. The expression in his brown eyes bolstered their confidence. The set of his jaw showed a resolve to see them safely home no matter what must be faced.

'Emma! What on earth is thee doing here on a night like this?' Joe slid from the saddle and came quickly to her. He took her hands in his. She felt heartened by their work-roughened touch.

A pang of jealousy struck at Amy as Joe focused his attention to her sister. Secretly Amy loved him. Though she had tried to cast him from her heart because of Emma, his handsome features, his manliness touched with gentleness, straight nose, strong jaw and dark hair with a slight wave at the temples, all combined to fill her with longing.

'We've been visiting our relatives in Whitby and stayed longer than we should,' explained Emma. 'And we didn't expect fog.'

'Thee knows it can roll in at any time.' There was a mild rebuke in Joe's voice, but it was stemmed only from concern for the safety of the girl he loved.

'I know,' she admitted. 'And I'm so thankful to see thee. We've had a terrible fright.'

'Fright?' Seeing the pallor of Emma's face, he reached out with a comforting touch to her arm.

'We saw Marten's Ghost and thought thee was it returning, and thee knows what that means!' put in Amy, wanting to draw Joe's attention to herself.

'Nivver.' He gave a half laugh of doubt trying to dispel such thoughts from the minds of his friends. He knew the story as did all folk around Whitby, Robin Hood's Bay, the outlying villages and remote habitations.

'It's true,' insisted Amy. 'We all saw it, didn't we?'
Emma and Jay confirmed this.

'Then we'd best be getting home,' asserted Joe.

'Thee's sure of the way?' asked Emma.

'Leave it to Bonny here.' He patted the horse's neck. 'As long as I'm on her back she's sure-footed across these moors. Knows her way instinctively. Keep close.' He swung into the saddle, and when he was sure everyone else was ready, put Bonny into a walking pace.

Emma was thankful for Joe's presence and for the good fortune which had taken him to Whitby today, to return at this time.

Joe was the only child of David and Kate Wade who farmed Drop Farm in the next valley, two miles across the moors from the Dugdales. He was the same age as Emma. They had grown up together and shared many interests. Joe loved the land, loved exploring the countryside. From their early years he had encouraged her to accompany him on his explorations. It had gone on through their years of growing up. She had come to know the ways of the countryside largely through him as he passed on information taught to him by his father who had devoted much time to his only child. Joe showed her how to stalk deer, get close to a badger's sett, take salmon from the river; she learned which berries and roots were edible, and how to build a shelter from whatever was available.

Their parents expected the deep friendship to blossom into love and marriage, and for the couple to move into Drop Farm which would eventually be Joe's.

He loved Emma, had from his youth, but whenever he started to express his feelings or approach the subject of marriage, she always diverted his attention to something else.

Emma thought a great deal of him but her feelings did not run as deep as those she knew he held for her.

She liked Joe a lot. He was kind and thoughtful, ever ready to offer a helping hand to anyone in need. He was handsome in a rugged sort of way, his face browned by the sun, beaten by the wind and rain. A man used to the open, he liked nothing better than to be striding the moors, close to nature. He had a natural affinity with animals. Dogs, horses, cattle, and sheep all seemed to sense that understanding, while any moorland animal or bird trapped or hurt seemed to know he meant them no harm and succumbed to his gentle care. His far-seeing deep brown eyes showed joy when a vast landscape lay before him. Those same eyes looked tenderly upon Emma and only clouded over with frustration when she refused to make the final commitment to be his wife.

Emma knew that life with Joe would be safe and secure, that he would work hard at a job he loved to keep it that way. She would have his undying love and devotion and that would extend to any family they had. She knew him as a determined man who would keep on trying to persuade her to become his wife, but though she had nearly given way several times, always she had been held back by a memory from the past.

If people knew they would say that she was foolish to hold on to a love she had formed in childhood; a love, they would add, which had no chance of being reciprocated. But Emma still hoped that one day it would, and clung to her dream in spite of the fact that logic told her it was most unlikely.

She had first met Mark Roper when her longing to study Latin and Greek could not be answered at her own school. She had been directed to a house-bound scholar in Whitby for special tuition and found that Mark, son of Edwin Roper, a well-to-do Whitby merchant, was also receiving extra instruction in those languages which were beyond the scope of the private tutor he had at home. He had attracted Emma from the first day they met, for even at that early age his likeable personality and self-assurance were noticeable. For his part Mark liked the girl whom he saved from teasing town bullies, as they left the tutor's house, and soon they became firm friends. On Emma's part the friendship developed into a girlish love, one which suffered a bruising when Mark announced that his father was sending him to St Peter's School in York. There he would board and would only see her during the holidays. Even then their meetings were infrequent for he was in Whitby and she five miles away across the moors. But she was happy with their brief reunions, and the love which had come to her so young would not subsequently be extinguished.

It had, however, suffered one severe setback. When they were both fifteen Mark told her that his father was taking all the family to live in London. Emma was shattered and barely heard his explanation that his father had seen an opportunity to expand his firm, though it meant making a home in London and leaving a reliable manager in charge of the Whitby business. Grief-stricken, she kept her love a secret, told him she would never forget him, and ever since had carried his memory in her heart, the final barrier to committing herself to Joe. Even after five years, with never a word from Mark, she still clung to the hope that one day he would return to Whitby.

She had told herself over and over again that this hope was foolish. There might never be a reason to bring Mark back to Whitby. Besides, he had never shown any indication of loving her, only feeling as a friend should. Now he would be a grown man, brought up in the ways of the great city, and had probably forgotten her. He might even be married, would certainly have had a chance to pick and choose among the fine young women in London who no doubt would be more sophisticated than her, better suited to fit the new life he must have found in London.

Yet Emma could not forget those childhood days and the love which had been secretly in her heart all these years.

The fog thickened but Bonny unerringly kept to the track. Emma realised but for the timely arrival of Joe they would have been lost, and that could have had dire consequences. Joe kept up a stream of encouraging chatter to divert them from thoughts of their ordeal. They were only too pleased to have this reassurance.

As Emma listened to his gentle encouraging voice and saw in his presence a symbol of a secure and certain future, she wondered if she was being foolish not accepting his proposal. If she wasn't careful she could be left a spinster, facing a bleak and lonely future. It would never do to throw away the chance she had. Maybe she could come to love him in the way he would want her to as his wife, as devotedly as he undoubtedly loved her. Yet . . .

Her thoughts were interrupted as the track dipped and she guessed that they were moving down towards their farm but a few more minutes passed before Joe called out, 'We're there,' and she was able to make out a darker shape against the greyness of the mist.

The sound of Bonny's hooves on the cobbled yard

brought the door of the cottage swinging quickly open. Light from a lantern held high pierced the gloom and extended warmth and welcome. John and Grace Dugdale, anxious for their children, crowded the doorway. She moved in front of him, for his big frame filled the opening.

'It's them,' said John, his restless eyes piercing the mist. He laid a comforting hand on her shoulder and felt her relief. She wiped her hands down the white apron which, tied at the waist, covered her grey poplin dress, its sleeves turned back at the wrist.

'Ma! Pa!' Amy and Jay rushed to greet their parents while Emma stopped beside Joe.

'Thanks,' she said. 'I'm glad thee came along when thee did.'

Joe swung from the saddle. 'Only too pleased to be of service.'

'Come in until the fog clears,' offered Emma.

'That's tempting,' he returned, 'but it might last all night and Ma and Pa will be wondering what's happened to me.'

'Well, a warm drink afore thee gan on?'

'I wouldn't say no t' that. This fog gets into the bones.'

They hurried inside the house and closed the door on the unwelcome weather which shrouded the valley and the moorland heights.

'Where's tha been?' fussed Grace as she helped Amy out of her coat. 'We were worried sick when the mist came in.'

'My fault, Ma,' said Emma quickly before either of the others could make their accusations. 'Thee knows how it is when Meg and I get chattering.'

'There's some mulled wine in the pantry, Amy, warm some up for Joe,' said John, reaching for his pipe. 'How come thee was on the moor?'

'Been to Whitby,' he replied. 'Caught up with these three.'

'Glad thee did. We were worried . . .'

Jay's efforts to get a word in were going to be held

back no longer. 'Ma, Pa,' he interrupted. 'We saw Marten's Ghost!'

'Nonsense,' rapped John, his eyes reflecting his doubt.

'We did, Pa, we did,' cried Jay excitedly. 'Didn't we, Emma? Didn't we, Amy?'

John and Grace looked questioningly at their two daughters.

'He's right,' agreed Emma seriously.

'We did, Pa,' said Amy, a bottle of wine in her hand.

'Joe?'

'No, I didn't see it, but if the three of them . . .'

'Thee'd better stop here,' interrupted Grace, concern in her voice.

Joe gave a half smile. 'I'll be all right, Mrs Dugdale. I'll have that drink and be on my way.'

Amy was already attending to the wine but Grace, uneasiness showing on her face, went to take over as if she could hurry its warming.

'Where did thee see this ghost?' asked John with a frown.

'Across the moor on the main Whitby, Pickering track,' said Jay, eager to impart information.

'Could it have come fra Baytown?' his father asked, using the local name for Robin Hood's Bay.

'Might. Couldn't tell,' replied Jay.

Joe took his wine and drank it quickly, enjoying the warmth it sent down his throat and into his stomach. 'Thanks, Mrs Dugdale. Now I'll be off.'

'If thee's sure, lad?'

'Aye, I'm sure. Goodnight to thee all.' His gaze met Emma's and lingered for a moment.

Amy opened the door for him. 'Take care,' she said with quiet concern as he passed her.

The fog swirled, trying to encroach into the wellbeing of the cottage. Amy closed the door quickly.

'Hast thee see Marten's Ghost, Pa?' asked Jay with eager curiosity.

John and Grace exchanged glances.

'Aye, lad, I have more than once. It ain't a pretty sight close to.'

Jay's eyes were wide with astonishment. Emma and Amy had stopped what they were doing and were hanging on their father's every word.

'And I kept out of the way in case it came back.'

'Put the shutters up, John,' put in Grace seriously.

'Aye, lass, I will.' His glance took in his three children. 'And none of thee look outside 'til morning. Better not to see what thee might see!'

Chapter Two

Zac Denby's chest heaved as he hurried up the steep pathway which climbed between the cottages clinging to the
cliffside. He paused at the top to get his breath and glanced
over the red roofs, across the huge bay to the cliffs rising
to an awesome height at Ravenscar.

Baytown, or Bay as it was called by most local folk, had
been his home all his life. It had been a life of poverty, his
father earning little from his trade as a fisherman, and the
small amount of money he did get soon disappeared in
drink which he could not resist. It had eventually been his
undoing. In a drunken fit he had taken his boat out to sea
and had fallen overboard. The boat had been found empty
by two brothers from Bay who towed it back. Zac, though
only fifteen at the time, persuaded his mother not to sell
up and to let him take on the role of fisherman for the
family – his mother, and three brothers and two sisters, all
younger than himself.

The money he earned was often not enough but it was
more than they had ever had when his father had held the
responsibility. Life had been tough for Zac as a youngster
when he was often the butt of jokes because of his size;
even now at thirty he stood no more than five feet six. But
those who mocked and those who challenged soon learned
to their cost that Zac could take care of himself. The scar
down his left cheek and the black patch over his left eye
were evidence of his toughest battle but Bay people knew
they were a sign of victory, for his opponent had never
been seen again.

Word of his toughness, physical prowess and sharp,
nimble mind spread beyond his home territory. One day

when he brought his catch into Whitby to sell he was approached by a well-dressed stranger. Zac regarded him with suspicion as he climbed down from the quay on to Zac's vessel. Half an hour later, when the stranger left, a meeting with someone called The Fox had been arranged for the following evening at a cottage close to Sam Armstrong's farm near Stainsacre, between Robin Hood's Bay and Whitby. After that meeting Zac knew that, though the future would hold more risk, he would never be faced with poverty again. It had proved to be so over the last five years. Though his family was better off, Zac saw that they all kept up an outward appearance befitting his trade of fisherman, one he still kept as a cover for what he now regarded as his real occupation – smuggling.

At The Fox's behest he had organised a gang to run the land operation out of Robin Hood's Bay. Its isolation in the cliff-bound bay made it an ideal place in which to run contraband. The narrow streets, some little more than wide enough to allow the passing of a man, the houses and cottages climbing almost one on top of the other up the cliff face, made ideal hidey holes and escape routes whenever the Preventive Men or dragoons appeared.

Zac and his gang had Baytown in their pockets. From all outward appearances strangers would have thought this was only a community of fishermen plying their trade from the beach, sailing into Whitby with their catch and selling it before returning, or else taking it to Baytown from where their wives and daughters would transport it by pannier pony, often across the moors along the trackway known as the Fish Road or Old Wives' Trod, to the market town of Pickering.

In fact there was hardly a family who, either directly or indirectly, was not connected with the smuggling trade. They, like many of the recipients of the smuggled goods, no matter where they lived, regarded the flow of illicit merchandise as a necessity. The smugglers looked upon themselves as free traders and saw nothing wrong with avoiding obnoxious taxes imposed by the government. Besides, they were well paid by the unknown faces behind the smuggling, the men who had the influence and the brains to organise the whole operation from collection to distribution, the men who were out to make fortunes from backing this illegal trading.

But there were dangers attached and Zac knew them. He kept a tight grip on the people of Baytown and the surrounding area, smugglers or not. The community was so close-knit that no one would betray their neighbour, or if the thought ever crossed anyone's mind it was quickly dismissed for they knew Zac would show no mercy to an informer and their fate would be 'drowned at sea'. The same end awaited any one of the smuggling fraternity who tried to break free. Once connected with the smugglers, always connected.

Zac had his spies everywhere, not only to report the movements of the Preventive Men and dragoons but also to keep his eye on his own followers. His organisation had been such that in the five years he had been running the gang, no one had ever been caught by the authorities.

In the early days he had been tempted to check on the stranger who had approached him, and on The Fox, but had thought better of it for he soon realised that such a course would jeopardise his own livelihood. He realised that powerful and influential people must be behind the smuggling, for who else could arrange for contraband to be picked up on the Continent and know when it was due? And who else could set up a distribution network once Zac and his gang, a vital link in the chain, had run the goods to the lonely inn at Saltersgate between Whitby and Pickering, from where it could be spread throughout the surrounding countryside and beyond?

Whenever Zac received a message that 'Armstrong's cow was calving' at a specific time he knew that the Fox wanted to see him at the cottage near Sam Armstrong's farm.

He was on such a mission when he paused to look back over the bay to the frowning cliffs of Ravenscar.

His gaze moved northwards and he grunted with dissatisfaction to see the darkening clouds gathering in the granite sky. An irritating little breeze flicked him with clammy fingers, and from the pallor which was settling across the horizon Zac knew his return to Robin Hood's Bay would not be a pleasant one.

By the time he reached Armstrong's farm the first spots of rain were beginning to fall. He made his way to the cottage standing about two hundred yards from the farmhouse. Nothing stirred around the buildings. It was as if no living creature dared shatter the silence.

He skirted the farmyard wall, following his usual routine on these occasions. He entered the cottage by the front door, paused inside after he had closed it to become accustomed to the gloom, more marked this evening because dark clouds had closed in quickly on the last remnants of daylight. He crossed to the chair beside the table and noted, as he sat down, that as usual the connecting door to the back room was open. Armstrong had set the scene as he always did and Zac wondered once again if Sam was more deeply involved in the smuggling or whether his unused cottage was used merely as a convenient place for these meetings.

The wind freshened, moaning through the thatch and driving the rain with more ferocity. It penetrated the interior, adding a chill to the damp rooms.

The lifting of the sneck on the back door startled him. He had not heard the sound of horse's hooves which usually heralded the arrival of the man he knew to be the brains behind the smuggling but whom he had never seen. That was something The Fox had insisted on at their very first meeting here in this cottage. Though Zac had not liked the arrangement then, and never had, he knew he had to go along with it. And there was something in, 'What you don't know, Zac, can't harm you,' as the leader of the gang had told him.

Zac had wondered why The Fox needed to make contact with him personally but once again saw the wisdom of the man's words: 'Too many go-betweens can be trouble. If I give you instructions I know you've got them, and when I get your report I know I've got it exact.'

Zac heard the door close, heard footsteps move into the room and then a chair scrape as it was moved. Zac glanced towards the doorway but could see no one for, with his usual efficiency, Armstrong had placed Zac's chair so that he could not see the back door nor the chair on which the new arrival sat.

'Good evening, Zac.' The voice was firm and deep with a touch of harshness, a voice which spoke of authority, of one who would stand no nonsense, a man who must not be crossed.

'Evenin',' he returned. 'Ain't a pleasant one to be abroad.'

'It isn't. When I go I'll leave you a flask of brandy. Warm you for your walk back to Bay.'

Zac brightened at the thought. 'Thank thee. It'll keep the damp out my bones.'

'Any trouble last night?'

'None at all, Fox.'

'Ed Crosby was ready?'

'Aye. The goods were soon off the pack-horses and out of sight.'

'Good. Marten's Ghost ride?'

'Aye,' chuckled Zac, 'worked a treat again. Nivver saw a soul. Gullible folk are scared stiff and don't stir out of their homes. Those that know it as a sign of smuggling activity keep out of sight and keep their curiosity to themselves.'

'Good.' There was satisfaction in The Fox's voice. 'The ghost has served us well over the years. A good idea of yours.'

Zac strained to catch an intonation which would reveal The Fox's identity. He had often puzzled over it. Well spoken, well educated ... Landed gentry? Whitby merchant? Who? The question was still in his mind as The Fox broke some disturbing news.

His tone became serious. 'I've some bad news. More dragoons are being brought into the area.'

'Damn!' Zac's lips tightened with annoyance. It was bad enough having to avoid the three who had been drafted into the area to help the Preventive Men a couple of years ago, but now extra care and vigilance and cunning would be needed. 'Know where they're ganning to be stationed?'

'Two at Sandsend, two at Hinderwell, two at Runswick, two at Staithes.'

'All north of Whitby so won't bother us too much,' commented Zac, marvelling that The Fox had such detailed information even before the dragoons had moved in.

'But ten are to patrol the area between Whitby and Bay and they're in addition to those already doing so.'

Zac gasped. This number was totally unexpected. 'Seems the Revenue Men are alarmed by our activities. But we'll cope with 'em.'

'See that you do. There's a run from France a week today.' His voice hardened. 'You know what failure means – someone will have to pay.' The menace and threat were unmistakable. In spite of his own merciless attitude it sent a chill to Zac's bones. He knew from the past that The Fox showed no mercy to failures and that his sadistic streak revelled in hearing reports of how Zac had dealt with those who went against the smuggling fraternity.

'I'll find more secure places for the contraband in and around Bay.'

'They'll need to be good,' warned The Fox. 'More dragoons will mean more patrols, more search parties.'

'I may use another method of moving contraband as well as the pack-horse trains.'

'What's that?' asked The Fox guardedly.

'Pedlars returning to Pickering from Bay and Whitby.'

'Risky,' snapped The Fox. 'More people involved.'

'I'll be careful in my choice.'

'You'd better be, or you'll answer for any mistakes,' assured The Fox, his voice spelling doom if anything went wrong.

'I know several pedlars who wouldn't say no to some extra money, no matter how they make it. And there'll be others.'

'It could work.' The Fox's nimble mind had been visualising the possibilities. 'It would mean some of the contraband could be moved straight to Pickering without using Crosby at Saltersgate. We'd have a greater dispersal of goods. Try it.' He paused then went on icily, 'But whoever you use, warn them of the consequences should they fail, and you keep it in mind too.'

As Amy straightened from filling the bucket at the stream, a movement at the top of the hill beyond the cottage caught her attention. She shielded her eyes against the afternoon sun and saw the figure of a man break the skyline. Followed by two laden ponies, he set off down the hill towards their house.

Excitement coursed through her and she broke into a run, not caring that the water which slopped from the bucket was drenching the bottom of her dress.

'Ma! Ma!' she yelled breathlessly as she raced into the cobbled yard.

Grace, roused by the commotion, left her ironing and flung open the kitchen door. 'What is it, Amy?' she cried, brushing a wisp of hair from her forehead with the back of her hand.

'A pedlar, Ma! A pedlar!' She dropped the bucket, splashing more water over the side.

'Calm thyself, lass. No need for syke ganning on,' said Grace. Even though she too felt a surge of pleasure at the visit of a pedlar, she did not want to show it. Her visits to Whitby and the shops were very infrequent and she made most of her purchases from pedlars who called at the farm on their way to and from Baytown and Whitby.

'Pedlar coming?' Emma queried excitedly, her eyes lighting up at the prospect as she burst into the kitchen from the house where she had been dusting.

'He'll be here soon,' cried Amy, unable to keep still.

'Thee ganning t' buy some curtain material, Ma?' asked Emma.

'Aye, and maybe summat else,' she replied, a twinkle in her eye.

'What, Ma, what?' cried both daughters with enthusiasm for they sensed a secret project in Grace's mind which would see fulfilment with the pedlar's visit.

'Never thee mind,' she said. 'Now in with thee, get the kettle on. He'll be ready for a drink.'

Amy filled the kettle and hung it on the reckon over the bright red fire in front of which irons were heating. Grace removed the basket of unironed clothes from the scrubbed table in the middle of the room while Emma set plates and cups for them all.

By the time they heard the footsteps in the yard the kettle had boiled, the tea was mashed and there were plates of bread, scones and cakes on the table.

Grace adjusted her white mob cap and opened the door. 'Ah, it's thee, Tom Oakroyd. Glad I am t' see thee. Come away in. Kettle's just boiled.'

'Thank thee, ma'am,' said Tom, slipping out of his leather jerkin. He was a tall well-built man of more than average proportions, and in spite of his itinerant life he was clean and tidy. His ruddy face broke into a broad smile when he saw the array of food on the table. He always got a warm welcome at Beck Farm and liked the taste of Grace's baking. He stepped into the kitchen to be greeted by Emma and Amy, eager to wait on him and get the refreshments over so that they could clear the table for him to display his wares. 'Thee all gets bonnier every time I come here.' Tom knew how to get and keep his female customers in a good mood and increase the likelihood of a better sale.

He lowered his broad frame into the chair Amy had pulled out from under the table. Emma poured his tea and Grace sat down opposite him.

'I hope thee has summat nice to show us?'

'I have. Oh, I have,' replied Tom, reaching for some bread.

'But?' Grace frowned, suspicious of the haste he had made to reassure her.

Tom looked sheepish. 'Well, I'm on my way back from Baytown so . . .'

'Thee hasn't much left,' Grace finished his sentence for him with a touch of admonishment. 'Shame on thee, Tom Oakroyd. Aren't I always a good customer?'

'Oh, aye, thee is, but I couldn't call on my way to Bay as I usually do, I'm sorry, but I still have a few nice pieces of cloth left.'

'And some ribbon?' put in Amy hopefully.

Tom brightened. 'Oh, aye, lassie, I've a rainbow of ribbons, just right to set off that fine hair.'

Amy's face broadened into a smile but Emma's remained doubtful. Her mother had promised her new curtains for her bedroom but maybe Tom wouldn't have what she wanted now the choice was restricted.

She watched him eat his fill, and listened to the news he brought, with her mind on the material she hoped he might still have.

'All right, lasses, clear the table,' said Grace when she saw that Tom had eaten his last cake and drained the final drop of tea from his cup. 'Tom, thee bring in what thee has to offer, less though it may be.' She put a note of disappointment in her voice, hoping it might give him a guilty feeling and thereby make him generous with his charges.

He pushed himself up from the table and when he returned to the house the table was clear.

Amy gasped and her eyes widened with awe as he scattered ribbons of every colour across the table, making a shining rainbow against the wood.

'Take thy pick, lassie,' laughed Tom, delighted at the reaction he had caused.

Amy glanced at her mother. 'Can I, Ma?'

'Of course.' Grace could not dampen her daughter's desire for she too was attracted by the colourful display.

'Thee choose, and the first one is free. One for thee too, Emma.' Tom glanced at Grace. 'Anything thee's really needing?'

'Some cloth, for curtains and dresses,' she replied fingering the ribbons.

Emma and Amy exchanged astonished glances. Was this the surprise their mother had kept secret. 'Dresses, Ma?' they both cried excitedly.

'We'll see,' replied Grace calmly, with a wry smile.

The pedlar left the house and returned with four bolts of cloth. 'There's not much choice, sold most of it in Bay. Sorry about that.'

As he placed the cloth on the table disappointment filled Emma. There was nothing like the curtain material she had been hoping for.

'Oh, Ma.' She bit her lip as she looked at her mother, who knew how her daughter felt.

'Tom, there's nowt here for the curtains I want for Emma's room. She has her heart set on a yellow print like her cousin has in Whitby.'

'Sorry,' he apologised. 'I know exactly what thee wants. I'll bring some next week.'

'Very well,' said Grace. 'Don't thee go forgetting. And call here before thee gans to Bay.'

'I will,' replied Tom. He glanced out of the window. 'Is thee interested in any of this cloth?'

Grace was examining the material. She looked over her shoulder at Emma. 'This would make thee a nice winter dress,' she suggested, wanting to alleviate her daughter's disappointment.

Emma's eyes brightened.

'Does thee like it?' Grace prompted.

'Yes, Ma.' She held the dark green cloth against her. 'Suit me?'

'Aye, lass, it does,' her mother confirmed. 'It sets thy hair off beautifully, and if thee crochets thyself a nice white collar it'll look reet grand.'

'Thee'll be a picture in it. I can just see that young man of thine takin' a fresh fancy t' thee,' put in Tom, eager to make a sale. He turned his attention briefly to the yard.

'Very well, and what about this for thee, Amy?' Grace indicated a plum-coloured worsted.

Amy diverted her concentration from the kaleidoscope of ribbons. 'Oh, Ma, can I have it?' she asked eagerly as she took the cloth which her mother had chosen. She would have liked something more patterned but this was Joe's favourite colour and she'd make sure he noticed it in spite of what the pedlar had said about Emma's material. She fingered it. 'It's lovely, and just my colour.'

'Very well.' Grace nodded at Tom.

'Thank thee, ma'am,' he confirmed the sale.

'What about thee, Ma?' asked Emma. She noticed Tom look out of the window again as she turned to her mother.

'I'll wait 'til Tom's next visit,' she replied.

'And I'll bring thee cloth that'll mak' thy blue eyes sparkle,' he said with flattering exuberance.

'Ah, thee'll say that to all thy customers!' Grace smiled.

'I'll fetch in some pins, needles and cotton,' he said, glancing out of the window again as he went to the door. He stepped outside, closing the door behind him.

Curious to see why Tom kept glancing out of the widow, Emma watched him cross the yard and saw her father approaching the house. She saw the two men exchange greetings and then go into a deeper conversation which from the look on their faces had a much more serious tone than friendly banter. Had Tom wanted a quiet word with her father? Though why he should want to she could not guess. Maybe she was imagining things. She turned her mind and eyes back to her green material and imagined what the dress would be like.

'Good day, Tom.' John Dugdale eased his muscles as he gave the pedlar a friendly greeting. 'Hope thee isn't making the women folk spend ower much money,' he added with a grin.

'Every man to his trade,' returned Tom with a smile. 'But it's thee I wanted to see.'

'Me?' John was curious. He had never had much to do with the pedlar though knew him from previous visits so he was puzzled by the seriousness which had clouded the man's usually bright and amiable expression.

'Aye. I was hoping thee'd appear while I was here otherwise I'd have had to hang around waiting for thee and that wouldn't have looked right.'

'So, what's this all about?' pressed John.

'I have a message from Zac Denby for thee.'

'Zac Denby? For me?' John was even more puzzled.

'Aye. Thee knows him?'

'Knows of him. Who wouldn't around these parts?'

'Fisherman.'

John gave a little laugh. 'Aye, and more besides as I think thee well knows. No regular visitor to the Bay could escape knowing Zac's true occupation.'

'Least said about that the better,' returned Tom.

'Aye, I agree,' said John. 'So what's the message he's sending me?'

'He wants to meet thee.'

'Me? What for?'

'He didn't tell me that. Just said to say he'll meet thee tonight in Black Wood after the owl hoots three times, followed by four sharp hoots and one long one.'

John frowned. Why was a known smuggler, leader of

the notorious gang which operated out of Robin Hood's Bay, wanting a meeting with him under such strange circumstances?

'Thee can't tell me more?'

'I know nowt else. Thee doesn't query the likes of Zac Denby. Thee does as he asks without question. I've done that, now it's up to thee.' With that Tom hurried back to the house with the goods he had extracted from one of the baskets strapped to the side of his lead pony.

John followed him, his mind on the mysterious demand.

Chapter Three

Emma turned in her bed to gaze at the small four-paned window. Unusually, sleep eluded her. After a day helping her mother with household chores and carrying out her outdoor duties around the farm she was usually asleep as soon as she laid her head on the pillow and was not awake until her mother's call the following morning. At first she put it down to the pedlar's visit and the excitement of a new dress and new curtains for this room after his next visit. But tonight she had been uneasy, restless, and it annoyed her not to know why.

Something was not right. She could not say what it was but instinctively she felt the usual nightly calm which settled over the farmhouse was not there. Maybe she was being foolish. Maybe the feeling was being created by an overactive mind unable to banish everything in sleep.

The pedlar came constantly to mind and she recalled his frequent glances out of the window and what had appeared to be a serious conversation with her father. It was almost as if Tom had been looking out for his arrival so that he could speak with him alone.

She tried to banish such thoughts, blaming an overactive imagination.

The moon sent a stream of silvery light through the window. Emma's eyes flicked around the room. The oak chest of drawers and its matching wardrobe seemed to mock her with their sense of solidity. Nothing was wrong, surely? The small table with its bowl and ewer filled with water, ready for the morning, indicated a routine which wouldn't be disturbed.

An owl hooted. She turned her gaze back to the window

as the light was momentarily usurped by the shadow of a passing cloud. She shuffled in her bed, trying to find a more comfortable position to induce sleep.

The owl hooted again, paused, then sent its eerie note across the countryside once more. Four sharp hoots followed and then one drawn out.

Emma was alert. That was no owl. If she hadn't been wide awake she would not have noticed the unusual aspect of what should have been a natural sound. No one unfamiliar with the ways of nature and especially of owls would have noticed, but she loved the countryside and its life and knew far more than most about the ways of animals and birds.

A signal? But why? Who? She slipped from her bed and tip-toed quietly to the window. Moonlight flooded the yard at the back of the house and patterned the ground with shadows from the stables, byres and barns.

She froze, hardly daring to breathe as she heard footsteps, trying so hard to proceed without a sound, pass the door of the bedroom. She inclined her head listening intently. The footsteps went down the stairs.

Who was moving about at this time of night, for she reckoned it must be past midnight. Mother? Father? Amy? Jay?

She heard the sneck on the back door give a faint click. She would not have heard it if she had not been listening so hard. The door shut and she saw her father cross the yard quickly to the gate in the low wall. What was he doing? Where was he going? He was dressed as if for work. Was this unusual occurrence at the bottom of her disturbed night? Was it something to do with his talk with Tom? Had something impinged on her mind to alert her to these strange happenings?

Emma was not a person to ignore something unusual. Her curiosity had been raised and she wanted answers. Though she knew she should creep back into bed and forget everything, she also knew she was not about to do so.

30

She saw her father head across the field in the direction of Black Wood.

She dressed quickly, opened the door quietly and, being extra careful, reached the bottom of the stairs without making a sound. She took her woollen cloak from a peg beside the door, wrapped a shawl around her head and stepped outside.

As she moved into the field, clouds unveiled the moon to reveal her father still on the path for Black Wood. She paused, weighing up the best way to follow him. If she kept to the path and he looked back he was sure to see her. The hedge a hundred yards to the right, which ran as far as Black Wood, could give some cover and provided she was careful, using all the skill Joe Wade had taught her, she should be able to stalk him as far as the trees. After that she would have to take things as they came.

She moved swiftly alongside the dry stone wall which ran from the farm to the hedge, keeping to a crouched run so that she did not break the height of the wall with her figure. Joe had always taught her never to break a skyline and to be sure to merge in with the countryside as much as possible.

She reached the hedge and, using its shadows and cover, started after her father. As he neared Black Wood, she quickened her pace. She must not lose sight of him. There were several ways out of the wood and unless she saw which one he took she could miss him.

Clouds moved across the moon plunging the wood into impenetrable darkness. She stepped more cautiously. Then she was amongst the trees. Five more yards and she stopped, wary of going on when her father was not in sight. If only the clouds would allow shafts of moonlight to filter through the trees. She cursed her luck. So far everything had gone well but now the advantage she'd had was slipping away. She recalled Joe's advice: 'Be patient. If things are difficult for thee then they are just as difficult for the person thee's following.'

Emma waited, listening with deep concentration for any sound which might indicate where her father was. Slowly moonlight moved across the fields. Then it was weaving through the trees, penetrating the canopy of foliage. It filtered revealingly into the spaces. She stiffened as it showed John Dugdale standing about twenty yards ahead and a little to the left. Another yard either way and he would have been hidden by a tree. Emma blessed her good fortune. She stepped carefully to her right to the shelter of a tree and, crouching in the undergrowth, concentrated her observation on her father.

Questions pounded in her mind. Why had he stopped? He was showing no inclination to move on. Was he waiting for someone? Maybe the person who had imitated an owl? But more than anything, what was he doing here at this time of night? He remained perfectly still only turning his head now and again as if looking for something or someone to move from the shadows of the wood.

She stood, her ears straining, listening for the slightest sound. When it came she almost missed it. Only someone trained to catch those tell-tale intrusions on silence would have heard the faint snap of a fallen twig. Her father had not heard it for he remained with his head turned to the left, oblivious to the sound which had come from the right and a little ahead of him.

Emma glanced skywards, hoping that the clouds would not cast a gloom over the meeting. The moon remained clear and no clouds would blot out its light for a little while. She intensified her gaze on her father and beyond.

'John Dugdale?' The whisper, barely audible, cut through the sharp night air.

Emma saw her father start, taken by surprise, and turn sharply in the direction of the voice.

'Aye.' His reply was low.

A moment passed and a figure stepped from behind a tree. Whoever it was had come within ten yards of him without his knowledge. Even Emma was surprised how close the stranger had got without another sound after that distant, unintentional breaking of a twig.

The man was short and stocky, probably six inches shorter than her father who touched six feet. Even in the moonlight she could detect the power in him and reckoned he was a man who could take care of himself. He half turned and the moonlight revealed a craggy face with a scar down his left cheek and a black patch over his left eye. She gasped for she recognised Zac Denby, a Bay fisherman, reputed smuggler, head of a gang who had escaped any attempt by the Preventive Men to catch him.

Her father associating with a smuggler! What was he thinking about? What was he risking? Deportation! She shuddered at the thought. The family would be ruined. They would be outcasts with no one to turn to, nowhere to go. Their life was good, certainly much better than the poverty she had seen in Whitby, and though they may not be as well off as the merchants and whaling captains in the busy port, they were comfortable. Why was her father risking all he had worked for, all that her mother did to see that he and his family were well clothed and well fed with a comfortable home to live in? It may not be as luxurious as that which her uncle Robert had in Whitby, something she occasionally envied in a small way without being discontented with her own lot. But now that life was being jeopardised by, of all people, the father who had formed the solid foundation, the core, of their comfort and wellbeing.

Emma shuddered. She was not cold but instinctively she pulled her shawl tighter around her as if seeking protection from the unknown which in her mind heralded the worst.

The two men appeared to be deep in conversation, their voices low. She strained to hear but, although she could hear the murmur of voices, could not distinguish one word. How she wished she had been nearer, but to move now might mean discovery and that could be fatal. Her father would drum up some excuse and she would never know the real reason for his rendezvous with Zac Denby.

She saw him point to the left and Denby nod. A moment later both men set off in that direction. They moved stealthily but without attempting to disguise their passage. Emma immediately seized on the advantage it gave her for, although she would follow with much more caution, their sound would disguise any that she might accidentally make. She blessed her luck that they thought they were not followed.

John and Zac reached the edge of Black Wood and stopped to survey the open ground ahead. Satisfied, they moved sharply forward with the air of determination which comes from wanting to reach an objective as quickly as possible. Emma realised they were making for a small stone barn which stood close to the edge of the land farmed by her father.

She was puzzled. The barn was in a state of disrepair and her father never used it. So why was he going there in the company of a known smuggler at this time of night? She must find out, but to cross the open ground risked discovery.

She weighed up the situation quickly but without the hurry which might lead to a wrong decision. She saw she could make her way closer to the barn by using the wood to the right. It swung round to the hedge which ran behind the barn and from there she would be about fifty yards away. The two men were halfway across the open ground. She must hurry.

Keeping to the edge of the wood she weaved her way quickly through the trees. She was a little over halfway to her objective when she saw the men reach the barn. They disappeared inside. She broke into a run, reached the hedge and, with the side of the barn affording her security from being seen by anyone inside, sprinted the last fifty yards. Trying to stifle any sound of her heavy breathing she edged her way along the wall to the front of the barn. She paused at the corner and listened. Hearing no sound from inside the barn she moved quietly to the doorway.

The old wooden door had long since fallen down and been thrown to one side. She moved with the utmost caution to the opening. She paused and listened. Her heart beat faster. It seemed to thump with a thunderous sound and she felt sure her father and Zac would hear her. Her whole body was tense with the fear of being discovered. A desire to flee, to run and get away from it all, seized her but she fought it down. She must know why her father was here. Voices reached her but they seemed muffled. She sank slowly to her knees and bent forward to look round the corner of the doorway. In that position, below eye level, she would be less noticeable.

She started with shocked surprise when she peered into the dark recesses of the barn. A flickering light came from one corner but it was coming from below the ground! There must be a cellar, a cave or an underground passage, and her father must have had a lantern hidden here. She scrambled to her feet and stepped cautiously into the barn, inching forward until she could pick up the conversation coming from the depths of the earth.

'This place is perfect. If I'd known it was here I'd have recruited thee long ago. Thee could have been makin' a fortune all this time.' Zac's chuckle, touched with delight, came from deep within his throat.

'I wanted nowt to do wi' smuggling, but now I hear there might be a chance to buy my farm I'm willing to listen to thy proposition.'

'Thee'll be well paid for the use of this place.'

'Aye, maybe, but what do I have to do?'

'Thee'll get to know when goods are being landed. See that some of them are stored here. We're altering our arrangements to move the goods inland. All thee needs to know is that when a pedlar calls on thee, if he has red, white and blue ribbons tied to the left hand basket on his lead horse, thee gives him contraband according to the list he'll give thee.'

John hesitated then said, 'Right.'

'Good.' There was satisfaction in Zac's voice.

Emma stifled her gasp at the news she had just overheard.

'Anyone else know about this place?' asked Zac cautiously.

'No,' replied John.

'Not even thy family?'

'No. I discovered it shortly after I took this farm. Came to see if the barn was any use. It wasn't worth repairing so I was prepared to forget it. But I took a look round just before I was leaving and stumbled across this cellar, cave, call it what thee will. I covered the entrance up and have only been down here occasionally to keep an eye on the place. Kept a lantern hidden down here for that purpose.'

'And thee did a good job. I'd never have suspected there was an underground chamber.'

'Aye, an' we'll leave it like that when we gan. No one will find it.'

'Good.' Emma heard the note of glee in Zac's voice as he went on, 'Off the ship, on to the beach, through Bay and Black Wood to here. There's only that one piece of open ground. It's ideal!'

'So, how much?'

'Ah, I'll have to check that with The Fox.'

'Fox?'

'That's the only name I know him by.'

'Can I meet him?' asked John.

'Nay. No one outside his group of gentlemen know him. I've never seen him face to face but he'll not deal with anyone else but me. Leaves all the arrangements to me except disposing of the goods and of course the dates when they're due. He tells me when and I set up the operation. Once the goods are hidden I wait 'til he tells me how and when to dispose of them. So they might be cleared out of here quickly or they might be here awhile.'

'Price he'll give me?' John asked again.

36

'Leave that to me. We have a string of hiding places but this is the best. He'll pay well for this.'

'All right.' A note of warning came into John's voice. 'But don't thee try to outdo me over the money.'

Zac laughed harshly. 'Nor thee ower the contraband. Try to an' the Gentlemen will wreak an awful revenge.'

The ominous words bit deep into Emma's mind. Her father had committed himself through this meeting and he was caught between two threatening forces. Annoy the smugglers and he was doomed. Get caught by the Preventive Men and he would face transportation. If either of those courses happened she and the rest of the family would suffer, their life would be torn apart. Oh why had he done it? He wanted his own farm, she knew that, but it had always seemed a distant dream. More than likely that ambition had been spurred on by seeing the success of his brother. There had never been any sign of envy or jealousy, the brothers had always been close. So why was her father prepared to risk the safe and comfortable life they had for the sake of having his own farm?

'When's the first time thee'll be using this place?' John asked.

'Now that I can't tell thee but it'll be fairly soon. I'll get word to thee, then that night thee waits for my signal, same as tonight. Thee then comes straight here and waits the arrival of the contraband. Stack it in the barn and when everyone's gone thee and I will put it below ground. That way only us two and the leader of the Gentlemen will know about it. Now, let's be away.'

Emma scurried quickly out of the barn and raced for the nearest covering of trees. She figured she'd be out of sight before her father and Zac left the barn. They had to make sure the entrance to the cavern was undetectable.

Once in Black Wood, she paused to regain her breath. She knew she must be home before her father, and once she set off lost no time in reaching the house where the comforting silence seemed to breathe an air of doubt about what she had witnessed. Had she really heard her father make a deal with the smugglers?

She moved silently to her room and slipped into bed but sleep did not come for she was listening for footsteps. They came about twenty minutes later. Her father was back. But even then she could not settle. Her mind was disturbed by the horror of what might happen to the family.

She wished there was some way of stopping her father. But what could she do? If she confronted him with what she knew he would swear her to secrecy. She could not confide in her mother. Maybe she knew about it and either condoned it or, if she didn't, was helpless to prevent it. And if her mother knew nothing about her father's plans, Emma could not bring her the worry which would go with the knowledge. Amy? Jay? She couldn't betray her father to any of them. Joe? No. Although she felt she could trust him implicitly it would mean someone outside the family knew and that must not happen. Emma was lost for a solution.

Chapter Four

Tom Oakroyd had been gone from Beck Farm only half an hour when he realised that he would not make the fifteen miles to Pickering before nightfall. Waiting for John Dugdale had delayed his journey longer than he had hoped. However he had made a good sale and had an order which he would fulfil on his next journey so he was in good spirits when he decided to seek shelter for the night at the cottage on Deadman's Howe.

He had never used it before, always timing his journey so that he was across the moors before the light faded. But he had heard of pedlars who had stayed there so when he sighted the howe he left the main trackway and followed a narrow path which weaved across the bleak landscape.

Little wind stirred the heather and even that ceased as he neared the howe. Clouds hung low like a grey pall. Tom paused to get his bearings for as yet the cottage was not in sight. His usually cheery whistle had faded from his lips and his bright countenance had dimmed with a serious appreciation of the loneliness of this place. Silence enshrouded the howe, as if nothing dare break the mysterious atmosphere which Tom felt seeping into his mind. Deadman's Howe. Why so named? Tom had never bothered to raise the question but now he wondered. He shuddered and then cursed himself for allowing his mind to entertain such thoughts.

He started forward but his two pack-horses resisted. He tugged at the rein. 'Not thee too,' he muttered to himself. He almost decided to turn back but then taking a grip on his feelings he said, 'Come on, there'll be shelter for thee.' His gentle tone soothed the animals and although he could still sense some reluctance in them they followed him.

Darkness was gathering as he reached the howe, a large rounded rise encroaching on the surrounding moorland plateau. A finger-like extension ran towards him and turned as if attempting to put a barrier across the path to keep out intruders.

His step faltered. He felt uneasy. The atmosphere around the howe seemed to press down on him. He felt a presence as if someone was close by. He glanced around tentatively, half expecting to see a stranger, but there was no one. He straightened, taking a grip on himself. Ridiculous for a man like him, a match for anyone, to be feeling like this.

He moved on, more slowly. The path curved to the right then swung to the left, and as he rounded the howe some relief eased the beating of his heart. A light shone from the window of a cottage a short distance away. His step became brisker with the thought of food, rest and shelter for the night.

Reaching the tumble-down stone wall which surrounded an unkempt piece of land on which the cottage stood, he paused and surveyed the property with some misgiving. As far as he could make out in the gloom the cottage was not in a bad state of repair though a few stones were missing from the walls and a piece of sacking hung over the window on the left-hand side of the door. The light from the right-hand window revealed a tattered curtain and spilled out to make the dark purple berries of deadly night-shades, which grew beneath the window, twinkle with a sheen which seemed to be mocking him. Tom shuddered.

He would have turned and left in spite of the difficulty of returning to the main track in the dark but the door opened and a voice called out with a harsh cackle: 'Come away in wi' thee.' Tom started. It was as if he had been expected, as if he was known to be there, but he had seen no one look out of the window. 'Come, young man, the moor's no place t' be on syke a dark night.' Tom thought he detected a chuckle of satisfaction in the words.

He stepped through the opening in the wall where once there had been a wooden gate which now lay broken beside the path, with two shattered spars pointing upwards like a bird's broken wing.

The woman who greeted him was small and thin. Her shoulders stooped, giving the impression that she was hump-backed. The light from the oil lamp touched half her face leaving the rest in deep shadow accentuating the hollow cheeks and deep eye sockets from which large eyes peered with a malevolent pleasure. 'Welcome to the cottage on Deadman's Howe,' she said in a low voice which cracked with a harsh lilt. She stepped to one side allowing Tom to enter.

He found himself in a large room with a fire burning cheerily which counteracted his sombre arrival. Though the furnishings were not all they might be they seemed serviceable and comfortable enough. Three chairs, one of them a rocking chair, stood in a semi-circle before the fire. A large scrubbed table occupied the centre of the room and on one wall there was a dresser on which there stood a scattering of pots. On an oak chest of drawers a clock ticked with an hypnotic rhythm.

There were feminine touches about the room which he thought could not have come from the woman who had greeted him. He realised he was not wrong when from a door on the right a tall young woman appeared, moving with a certain gliding grace. She held herself erect and smiled at him with a welcome which put him at his ease and instantly banished all the doubts and forebodings he had had. And yet after a few moments the contrast between her and her surroundings, and between her and the figure which had come to the door brought back an uneasiness.

'Welcome to the cottage on Deadman's Howe.' She made the same greeting, but her voice was soft and caressing. 'Thee'll be wanting a bed for the night? The moors are no place to be at this time.' Her blue eyes sparkled as she assessed him.

'Aye, lass is reet.' The older woman had come up beside him. 'Mak' thissen at home. Thee's welcome.'

Tom glanced at her and saw her hair was lank and unkempt, in marked contrast to that of the younger woman. Hers tumbled to her shoulders like a moorland stream browned by the peat.

'Thanks,' he replied. 'I was late leaving Bay, realised I wouldn't make Pickering before dark. I heard thee had accommodation for pack-horse men?'

'So we have,' cackled the older woman. 'So we have.' She gave a deep-throated chuckle as she started to shuffle towards a rocking chair at one side of the fire. She stopped and half turned and flung a question at Tom. 'What's thy name?'

'Tom Oakroyd,' he replied.

She nodded. 'I'm Eliza Petch and this 'ere's me daughter Phoebe.' She went to the chair, sat down and started to rock which sent up a monotonous squeak to combat the ticking of the clock.

'Thee'd like something to eat?' asked Phoebe.

'Aye, I would that,' replied Tom. 'This moorland air makes me hungry.'

'The stew is nearly ready for thee.'

She disappeared through the door from which she had appeared and soon an appetising smell was drifting into the room.

'Thee been a pedlar long?' Eliza asked.

'All my life. Followed my father.'

'So thee finds it a good trade?'

'Aye. And this time it's been one of my best ever.' Tom was so pleased with the sales he had made that he readily admitted it.

'Good, good,' said Eliza. She rubbed her bony hands together.

Phoebe came into the room and quickly set the table for him before returning to the kitchen.

'I'd better see to my ponies,' said Tom, rising from his chair.

'No need,' replied Eliza. 'My son Dick will see to them. He'll be here in a few minutes. Went to get the stable ready when we reckoned thee'd be coming.'

A chill touched him. There was something uncanny about the whole thing. Eliza had greeted him as if he was expected. Phoebe had the stew nearly ready and Dick had started on the stable before he had arrived. It was as if this family, or one of them, could see into the future witch-like. He stared at the woman rocking in her chair. Could she be?

A meow startled him from his thoughts but then added to them when he saw a long-haired jet black cat come into the room. It walked slowly towards him, stopped and stared straight into his eyes, turned, jumped on to Eliza's knee and settled itself so that it could watch him with unblinking eyes. Tom felt unsettled by the cold malevolent stare.

'It won't be long,' said Phoebe as she returned to join them. Able to direct his attention to her Tom felt some relief. She seemed an oasis of normality amidst the strange atmosphere which surrounded the cottage.

He saw she had a lithe body with small, firm breasts accentuated by a thin blouse drawn tightly across them. As she sat down she imperceptibly raised her wide skirt so that he could see her shapely calves. They were bare and she wore nothing on her feet. In the same movement she drew the skirt tight across her thighs.

Tom felt stirrings within him, and when he glanced up to meet her warm, enticing smile he realised she knew the effect she was having. Embarrassed, he glanced at Eliza and from the half grin which touched her lips had no doubt she was finding pleasure in the effect her daughter was having on him. He looked back at Phoebe and her impenetrable stare from glinting green eyes matched that from the inscrutable cat.

Startled, he shuddered.

'Our guest is cold,' cackled Eliza. 'Stir the fire, Phoebe.'

She uncurled herself from her chair, her eyes all the time fixed on Tom. 'Maybe thee'd like a different kind of warmth later on?' she said with a low seductive whisper. She smiled at him and Tom was taken aback when he saw the invitation coming from alluring pale blue eyes.

A witch! One who could change the colour of her eyes at will! What had he come to? Tom tried to shake the thoughts from his mind. It must have been a trick of the light or his concentrating on the stare of the cat. Someone as attractive as Phoebe couldn't possibly be a witch and yet he had heard tales of hags who could turn themselves into beautiful forms to win the soul of a man.

He shuddered again.

'Still cold?' Phoebe reached out to him. 'Come sit nearer the fire.'

Tom was startled by her touch. It was gentle, soft, inviting. It sent his blood coursing through his veins with an excitement he had never felt before and sealed the invitation at which she had hinted earlier. She gave a slight nod as she looked mesmerisingly into his eyes and he read an agreement to fulfil the desires she had stirred in him.

'Has thee much to sell us?' she asked casually.

'Sorry, I ain't. Sold most everything in Robin Hood's Bay,' replied Tom apologetically.

'Maybe next time?' Phoebe turned towards the kitchen. 'The stew must be nearly ready.' As she glanced at her mother she saw her bony fingers stroke the cat twice. Phoebe knew her mother approved and knew what she should do next.

She went into the kitchen, stirred the stew in the big black pan which hung from a reckon over a fire. She took a small pan and spooned sufficient stew for one into it. Satisfied she took a jar from a shelf and poured a good measure of the liquid her mother had brewed from the berries of the deadly nightshade into the small pan. Chuckling to herself, she stirred the stew until she was satisfied that all traces of the liquid had been absorbed into the mixture of rabbit, hare and vegetables. She tipped the stew on to a big plate, spooned some potatoes beside it and took it through to the other room.

'Here thee is, Tom. That'll warm thee.'

He rose from his chair and crossed to the table. 'By gum, that smells good. Thanks.' He smiled at Phoebe whose eyes teased him.

He smacked his lips at the first taste and then tucked into the meal with relish.

He was halfway through his meal when he heard the kitchen door open and looked up to see a big, broad-shouldered man filling the doorway. He wore a woollen jerkin over a tattered shirt. The sleeves were torn and revealed thick muscular arms. Tom could almost feel the power in them. His trousers, fitting into the tops of calf-length boots, were held at the waist by a broad leather belt with a big brass buckle. A thick short neck supported a square head from which dark eyes peered with a half-vacant look. He looked in Tom's direction and leaned slightly forward as if his hawk-like nose would ensure communication.

'I've put thy ponies in t' stable.' His speech came as a half reluctant grunt.

'Thanks,' Tom managed to mutter, still taken aback by the impression of immense power which emanated from the man.

'My son Dick,' said Eliza.

'Stew?' asked Phoebe.

'Aye.'

'We've really had ours, but Dick'll eat more any time,' offered Phoebe, thankful that her brother had played his part in accepting what Tom would think was the same stew as he was having should he detect any touch of bitterness about the meal.

Dick ate his stew with a vigour and little thought for manners which Tom reckoned had never been prominent in this household. From the remarks which passed between mother and son he figured that Dick was only 'ten to the dozen', that all his decisions were made for him by her or sometimes by Phoebe. He seemed to have no opinions of his own and it therefore surprised Tom when he suddenly looked at him and said, 'Those are a couple of fine ponies thee has.'

'Aye. I'm pleased with them.'

'They're strong, well-built. Carry a good load for thee. Black one's best and nicest pony.'

Tom realised that whatever else he was Dick knew his horses and had a soft spot for them.

'Some jam pie?' asked Phoebe, halting the exchange about ponies.

'Thanks,' said Tom.

'And a drop of ale, home brewed?'

Tom licked his lips. 'Will go down well.' As Phoebe served the pie and ale he asked, 'Why is this called Deadman's Howe?' and immediately wished he hadn't when he heard the witch-like cackle come from the rocking chair.

'There's some that say this 'ere howe's an ancient burial ground. Lots of bodies,' said Eliza with a touch of amusement in the rattle which came from her throat. 'And there's those that say there was a suicide in this very house, others say it was murder, and some say it's because Jonas Marten lived here. Thee's heard o' Marten's Ghost? Rides these here moors, searching, always searching for his way home.' She chuckled. 'Whatever, it's a name I like. Wouldn't change it.'

With the meal finished, Tom, at Eliza's invitation, moved to a more comfortable chair. Settled, he felt highly contented. His stomach was full, the fire now seemed much warmer than before and the unsettling atmosphere had eased. It must have been tiredness which had made it seem oppressive and foreboding when he arrived. Eliza seemed a much more jovial person now, less of a hag, and her laugh did not have the harsh cackle to it. That cat on her knee looked friendly. And Phoebe? Why had he ever

46

thought her a witch? His mind must have been playing tricks with him. It couldn't be doing that now.

He looked across at Dick who gave him a friendly smile, nothing like the uncouth, objectionable lout whose only saving grace had been that he liked horses.

As he leaned back in his chair contentedly, Tom figured he must have been suffering hallucinations before he had that meal.

They talked but Tom's mind wasn't concentrating at all on what they were saying. He answered automatically without any idea of his replies.

'Thee looks ready for bed,' said Phoebe. 'I'll show thee where thee's sleeping.' To Tom the invitation in her voice was unmistakable.

He pushed himself to his feet, steadied himself, and with Phoebe by his side seemed to walk on air as she guided him through the kitchen to a room beyond. The room held a bed, a chest of drawers, a chair and a washstand with a bowl and ewer on it. But to Tom the whole room had a shining aspect, it seemed to glow and exude comfort. The bed looked soft and inviting and was big enough for two.

He looked at Phoebe. She held her body provocatively as she loosened her blouse. Tom's eyes widened in anticipation. She slipped the blouse from one shoulder and then held it from her, revealing more.

'Race thee to bed,' she said seductively, her voice holding out all the promise he could wish for.

Tom's head spun. That he should be so lucky as to have to break his journey across the moors! Why had he never done so before? As he frantically shed his clothes he was unaware of Phoebe leaning back against the chest of drawers, laughing to herself at his haste.

He flung himself naked on to the bed. 'Beat thee!' he cried. A grin of triumph crossed his face. The room seemed to turn slowly before him and in the movement a beautiful girl with bare breasts came slowly to him. He held out his arms. She leaned forward.

Phoebe, with a practised dexterity, scooped up a pillow and in the same movement pressed it across Tom's face. She fell on top of him, holding the pillow down with all her strength. Tom's mind reeled. The girl was taking him so quickly that he was gasping for breath. Then momentarily his mind cleared. He was not gasping at the exertion, he was being smothered!

He fought but was weak. His mind slipped back into the hallucination. He gave way to the wonder of the girl's body. Fight! Something deep inside him drove a modicum of reality back into his mind but it was only sufficient for him to realise that a huge pair of hands were pinning his arms to the bed. He could not fight.

'Well done.' Eliza clucked in the doorway as she stared at the body.

Dick relaxed his hold on Tom's arms. Phoebe pushed herself from the bed, threw the pillow on to the chair, picked up her blouse and covered her naked breasts.

'Thee's a fine lass,' chuckled Eliza, admiring her daughter's body and thinking of the day when she herself attracted the eyes of men. 'I'll bet he was disappointed.'

Phoebe fastened her blouse and swung past her mother with a touch of disgust. One thing she did not like about this whole business was when her mother eyed her as she had just done, for she always saw jealousy in those sharp eyes.

'Now, Dick, finish the job.'

He grunted and nodded. It was the same phrase every time. He picked up Tom with no effort and walked from the house.

The air was damp. The cloud hung low obscuring the moon, but Dick knew his way in the dark to the bog as if it were daylight. He had been instructed by his mother, knew the two turns in the path and counted the paces as he had practised when it was light.

After three hundred and twenty he stopped. He then moved twenty paces to the right and heaved the body forward from his shoulder. For a moment its white skin contrasted with the dark. There was a splash as it hit the soft ground. For a brief moment it seemed to lie there staring up at him, then there was a sucking sound and the body slowly sank, drawn into the dark unyielding depths of the bog.

Chapter Five

'Hurry up, lasses, thee'll be keeping Joe waiting and thee's breakfast to have afore thee leaves,' Grace called from the bottom of the stairs, sighed with exasperation and returned to her kitchen.

The girls were slow this morning. John had done the early morning milking, helped by Jay, and the pair of them had finished their breakfasts and were away to check on the sheep.

Grace went to the pan hanging on the reckon above the fire which burned brightly in the grate. She stirred the contents, laid the spoon down and wiped her hand across her forehead as she straightened and turned to the long scrubbed wooden table which occupied the centre of the large, square kitchen.

A slim woman of forty-five, she said it was leading an active working life that kept her that way. Now with the family all grown up, able to help with some of the chores, she could take things a little easier and felt at times that she was putting on a little weight, She was happy to do so so long as she felt no worse for it and it didn't get out of hand. She'd smiled to herself when she first noticed it and John had said, 'No worry, it's a bit more to cuddle.' She wiped her hands down her white apron as she muttered, 'Where are those lasses?'

She was picking two bowls from the table when the door opened and Emma and Amy came into the kitchen, Emma determined to hide the troubled thoughts about her father which had worried her all night.

Immediately she saw them, irritation at the delay left Grace.

'Ee, tha both looks reet bonny.' She could not but admire her two daughters.

Emma reminded Grace very much of herself at that age. This morning she was wearing a brown fustian dress, practical for the outing to Whitby. She had piled her long copper-coloured hair on top of her head and pinned it securely in place.

It was in marked contrast to Amy's dark locks which tumbled to her shoulders. Their seeming disarray matched the casual way she wore her blue check woollen dress.

'Sit thissens down. Joe'll soon be here.' Grace ladled the frumenty from the pan, and as soon as she had placed the bowls in front of her daughters she started to spread butter on some oatcakes. 'That material we got yesterday is just making my fingers itch,' she said, thinking of the pleasure she would get from making the dresses. Creating something of beauty from a piece of cloth was something which brought joy to her. She stopped buttering the oatcakes and looked at her daughters. 'Amy, thee stay at home today and I'll get on with thy dress. Emma can manage on her own. There's not so much to take today.'

'Aw, Ma. I'm all ready to go to Whitby,' Amy protested. 'Emma can stay.'

'No,' said Grace firmly. 'I want to make thy dress first. Thee's in more need of it than Emma.'

Amy pouted. She knew it was no good arguing with her mother. She would be delighted to have the dress but she did want to go to Whitby with Joe. She always enjoyed being with him even if her sister was there, for there were times when Joe just had to take notice of her. 'Very well, Ma,' she agreed reluctantly.

'Good, now get on with thy breakfasts. Emma, the butter's all ready made up in the basket. And see thee gets no less than a shilling a slab for it.'

'Yes, Ma.'

'There's eggs in another basket. And don't break half of

them as Amy did last time.' She glanced teasingly at her youngest daughter.

'Ma, ain't thee ever ganning to let me forget that?' Amy, recalling the incident which had occurred as she was getting into Joe's trap, objected to the chaffing.

Emma paused as she scooped up some frumenty. 'Do thee want me to get anything in Whitby, Ma?'

'Aye. I've made a list. It's in butter basket.'

Grace poured some tea as the girls switched their attentions to the oatcakes and spread them with honey.

With the meal finished the girls cleared away and washed the dirty pots. Emma took the two baskets outside and turned back to the house when she heard the clop of a horse's hooves on the trackway which passed the farm. She waited a few moments until the trap came in sight. She waved to Joe who raised an arm in acknowledgement. As she hurried into the house she called, 'Joe's here.'

Amy ran outside and was through the gate as Joe pulled his horse to a halt.

''Morning, Joe,' she called, her face bright with a smile of pleasure.

''Morning, Amy. How's thee this fine morning?' he asked.

'Well, Joe, but sorry I ain't coming with thee to Whitby,' she replied.

'Why's that?' He looked concerned, but secretly he was pleased for it meant that he would have Emma to himself.

'Ma's making me a dress, wants me at home.' Amy screwed up her face in annoyance. 'Will thee miss me?'

'Of course I will,' replied Joe.

'Thee will? Thee means it?' cried Amy, wanting to read more into Joe's reply and doing so.

Before he could answer, Emma, a cloak around her shoulders, came from the house. 'Hello, Joe,' she called as she picked up the baskets.

'Hello, Emma,' he replied with pleasure. ''Morning, Mrs Dugdale,' he called on seeing Grace come to the door.

52

''Morning, Joe,' she replied. 'Nice morning for a drive into Whitby.'

'Aye, it is that, and the weather looks fair for the day.' He cast a quick glance skywards to confirm his observation. He leaned forward to take the baskets from Emma and placed them in the trap beside his own, before helping her to her seat.

She settled herself and nodded to his query about her comfort. He flicked the reins and sent the horse forward. Emma waved to her mother and to Amy who had joined Grace in the doorway.

They watched the trap moving further and further away.

'Wish Emma would make up her mind about Joe,' Grace said quietly. ''T ain't fair to keep him hanging on.'

It ain't, thought Amy to herself. If her sister wasn't sharp enough to see the fine husband Joe would make then she'd better watch out for here was someone who'd have him and Amy was sure she could capture his interest. She had only to show him that she was grown up, that she was a woman and could make him love her with all the same feelings she held secretly for him.

'Thee's quiet, Emma,' commented Joe. 'Something the matter?'

She started. She had been preoccupied with thoughts of what she had witnessed and overheard at the old barn. Her father was taking great risks. Why hadn't he refused? Maybe he couldn't. She had heard how persuasive the smugglers could be, often using threats to get their way. Maybe that had happened as her father and Zac had walked through the wood. Her mind was deeply troubled. If only she had someone in whom she could confide. Joe? He was dependable, she was sure he would be discreet, but she hesitated to tell him. She would be betraying her father whom she loved and she would never forgive herself if anything happened to him because of her.

'Sorry, Joe. I was miles away.'

'Thinking about us?'

Emma gave a half smile. 'In a way.'

'I hope I came out favourably?'

'Of course thee did. Thee's a very, very dear friend.'

'I hoped I was more than that.'

'Maybe. Maybe,' replied Emma quietly.

'Then thee still thinks about what I've asked thee more than once?'

'Of course.' She hesitated.

'And?' prompted Joe.

'Oh, I do love thee, Joe, but it's as a dear, dear friend, not in the way I should to be your wife.' Emma felt the pain of not wanting to hurt him.

Joe pulled the horse to a halt. He turned to her and took her hands in his. She did not resist his touch. 'My lovely Emma, that love thee has could grow into what we both would want as man and wife, I know it could. I know I could make thee love me in the way thee says thee would want to as my wife.'

Emma looked into an expression which was gentle and at the same time willing her to say yes. She bit her lip as she hesitated. To her mind sprang a picture of the young boy saving her from school bullies, an event from which had grown a love which haunted her even through parting and beyond, through the years without a word from him. But they were years when she'd pictured him growing into a fine handsome man. Now, with Joe beside her, earnest in his love for her, she began to think herself a fool to turn him away. There would be security and happiness with him. If only she could tip her love that little bit further into an all consuming passion which would swamp all thoughts for anyone else. Maybe he was right, maybe that would come.

'Joe,' she said softly, meeting his enquiring and hopeful gaze, 'don't press me right now, but I promise I'll give thee a definite answer a month from today.'

The pleasure in his smile and the joy in his eyes touched

Emma for she knew that her answer had set his heart soaring. She had gone further than she had done on any other occasion when he had proposed.

He bent to her and kissed her gently on the lips. 'I love thee, Emma.'

'I know thee does, and I'm honoured.' She ran her fingers down his cheek. 'Please be patient with me.' She returned his kiss.

'The next four weeks can't go quick enough.' He picked up the reins and sent his horse forward.

Reaching Whitby, Joe guided the horse and trap down the hill and alongside the River Esk which ran between cliffs to the sea. Some houses, inns and warehouses clustered along the west bank, while higher and beyond the bustle of the busy port new houses, built by well-to-do merchants and ship owners, were springing up. But the greater part of the town lay on the east side where the red roofed houses seemed to stand one on top of the other as they clung to the steep cliff and climbed towards the parish church and ruined Norman abbey on top of the wind-swept cliff. Smoke curled from many chimneypots and Emma thought the houses near the top of the pile must never be free from the smoke of those below. Though she liked to come to Whitby she knew she could not live in the claustrophobic conditions of the old town but it would not be too bad in the more salubrious area where her merchant uncle lived.

Joe held his horse to a walking pace as they made their way alongside the bustle of the quays along the east bank.

'Expect they're spices from Africa,' he said, indicating the sacks which were being carried by a line of men from a merchantman tied up at one of the quays.

Emma enjoyed seeing the active life of the port. She commented on the timber being stacked from a vessel recently arrived from the Baltic and admired the dexterity of the women who wielded sharp knives gutting fish from large panniers. Gulls screeched overhead and fought over the guts which dropped on the quayside amidst glittering fish scales.

The river flowed easily, swirling around ships tied to the fixed dolphins in mid-stream. It swished alongside the vessels moored to the quays, eddied around the timbers of staithes and jetties, and rolled under the drawbridge which connected the two banks.

Across the river were the shipbuilding yards where many of Whitby's ships were built. Emma could see two nearing completion.

Joe directed the horse to the White Horse Inn on Church Street. He had an arrangement for his horse to be cared for there on market day.

It was but a short distance to the market-place, and the butter cross as it was known because here gathered people from outlying farms to sell their produce.

Joe lifted Emma's two baskets to the ground and placed his own beside them. 'Here,' he called to a bare-footed boy who was hanging around the inn yard seeking jobs from customers. 'Carry these two baskets to butter cross for Miss Dugdale.'

'Aye, aye, sir.' His eyes brightened at the prospect of receiving some money as he mimicked the response of sailors to an order.

Emma smiled at his enthusiasm. 'Be careful with that one,' she said gently. 'It's got eggs in it.'

'Yes, ma'am,' the boy replied and picked up the baskets.

Joe grasped his and they left the inn yard and moved among the crowds in Church Street. Housewives hurried about their shopping or stood gossiping, taking little notice of the people who flowed around them. Artisans hastened about their work, sailors made for their ships or headed for their favourite inn. Urchins in ragged clothes played chase among the crowd bringing curses on their heads from men they bumped and sharp rebukes from stern-faced dames.

The market-place swarmed with people pressing in and

out of it from every direction. Women milled around the cross where farm produce was being sold. Joe forced his way through the throng closely followed by the boy and Emma to find them a position at one corner of the steps which formed the base of the cross.

He gave a coin to the boy who glanced at it and ran off delighted with his payment.

They barely had time to exchange greetings with familiar faces around them before they were dealing with customers, stating a price and upholding it in spite of the efforts of some buyers to try to beat them down.

Within two hours Emma had sold all her butter and eggs but Joe still had some to dispose of.

'I've some shopping to do for Ma,' she said. 'I'll do that and meet thee at Aunt Matilda's.'

It was an arrangement that they had every market day with her aunt who always had a meal ready for them. Emma looked forward to spending time with her cousin.

'Right,' replied Joe. 'I'll take all the baskets back to White Horse. Careful with thy money. Watch out for purse snatchers.'

Emma nodded, took a firmer grip on her bag and set off. She had dealt with the part of the visit she liked least of all and now she could enjoy looking at the shops, purchasing what her mother wanted and letting her mind dance among the goods deciding what else she would buy if she had enough money. Dresses, cloaks, some lace for her new dress, sweetmeats, paste necklaces, colourful beads and jet brooches all came under imaginative scrutiny as she made her way among the shops in Church Street.

In her enjoyment, thoughts of her father and smuggling had been pushed to the back of her mind until they seemed unreal, figments of her imagination, dreams which should not be encouraged.

Having obtained everything her mother wanted, she headed for the bridge, crossed the river and walked to

Bagdale where several new houses had been built, the first of which was her uncle's.

She turned through the gate on to a stone path running beside a neatly kept garden to the four steps leading to the front door. An elegant fanlight topped the narrow architrave and the six-panelled door was painted a dark blue. Emma saw the sash windows on the three-storey house as friendly eyes ever watchful to extend a warm welcome.

That welcome was matched by the one she received from her cousin Meg when she opened the door in answer to Emma's pull on the door bell.

'Emma!' Laughter filled the hall as Meg held out her arms. The cousins hugged each other, happy to be together again.

Emma stood back. 'I like thy dress,' she commented, her eyes sparkling in admiration of the green taffeta dress which was drawn tight at the waist, emphasising Meg's slimness. 'New, isn't it?'

Meg swung round to give Emma a full view. 'Yes, got it last week.' Her large dark eyes, set in an oval face, reflected the pleasure she felt at Emma's comment. They always shone as if she was enjoying that very moment. They were attentive to anyone with whom she was in conversation and were expressive of her understanding of people's views and arguments. Her fair hair, shining with regular brushing, had a natural curl which she cultivated to the nape of her neck.

As Meg was closing the door a young girl dressed in black with a neat white apron tied around her waist hurried into the hall. She stopped when she saw Meg. 'Oh, I'm sorry, miss,' she apologised timidly.

Meg smiled. 'That's all right, Anna. I was watching out for my cousin.'

'Yes, miss.' Anna bobbed a small curtsey and left the hall.

'Amy not with thee?' asked Meg as Emma put her bag and purchases beside the chair which stood at the bottom of the staircase which swept gracefully to the next floor.

'No. Ma's making a dress for her so she wanted her to stay behind. The pedlar called yesterday.'

The mention of the pedlar brought back thoughts of her father's connection with the smugglers. Should she tell Meg? Emma had shared secrets with her in the past, but those had been merely her own thoughts and feelings. This was different. It involved other people and would betray her father, and that she could not do.

'Come, tell me all about it.' Meg led the way into the withdrawing room. 'Joe will be coming? I presume he brought thee into Whitby as usual?'

'Yes. I'd sold everything before he had, then I went shopping. I thought he might be here before me.'

The cousins seated themselves opposite each other in easy chairs on either side of the fireside in which a cheery fire added more life and brightness to a room which was homely and cosy.

Meg straightened her dress as she sat down. As she leaned back in the chair she fixed her eyes on Emma.

'Well,' she prompted, 'are thee getting a new dress too?'

'Yes.' Emma threw off the thoughts which had troubled her at the mention of the pedlar.

'Thought thy ma wouldn't make one without the other,' laughed Meg, pushing back a wisp of hair from her forehead. 'What's it like?'

Emma described the material enthusiastically. 'And I'm getting new curtains for my bedroom. Pedlar's bringing the material when he returns next week. Thee must come and visit when it gets done.'

'I'd love that.' Though they had moved up the social scale since her father had become a successful merchant, enabling them to buy this fine house with all the accompaniments of fashionable furniture, Meg had never lost her delight in the homely atmosphere of Beck Farm.

'So Joe had thee all to himself today?' she said, changing the subject with a teasing look in her eyes.

'Yes.'

'So?' Meg pressed eagerly, knowing the feelings Joe had for her cousin.

'He proposed again.'

'And this time?'

Emma hesitated, then said with a twinkle in her eyes: 'I said I'd give him an answer four weeks today.'

'Oh, Emma, thee didn't?' exclaimed Meg excitedly. She leaned forward in her chair as if that would draw forth the answer to her next question. 'And what will it be?'

Emma's expression became more serious. 'I don't know yet.'

'Oh, Emma!' said Meg, a touch of disgust in her voice. 'There's a fine man like Joe wanting thee, and thee doesn't know? Thee knows he'll make thee a good husband. Thee'll want for nothing. Surely after all these years thee isn't still thinking about Mark Roper, that one day he'll return to Whitby and sweep thee into his arms? If thee is, then more fool thee.'

Meg was the only one whom Emma had told about her love for Mark Roper.

'And I'll tell thee another thing,' Meg went on when Emma made no reply. 'And I'm telling thee this to try to bring thee to thy senses. If thee doesn't take Joe, Amy will.'

'Amy?' Emma was astonished by Meg's suggestion.

'Yes, Amy. Thee's too close to her to notice the way she eyes Joe, certainly whenever they've been here. That girl's in love with him, and now she's coming a woman she'll make Joe notice her. I think she's only held back because of thee.'

'Me?' Emma was even more taken aback by what her cousin was revealing.

'Yes. Amy may not show it on the surface but she thinks the world of thee. Oh, the pair of thee may fratch and quarrel and not always see eye to eye, but deep down thee cares for each other. It's because she loves thee that she hasn't already set out to snare Joe. She's an attractive lass and could do it. She doesn't want to hurt thee by taking Joe from thee if thee has a mind to marry him.' Meg paused for breath. 'There, I've said it. Something I should have told thee before when I realised thee was too blind to see it. Now all I say to thee is, accept Joe in four weeks' time before it's too late.'

Emma looked thoughtful. 'Maybe thee's right. Maybe I'm living too much on a dream.'

'I know I'm right. Thee heed me.'

'All right, I'll mind thy words and I'll give Joe his answer in four weeks,' said Emma, then added to divert attention from herself, 'But what about thee, no beau yet?'

Meg gave a little laugh. 'No one special. There are those who come courting but there's no one that takes my fancy. Maybe we're both too particular. Ma sings the praises of nearly everyone who comes. I think she's afraid I'm going to be left on the shelf.'

Emma knew her cousin had no end of suitors for the pretty girl had grown into an attractive young woman who knew how to make the best of her fine, delicate features. She'd be attractive to any man. But Emma also knew that Meg was not a person to give her undying love easily. She would save it for the man she'd marry.

'I'm sure the right man will come along before long,' said Emma.

The tack of their conversation and the sharing of intimate feelings were ended when Matilda Dugdale came into the room.

'Hello, Emma. Anna told me thee was here.' The well-built woman, looking smart in a pale green poplin dress, bustled across the room. She was not tall but held herself erect in an attitude which did not lessen the homely impression which emanated from her. She gave Emma, who had risen from her chair, a hug and a kiss. Emma returned the greeting with a smile of pleasure at seeing her aunt. They had always got on well and Emma was always grateful for her care during her schooldays in Whitby. 'How's thy ma?'

'Well, thank thee.'

'Amy and Joe not with thee?'

'Amy stayed at home and Joe should be here soon.'

'Good. It's a cold meal so we can have it whenever he comes. Thy uncle and cousins won't be here today. They've a ship in from the Baltic to see to so will get something at one of the inns.'

Joe arrived ten minutes later, apologising for his lateness. The cold meal of beef and ham with salad and potatoes passed in genial conversation, imparting all the local gossip.

Afterwards the three young people walked on the west bank of the river where Joe, knowing the girls would like to chatter on their own, stopped to watch the activity on one of the merchantmen while they walked along the pier enjoying the tang of the sea borne on the gentle breeze.

'Oh, Joe, I've had such a pleasant day,' Emma remarked as they drove home. She had been enjoying herself so much that thoughts of her father and the smugglers had not troubled her.

Joe pulled the horse to a halt. As he turned to Emma he drew a small packet from his pocket. 'I hope this makes it more pleasant, and in four weeks' time is a reminder of what thee promised this morning.' He handed it to her.

'Joe, thee shouldn't be buying me presents,' Emma protested, feeling that it might be putting her under an obligation to say yes.

'Who better to buy them for?' he said quietly.

Emma took the neatly wrapped package and glanced at Joe. She met the love in his eyes. 'Thank thee.' She leaned towards him and kissed him.

'Open it,' he prompted, eager to see her reaction when she saw his gift.

She undid the wrapping paper carefully to discover an oblong box with a hinged lid. She raised it slowly, her eyes widening as she revealed the contents. A jet pendant with silver chain lay between two jet bracelets.

'Oh, Joe!' she gasped, 'They're beautiful.' She stared at them for a moment then looked up at him, her eyes misting over. 'Thee shouldn't.'

'Anything for thee, my love.' He kissed her and she held his kiss.

Her mind was awhirl. Joe was so good, so thoughtful, and she knew she could be happy with him. Should she heed Meg's words and say yes now?

But the decision was made for her when their lips parted and Joe said, 'Four weeks today, I'll expect thee to keep thy promise.'

Chapter Six

'Someone's coming, Pa.' Jay had spotted a figure striding across the heather as he was helping his father to repair a hedge on the east side of his land.

John Dugdale straightened, stretching as he did so, and eyed the man who was moving purposefully as if he was intent on reaching them.

'Who is it, Pa?' Jay asked.

'Looks like Pete Bray,' commented John, rubbing his back to ease the muscles.

'Wonder what he's doing out here?' said Jay. 'Thought he was a fisherman.'

'Aye, lad, he is, but fishermen have a right to walk the moors.'

'G'day, John,' Pete called while still some distance away.

'G'day Pete,' returned John heartily. He knew Pete Bray as a competent fisherman, a likeable man in his thirties, well built and muscular through coping with his lines and sailing his coble. His eyes had the brightness of a man who tries to see beyond the horizon, and his face, tanned and beaten by the sun and sea, was angular with an attractive ruggedness.

The unusual sight of Pete Bray on the moor, away from his beloved coble, sent a warning to John's mind. Pete must be here for a purpose. Was it connected with Zac's instruction that he would get a message to John when they next had to meet? John glanced at his son who was intent on watching Pete approach them.

'Jay, get thee down to yon hedge, see if it needs any attention.' John indicated to the right with a casual wave of his arm.

'We've just done that, Pa,' he protested.

John was annoyed with himself for not concentrating on directing Jay to an unexamined part of the hedge. 'Then gan and check it again t' see we've missed nowt,' he added with a sharpness which would brook no disobedience.

'Aw, Pa.' Jay groaned, moving off reluctantly.

John turned his attention back to Pete. 'What brings thee on t' moors?'

Pete hesitated and glanced in Jay's direction. Satisfied that the boy was out of earshot, he said, 'Message for thee, John. Tonight.'

John nodded. He understood. No more need be said and the two men lapsed into casual conversation until Jay returned.

'Find anything, lad?' asked John.

'Nay. Knew I wouldn't,' replied Jay.

Pete smiled at the youngster's assurance. 'Must be good to have a son who tak's an interest. I'm landed with four girls.' He eyed Jay. 'Like t' come fishing with me some time?'

Jay's eyes brightened with eagerness. 'Can I?' The enthusiastic note in his voice broadened Pete's smile even further.

'Aye, if thy Pa says so.'

'Can I, Pa?' Jay swung round on his father with a pleading excitement which could not be denied. 'Can I?'

John smiled, recalling himself as a youngster facing the same situation. 'Aye, all right.'

'Thanks, Pa.' Jay was bursting with enthusiasm. 'When, Mr Bray, when?'

'I'll let thee know, lad. Maybe next week.'

'Thanks, Mr Bray, thanks.'

Pete nodded at John. 'I'd best be getting back. Nice t' have a chat.' He turned and strode out across the moor.

'We'll just finish this piece here and then we'll gan home,' said John.

Enthused by the prospects of a fishing trip with Pete Bray, Jay worked willingly and chatted all the way home

65

about what he might catch. His father was pleased that Jay was happy and he was not surprised when he ran ahead on seeing Emma filling a bucket at the stream.

'Emma, Emma, I'm going fishing with Mr Bray,' he shouted.

She straightened and turned to her brother who reached her panting with the exertion.

'I'm going fishing,' he gasped, swallowing to catch his breath.

'When?' asked Emma, smiling at the sight of his red face and wide-eyed excitement.

'Maybe next week. Mr Bray will let me know.'

'Where did thee see him?' Emma's curiosity was aroused. She knew her father and brother had been working close to the moor and recognised that it was an unusual place to be encountering Pete Bray. She wondered what he had been doing there and waved to her father who was making straight for the house.

'He came across the moor. I might have missed the invitation, Pa sent me off to examine a hedge when Mr Bray arrived,' he explained. 'Funny that,' he added with a quirk of his eyebrows, 'we'd just done that piece of hedge.'

'Why did Pa do that?' asked Emma.

Jay shrugged his shoulders. 'Dunno.'

She made no further comment nor enquiry but reached for the bucket. Jay beat her to it. 'Let me,' he said.

As they walked to the house, Emma's mind was on what Jay had told her. It almost seemed as if Pete Bray had come deliberately to see her father. If so, had he brought a message which her father had not wanted Jay to hear, and could it have been from Zac? She had heard him say that he would get a message to her father when contraband was to be brought ashore. Could it be tonight?

By the time they reached the house Emma had made up her mind to stay awake that night and had no doubt about what she would do if she heard the signal.

*   *   *

Dusk was settling over Baytown as Zac Denby hurried down the steep street towards the beach. He glanced skywards and grunted with satisfaction. The weather was good. The slow-moving clouds were thin and patchy enough to allow the young moon to give some light, which would help the night's work. But here, in the narrow street where houses rose high as if vying with each other to reach the light, little of the moonlight penetrated. On either side the narrower streets, yards and garths ran like a maze across the cliff. They crowded in upon each other with houses on one side looking on to the roofs of those on the other. So close were they that from below they seemed to be standing one on top of the other as they climbed the cliff.

Zac strode on, ignoring the occasional person he passed. He was satisfied that all was ready. The previous evening at Armstrong's Farm The Fox had given him details of the contraband which would arrive from France: gin, brandy, rum, lace, silks, tobacco and tea.

A cargo which would enable many local gentry to enjoy their brandy and gin, dress in silks and lace, and save money doing so. The parson could preach against illicit trading but secretly thank the free-traders while enjoying tobacco which would be run ashore this night. Innkeepers would make an extra profit on the spirits they would obtain. The land smugglers and their helpers would benefit from the goods they would receive in addition to their pay, while the men behind the smuggling, those who organised and financed the whole operation, would add to the fortune they were making while remaining anonymous and apparently innocent bystanders should the law close in.

Zac had spent the day organising and checking that everything was ready to receive and dispose of the contraband in line with his new scheme of using pedlars to move the goods inland.

At the end of the street close to the beach, he opened the door of the Fisherman's Arms and stepped into a corridor in which only one lantern's flickering light attempted to relieve the dark. He opened a door on the right and entered a room in which ten men were seated around upturned barrels which acted as tables. A fire glowed red in a grate adding to the warmth of human bodies. Four metal lanterns hanging from the beams gave the room some semblance of light which tried to penetrate the haze from pipe smoke which drifted across the room.

The men, tankards readily to hand, acknowledged Zac's arrival while he gave them a cursory nod as he crossed the flagged floor to a hatch which gave into a kitchen.

''Evening, Nell,' he called as he leaned on the shelf in front of the hatch. His usually hard voice had softened a little.

Nell Randall straightened from the table in the middle of the kitchen on which she had set eleven plates.

She was a woman in her early-forties who ran the Fisherman's Arms with a firm hand. No one took liberties with Nell Randall, or if they tried they soon knew better. She had run the inn since her mother died fifteen years ago, following the loss of her father one night at the hands of Preventive Men. Nell had hated them ever since and was a willing ally and confidante of Zac Denby. He was the only one who could get close to her, the only one who could penetrate the shell she had put up around herself. Not that she was stand-offish, far from it. She was the genial landlady who would laugh and joke with her customers. But she was ever wary, especially of strangers, though not many of them penetrated the close community of Baytown.

Nell's brown eyes lit up with pleasure as she approached Zac. He was not a man given much to speaking words of admiration but she saw it in his eyes as they ran across her bodice and outer skirt of cerulean blue. Her sleeves were tight at the elbows, leaving her forearms bare. The yellow wrap around her shoulders was tucked into the top of her bodice which was drawn tight accentuating her small firm breasts. Light brown hair peeped from beneath a white bob cap.

"Evening, Zac.' Her smile revealed a row of perfect teeth and lifted the corners of her full lips. The deaths of her parents had brought lines to her face, ageing her prematurely, but since then time had been kind to her and now she was an attractive woman.

'Everything ready?' she asked.

'Aye,' replied Zac, and lowered his voice. 'I'd be happier if we were using the pack-horse trains instead of the pedlars. Means we've to store the contraband longer.'

'But thee's got extra storage places,' Nell pointed out.

'Aye.'

'Then what's thee worried about?'

Zac shrugged his shoulders. 'Just have a feeling.'

'That's not like Zac Denby.' She filled a tankard with ale as she was speaking. 'Here, get that down thee, and with some of my pie thee'll be as reet as rain for the night's work.' She leaned forward to put her question so only Zac could hear it. 'Do that lot know about the dragoons?' She inclined her head in the direction of the ten men.

He shook his head. 'Better not to worry them with that tonight. Besides, dragoons ain't here yet. And thee keep it to thissen.' Zac added the advice in spite of knowing that Nell was probably the one person he could trust implicitly. He took his tankard and joined the others.

'Everything ready?' he asked as he sat down. His glance took in everyone.

'Aye.' The murmur ran through them all. Each one knew his job, knew the people they would have to supervise and, in view of Zac's new scheme for the disposal of the contraband, had laid their plans accordingly.

'The two dragoons?' asked Zac, concerned about the two men who were stationed in Baytown.

'No trouble,' chuckled Pete Bray. 'Nell plied them well with spirits, with a little something added. They're upstairs now. Won't awake 'til midday I reckon.'

'Aye, and then they'll have such thick heads they won't remember anything,' laughed the man next to him.

Relaxed banter and leg-pulling filled the next few hours as they all enjoyed the rabbit pie which Nell always made for them on the nights that contraband was to be run ashore. This time also enabled Zac to check everything with these men who were the lieutenants in his smuggling gang and issue any last minute instructions.

They were curious about the fact that he had decided to store the goods in more places than usual, and some at farms a few miles inland. But they knew better than to question him. They were here to carry out orders, and being well paid in cash and kind, they knew it was wise to keep a still tongue.

Zac fished inside a pocket in his short jacket and pulled out his watch. He glanced at the time.

'Time we were ganning,' he said as he stood up. He replaced the watch, drained his tankard, wiped his hand across his mouth and shrugged himself into a knee-length woollen coat fastened with a broad leather belt around his waist. He turned to the hatch where Nell had laid out eleven pistols. He chose one and tucked it securely into his belt. He adjusted his woollen cap over his thick black hair and turned to await the others.

They were in various stages of readiness. Some preferred waistlength coats, others thick jerseys; most wore caps similar to Zac's but two chose to have a short shoulder cape with a hood. All wore knee-length boots, stout enough to keep out the sea yet sufficiently pliable to be comfortable and not hinder movement. Once they were dressed they each selected a pistol and some produced knives which they also secured into the belts at their hips.

When everyone was ready they slipped quietly out of the inn and made their way to the beach. Reaching the sand they paused as a group and eyed the sea.

It was calm with only small waves breaking on the beach, to run hissing on to the sand until they lost momentum and slid back to be lost in the oncoming water. The moon peeped from behind the clouds and sent a silvery trail shimmering across the sea. The dark mass of cliffs rose and soared to the forbidding heights of Ravenscar across the bay. Behind them Baytown rising on the cliff-face was dark and quiet. Only those who needed to be abroad were; the rest wisely kept to their homes for they knew that smugglers would be active tonight and would brook no interference or curiosity.

Zac grunted with satisfaction. The weather couldn't have been better. 'Half an hour.' His observation was a signal for the men to move off.

Three went to the six cobles drawn up on the beach close to the sea. Each was responsible for two cobles when they brought the contraband ashore. By each coble were four men well wrapped against the night air. Six made their way to the low cliffs up which some of the contraband would be taken. There awaiting them were six groups of men, mostly from Baytown but also some farm hands, eager to make an extra coin or two for a night's work moving contraband. Pete Bray stayed with Zac and as the time for the expected arrival of the lugger from France drew close their eyes concentrated on the sea beyond Ravenscar.

Each man never failed to become tense as the moment drew nearer, and sensed that same tension along the beach. Only the sound of the waves broke the silence which hung over the scene. The odd shuffling sound, movements among the men, came from an impatience of wanting to be in action and added to the tension which charged the air.

'There!' Zac's exclamation came with a sharp intake of breath.

Silhouetted against the lighter sky above the horizon, a two-masted lugger, distinctive by its square sails, turned the headland.

Zac glanced quickly at a prominent position some distance along the cliffs. The darkness was marked by a bright flash from a primed but uncharged flintlock pistol with its barrel sawn off. The signal to the lugger that it was safe for it to make its run into the bay had been made. Some of the tension left the men on the beach. Soon they would be in action.

They watched the black mass of the lugger come slowly across the bay, edging nearer the shore. Knowing the bay from their roles as fishermen, the three men in charge of the cobles watched its progress with skilled eyes and ordered their cobles away shortly before the lugger proceeded to heave to.

The four men operating each coble immediately pushed the flat-bottomed, clinker-built boat, with its deep forefoot helping to keep it straight and steady, through the few feet of sand to the sea. Once it was floating three men were at the oars while the fourth positioned himself in the stern. With powerful strokes the six cobles headed for the lugger which was being brought-to. By the time they were alongside, it lay motionless head to wind.

'Pete, I'm away. First time for John. I'd better be there.' Zac was satisfied that all was well here at the beach.

'Right. I'll see to things here.' Pete's voice was firm, reassuring.

With one last glance to sea, Zac hurried up the low cliff and headed for Beck Farm.

Emma, feeling that there was something behind Jay's account of the meeting between her father and Pete Bray, had struggled to keep awake but was startled when she heard the dying hoot of an owl on the still night air. Awake, she tensed herself, listening for the rest of what she remembered of the signal. But nothing came. Had there been any more hoots before that final one? She cursed herself for dozing off.

She lay for a moment, listening, trying to detect some sound of movement. Nothing. The house was as silent as the grave. Then, as the thought struck her that maybe, knowing of the liaison, her father had not gone to bed, she threw the bedclothes back and was at the window straining her eyes against the blackness. Only just in time she saw the movement beside the wall leading away from the farm.

Emma dressed quickly, thankful that she hadn't to keep her father in sight. She knew where he was going. Avoiding the squeaking stair, she took her warm cloak from the peg in the kitchen and left the house. She hurried across the fields towards Black Wood which she approached with caution. Nearing the trees, she moved slowly, trying to catch a glimpse of her father in case he was meeting Zac Denby here as he did before. She paused, her head inclined, trying to catch a sound. She inched her way to the right and stopped again. A whisper? Could it be? Crouching low she carefully moved again in the direction from which she thought it had come. Yes, she was right. Two voices. A few more feet and she froze. Two shadowy forms stood among the trees.

'Shouldn't be long now. All was going well when I left the beach.'

'The goods will be placed in the barn and we'll put them in the cellar. I want no one else to know of its existence.'

'Nor do I. With a valuable hiding place like that it's better only we know about it. If anyone gets to know inform me and I'll see they soon forget.'

Emma shivered at the implications behind that threat.

By the time the cobles were alongside the lugger its crew was ready and operated quickly to unload the cargo. As soon as one boat was filled, backs bent and muscles strained to bring it quickly to the shore where it was turned so that it could be brought stern first on to the sand. Each gang of men met the boat to which they had been assigned and dragged it from the water.

Barrels, bales, boxes and chests were taken from the cobles with the utmost speed. Under the eerie light of the pale moon, the beach became a moving mass of men as the gangs, supervised by the landers, carried the goods to houses in Baytown where the inhabitants were ready to store it in all manner of secret places, hidden rooms, concealed tunnels and secluded crannies. Nell Randall had the doors to the cellars of the Fisherman's Arms unlocked for contraband to be taken by a short underground passage to a cavern which extended under the buildings on the opposite side of the road.

Hardly a word was spoken, only the harsh breathing of physical exertion mingled with the murmur of the waves and the shuffling of feet through the sand.

Carts were loaded with goods to be transferred to farms which had convenient tracks leading to them from the cliff top. The horses' hooves and the wheels were wrapped with rags and the leather harness well greased to make for silent progress up the steep hill through the town.

Without a convenient cart track leading from Baytown to Beck Farm, the goods had to be moved by foot and Zac had picked a special gang of strong fit men to do the carrying. Pete gave this gang his special attention for, with Beck Farm being used for the first time, nothing must go wrong.

Tubmen, used to carrying tubs of brandy or rum, roped them in pairs across their shoulders with one across the chest, balancing it with another positioned on the back. Other men took charge of bales of silk and lace or boxes of tea. Pete and the gang leader, who would guide them to Beck Farm, moved among the men supervising the disposition of the contraband and making sure that it was secure for transportation. When all was ready to their satisfaction, the leader with his own load started up the path which Zac had taken earlier. He had familiarised himself with the path by walking it several times since Zac had instructed him he was to lead a gang to Black Wood where he would be met.

Sure-footed, he made a good pace, matching it to the ability of his gang, and only eased it when the wood came in sight.

*   *   *

Crouched in an unnatural position, fearful of betraying her presence, Emma's muscles began to ache. She was longing to ease her back and legs but strengthened her determination to hold out. She had heard Zac say it wouldn't be long and she hoped it wouldn't be.

'Listen!' The short sharp intonation from Zac came as some relief to her.

She could hear nothing and wished she had Amy's fine sense of hearing. But a few moments later she heard the muffled footsteps in the short undergrowth of the gully leading to Black Wood.

All thoughts of aching limbs vanished when a few minutes later a line of men came in sight. Emma's heart beat a little faster when she saw they were all carrying some form of container and she realised she was watching a smuggling run. The excitement of the adventure almost drove the concern that her father was involved from her mind.

Once contact with Zac and John had been established, the smugglers were soon following them in the direction of the barn.

Thankful when the last man passed her, Emma straightened up. She had seen enough to know that her father was now inextricably involved with the smugglers, she should go home, but her sense of adventure was too strong. She must see the goods stowed in that cellar. She moved warily through the wood and paused at the edge. Shadowy forms still walked across the field and would most likely return this way. She must use the hedge as she had done before and accordingly moved along the perimeter of the wood until she reached the covering shadows of the hedge. As she headed in the direction of the barn she kept her eyes on the smugglers. She had counted twenty-four in the gang, she must be sure twenty-four returned before she reached a position from which she could see her father and Zac.

As she came round to the side of the barn she counted the last man away and waited until he had caught up with some of the others halfway across the field.

She inched her way forward around the side of the barn to the opening which had once supported a door. She crept the last few feet so that she could peer into the barn at ground level as she had done before. She was surprised how calm she was compared to the previous time. Then she had faced the completely unknown; now she knew something of what she expected to see.

A light had already been lit in the cellar and she saw her father and Zac in the process of taking the contraband below ground. The two men worked hard, and in spite of the cool night were soon complaining to each other of being too warm.

'It'll be worth thy while,' chuckled Zac as he stretched his back and wiped his forehead with a large red handkerchief. 'Leave that tub, John, tak' it home wi' thee.'

'A tub of brandy? I couldn't do that!'

''Course thee can.' Zac laughed at John's bewilderment. He had been opening a box as he spoke. 'And this,' he added, pulling out a roll of silk which he dropped on the tub he had indicated. 'Thy wife and grand lasses will look well in it. And this'll finish it off.' He took some lace from another bale.

Emma stifled her gasp just in time. Exhilaration at the thought of wearing that silk coursed through her veins. Surely her father wouldn't refuse it? He couldn't! Thoughts of the benefits from smuggling had driven from her mind all reminders of the consequences if her father was caught. He was so deeply involved now he may as well reap some of the benefits until she found a way of extracting him from his folly.

'I can't accept them,' said John. 'Thee's paying me for use of this barn.'

'Aye, we are, but whenever there's a good run, and tonight's is one of those, The Fox doesn't mind if I present gifts where I think best.' Zac laughed. 'Don't look so dumbstruck. Thee knows as well as I nearly everyone around here benefits in some way from we free traders, and that's what we are – offering goods more cheaply than thee can buy them elsewhere. There's many a fine lady walking round in silks that we've run ashore and many a fine gentleman drinking brandy that's been humped on the back of a free trader. Thou tak' the brandy and the silk and enjoy them, John Dugdale. Now say no more and let's get this job finished.' He picked up a chest and started towards the cellar.

John glanced once more at the tub, silk and lace which had been set aside and then picked up a box and followed Zac.

Emma knew it was time she was going. She had seen and heard more than she had expected tonight.

Sleep did not come easily to her once she was back in bed. Her mind was too full of what she had witnessed and discovered. She heard her father return and could make out whispering from her parents' bedroom. She wished she could hear what was being said.

Grace Dugdale stirred when the bedroom door opened. She had awakened a few minutes previously to be surprised that her husband was not in bed.

'John, why's tha been so long?' she whispered.

'It took longer than I thought,' he replied quietly as he sat down on the side of the bed and started to undo his shirt having left his coat and boots downstairs.

Grace was not to be taken in by that. Besides she hadn't been married to John Dugdale all these years not to know when he was trying to cover something up.

'And what might it be that took thee longer than tha thought?' she demanded, pushing herself up in bed. 'And don't tell me it's thy concern for sheep as thee said. There's summat afoot, John Dugdale, and I mean to know what. So tha may as well tell me reet now.'

John had slipped quickly out of his clothes and into his nightshirt as she was speaking. He slid into bed and started to cuddle up close to his wife.

She fended him off, saying, 'That'll not let thee off. I want to know what's ganning on and I want to know now.'

John knew he was beat. He knew Grace for a determined woman once she had her mind made up and realised there was no way that he was going to be able to keep his latest activity a secret from her, especially as there was a tub of brandy and a roll of silk in the stable.

He propped himself up on one elbow so that he could face his wife and told her all that had happened since the first contact by Zac.

'Thee's mad, John Dugdale, to get thissen embroiled with the smugglers,' cried Grace. 'Mad!' Disgust and concern filled her voice.

'Now calm down, luv. We're in no danger.'

'Of course we are,' she snapped as the awful consequences of being caught rose in her mind.

'The smugglers could have made it hell for us if I'd refused,' replied John. 'Thee knows what they could do – burn crops, kill animals, maybe waylay me out in the fields and even get at us through the children. Thee's never thought of that, has thee?'

Contemplating the terrifying results of falling out with the smugglers shook her. She had seen only one threat to them, the law, but now, from what John had pointed out, she realised he had consented to help the smugglers to save them from what could have become a terrible ordeal. She had heard of people who had suffered that way and certainly did not want her family to experience their wrath.

She nodded slowly. 'All right, John, but thee be careful.'

'I will, luv. There's good pay in it, and thee knows it'll help us buy this farm.' He gave a little smile and Grace knew from his expression that he had some surprise in store for her. 'And I got some extra pay in kind tonight.'

'What's thee mean?' she asked when he paused with a twinkle in his eye.

'There's a tub of brandy, a roll of silk, and some lace in the stable.'

'What?' Grace gasped with alarm. 'Thee's taken them?'

'It's all right, luv, Zac Denby gave them to me. It's the practice if it's a good run.'

'But how are we going to explain them to the children?'

'I'll gan into Whitby one day. The brandy can be a present from brother Robert and the silk I can bring thee as a present.' He smiled. 'Now come here, luv, stop looking so bewildered and worried.' He put his arm round her and pulled her down into the bed.

Chapter Seven

'Emma!' Joe's call stopped her in the midst of sweeping the flagged kitchen floor and brought her to the open door. 'Fancy a ride to Whitby?' he asked when she appeared. Seeing her mother through the window, washing up at the sink, he added, 'That's if thee can spare her, Mrs Dugdale.'

Before she could answer, a shout came from an upstairs window. 'If my big sister doesn't, I do.'

Wiping her hands on a piece of towelling, Mrs Dugdale came to the door and glanced upwards. 'Amy, thee get back to making the beds,' she ordered sharply. There was something in Amy's tone which disturbed her. She turned her attention back to Joe. 'Aye, if she wants to, she's about finished. Besides I have some jam here that she can take to her aunt's.' If Emma wanted an excuse to go she had made one for her.

'I'll be with thee in a couple of minutes,' called Emma enthusiastically. She turned back into the house and pushed the sweepings on to a shovel, took them outside and tipped them into a rubbish bin.

'I could be ready sooner, Joe.' There was merriment in Amy's voice.

He looked up with laughter in his eyes. 'Maybe one day I'll let thee two race to get ready and I'll tak' the winner.'

'I'd win! Sure would to ride with a handsome chap like thee.'

'Amy! What did I tell thee to do?' Mrs Dugdale paused as she turned in the doorway to look up and admonish her daughter who had so openly flirted with Joe. She must have a word with her about it. It was almost as if she was attempting to rival her sister for his affections.

'Yes, Ma,' Amy replied lightly. She smiled and waved to Joe which brought a matching response from him.

Emma hurried from the house. She had put on a dark blue cloak over her fustian dress and had placed a small matching bonnet on her head.

'Thanks, Joe,' she said with a warm smile as he reached down for the basket containing six jars of jam. 'And thanks for calling for me,' she added as she climbed on to the seat beside him.

He flicked the reins and sent the horse forward along the track towards the main trackway to Whitby.

'What takes thee to Whitby?' asked Emma as she settled down.

'Pa wants some rope,' he replied, happy that he had had an excuse to invite Emma to accompany him. 'And I've no need to hurry back. Maybe we could take a walk on the cliffs after I've got the rope and thee's delivered the jam?'

It was a warm bright day with wisps of white cloud gentled by a light breeze, a day to enjoy the ride and spend a few hours in Whitby.

'That would be nice, Joe. We'll meet on the bridge.'

'Right. No doubt thee'll want a bit of time with Meg so let's say a couple of hours after we get to Whitby,' he suggested. 'Thee get something to eat with your aunt and I'll get something at one of the inns.'

'Very well,' replied Emma, pleased with Joe's thoughtfulness.

'That Amy's a tease,' he grinned, recalling the smiling figure at the upstairs window. 'She's becoming an attractive lass. Soon be having the lads around her.'

Emma was surprised. She had not really noticed how appealing her younger sister had become; she supposed it was being with her every day, but Meg had seen it and warned her that Amy could easily set her sights on Joe. And now she had attracted his attention. Emma had seen her flirt with him that very morning and Joe had liked it.

'Aye, and thee keep thy eyes off her, Joe Wade,' she said

with a sharp light in her eye. She slid nearer to him on the seat and slipped her arm through his as if claiming possession.

'She can't hold a candle to thee.' He smiled as he turned to look at her.

He met a depth of admiration in the deep brown eyes and could not resist the temptation. As he leaned to her and touched her lips in a gentle kiss, he pulled on the reins and let them slide from his fingers when the horse stopped. He turned, put his arms round her and pulled Emma gently to him. This time his lips held more passion and burned with love. She responded and met his kiss with equal fervour.

'Oh, Emma,' Joe gasped, 'I love thee so much. Say thee'll marry me.'

A sudden chill gripped her. That word: marry. Commit herself to Joe for life. She would have undying love, devotion, respect, and a stable life based on the farm which would be his one day. But was that what she wanted? Why not? It was a life she knew. She had never yearned for any other and yet she held back. Why had she carried a schoolgirl's love in her heart all these years when there was no chance of its fulfilment? Surely she should say 'yes' to Joe? Everything seemed to point that way. The word started to form on her lips but came out as, 'I told thee when I would give thee an answer. Be patient, Joe.'

'But thee loves me! Thee couldn't kiss me like that if thee didn't. There's no reason to wait. Say yes, Emma, please.'

'A little more time,' she replied quietly, and drew away from him as if trying to put an end to the moment.

The movement annoyed him. He grabbed the reins and shook them irritably to send the horse forward. His lips set in a tight line and exasperation lurked in his eyes. 'Maybe I should have asked Amy,' he snapped.

Emma stiffened. 'Maybe thee should,' sprang to her lips in retaliation, but she stifled the words before they could be uttered. Instead she said, 'Oh, Joe, don't be like that.' Her voice was soft and caressing, trying to ease the hurt she knew he was feeling. 'I've promised to give thee an answer soon, and I will. See, I wear the jet pendant and bracelets every day to remind me of thee and my promise.' She unfastened her cloak so he could see the pendant and held out her hands so he could see the bracelets around her wrists.

He glanced at them and his face softened as he looked at her.

'Don't let's spoil today,' she requested.

'I'm sorry,' he said quietly. He leaned to her and kissed her lightly on the cheek, a kiss which asked forgiveness.

She rested her hand on his arm, in token that she had forgotten his sudden outburst.

They rode on, enjoying the sun, the air and each other's company and Joe spoke of his work and his plans, hoping they might assure Emma of the good life she could expect if she married him.

She was attentive to his scheme of tilling more land and enlarging the flock of sheep which his father was allowing him to run on the moor, but Emma was only half listening. Her mind, worried about giving him an answer, also dwelt on Meg's observations about Amy and on her father's connections with the smugglers. Her life which only a few weeks ago had been stable and undisturbed now seemed threatened on all sides.

Joe dropped Emma at the end of Bagdale and she hurried to her aunt's with her basket of jam.

'Thee's meeting Joe in two hours?' said her aunt after Emma had explained her visit. 'Then we'll have lunch in an hour's time.'

'That gives us time for a walk,' said Meg brightly. 'It's such a beautiful day.'

The cousins left the house and made their way to the top of the west cliff. Far below, the river carved its way between the heights to slip quietly beside the two stone piers into the sea. Beyond the red roofs, climbing the cliff on the east side, stood the ruined abbey looking gaunt even in the mellowing sunshine. Ships of all sizes were tied up at the quays and wharves and Whitby bustled with a purposeful air.

'Thee and Joe going straight back?' asked Meg as they strolled along the cliff.

'He suggested a walk,' said Emma.

'Has thee made up thy mind about him?'

Emma shook her head. 'Not yet. I nearly said yes on the way here.'

Meg threw up her arms in dismay. 'As close as that? So why didn't thee?'

'Oh I don't know, something just held me back. Maybe because I promised him an answer at a certain time.' She paused, then added with irritation at herself, 'Am I being stupid?'

'Only thee can answer that,' replied Meg sympathetically.

Emma looked wistful. 'Oh, for our schooldays when life seemed so simple!'

'Was it? Even then thee liked two boys,' pointed out Meg. 'Who would thee have chosen then if thee had had to make a choice?'

'Mark,' replied Emma without hesitation.

'And thee's clung to that dream ever since, expecting him to return to Whitby? Get a hold of thissen, Emma. Times and circumstances change and what is there to bring him back? His father's company is well-run in Whitby, I've heard Pa say so. Forget thy dream and get back to reality, one in which thee's loved by a good man for whom thee has a deep feeling.'

Emma gave a small laugh as she gave a slight inclination of her head. 'Maybe thee's right, Meg.' She linked arms with her cousin. 'Now let's forget it and enjoy the walk and tell me all the latest news in Whitby.'

They strolled along the cliff chatting as if they had not seen each other for months. They were on their way back when Meg brought them to a stop as she eyed a ship beating in towards the piers.

'She's a revenue cutter,' said Meg, admiring the clean-cut form of the single-masted vessel. She looked built for speed with her gaff mainsail catching the wind. 'Come on, let's get to the end of the cliff. We'll have a better view of her as she comes into the river.'

Emma was swept along by Meg's enthusiasm as they hurried along the path. She knew of her cousin's delight in ships through living in Whitby. Though shipping was regarded as a man's world, Meg's knowledge would stand against anyone's, a fact which her father and two brothers had been forced to admit. Her father was delighted at the interest she showed, not only in ships but also in the family business, something which her brothers acknowledged.

They reached the edge of the cliffs just as the cutter was moving slowly between the piers. They watched her proceed along the river towards a quay on the east bank.

'Yes, she's a revenue cutter,' observed Meg. 'See the jack she's flying.'

'Those men lining up on deck, they're soldiers,' said Emma with a surprised curiosity. 'Why on a revenue cutter?'

'Must be dragoons. And being on a revenue cutter they must be being brought in to strengthen the campaign against smugglers. I've heard tell it's getting a serious problem for the government, though how they'll put a stop to it when so many people benefit from it, I don't know.'

Emma hardly heard her cousin's last words for the sight of the dragoons and Meg's explanation of their presence had sent a chill through her heart. Her father was in greater danger and there was nothing she could do except casually warn him by telling him she had seen dragoons come into Whitby.

During the rest of her stay her mind was preoccupied

with the shadow which she imagined hung over Beck Farm. It spoiled her walk on the cliffs beside the ruined abbey with Joe though she hid her feelings and kept off any topic which she sensed would betray her thoughts. In spite of the beautiful day and a gentle sea lapping the foot of the precipitous cliffs, she was thankful when it was time to go home.

George Stackpole, Collector at Whitby, watched with satisfaction from the window of his office in the Custom House. His attention was on the revenue cutter coming slowly up the river towards its berth for he knew that on board were the eighteen dragoons he had requested to help in his fight against the smugglers.

With so many goods being brought ashore illegally along the Yorkshire coast, especially in the Robin Hood's Bay area, the revenue he was collecting was not as much as it should be and that was restricting his plans for the development of the port. He knew that he had a difficult task to stamp out smuggling altogether for so many people condoned the role of the smuggler, seeing him as a necessity in the days when the government were bent on taxing goods to raise revenue.

He smiled to himself as he noticed little knots of people gathering to watch the cutter for he knew they would be murmuring among themselves. There would be complaints at the presence of a revenue vessel in Whitby and abuse thrown at it and its occupants for the revenue officials and the Preventive Men were hated almost as much as the press-gang.

A man in his late-forties, Stackpole turned from the window, pulling his embroidered waistcoat more comfortably over his stomach where he was beginning to put on a little more flesh. The embroidery of yellow, green and mauve was in contrast to his dark-plum tail-coat. His breeches matched his coat and were buttoned at the knee above white stockings. He glanced down at his black leather shoes and was satisfied that they and the buckles shone as he liked them to. He picked up his black velvet tricorne hat and left his office, calling to one of his clerks to accompany him.

By the time he reached the quay the cutter was tied up and the dragoons were drawn up on deck ready for disembarkation. George cast a quick glance over them as he hurried to the gangway. He was pleased. They looked a capable body of men, smartly turned out in their thigh-length red coats over plain waist-length undercoats. A sash over the right shoulder held a sword on the left side, while the sash from the left shoulder supported pouches on the right side just below waist height and positioned so that they were not an encumbrance. Their brown breeches were fastened at the knees, the fastenings hidden by the knee-length boots which befitted men who were used to riding as well as acting on foot. Each man carried a musket, and the officer, who was about to give them the order to leave ship, had two pistols tucked into a sash tied tightly around his waist.

George hurried on board. 'Lieutenant Henry Boston?' he asked.

The officer swung round on hearing his name. He came smartly to attention and saluted the newcomer. 'Yes, sir,' he replied sharply.

'George Stackpole, Controller.' He held out his hand in greeting.

As Boston took it, he relaxed. He had been wondering what the man from whom he would take orders would be like and was pleased to see an open friendly face and a genial smile. Some Controllers with whom he had worked could be real sticklers with never a smile, regarding the dragoons as well beneath their dignity. He had not looked forward to this posting to the north, a God-forsaken part of the country he had been told, but his first impressions on sighting Whitby had been favourable and now meeting the Controller had eased his apprehension.

'Welcome to Whitby,' Stackpole went on. 'I trust you had a pleasant voyage?'

'A good one,' replied Boston. 'Calm sea, which was a blessing.'

'Splendid,' said Stackpole. 'I have your accommodation all arranged and also horses for you. My clerk is waiting on the quay.' He indicated the man. 'He'll direct you. I suggest you come to see me in my office in the Custom House eight o'clock in the morning.'

'Yes, sir. And thank you for all the trouble you have taken.'

Stackpole smiled. 'No trouble at all. And I hope we can get some result in curbing the smuggling along this coast.'

'We'll do our best, sir.'

'Good. Until tomorrow then.'

The two men shook hands again, Boston saluted and Stackpole left the ship.

He had a word with his clerk as they watched the troops disembark and fall in line ready to march off.

As they did so, George heard unfavourable comments about the presence of troops in Whitby come from the groups of sightseers who had gathered along the quay. They regarded this as a formidable force and guessed it had been brought in to combat the smugglers. Even if the onlookers had no direct connection with the smuggling fraternity, they were antagonistic to any opposition, for there was hardly one of them who, in some way or another, had not benefited from the contraband trade. Brandy, lace, tobacco, wine, tea ... something of untaxed goods had found its way at some time or other into most homes. Sailors, artisans, housewives, farmhands, innkeepers, parsons, gentry, no one would resist the temptation of cheaper goods which, to salve their consciences, they regarded as legal wares brought in by free traders.

'Where's thee off?' asked Grace as Amy took a shawl from the peg beside the door.

'There's a trap coming,' she replied.

'I can't hear anything,' said her mother, but she did not doubt that Amy was right for she had the sharpest hearing of any of the family.

Amy went outside and stood by the gate where her mother joined her a few minutes later just as the trap was coming into sight.

'They've picked up your pa and Jay,' observed Grace. 'Good, we'll be all on time for tea.'

Amy concentrated her gaze on Joe. She wondered how he and Emma had got on and felt jealous of the time they had spent together.

'Had a nice day?' asked Grace as the trap came to a stop.

'Lovely, Ma,' replied Emma, hiding the worry which knowledge of the arrival of more dragoons had brought.

'Good. Going to stay to tea, Joe?'

'Thanks, Mrs Dugdale. That would be nice.' He clambered down from the trap quickly and came round it to help Emma down. 'Got the beds made, Amy?' he asked chaffingly as he passed her.

'Aye,' she replied. 'Want to inspect them?' she added with a teasing twinkle in her eye as their gaze met for one brief moment.

Emma frowned as she caught the short exchange.

'Amy!' Grace made her disapproval known with a sharp reprimand in her tone.

Amy did not miss the slight twitch of Joe's eyebrows and the admiring glance which flicked over her. She knew she had captured his attention and then felt remorse at flirting with her sister's beau when Emma handed her a packet.

'Your favourite,' she said.

Amy peeped into the packet. Her eyes widened with delight. 'Oo, treacle toffee. Thanks, Emma.'

'And some sweetmeats for the rest of us,' added Emma, passing a bag to her mother.

'What are they?' cried Jay excitedly.

'All sorts,' replied his mother.

'Can I have one?'

'Not now,' put in his father. 'It's tea-time. Come on, get thissen washed.' He led the way to a bowl which rested on a stone slab outside the back door.

'Come in, Joe. Everything's ready.'

During the meal Emma passed on messages from her aunt and told them how she had spent the day. When she mentioned walking on the cliffs with Meg she casually dropped in the news of the arrival of the revenue cutter with dragoons on board. Although she appeared to be directing her attention at no one in particular she was watching for her father's reaction to the news and caught the momentary glance exchanged between him and her mother. Now Emma realised her mother knew her father was involved with the smugglers. Whether she approved or not was another matter.

'Did they disembark here?' asked John casually.

'Aye, they did,' put in Joe. 'I was down on the quay. Likely-looking bunch. The Controller was there to meet them. He must have asked for them to help stamp out the smuggling. I hear it's become pretty rife of late, especially in Baytown.'

'Aye, so they tell me,' said John.

'Well, I think the government's right in trying to stamp it out. It's depriving them of a lot of money. Free traders they call themselves.' Joe gave a little grunt of derision. 'Say they benefit folk by selling the contraband cheaply. They ain't concerned with folks. All they're bothered about is lining their own pockets.'

Emma's heart missed a beat at Joe's outburst. She was thankful she had not confided in him and sought his help, as she had been tempted to do when she first knew of her father's involvement with the smugglers.

'Aye, maybe thee's reet, lad,' said John, wanting to put an end to the matter.

'Joe tells me his father's letting him run a few sheep on the moor,' put in Emma, changing the subject.

'Aye, Pa's given me a tup and three ewes. I aim to build up a good flock,' explained Joe.

The rest of the meal passed off without any further mention of smuggling or the dragoons.

That night by lantern light, John dug a deep hole in the pig sty on the far side of the stable out of sight of the house. He lined it with stones, and after carefully wrapping the roll of silk and the lace in a protective covering, buried it with the tub of brandy, figuring that no one would care to dig up a pig sty unless they were almost certain of finding smuggled goods. They should be safe there until he judged the time right to produce them as he and Grace had discussed.

The following morning Lieutenant Henry Boston was aware of the stares, some of them hostile, he was receiving as he walked briskly to the Custom House. He found George Stackpole already at work and felt a sense of efficiency emanating from the building. He figured Stackpole ran a tight crew but that while he could be firm, he would be fair and understanding.

'Sit down, Lieutenant,' said the Controller after he had greeted the officer with a firm shake of the hand.

He eyed the dragoon closely, seeing a smartly turned out young man whom he estimated had the respect of his men. He had a firm chin, bright eyes which were sharp and missed nothing, and held himself with a degree of assurance. His broad shoulders spoke of power and Stackpole judged him a man who could look after himself.

'I'll tell you the situation, shall I? Smuggling along this coast has become rife and is raising concern as far away as the Board in London. We aim to stamp it out completely, though I realise with so many people involved – the majority of the populace in some villages – it will be a difficult thing to do. So the best we can hope for is to contain it as much as we can. That's why I asked for more dragoons for this area.'

'We'll do our best, sir.'

'Now, two of your men are to be posted to Sandsend, two to Hinderwell, two to Runswick and two to Staithes. I've made out the necessary authority for them to take over the cottages I've allocated.' Stackpole handed over the appropriate pieces of paper then went on, 'The rest of your troop will be based in Whitby to patrol the area between here and Robin Hood's Bay. Bay is notorious for smuggling and that's the place I want you to concentrate on. I give you a free hand, but keep me informed.'

'Yes, sir. Can you tell me anything about the smugglers there?'

'The leader is Zac Denby but we've never been able to prove it. The only way would be to catch him red-handed but we've never achieved that even though I have two men stationed in Bay. The whole village is behind the smugglers. You'll get no one there to betray them. If they did, they know the consequences.' Stackpole drew his finger across his throat.

'In some places the leader of the land operation is not the main person behind the smuggling. Is it the same here?' queried Boston.

'Most certainly, but no one knows who. I don't even have a suspicion and that's the frightening thing about it – it could be anyone. But of one thing I'm certain. It must be someone with influence and the means to finance the purchases on the Continent before smuggling them in and disposing of them over here.'

'Do you expect me to pursue that line of enquiry?' asked Boston.

Stackpole shook his head as he leaned back in his chair. 'No, that would be too big an operation for you. Of course if you get a hint or a clue let me know, but what I really want you to do is to curb the land operation. That may help us to flush out the man behind it all.'

'Very good, sir. I'll do my best. I'd like you to withdraw your two men from Robin Hood's Bay. They aren't doing much good if they haven't found anything out so far.'

'Very well. That will be done today.'

'I'll deal with the postings you want and this afternoon my men will familiarise themselves with the horses you've allocated. Tomorrow I'll ride with my troop through Robin Hood's Bay, make a show of strength, and also visit some of the farms in the area. If they are in league with the smugglers and storing goods for them it may make them think again.'

When Lieutenant Boston had departed Stackpole felt reassured. They had been at stalemate for so long, something he had found frustrating. Now something was being done.

Chapter Eight

Lieutenant Boston drew his troop to a halt on the cliffs above Robin Hood's Bay and eyed the prospect before him. Most of his time in the service to date had been spent operating against the smugglers of Romney Marsh and the south-east. He had never seen a coastline dominated by such precipitous cliffs as these.

Houses, lying at all angles as if grabbing what little ground they could, appeared to be standing one on top of the other as they tumbled down the cliff towards a tiny beach. Some were three storeys tall, trying to catch a glimpse of the sky before a neighbour blocked it out. Deprived of the sun by grey clouds, the red roofs held no sparkle today. Why anyone should want to live in such an isolated, God-forsaken place Lieutenant Boston could not imagine.

The high tide filled the bay with a sea which, though calm, looked cold and uninviting. The cliffs swung round in a huge arc, climbing to the heights of Ravenscar on the opposite side of the bay. The lieutenant could see why this made an ideal place for smugglers. Luggers could run into the bay in comparative safety and, with such promontories ideal for lookouts and warning systems, could be in full sail before their escape was blocked.

The lieutenant could sense a growing unease amongst his men at the bay's forbidding atmosphere. He must put them into action immediately. He sent his horse forward to the uneven trackway, muddy from last night's rain, which served as the main street of Baytown. He kept it to a walking pace, giving it a chance to hold its footing among the squelching mud and stony ground. The men behind him rode two abreast matching their pace to his.

The main street swung towards the cliff edge where it hung precariously above the sea before swinging back in front of a row of houses and then turning between stone buildings of various sizes to run downwards towards the shore.

Boston's eyes were everywhere, mentally noting anything worthwhile, especially the layout of the village. Narrow streets ran right and left and the short connecting alleyways turned the whole cliff-side into a warren in which it would be easy for any human to escape pursuit.

He saw that the first-floor windows on one side of these streets looked into the ground-floor windows of those on the opposite side and realised how easy it would be to pass smuggled goods from one to the other all the way up the cliff.

The whole place was made for hidey holes and the task of catching anyone red-handed with smuggled goods would not be easy. Maybe the only way would be to engage the smugglers in the act of offloading on the beach or destroying the distribution network once the contraband had been landed. Boston realised he had a formidable task ahead for he knew how close-knit smuggling communities were and guessed they would be no less so on the wilds of the Yorkshire coast.

Today he was here to establish a presence. To show strength and let these folk know that the government meant business in its attempts to stamp out smuggling, and that he, Lieutenant Henry Boston, was no fool, a man to be reckoned with.

He sat tall in the saddle, with an air of authority, yet relaxed and at ease with his mount. His men, knowing their commanding officer, took their lead from him. They knew what he expected of them – to show themselves as a threat to the smuggling gang.

The buildings lining the main street had no set pattern to them. Roofs started at various heights; the houses, some set a few feet back, others protruding across the roadway, were in diverse states of repair, according to the pride or finances of their inhabitants. Their sash windows, of a variety of sizes, were like so many eyes watching the troop.

And Lieutenant Boston knew that behind the net curtains, dirty or not, onlookers were hostile to his soldiers. That hostility hung on the air of Baytown like a defensive cloak. No one was on the street. No one was going to offer a word of welcome nor pass the time of day. Word of their coming must have gone through the village like flames through chaff. Everyone had gone indoors and locked themselves in and he knew no amount of hammering on doors would bring the occupants to see who disturbed them. If he wanted a word he would have to break a door down, and at this stage he was not prepared to raise any more antagonism than was already here. Maybe the only place he would find someone was in one of the inns.

The trackway narrowed towards the bottom, squeezing between gaunt buildings on to the beach.

Lieutenant Boston called his men to a halt, ordered them to dismount and then to stand at ease. He handed his reins to his sergeant.

'Hell of a place this, sir,' the man observed. He had served with Boston for six years and knew just how familiar he could be. 'They know how to tell us they don't want us. There ain't even a child about.'

'Aye, and they've even given up mending their nets,' returned Boston, nodding in the direction of the deserted cobles drawn up on the sand. 'Still, they know we're here.'

'Aye, I'm sure they do, sir.'

Boston glanced round. 'I'll see if there's anyone in the Fisherman's Arms yonder. The men can relax and then we'll ride inland and circle back to Whitby. Let the neighbourhood know we're here.'

Henry Boston walked briskly towards the Fisherman's Arms. He half expected the door to be locked against him but found it was not so. He had no doubt that their arrival on the beach had been watched. Had someone purposely unlocked it to allow him to get in?

He pushed it open and stepped into the corridor. He paused and listened. There was not a sound. He waited, letting his eyes become accustomed to the gloom, then moved to a door on the left and pushed it open slowly. He looked into a room furnished with upturned barrels and chairs and high-backed settles against the walls, but no one was there. The mute objects seemed to mock him. He closed the door and opened the one opposite. This too was empty and he was about to withdraw when a slight sound drew his attention to another door. Six quick steps took him to it. He opened it quickly and found himself confronted by a middle-aged woman who straightened from a table on which she was kneading dough.

Her eyes held hostility at the intrusion but as they swept over him, noting his uniform and insignia of rank, softened slightly.

'Good day, Lieutenant.' Her voice was flat, uncharged with either friendliness or antagonism.

'Lieutenant Henry Boston, ma'am.' His deep voice smacked of authority.

'Nell Randall,' she returned.

'Robin Hood's Bay is like the grave. Where is everyone?'

'How should I know? I'm not their keepers,' Nell replied sharply.

'Then tell me, where's the owner of this place?' Boston demanded, stepping further into the kitchen.

Nell saw his eyes darting everywhere, taking everything in. She knew he was a man to be wary of.

'Here,' she replied, wiping the flakes of dough from her hands with a towel.

'Then get him,' Boston rapped haughtily.

'She's here,' replied Nell.

Boston swung round. 'You?' He showed momentary surprise but had his reaction quickly under control. 'Ah. And no doubt with such an attractive landlady as you you'll not lack customers.'

'I do nicely.'

'And you'll know most folk, if not all, in Robin Hood's Bay.'

'Aye.' She smiled. 'Thee's new here, from the south? Must be with an accent like that. If thee's ganning to be up here long thee'd better get used to calling it Baytown or just Bay.'

Boston nodded his acknowledgement of the information and said, 'No doubt you know Zac Denby. Where can I find him?'

Nell was immediately on her guard. She shook her head. 'He's out of Bay today.'

Boston grunted. He didn't believe her but realised he would get nothing more from her. And it would be useless to search the warren-like village. Denby could be gone from one house to another before his soldiers knew it.

'Smuggler, isn't he?' The question came quickly after a moment's pause, trying to catch her off her guard.

'Fisherman.' Nell's retort came equally fast.

'And smuggler.'

Nell shrugged her shoulders. 'That's what thee'll believe no matter what I say.' She glanced in the oven and as she opened the door the tangy smell of new baked bread wafted into the kitchen.

'You bake a good loaf and a good pie, I would say,' he commented as she stepped to a table on which several pies were cooling. His casual comments were suddenly replaced by an incisive tone as he swung round on her. 'And this place, close to the beach, is ideal for smugglers.'

'What on earth is thee talking about?' demanded Nell indignantly.

Boston gave a short, harsh laugh. 'Everything is too neat, too straightforward. You'll deny anything connected with smuggling.' He came to her, his eyes cold. 'Listen to me, Nell Randall. I'm here to stamp it out in Baytown, and stamp it out I will. You tell Zac that.' He straightened, looking down on her. 'And there'll be no mercy shown to anyone connected with smuggling.'

'Don't thee threaten me.' Nell's eyes narrowed as she met his stare. 'And don't accuse until thee has proof.'

Without a word Boston strode quickly from the kitchen. She heard his footsteps head for the front door but only when it had slammed shut did she relax. She leaned against the table, knowing that everyone in Baytown would have to be a little more on their guard in future.

Then she heard a shout and her body stiffened in response.

'Sergeant! Leave one man with the horses and get the rest over here.'

A few moments later Nell heard the front door flung open and the tramp of feet in the corridor.

'Search this place.' The lieutenant's order was not amplified and she realised this was nothing new to these dragoons. Wherever they had come from they had experience of combating smuggling.

She rushed to the corridor and faced Boston with indignation but before she could speak he put in, 'There's nothing you can do so let you and I return to the kitchen and await my men's report.'

Seething with frustration at being unable to prevent the search, she turned and preceded him to the kitchen.

'Don't let your bread burn,' said Boston smoothly, with a sardonic twitch of his lips as he sat down on a chair. He watched her closely, amused by her suppressed indignation and anger.

She heard chairs and tables being tumbled about, settles dragged from their places, beds and drawers moved across the upstairs floors and walls tapped. Seething inside it took all her will-power to hold back her temper, to stop herself from telling this upstart officer what she thought of him. She must keep cool, she must not let this violation of her home bring to the surface all the antagonism she was feeling, for to do so would weaken her resolve and maybe bring about a slip of the tongue which the officer would seize on. She ignored him and went on with her baking as if nothing was happening.

One by one the dragoons reported to the sergeant that they had found nothing. When they had all done so he informed his superior.

Boston nodded and smiled at Nell as he got slowly from his chair. She felt a shiver run down her spine. The smile was smug and self-satisfied. Her confidence dipped.

He walked slowly across the room. He knew an inn such as this must have cellars yet all doorways had been examined and none led downwards. As he had sat in the kitchen while his men searched he had realised where the entrance might be. He paused beside a large clip-rug, looked once more at Nell who was watching him intently whilst trying to appear casual. With a sharp movement he kicked the rug away. The sudden action startled her. She glanced down at the trapdoor which had been covered by the rug, then back at Boston who stood smiling triumphantly at her.

'Search it!' he ordered without taking his eyes from her. If he hoped to detect even the slightest hint of alarm he was disappointed.

The sergeant brought his troop into the kitchen. The trapdoor was raised to reveal a flight of stone steps. Three lanterns which had been on a windowsill were lit from spills ignited at the fire. The sergeant led the men down the steps. Lieutenant Boston paused, gave a slight bow to Nell and said, 'After you, ma'am.'

She said nothing but her heart was beating faster by the time she reached the bottom of the steps. The men were already beginning their search with the aid of two lanterns. Boston held the third and from the dancing light saw that they were in a square cellar which seemed to hold nothing of consequence. Some chairs in need of repair were stacked in one corner. A table stood beside one wall while another was taken up with beer barrels.

'Test them, Sergeant,' Boston ordered.

'They're all full except those ten,' protested Nell, indicating ten barrels which were apart from the others.

No one took any notice of her.

In a matter of moments every barrel had been tested and found to be exactly as Nell had said. She gave a little smile of satisfaction and a moment later regretted that she had given way to this expression when the lieutenant rapped out his next order.

'Move them!'

As his men went about the task, she held her breath, hoping that the wall across the mouth of the tunnel, which the barrels had been covering, had been replaced satisfactorily, for it had not been supervised by Zac. But she need not have doubted Pete Bray's thoroughness. As the section was revealed she saw that it looked no different from the rest of the cellar wall.

She smiled to herself when she saw Boston's lips tighten with frustration. She sensed he had hoped to find some contraband or at least something which might serve as a hidey hole. It would have been a triumph for him on his first day on duty on the Yorkshire coast.

'Fall the men in with their horses, Sergeant,' snapped Boston, his face clouded with annoyance. He'd felt sure that he would find something here at the Fisherman's Arms. Its situation was ideal for the smugglers. There must be some place to hide contraband. He felt outwitted by this woman and it irritated him. He stormed up the stairs after his men. Nell followed, hugging herself with glee.

In the kitchen Boston turned to her. 'Tell Zac Denby to watch out. He has me to deal with now, not the halfwits who have been stationed here before.' He swung on his heel and hurried from the inn.

Nell chuckled to herself when she heard the door slam.

Although annoyed at the upset which had taken place, she knew that once the dragoons had left Baytown she would have all the help she needed to set the inn straight again. But she also knew that the situation had changed with the arrival of this troop of dragoons under Lieutenant Henry Boston. Much more caution would have to be exercised, but she believed that Zac was wily enough to outwit this officer who thought so much of his ability to stamp out smuggling.

Back at the beach Boston studied the map of the area which George Stackpole had supplied. It was crudely drawn but was better than nothing. Trackways were marked, and if they were accurate they provided a route which would take in isolated farms on a circular ride to Whitby. A show of strength to the farmers and their families would do no harm and serve as a warning if they were in league with the smugglers. He had no doubt that some of them would be, for their farms, secluded as they were, would make ideal hiding places for contraband.

Satisfied with his study, Lieutenant Boston ordered his troop to mount, and led the way from the shore along the track which climbed the cliff to the farmland and the moors beyond.

Jay, intent on resetting his rabbit snares on the east side of the beck about a mile north of Beck Farm, was unaware of the approaching riders. They were out of sight on the west moor but Jay would have heard their movement had he not been concentrating on his job and thinking of the mouthwatering rabbit pies his mother would make with today's catch.

The rustling noise of movement through the undergrowth on the opposite side of the beck startled him. He looked up and a wave of alarm swept over him at the sight of a man on a horse. But this was no ordinary man, he was a soldier. Jay knew it from his red coat, his sword and musket. One of the dragoons he had heard Emma and Joe talk about? Jay cowered, overawed by the presence which seemed to tower over him. The man steadied his horse and surveyed the prospect before him, as if he was looking for an easy way across the stream which he found did not offer an obstacle to the troop's progress. He started to turn in the saddle to signal to Lieutenant Boston when he saw the boy.

'Hi, you there.'

The harsh, gruff tone sounded threatening. Jay's instinct was to run to the protection of home. He jumped to his feet and started off alongside the beck.

'Hi, come back!' The soldier who had been sent to scout the direction, stood in his stirrups. 'Lieutenant, over here!' he yelled. Seeing the troop respond immediately to his urgent call, the soldier put his horse down the slope, sending stones and soil slithering beside him. Water sprayed from beneath its hooves as the horse splashed across the running water. On gaining the bank, the trooper turned his horse quickly and urged it after Jay.

The boy heard him coming and pumped his legs faster. His chest heaved, gulping in air. His brain pounded with the thumping of his heart. Fear gripped him. The horse was beside him. Hooves thundered in his ears. He tried to twist out of the way but in the restricted, uneven space of the gully he could not escape. He felt a sharp blow on his back as the stock of the man's musket struck him. He lost his balance, stumbled and went flying forward to pitch face first to the ground. He lay gulping on the air, his mind trying to cope with the pain that fused through his body. Tears of fear and hurt welled in his eyes but he fought them back. He was not going to let this man see him crying. He heard the noise of the horse's hooves fade as the soldier pulled it to a halt and turned it back.

Jay rolled slowly over on to his back and saw man and horse towering above him. The man's grin showed uneven, broken teeth. His eyes, gleaming with triumph, had a threatening evil behind them.

'Thought you'd get away, did you?' the soldier's chuckle mocked Jay from deep in his throat.

'Mister, I ain't done nothing wrong,' he gasped. 'I was only . . .'

'Nobody said you had,' cut in the trooper, leaning forward in the saddle and peering hard at Jay, who shrank back from a stare which frightened him, 'but you shouldn't run. The Lieutenant'll want to talk to you.'

Jay said nothing. He toyed with the idea of trying to make his escape but the man was watching him intently. Then he heard the sound of horses crashing through the undergrowth. More of them. It would be useless to run.

He looked towards the noise and saw more soldiers riding along the bank side. He saw the man in front wore insignia on his shoulders and the second one had stripes on his arms. The rest were clothed similarly to the man who had run him down. Jay had no doubt this was the troop of dragoons who had newly arrived in Whitby.

The leading horseman pulled his mount to a halt and sat staring down at Jay while the others came to a halt round about.

'Name, lad?' Lieutenant Boston's voice bore no concern for the fright his men had caused.

Jay stared, his eyes wide, at the men who seemed to tower over him.

'Name!' The lieutenant liked instant obedience, not silent insubordination. He did not consider that Jay might be too scared to speak. 'Name, or I'll have it beaten out of you!'

Jay gulped. 'Jay, sir. Jay Dugdale,' he spluttered.

'Where do you live?'

'Beck Farm.' He drew on his courage and pushed himself to his feet. He glanced down at his trousers, mud-stained from his fall, and wiped his hand roughly over them.

'Why did you run when you saw my trooper?' asked Boston, eyeing him with suspicion.

'I was frightened, sir.' Jay brushed his hand across his face and pushed his hair from his forehead.

Boston grunted in disbelief. 'More likely running to warn your folk that we were coming.'

'No, sir,' protested Jay, wondering why this soldier should think that.

'I think you were.' He leaned forward in the saddle, setting his bright eyes in a penetrating stare which chilled Jay. 'What has your family to hide?'

'Nothing, sir.'

Boston straightened with a chuckle. 'We shall see, we shall see. Sergeant, take this lad up and lead the way. Boy, lead us to Beck Farm.'

'Just follow the beck, sir.'

'Come here, lad.' The sergeant barked his order.

Jay reluctantly shuffled towards him, stumbling over a clod of earth and startling the lieutenant's horse.

'Watch what y' doing,' snarled Boston as he brought his stamping mount under control.

Jay avoided the trampling hooves and grabbed the sergeant's arm who swung him up behind him. The trooper tapped his horse and sent it following the twisting beck.

Jay, still shaking from his experience and wondering what his father would say at the arrival of the dragoons, directed the sergeant away from the stream as the tiny valley they had been following widened. The land, sheltered by the moorland slopes on either side, became more fertile and even before the buildings came in sight Lieutenant Boston knew he was approaching a well-run farm.

As they rode towards the house with its stables, byres, barns and pig sties nearby, he saw that everything was well cared for. There was an air of wellbeing about the place and he began to wonder how much money from smuggling had gone to making the farm look so prosperous. He became even more convinced that the boy had run to try to warn his family of the presence of the dragoons. Well, he had been stopped, so Lieutenant Boston figured that on this, his first day in action, he might just uncover some contraband. Beck Farm certainly had the buildings in which to hide smuggled goods. He had found nothing in the Fisherman's Arms though he was sure that Nell Randall knew more than she cared to let on. Maybe he would gain more satisfaction here.

'That your pa?' asked the sergeant when he saw a man appear at the door of the house.

'Aye,' replied Jay as he peered past the man's broad back.

'Your ma?'

'Aye, and my two sisters.' He had seen them all appear and stand watching the group of horsemen.

'Any more?'

'No.'

'Any hired hands?'

'No. Only when we need 'em.'

The sergeant grunted and when his superior came alongside, reported, 'All the family, sir. No hired hands.'

'Good,' replied Boston with satisfaction.

Emma was working at the kitchen sink when she glanced out of the window. She stiffened. Her breath caught in her throat and she could feel her face draining of its colour. 'Ma, Pa, a troop of dragoons.' She could scarcely get the words out.

Amy dropped the cloth she was folding and ran to the door.

John and Grace exchanged a quick questioning glance and he saw worry in her face. He stepped beside her, squeezed her hand reassuringly and whispered, 'There's nowt to worry about, just be normal.'

She bit her lip and nodded, took a deep breath and drew on the inner strength which had seen her support her husband through hard times to get where were today. Nothing must destroy it now. She followed him to the door where he stepped outside.

Emma's heart was racing as she joined her parents and sister. Her hand fiddled nervously with her apron strings. What if they should make a thorough search and find the contraband? She dared not think of the consequences. She glanced at her parents and marvelled at how calm they appeared. She was suddenly aware that she was twisting the apron strings and stopped immediately. She must be like her mother and father, giving nothing away through nervous reactions.

'Ma, there's Jay,' Amy gasped.

'Jay?'

'Aye, behind the man on the left.'

They all saw him.

'What's he doing with the dragoons?' Grace was stunned. What might have happened to him? 'Where's he been?' she asked, turning to her husband.

'He went to his rabbit snares,' John replied.

'Up the beck side?'

'Aye.'

Apprehension seized Emma's mind as she watched the soldiers approach. She had never seen such a menacing body of men. They were a threat to the whole family, to their lives and their future. If only her father had not involved himself with the smugglers she would have been standing here without a care in the world knowing this troop could do nothing to bring upheaval to Beck Farm.

The lieutenant brought his troop to a halt. No sooner had he done so than Jay slid to the ground from behind the sergeant and ran to his family as if the devil was behind him.

'Thee all right, son?' his father asked with concern.

'Aye,' panted Jay.

'What happened to thee?' his mother queried anxiously. 'Thee's in a mess.'

'I fell, Ma. I'm all right.' He moved closer to her and took her hand to reassure her. He wanted no scene in front of these soldiers.

Before anything else was said Lieutenant Boston broke in.

'Are you Dugdale?' His gaze scrutinised John.

'Aye, John Dugdale.'

'Why did your son want to warn you?'

The question took John by surprise. He was immediately wary. This man may be an efficient soldier but he was a haughty one who would stand no nonsense. And being on a new posting was no doubt wanting to prove himself to his superiors as soon as possible.

'Warning? About what?' asked John.

'That we were coming.'

'Why should he want to do that?'

'To give you time to make sure all contraband was adequately hidden.' Boston's watchful eyes were on the group hoping to see some reaction in their expressions which would prove him right. But there was none.

Emma's heart fluttered at the lieutenant's statement. Did he know something or was this a trick?

'Contraband? What would I know about contraband?' protested John.

'You tell me. You've a farm here, plenty of buildings, not too far from the coast. An ideal hiding place. Just suit the smugglers, and they pay well, I believe.'

'Wouldn't know,' replied John.

'Wouldn't you?' Boston leaned forward in his saddle, and turned his sharp, bright eyes on Grace.

She shuddered inwardly under their cold stare, a penetrating gaze she felt could almost read her thoughts.

'What do you say, Mrs Dugdale?' His voice carried an unveiled threat should he find she was not telling the truth.

'I don't know what thee's talking about.' Grace kept her voice steady. She drew herself up and met his gaze. 'And what's thee been doing to this poor lad to frighten him so? He was innocently seeing to his snares, and comes back with his clothes soiled and marked and scared out of his wits.'

Boston gave a half smile of derision. 'He wouldn't be marked if he hadn't run. We had to stop him warning you. And I don't think he's all that scared. He's an intelligent lad and had the presence of mind to try to get here before us.'

'See here,' put in John indignantly as he fought to keep his real attitude under control, 'we don't know where thee's got the idea that we might be hiding contraband, merely from a boy running at the unexpected sight of soldiers it seems, but I can assure thee that thee won't find any on my farm.'

Boston ignored him and turned his eyes on Emma and then on Amy. 'Is that right?' he snapped.

'Aye.' Emma forced her voice to be firm though her throat was dry.

'It's reet,' said Amy, overawed by the presence of so many soldiers and the hostility of the man who led them.

Boston swung from the saddle. 'Then you won't mind if we search the place.' Without waiting for permission, he barked over his shoulder, 'See to it, Sergeant!'

'Sir.' The sergeant acknowledged the order and half turned in his saddle. 'Dismount and fall in,' he roared.

The troopers quickly formed a line while one of them took charge of the horses. The sergeant allocated the men in twos to search the barns, stable and byres.

John started to move forward in protest but he checked himself. Better to let them get on with it. It would only make matters worse if he raised any objection. They would do it no matter what he said. The sooner they were through with their search the sooner they would be away and the family would be left in peace. Peace? He wondered if they would ever know peace again. Would they now be ever on edge lest the authorities discover his connection with the smugglers? If he tried to break away from Zac and his gang it could have dire consequences. He was caught and all he could do was to make the best of it.

'Sergeant, you and one other in the house!' Boston's order tolerated no protest from Grace.

She would have to endure these men tramping through her house, turning over her things in what she knew was a vain search for contraband. To voice a protest would only make matters worse and probably lead them to make their search more thorough, despoiling the house in which she took a pride.

'Shall we go inside too?' said Boston. His politeness was accompanied by a smile of satisfaction that he was making these Yorkshire folk feel uncomfortable.

Grace, her arm round Jay's shoulders, led the way followed by Amy and Emma with John a step in front of Boston.

The kitchen was warm and under different circumstances they would have found it homely. The smell of baking was enticing and Boston, seeing three pies on a table, picked up a knife and cut himself a quarter from a tea-plate-sized pie. He sat down on a chair and took a bite. After he had swallowed his first mouthful he wiped his hand across his lips and said, 'You bake a good apple pie, Mrs Dugdale.'

No one spoke. They all stood awkwardly around. Grace was not in the mood for compliments as she listened to the sergeant and a trooper pounding overhead, moving furniture and tapping walls.

'Emma, thee make some tea,' said Grace. 'Amy, thee get the cups.' She knew it was better for the girls to be occupied.

'Cheap from the smugglers?' commented Boston with a gleam in his eyes.

'Certainly not,' replied Grace, wishing she hadn't given him a chance to point the finger of suspicion at them again.

He grinned and took another bite at his pie.

Emma was thankful to be busy. It helped to hide her nervousness.

Fifteen minutes later the troopers reported that they had found nothing.

'Any other building on your farm?' Boston demanded of John, disappointed that not even the slightest bit of evidence had been found. He had so wanted to make his mark.

John was about to say no when he thought better of it. It would be easy for these troopers to ride his land, and to be found denying the existence of another building, no matter how dilapidated it was, would only lead to further suspicions.

'Only an old brokendown barn which is never used,' he replied.

'Never used. I wonder?' Boston grinned. 'Maybe you have something to hide after all.' His grin disappeared. 'Take us to it,' he snapped.

The troop mounted and followed John who led them towards Black Wood.

Emma watched them go with a heavy heart. She began to feel that this was the end, that the troopers would find the hidden cavern and all would be lost. She glanced at her mother and saw worry lines creasing her face. Emma was certain she knew about the contraband. She wanted to reach out and comfort her, to let her know that she was not alone with her anxiety, that Emma too shared it. But to do so would only add more concern, for her mother would then have the additional unease that someone else knew, even though it was a daughter she could trust.

When they reached the barn Boston dismounted and threw his reins to the sergeant. From the look of this building – holes in the wall, no door, tiles missing from a quarter of the roof – it was hardly likely to be a place to hide contraband. But having ridden here, he decided he may as well have a look.

He walked into the barn and glanced about then swung

round on John with a grunt. 'How long since you used this place?'

'I never have.' He found himself answering much more calmly than he had expected with the soldiers only a few yards from the contraband. He was thankful that he and Zac had been meticulous in covering footmarks leading to the cavern and that its entrance had been carefully disguised. 'It was in little better state when I came to Beck Farm and I decided it was of no use to me.'

Boston nodded, glanced around once more, then strode quickly from the building. When John got outside he was swinging into the saddle. He said nothing but rode off with his troop behind him.

John watched them for a few moments, then without a glance at the barn, strode off in the direction of home.

Though they tried to busy themselves, both Grace and Emma waited anxiously for the outcome of Boston's search. Amy had got out the board and pegs and was playing merrels with Jay to take his mind off the ordeal when Emma spoke. 'Here's Pa!' She had spotted him crossing the field from Black Wood and felt relief that he was alone. If the troopers had found anything they would certainly have taken him with them. They were safe, at least for the present. Though she knew her father would be much more on his guard now that he had seen the strength of the dragoons and knew the type of man he was dealing with in the lieutenant, she drew little comfort from the fact. She glanced at her mother and saw that her anxiety had lifted.

Grace brushed back her hair, straightened her dress, and with her children beside her went to the door to await the arrival of her husband.

Chapter Nine

'So they found nothing?' Zac's question sought confirmation of what Nell had just told him about the visit of the dragoons.

Her smile broadened. 'Not a thing. Word came into Bay that the dragoons were on their way. Everyone went to ground. The place was dead. I figured they might come looking here so I left the door open. Wanted to cast my eye over the lieutenant. Didn't expect them to make the thorough search they did, even moved the beer barrels in the cellar, but Pete had done a good job supervising the replacement of the wall.'

Zac chuckled and cut himself another piece of Nell's meat pie. 'If they'd known how near they were to all that contraband in the cavern . . .' His laugh deepened and she joined in his amusement as she filled his tankard with beer.

She replenished the jug from the barrel of beer standing in one corner of the kitchen and brought it to the table. Her face was serious as she sat down.

'We'll have to be careful of this lieutenant.' Her eyes were fixed gravely on Zac. 'He'll be a sharp one and I reckon he'll be out to prove himself to his superiors.'

Zac glanced up and met her gaze. 'There's nowt and none we can't handle, Nell.'

'Don't get ower confident, Zac. He could be a wily customer. And don't forget he's got a bigger troop and can deploy his men differently to what we've been used to.'

Zac nodded his head thoughtfully. He put a lot of store by Nell's views and opinions. 'Maybe thee's reet.' He drew the words out as he considered what she had said. 'The two Preventive Men who were stationed here have been withdrawn so we could be faced with strangers, spies in civilian clothes. With the strength of the troop, he could even post some of them along the cliffs to keep a watch on Bay.' He forked a piece of pie into his mouth and followed it with a swig of beer.

The hum of conversation from the bar room became louder as the door into the kitchen opened. The round, rosy-cheeked face of the barmaid peered round the door.

'John Dugdale's asking for thee, Zac.'

'Send him through,' he instructed.

The barmaid disappeared and a moment later John came into the kitchen.

Zac read the concern on his face. 'What brings thee here, John?' he asked easily.

He hesitated and Zac saw a query in his quick glance towards Nell.

'It's all right, thee can talk in front of Nell,' Zac was quick to reassure him. 'She knows as much about the smuggling as I do.'

'Sit down, John.' Nell smiled warmly as she indicated a chair next to her. 'Have some beer?'

'Thanks.' He nodded and, as she got up from the table to fetch a tankard, looked at Zac. 'I had a visit from the dragoons. Went through the house and all the buildings.'

'All of them?'

'Aye, even the old barn. Had to take them, Zac. If I'd denied its existence and they'd seen it they'd have been more suspicious.'

'Aye, thee's reet. Find anything?'

'No.' He mouthed his thanks to Nell who had poured him a tankard of beer. 'Only the lieutenant went inside. Didn't even bother to dismount his troop when he saw the state of the building.'

'Then what's thee worried about, John?' Zac raised his right eyebrow in surprise as if making light of the matter.

'They rode through Bay. They were only making a show of strength, impressing Bay folk and those in the neighbouring countryside that they mean business.'

John, taken a little aback by this attitude, spluttered his reply. 'Well, I, er, I thought thee ought to know.'

'Aye, thanks, but thee's nowt to worry about. They searched these premises, didn't they, Nell?'

'Aye. And like thee, John, I was too smart for 'em.' Nell smiled as she sat down again.

He was puzzled by the seemingly light-hearted attitude they were taking. It was as if they were not bothered about the presence of the dragoons. But he felt just a little flattered that Nell was accepting him to be as wily as she, and he only very new to the smuggling trade.

He took a drink of his beer and asked, 'When is thee likely to move some of the contraband?'

'I'm expecting it to be next week. So far I've recruited two pedlars but they will not be this way until then. But keep alert for any callers. You know the signal. If I can find any others willing to help I'll do so. It might be wise to get some of the goods moving as soon as possible.'

'And be suspicious of everyone, even friends,' put in Nell. 'But more particularly strangers. This lieutenant has sufficient troopers to send some out as spies.'

John nodded. 'Thanks for the warning.' He drained his tankard. 'I'd best be ganning.' He stood up. 'What do I owe thee for the beer, Nell?'

She gave a dismissive wave of her hand. 'Forget it, John. It's a welcome-to-working-with-us drink.' She smiled and gave him a wink of assurance.

Zac leaned back on his chair, his right eye gleaming as he looked at John. 'Thee has an exceptional hiding place. See no one knows about it except thee, not even the pedlars picking up the contraband, and thee can make thissen a fortune from what we'll pay thee.'

*   *   *

When John had gone and he had finished his meal, Zac took his tankard through to the bar room and found a chair beside Pete Bray.

'Fish run well today?' he asked.

'Aye. Good catch quickly and I was back, panniers packed and three of my lasses away to Pickering with them by noon.'

'So thee saw nowt of the dragoons?'

'No, but I hear tell the town put on its dead-as-the-grave act.'

'Aye,' chuckled Zac.

'Bit of difference to now with folk busy mending nets, packing fish, kids playing in the alleys and everyone toing and froing.'

Before Zac could make any comment his attention was drawn by the door opening. Two men walked in. He recognised one as Jim Harrison, a pedlar who sometimes called at Baytown on his way from Whitby market. The other was a stranger. Jim exchanged greetings with some of the occupants of the room as he crossed to two chairs close to Zac, pausing only to order two beers from the busy barmaid. As they reached the seats he saw Zac and nodded to him.

'Jim. Pull them chairs round here and join us.'

'Thanks,' replied Jim, a man of medium height, strong of leg through miles of walking with his ponies, and with an angular face marked by the wind and sun.

The two men swung the chairs round and sat down.

'This here's Fergus Pinkney.' Jim introduced the tall, thin man who was having difficulty in accommodating his long legs around the barrel serving as a table.

Zac made himself and Pete known to Fergus then added, 'Thee a pedlar too?'

'Aye,' he replied. 'Been to Pickering and Whitby often, but never been in Baytown. Jim persuaded me to come this way back to Pickering with him.'

'Bit of company,' put in Jim. 'Besides we might get rid of a few more goods before we move on.'

'And might do thissens some good in other ways,' put in Zac. His mind was already toying with the idea of using these two to move the first batch of contraband from Beck Farm. He knew Jim would keep a wise tongue in his head but he had to make sure of Fergus.

'How does thee mean?' asked Jim, his curiosity raised at the proposition hinted at by Zac.

'I'll show thee.' Zac stood up and with an inclination of his head indicated to Jim to follow him.

Zac led the way to the kitchen and paused just through the doorway. Nell recognised the mood when Jim joined him and after a cursory nod of recognition to him continued filling jugs with beer and taking them to the hatch for the barmaid to collect.

'What has thee to show me, Zac?' asked Jim, glancing round the kitchen puzzled as to what it could be.

Zac's reply of 'Nowt,' surprised him. 'Well, not here.' Zac hastened to banish the momentary flash of annoyance which glimmered in Jim's eyes.

'Like to make some extra money?' Zac put the question while keeping Jim under a scrutiny which saw the gleam come to his eyes. Before Jim answered he knew he had another man to run contraband to Saltersgate.

'Allus out for an extra coin,' he replied.

'What about Pinkney?' Zac inclined his head towards the door to the bar room.

'I reckon he'd be interested.'

'Can he be trusted?' asked Zac.

Jim knew of Zac's reputation as a smuggler and guessed that whatever he was going to propose would be running close to breaking the law. He also knew that the smugglers had a way of dealing with people who let them down.

'I've known him the past five years. I've travelled with him to Whitby from Pickering. He's never been to Bay. Generally goes on to Guisborough. He'll not let thee down.'

'Good. Bring him through here.'

Jim left the kitchen and returned with Fergus. Within a few minutes Zac had informed them of his proposal and an agreement had been reached, with Zac swearing the two men to the utmost secrecy and making it known in no uncertain manner that betrayal would wreak an awesome revenge.

'If thee needs any more pedlars and Luke Newell comes this way, I'll vouch thee can trust him,' said Jim as they were about to return to the bar room.

The following morning under the overcast sky which still persisted over north-east Yorkshire, Jim Harrison and Fergus Pinkney led their four ponies out of Baytown and were soon on the track for Beck Farm. Seeing money in their pockets now and in the future, they had complied with Zac's instruction to stay the night at the Fisherman's Arms so that they could collect contraband from John Dugdale the next day. They were happy with the arrangement for it meant that they could deliver the smuggled goods to the inn at Saltersgate and be back in Pickering in daylight.

John Dugdale straightened from milking the last of his three cows. He eased his back, pleased that he was finished. He picked up two pails and went outside. As he walked to the house his attention was drawn to a figure leading two pack horses. He paused, narrowing his eyes against the distance. He grunted and then went quickly to the house, set the pails down inside the door and turned back without a word.

He hurried to meet the pedlar and as he neared him saw that his first impression was right. There were three coloured ribbons tied to the left hand basket on the lead pony.

Emma gave her mother a quick glance of surprise when her father left the pails and returned outside without a word. Grace, who had looked up from the pan she was stirring at the fire, responded with a shrug of the shoulders and a grimace which indicated she was just as puzzled as her daughter.

Emma collected the pails and put them on the table near the window. She glanced outside, looking for a clue as to her father's behaviour. Her nerves tightened when she saw him hurrying towards the pedlar. She watched, saw a brief exchange between the two men and then they both started towards Black Wood. She bit her lip. Another pedlar for contraband so soon after Jim and Fergus?

Her mother joined her and was gripped by anxiety when she saw the direction John and the pedlar were taking.

'Where's Pa off to now with yon pedlar?' said Emma, trying to sound casual though she knew full well what mission her father was on. 'Why didn't he bring him to the house?'

'Maybe the pedlar was wanting to be on his way, it's getting late for him to cross the moors,' replied Grace.

'But why's Pa ganning with him?'

'Probably to show him the right track. Now let's get the table set.' Grace wanted no more questions. She knew what John was about but deemed it best to keep that to herself. It was safer for the family not to know their father was tied to the smugglers.

As he had done with Jim and Fergus, John left this stocky pedlar with a cast in his left eye, who had introduced himself as Luke Newell, in Black Wood while he went to the barn and brought the goods from the cavern. The task completed, he covered its entrance and signalled to Luke that all was ready.

Once Luke had the contraband safely hidden in the large baskets on his two pack-horses he was eager to be on his way.

'Will thee make it across the moors tonight?' queried John, eyeing the sky with some concern. 'There's rough weather coming.'

The pedlar cast a quick glance at the overcast sky where

more ominous clouds were piling in the west. 'Aye. I'm used to the moors, usually direct from Whitby, but I'll be back on that track before long. Dark doesn't bother me.'

'Easy to lose thy way, especially if the weather turns really foul,' warned John.

'I'll be all right. Want to get home tonight,' said the pedlar, gathering up the lead reins of his horses.

'As thee will,' said John. 'Good luck.' He watched the pedlar for a few minutes then hurried back to the farm.

Luke Newell made good progress to the main trackway from Whitby to Pickering but by the time he reached it the west wind had strengthened to gale force. It drove the thick clouds eastwards, darkening the sky prematurely. As he felt the first heavy drops of rain Luke stopped, took his long coat from the lead horse and shrugged himself deep into its protection. He turned up the large collar and crammed his wide-brimmed hat more firmly on his head.

He sensed restlessness in the horses and tried to calm them with soothing words. 'Steady now, steady. There's nowt to be afraid of. It's only the wind. Come on wi' thee.' He took the reins again and, hunched against the gale, started off again.

The wind hurled itself at him, howling like some demented hob haunting these moors. It bent the stunted heather and the dead bracken as if it would rip them from the ground and hurl them far beyond the moors. Its shrieking was interrupted by the roar of the rain as the clouds burst open with a deluge that lashed the horses and stung Luke's face and hands. In a matter of moments the trackway was a quagmire of mud pulling at his slowing steps.

The darkness, hastened by the clouds, now seemed total. Luke felt as if he was being dragged into a bottomless pit by the bullying wind and tormenting rain. How he wished he had sought shelter at Beck Farm. The ground became more sodden and mud squelched under his boots which, stout though they were, were beginning to take in water. He felt it soaking into his woollen socks and the dampness sent a shiver through his body. He tried to pull his coat more tightly around him but the wind mocked his effort as it curled the brim of his hat allowing the rain to drive under his collar and creep down his neck.

He stopped, panic gripping his mind. Was he still on the track? The ground felt rougher. Dare he move on? He knew there were areas of bog on the moors and to stray into one of those meant being dragged slowly to a choking death. In this awful darkness, where earth and sky were one, there were no stars to guide him. He was at the mercy of the storm, ripped by the wind and beaten by the rain.

His calls to comfort the horses were torn from his lips and cast into the darkness. He tightened his grip on the reins and plodded on, slowly, ever so slowly, aware that one false step could plunge him to death. How long he trudged in this fashion he could not calculate. Time meant nothing. All he could concentrate on was putting one foot safely in front of the other and making sure he held on to the reins, for a bolting horse, scared by the storm, would be doomed.

The thick pounding beat of the solid sheets of rain eased a little, though still combined with the howl of the wind to gnaw at his mind. What would he give for some shelter, crude though it may be, to spare him any more distress! He felt a tremor in the wind. Its continuous shriek was broken. He drew hope and courage from its ruptured pattern. Maybe the worst was over. He glanced skywards hoping to detect some change in the clouds as there had been in the swish of the rain and the wail of the wind, but there was none. They were as thick and as glowering as ever and threatened heavier rain.

As his eyes swept down again he started in disbelief. A light! He shook his head as if to purge it of all extraneous thoughts so that he could concentrate. He rubbed the rain from his eyes, clearing them for the search. He tried to force them to pierce the gloom, to verify that he had been right, that the light had not been a figment of a wishful imagination. Nothing. His heart, which had been buoyed on hope, sank on despair. His feelings choked in his throat. He cursed the foul weather which had played tricks on him.

The wind rose and fell and rose again with a sound which mocked him, but in that rise and fall it seemed to part the rain for one moment. There it was! The light! Luke tried to calm himself as excitement gripped him. Then the light vanished in a sudden downpour. But it must be there. He had seen it twice. Surely his mind couldn't play tricks again? He waited, longing for the rain to lose its wall-like appearance. He moved forward tentatively, keeping in mind the direction in which he had seen the light.

There it was again. Ahead and to the right. It remained there steady, a beacon of hope. Where there was light there must be shelter. But how to reach it? Where lay the path which would take him to safety, safety he must reach soon as the storm took on a new viciousness and thunder rumbled across the moor.

Carefully, through what seemed an interminable time, he checked the ground on his right as he moved forward. His search for a path took ten minutes which seemed like eternity as thunder pounded the heavens and lightning streaked the sky with forked fingers. Once on the path he gained confidence but with horses frightened by the boom of the thunder and the startling flashes from the sky it was no easy task to progress as quickly as he would have liked. Besides he was aware that there may be bogs around him.

The light seemed to get no nearer and Luke's mind felt uneasy whenever it disappeared in the rain thickening squalls which beat ferociously through the darkness. He feared he would never see it again but it reappeared, beckoning him to a haven of security. He walked on with hope.

Then the light disappeared. He waited for the squall to pass. The rain eased. His eyes strained in expectancy. His heart slumped. There was no light. Thunder boomed with an intensity which mocked his confidence. Despair began to fill him when lightning cut through the dark and revealed that the path had taken him close to a rise in the land. Eagerness gripped him once again for he realised that the light must have been blocked out by the howe. He moved on and as he rounded the howe, lightning revealed a cottage with a light shining in the window. Anxious as he was to find shelter he was oblivious to the condition of the ground around the cottage and of the unkempt garden now saturated by the rain. He hitched his horses to the broken gatepost and walked up the path. Shelter for the night, warmth and food.

He raised his hand to knock on the door but there came a moment's hesitation. He shuddered but hardly had time to wonder whether it was because he was cold or from a feeling of foreboding when the door opened.

He lowered his arm. Someone must have seen him from the window yet how could they? Unease gripped him but was dispelled when the man who had come to the door spoke in a deep voice. 'Come in wi' thee. Thee's letting the rain in.'

Luke stepped into the cottage. 'Sorry.' He muttered his apology for the man was intimidating. He was big and powerful and when he turned Luke almost shrank from the dark piercing eyes, for in their half-vacant stare was a look which was uncanny. Luke hadn't a moment in which to consider the matter further for the man brushed past him as he said, 'This is Ma,' directing Luke's attention to the small, thin woman who sat huddled in a chair beside the fire. Eyes peered at him from deep sockets.

'Ah, young man, this is no night to be out on t' moors.' Her voice was light but held a grating lilt. As if to emphasise her words thunder crashed around the cottage, seeming to shake the very stones of the building. Luke's eyes widened. Had the witch-like figure in the chair conjured up that thunder at the very moment she wanted it? She was rubbing her bony hands as if enjoying the situation.

'Dick, see to the horses,' she ordered sharply and the big man made no murmur of protest as he went to the door and stepped out into the rain. Again Luke was surprised. He had made no mention of his horses and yet this woman knew. 'Phoebe!'

Almost immediately a door opened and Luke received another surprise when he saw an attractive young woman come into the room. She seemed out of place in these sur-roundings.

'Yes, Ma?'

'Show this young man to his room. He'll want to get out of his wet things,' said the old woman, eyeing the pools which were forming round Luke's feet.

'Reet, Ma.'

'I'll need some dry things from my . . .'

'Thee needn't gan out in the rain again,' rattled the older woman. 'Look behind the curtain in the room, thee'll find something to fit thee.'

Luke raised his eyebrows in surprise but made no com-ment as Phoebe said, 'This way.' She smiled at him with sparkling blue eyes and as he followed her he found himself admiring her lithe body which moved enticingly and he wished he had her alone to himself.

A lamp was already alight in the room. The bed looked inviting and Luke felt sure he would have no trouble sleep-ing after the buffeting he had taken.

'There's water in the ewer.' Phoebe indicated the bowl and ewer on the washstand. 'And you'll find some clothes here.' She drew back a curtain to reveal a row of hooks which held all manner of coats, breeches, shirts and underclothes as well as a row of shoes and calf- and thigh-length boots.

Luke was surprised for he realised that these clothes would not fit Dick, who was too big and broad, but he thought it wise to make no comment. It did not matter to him where they had come from, but he might have thought otherwise if he had known he was looking at dead men's clothes. All he could think of at the moment was to get out of his wet things as they were driving a chill into his body.

'Don't be long,' said Phoebe coyly as she glided to the door. 'Thy meal is about ready.' She paused and looked back at him. 'And who knows what there might be after that?' The seductive tone of her voice sent Luke's pulses racing. Maybe he would receive a visit when her mother and brother were asleep.

He shed his wet clothes quickly, gave himself a vigorous rub down and revelled in the warm sensation which began to flow through his body.

Eliza and Phoebe sensed excitement in Dick when he returned to the cottage. He paused in the doorway, rain dripping from his clothes and running down his face from his hair which lay lank and sodden. But they ignored it all for they felt an exhilarating tension in him.

'Where is he?' he gasped, his chest heaving from the rush back from the stable.

'Changing,' replied Phoebe.

'Well, what is it? What's he carrying? Out w' it,' urged Eliza.

Dick squatted in front of them, his eyes darting from one to the other. 'There's tubs. Brandy and gin, I reckon. Baccy. Silks, lace, and some tea.'

Eliza's eyes brightened. 'Contraband!'

'Contraband?' gasped Phoebe.

'Keep thy voice down, lass,' warned Eliza with a frown of annoyance.

'We've nivver had contraband before.' Phoebe kept her voice low.

'We ain't, lass, we ain't.' A touch of glee had come to Eliza's cackle. 'If Zac Denby and his gang are starting to use pedlars to move their smuggled goods, then we could benefit.' She chuckled at the thought of the extra money they could make and looked at Dick. Her eyes narrowed. 'Reet, away wi' him now.'

'Ain't the condemned man allowed a meal?' smiled Phoebe with a sarcastic twitch of the lips.

'He won't know what he's missed,' chuckled Eliza. 'Away wi' thee, Dick.'

The big man straightened. He cracked his knuckles and strode to the kitchen. He poured some whisky into a glass and then went to the room where Luke was changing.

Luke carefully selected the clothes he would wear. The first two shirts were not to his liking but the third fitted well. He chose a pair of plum-coloured breeches, only to find they were too tight around his middle and had to settle for a grey pair. He was hitching them up when there was a knock at the door. Before he could answer, it opened and the whole doorway was filled with Dick's huge mass.

'Brought thee a drop of whisky.' His voice boomed around the room. 'It'll drive out the chill.'

'Thanks,' said Luke.

Dick pushed the door shut and came to Luke with the glass held out in his left hand. Luke reached for it but never touched it for Dick's clenched right fist swung fast and took him on the point of the jaw. It was a sledgehammer blow and Luke never knew what hit him, for he was unconscious before he landed on the bed. Dick stood looking at him for a moment. Satisfied that the pedlar would not open his eyes again, he raised the glass to the prone figure and threw the whisky down his own throat in one gulp. He licked his lips, put the glass down, quickly stripped Luke of the clothes he had been so careful to select and hoisted the naked man over his shoulder.

Ten minutes later, with rain lashing him, Dick watched Luke sink slowly into the bog. Vivid lightning illuminated the macabre scene and thunder boomed a death knell.

Chapter Ten

Ben Thrower looked up from the stew he was enjoying to his wife, sitting across the table in their small cottage on the outskirts of Pickering.

He put down his knife and fork and rested his broad arms on the oak table which stood beside the wall opposite the fire over which hung a black pan, its contents giving an occasional bubble. His face, tanned by his outdoor life, took on a serious expression which eliminated the laughter lines at the corners of his eyes.

Susan sensed him looking at her and lifted her gaze to meet his.

The movement jerked him out of his loving scrutiny of her. He never ceased to enjoy studying her homely charms. Her chestnut hair, gathered up at the nape of her neck, framed a round, open face from which deep-set eyes looked at him tenderly.

'Susan.' He hesitated when he saw her expression become touched with suspicion.

'Ben, when thee uses my Sunday name I know thee's up to summat. What is it?' She rested her hands on the table, ignored her food and waited for him to go on. After two years of courting and six years of marriage, she reckoned she knew all Ben's moods and idiosyncrasies.

His mother had died when he was a child and his father when he was twenty. Since the age of fifteen he had accompanied his father on the road between Pickering and Helmsley with regular calls at the villages and farms along the way, so it was natural for him eventually to take over his father's pack-horses and follow the trade of a pedlar.

His father, a wise and prudent man, had saved to buy

his own cottage. Small though it was, it gave him independence and when Ben inherited it he asked his 'bonny lass', whom he had known since schooldays and had seriously courted since they were both eighteen, to marry him.

Ben wondered whether to try a piece of subtle flattery or whether to come straight to the point. When he saw Sue's lips begin to set in a determined line he decided on the latter.

'I'm changing my journey, I'm ganning to Whitby.' He knew Sue was not one for change. But now it was out. The dye had been cast.

She stared at him without speaking for a few moments, her brown eyes revealing nothing of what she was feeling. Then she mouthed the word: 'Why?'

'There's more brass to be made. Whitby's bigger than Helmsley, a thriving port that's growing. And there's the villages along the coast all relying on pedlars.' Ben put all his enthusiasm into his words.

'Do we need more money?' asked Sue.

'Why not? I could buy things for thee that I can't now. We could get a bigger cottage.'

'I'm content. I'm happy here. This cottage is ours thanks to thy father. We're comfortable. Why want more?'

'I want to do things for thee, lass. Things I might have done for our children, but it looks as if we aren't ganning to be lucky, so thee's the only one I can spoil.'

Sue sensed the touch of pleading tinged with sadness in his voice. Her features softened. She reached across the table and took his hand. There was love in the grip which united them. Each wanted the other to be happy, to have their own way.

'It's wild country to cross to Whitby,' she pointed out gently.

'Nothing to be afraid of.'

'Who's telled thee that there's more money to be made ower there?' Sue frowned, worried that his informant had been unreliable.

'Jim Harrison and Fergus Pinkney.' Ben's enthusiasm rose again. 'Fergus always went on to Guisborough but says he'll always come back now by Baytown. They got rid of practically all their goods this last time.'

Sue pursed her lips thoughtfully without speaking. She knew the two men to be reliable, experienced pedlars. Should she protest? Had she the right to destroy Ben's ambitions and desires which she knew were only for her?

'If thee doesn't want me to gan, luv . . .'

'No, Ben. I can't hold thee back. Thee gan if that's what thee wants to do.' Her eyes expressed her deep love for him.

Ben rose from his chair and came round the table to her. He knelt by her, put his arms round her waist and drew her to him. 'I love thee, my bonny lass, with all my heart.' His lips met hers gently but the sensuous tremor which passed between them expressed the depths of their feelings.

When their lips parted she moved her hands to hold his face between them. She looked into the depths of his eyes. 'And I love thee, Ben Thrower, always have and always will.' She paused, her gaze tender, soft and loving. In return she received adoration. If the bond of love between them could be strengthened it was in that moment when time stood still for two people so deeply in love that nothing else mattered.

Sue broke the moment with the question, 'When will thee gan?'

'The Gals are fit, the panniers all packed – I'll leave early. I'll ride so I can make good time, and then I see no reason why I shouldn't be back tomorrow night.' Ben felt certain he could do it. His three Galloways were sturdy horses, their hard feet and sure-footedness ideal for the moorland journey.

Sue brightened. She had not thought of his riding. Ben usually walked with three horses carrying panniers. 'But that'll mean thee'll only have two horses for goods. Will it still be worth it?'

'Aye. According to Jim and Fergus they get good prices in Whitby. Besides I want to be back wi' thee as soon as possible.'

She kissed him. 'Be careful, Ben, those moors can be treacherous and thee's very precious.'

'I will, luv.'

Sue's mood lightened. She gave him a friendly dig in the shoulder. 'And watch the lasses in Whitby. Seaports have a reputation.' Her eyes sparkled teasingly.

'Well, I might just see what's on offer.' He grinned and ducked the playful blow she aimed at him.

Ben watched the eastern horizon streak with pale light as he climbed towards the moors from Pickering. He rode easily, holding his pace steady to allow the two horses behind him to feel easy with their loads. He was thankful the storms of the last two days had passed leaving behind a warmth which drew mist from the saturated valleys.

The immense Hole of Horcum was filled with vapour and as he rode round its rim it seemed as if he was riding on the edge of a cloud. The track turned and dipped and ran past lonely Saltersgate Inn where the creaking inn sign added its own eerie atmosphere to the lonely moors.

Ben studied the rough map which Jim Harrison had drawn him. He was also grateful for the information that the Dugdales at Beck Farm were wanting curtain material and that he would find a good customer in Zac Denby in Robin Hood's Bay if he was to mention Jim's name.

The mist was thinning in the secluded valley where he found Beck Farm without any trouble.

'Good day, ma'am,' he greeted, touching his hat, when Grace appeared at the door. 'Ben Thrower, pedlar from Pickering. Jim Harrison told me thee was needing curtain material. May I show thee some?'

'Aye, that thee may. I was expecting Tom Oakroyd to bring some. Don't know what's happened to him. I mentioned it to Jim, glad he told thee. Come away in wi' it.

I'll mash some tea.' Grace's welcome was friendly just as Jim had described it to Ben.

He took three bolts of material from one of the panniers and carried them into the cottage where Grace had cleared a place on the table.

'It's curtain material for my eldest daughter's bedroom I want,' said Grace, pouring some water from the kettle which was hanging on the reckon. When the teapot was full she placed it on the hearth and headed for the pantry. 'Emma will have to chose so we'll wait until she gets back from gathering the eggs. She won't be long.'

'Right, ma'am,' called Ben, glancing round the room and feeling the friendliness of a true home. It was no surprise when Grace came out of the pantry carrying two pies, for both Jim and Fergus had sung the praises of Grace Dugdale's apple pies after telling Ben to call at Beck Farm.

Ben was commenting on her baking when Emma hurried in, her eyes bright with excitement, having recognised a pedlar's horses as she returned to the house.

'This here's Ben Thrower from Pickering. First time this way. Jim Harrison told him we were wanting curtain material,' Grace explained.

Emma made her greeting and turned enthusiastically to the rolls of cloth.

'Let me open them out for thee,' said Ben, rising from his chair beside the small table at which he and Grace were sitting. He unrolled the bolts one by one, commenting on the quality and colours as he did so.

Emma made her choice, the cloth was cut and paid for, and after another cup of tea and piece of pie, Ben left for Robin Hood's Bay.

He drew his horses to a halt on the lower cliffs to the south of the village. He felt the isolation with the precipitous heights of Ness Point and Ravenscar hemming the bay in from both sides. Even in the mid-morning brightness they were dark and menacing as if they wanted to keep strangers out and preserve this lonely section of the coast for their own people – Bay folk. Houses, climbing higgledy-piggledy on top of one another, clung to a small section of the cliff. Smoke curled from chimney stacks, hung for a moment under the sheltering cliff and was then whisked away by the breeze.

Men were busy checking their cobles pulled up on the beach, or mending nets, their red and blue jerseys putting a dash of colour against the light brown of the sand and grey of the scars pointing finger-like towards the sea which would cover them as the incoming tide filled the bay.

He turned his animals along the edge of the cliffs on a track which swung round to join the steep incline into the village. He dismounted, deeming it wiser to lead the horses down the slope on foot. He was amazed at the way buildings had been crowded together, with snickets and alleys little wider than a man as the only means of access to rows of houses and cottages. In some, proud housewives swept the cobbles and flagstones; in others it appeared no one cared, for rubbish littered the ground and the houses looked shabby. Children ran at play, or on seeing the stranger raced into the house to hide or tell their mothers that a pedlar had arrived. Womenfolk peered at him with interest while the men, hanging out their brown nets to dry, or sitting in groups discussing the fishing prospects, eyed him with some suspicion. A stranger was in Baytown, the folk did not take readily to strangers and, though Ben did not know it, their attitude had been intensified after the visit of the dragoons.

He sensed the tight atmosphere in which only a few folk nodded to him or passed the time of day. Most just stared with curiosity but he would not be put off. Jim had told him not to let the initial mistrust bother him, that once Bay folk learned he was a genuine pedlar, there to serve them, a friend, he would meet none more loyal. Isolation had made them trust only one another but that trust spilled out on to others once they were no longer strangers. And Jim had told him he would probably get rid of most of his wares on his initial call at Bay and save having to go into Whitby. Housewives would test out a pedlar the first time he brought his goods to sell, so he had determined to show them good quality and charge a reasonable price. That way he figured he would win their trust for future visits.

On his way down the main street he pierced the air with shouts of, 'Cloth, ribbons, buttons, flour, butter, everything for thy needs!' Having in mind a sure way to draw people to him he added, 'Toys for the bairns.' He made these wooden playthings, certain sellers, in his time at home. Children couldn't resist the call and that, more often than not, drew their mothers too.

He smiled to himself when a string of children began to follow him, and soon women of varying ages came from the alleys and snickets. Word had flashed round Baytown and they weren't going to miss the opportunity to see what a new pedlar had to sell.

As he controlled his Galloways with an expertise honed over eleven years, he kept a look out for a man with a black patch over his left eye. Jim had told him to contact Zac Denby, for he was a man with influence in Bay, a man who could do Ben a lot of good, but by the time he reached the end of the street close to the Fisherman's Arms he had seen no one who resembled the man Jim had described.

He tethered his Gals to a rail outside the inn and turned to the crowd which had gathered around him. 'Please, just stand back a little and I'll show thee what I have.' He took a large cloth which had been rolled behind his small saddle, opened it out and spread it on the ground. He selected a variety of goods from the wicker panniers on the other two horses, which at no more than fourteen hands high held the containers at a very convenient height for unloading.

He showed the items around, praising their quality before placing them on the cloth. His banter was to the point, tempting as it extolled, and laced with dry wit learned in the shadow of his father. He sensed the wariness of these people begin to crumble, and saw the dour countenances which they had first presented begin to soften.

Soon a brisk trade was flowing and chatter reserved only for strangers for whom Bay folk had a liking began to break out. Ben vowed he would be back again soon. By mid-afternoon he realised that he would have little left and that there would be no need to go into Whitby. He should be able to reach home that night and there he would be delighted to tell Sue that his hunch to switch his route to the coast had paid handsomely and that this route was one which could be developed to embrace Whitby, other coastal villages and more farms.

When his customers became a mere trickle he turned at the sound of a voice beside him. 'Here, lad, selling's thirsty work. I think thee could do with that.'

Ben saw a foaming tankard of ale being held out to him by a slim though well-proportioned woman with a friendly smile, revealing perfect teeth.

Ben licked his lips. 'By gum, thee's reet, ma'am. Thanks.' He took the tankard and drank deeply. He swallowed, smacked his lips and wiped them with the back of his hand. 'That were reet good.' He took another drink. Offered a drink in this fashion, Ben knew he had made it with the folk of Baytown.

'Nell Randall.' The woman introduced herself.

'Please to know thee.' He smiled. 'Ben Thrower.'

'New in Baytown,' she commented.

'Aye, Jim Harrison said I'd do well here.'

'And he's been reet from what I've seen.'

'He has that,' Ben agreed with a grin.

'Where's thee from?'

'Pickering.'

'Ganning straight back?'

'Aye. Said I'd be home tonight.'

'When thee packs up here come inside. Have some meat pie before thee leaves.'

The invitation was warm and genuine, Ben couldn't

refuse. Besides he was a mite hungry and a good feed would set him up for the ride across the moors.

'Thanks,' he said. 'That's kind of thee.'

'Come straight through to my kitchen, there's someone wants a word with thee.'

Ben nodded and, as he packed the few items he had left into one of the baskets, puzzled as to who wanted to meet him. He knew no one in Baytown.

When he went into the kitchen he pulled up short for sitting at the table facing the door was a man with a black patch over his left eye. The man did not speak but stared hard at him with his one eye as if making an assessment of the pedlar who had just entered the kitchen, a stranger to Baytown.

Nell looked round from the oven out of which she was taking a deep pie-dish. 'Sit thissen down, Ben.' She inclined her head towards a chair at the table. 'This here's Zac Denby.'

Ben nodded at Zac whose eye still bored into him. Zac grunted a greeting and watched him as he came to the table and sat down.

Zac's eye still held a certain wariness but it softened with the easing of the tension in his body. 'Nell tells me thee's from Pickering and that Jim Harrison told thee to come to Baytown?'

Ben met Zac's gaze. From what had just been said he realised that whatever Zac's role in Baytown, he and Nell were close; anything said to her would be passed on to Zac.

'Aye, he did. Also told me to contact thee.'

Zac's eye narrowed with suspicious caution. 'Tell thee anything else?'

Ben shook his head. 'No.'

'Not why thee should contact me?'

'No, but I gathered thee have some influence in Baytown and therefore might make it easier for me to sell my wares.'

Zac leaned back in his chair and visibly relaxed. A smile

softened the scar down his left cheek and he exchanged a glance with Nell as she placed a plate of hot meat pie in front of Ben.

'Thanks,' he said, glancing at her. 'This smells good.' As he looked back at his meal he missed the slight nod which she gave Zac.

'Thee didn't need my help to sell thy goods from what I saw happening out there,' commented Zac.

Ben smiled as he cut into his pie. 'Folk seemed pleased with what I had to offer and with my prices.'

'Aye, they took to thee well. They don't do that with all strangers.'

'That's reet,' put in Nell, bringing a tankard of beer to the table. 'They can be reet obstreperous at times. Comes of being an isolated, tight-knit community.'

'Where did thee trade before?' asked Zac.

'Pickering to Helmsley. Jim said there was more money to be made here at Bay and in Whitby so I thought I'd give it a try. Seems he was reet.'

'Expect thee wanted more money to help thy family?' said Nell casually.

'Only me and Sue, my wife. I want what's best for her and brass can help.'

'It can,' agreed Zac. 'And Jim was reet, there's more brass to be made in Bay than thee's taken today.'

Ben glanced up from his plate. He saw Zac watching him intently. 'How?' he asked. What was this man hinting at? Was this the reason Jim had told him to contact Zac Denby?

'Smuggling.' Zac's eye held Ben's, seeking a reaction which would verify if Ben could be trusted.

Ben was aware that Nell had ceased peeling an apple and had her attention riveted on him.

He half closed his eyes as if trying to hide his thoughts. 'Smuggling?' He inclined his head and cocked one eyebrow. He knew smuggling was rife along parts of the Yorkshire coast, that goods found their way to all manner of people

136

who looked upon it as a legitimate trade. But beyond that he knew little about it and nothing of the organisation required to ship contraband from the Continent, run it ashore and dispose of it. He wondered why Zac had raised the subject.

'Aye.'

'What's it to do with me?'

'There's good money in it for thee if thee's interested.'

'But I know nowt about smuggling.'

'No need,' Zac reassured him. 'All thee would have to do is what I tells thee whenever thee visits Bay.'

Nell sat down and started to peel her apple again. 'Thee likes brass, wants more to treat thy wife. Well, now thee has a chance to mak' some.'

Ben hesitated thoughtfully before commenting, 'Ain't there a risk from government officials?'

'Aye, I'll not deny it,' said Zac. 'But there's no danger if thee's careful. And thy job would run hardly any risk. The biggest danger's here in Bay, when goods are run ashore or when the nosy Preventive Men, or dragoons come poking their damned noses in. But thee wouldn't be here then.'

'Good brass?'

'Aye, it varies, but I'll see thee gets well paid.'

'Thy organisation?'

Zac gave a half smile and shook his head. 'No. I run things here in Bay and that's all thee needs to know.'

'Do I get to meet the boss?' asked Ben, wariness creeping into his tone.

'No. And don't ever try to find out who he is. I'm the only one who gets to meet him. But I pays thee and thee'll get a good deal from me. Have no worries on that count. Thee does what I want and thee'll be well paid in brass and kind.' Zac leaned forward on the table. 'Thee makes the decision now, Ben, before I tells thee what I wants thee to do.'

'But how can I decide before I know what I have to do?'

'I know what thee'll have to do,' put in Nell. 'And I can tell thee it will be easy enough. It's a simple task but essential to the smugglers and as Zac says thee'll be well paid.'

'Nell's reet,' said Zac. 'I'm not telling thee now because if thee decides against it's better thee doesn't know what it is.' His voice hardened. 'If thee decides against thee'd better keep what's been said here to thissen.'

The implication behind this last sentence was not lost on Ben. He glanced at both Zac and Nell and seeing reassurance in her eyes made his decision. 'Reet, rely on me.'

Immediately the whole atmosphere in the kitchen became more relaxed. Ben could sense the tension drain out of Nell. She sliced a piece of apple and popped it into her mouth, swallowed and said, 'Thee'll not regret it.'

Zac leaned back in his chair and linked his hands behind his head. 'All thee has to do is on thy return tak' some goods to Pickering or to Saltersgate Inn. Landlord there knows what to do. Thee just delivers.'

'That all?' Ben was surprised.

'Aye, but it's a damned important part of the smuggling.'

'So, when do I start? Now?'

'Aye. Know Beck Farm?'

'Called there on the way here, delivered some curtain material.'

'Good. Thee calls on the way back. Contact John Dugdale. No one else. Not even any other member of the family. Just make it a casual visit. If John's in the fields or on the moor, contact him there. And all thee has to do is let him see that there are three ribbons tied to the left side of the lead horse. When he sees them he'll know thee has to pick up contraband. That's all thee needs to know. John will instruct thee once thee's met him. When thee's got the goods thee goes to Saltersgate this time.'

The bargain was struck. Nell produced the ribbons and Zac wrote out a list of the goods he wanted moving from Beck Farm. Ben finished his pie, drank his ale and left.

*   *   *

John Dugdale had been out on the moor between his farm and the fields which ran to the cliffs around Robin Hood's Bay. Satisfied that the sheep he ran there were in no trouble, he had turned for home when he saw a horseman leading two more horses with panniers fastened to their sides. Another pedlar. Could he be coming from Zac Denby? He waited and watched the rider get nearer. He saw the man check his horse and shield his eyes against the lowering sun which would soon be obscured by clouds thickening in the west. The pedlar had seen him for he turned his mount in his direction. As the man neared him John saw the ribbons tied to his saddle.

'G'day,' greeted John as the man pulled his horse to a halt.

'And to thee, sir,' replied Ben.

'Fancy ribbons thee has there,' commented John.

'Aye.' Ben eyed the stranger. 'Thee John Dugdale?'

'Aye.'

'Then thee'll know about the ribbons?'

'Thee's a stranger to these parts.' John avoided the question. He was wary as Zac had warned him to be of strangers.

'Aye. First time from Pickering. I called at Beck Farm with some cloth on my way to Baytown. Jim Harrison said thy wife was wanting some. Thee weren't about then. Name's Ben Thrower.'

John nodded. The man seemed friendly enough and he liked the open face and readiness to make himself known. 'Aye, I knows about ribbons. Thee got a list?'

The man fished in his pocket, drew out a sheet of paper and passed it to John.

He glanced at it, saw Zac's signature and looked up at Ben. 'Reet. Follow me.' John strode off across the moor. He was pleased that he had met Ben for there would be no need for them to be seen from the house and he didn't want anyone there wondering why he kept going to the top field near Black Wood.

*   *   *

'Come on, Emma, let's go and see the secret place we had as kids,' suggested Joe.

Her responsive laugh had a touch of merriment as she recalled their escapades when they were young. 'Reet.'

They had walked upstream from the house after Joe had called at Beck Farm in mid-afternoon and suggested to Emma that they go for a walk. Her chores were done and she was pleased at the prospect.

They had walked hand in hand, finding pleasure in each other's company. Joe was pleased to be with the girl he hoped to marry. He loved her deeply, always had. It was as he had grown up that he had realised his schoolboy friendship had really been love, and that he must have felt it from the first day he knew her. Sometimes he wondered if he really did know her, for there were times when she seemed to be holding him at arm's length, as if a barrier had risen momentarily between them. He had never been able to figure out what it was, nor why she always found some reason for not giving him a direct answer when he proposed. But now his hopes were high for there were only two more weeks before she had promised him a definite answer. And in that time he would do his best to make sure her answer would be yes.

Emma knew that Joe's chatter about Drop Farm and what he could do with it was made to paint a glowing picture of what life would be like for her after they were married. But, as she listened, she wondered if that life was what she really wanted. She had known farming all her life and though she helped around Beck Farm, she was never really enthusiastic about it. She realised that farm life with Joe would mean security but was that what she wanted? She could cope with it, be a good wife and helper to him. She knew both families would approve, and in fact sensed they were expecting it. Her mother would be saying she'd be getting left on the shelf if she didn't hurry up and make up her mind. No one knew what was holding her back — that secret was locked in her heart.

The valley narrowed as they moved further upstream. They passed the ford which carried the track from Baytown across the stream. Beyond it the water tumbled over rocks and stones and carved its way between banks whose slopes, steepening towards the moorland, were dotted with young oaks and ash. The stream ran clear, sucking at fallen branches and gurgling around exposed roots.

Joe stopped, frozen to the spot. Emma did likewise. It had happened hundreds of times throughout the years when Joe was showing her the ways of nature, teaching her to observe the rule of the countryside. She glanced at him and then followed his gaze. A red grouse paused in the act of feeding where the heather dipped into the valley. Its head jerked in small movements as if it was listening, aware of intruders.

They watched for a few moments then, when Joe took one careful step forward, the grouse rose in a flutter of wings and flew off, leaving a plaintive screech in its wake.

'Beautiful,' whispered Emma. 'Such delicate colours on the feathers.'

They moved on slowly, picking their way among the trees and over ground which was becoming much more uneven. Occasionally stones loosened by their weight tumbled into the water with a small splash and made one more obstacle to the flow.

Joe pointed to snail shells scattered around some of the rocks. 'Thrushes been feeding here, using the stones as anvils.'

'A tree creeper!' whispered Emma close to Joe's ear. They stopped and watched the tiny creature pecking at the bark for food and then move up the tree in short sharp bursts.

Emma was enjoying herself and recalled the many happy hours she had spent with Joe in similar circumstances.

The valley narrowed and steepened towards the moor at its end. The stream came off the moor in a tiny waterfall hiding an opening and small ledge behind it.

'Our secret place,' smiled Emma. 'How long since we've been here?'

'Maybe five years,' replied Joe. 'We just seemed to outgrow it. But it will always be special to me.' He turned Emma to him and looked into her eyes with a love that knew no limits. 'Our place. The place I first kissed thee.'

Emma's mind travelled back over the years. They had scrambled behind the fall, laughing because they had slipped into the pool at the bottom and, as she had threatened to stumble again, Joe had grabbed her and pulled her the last few feet. She had tumbled into his arms and he had held her. Their eyes had met in an understanding of more than friendship. He had bent forward and kissed her lightly on the lips. His mouth lingered for a few moments and Emma felt sensations course through her body, suffusing her with a wonderful warm glow which she had never experienced before. When he had drawn back she held him, pulled him to her and kissed him with a passion which had surprised him.

'I remember it very well.' She smiled at him with a knowing look of recollection. Joe moved to kiss her again but she turned away and said, 'I'll bet we can't get behind the fall now.'

Joe felt chagrin and annoyance rising in him. He sensed that Emma had deliberately broken the moment and raised the barrier again. Words of anger sprang to his lips but he curbed them. He did not want to antagonise her now, so near was he to receiving an answer to his proposal, an answer he felt sure would be yes. Nothing must jeopardise that. Instead he said, 'I don't suppose we could.'

'Well, I'm going to try.' She laughed, and leaving go of his hand stepped to the right. She scrambled up the slope, feeling the spray from the water dampen her. She moved further to the right, trying to remember the exact way they had used many times to reach their secret place. She remembered they had used a shrub as a marker for the point where they could start to get behind the fall. She saw it, now much bigger, and just beyond it the elder which they had used as a handhold. Within a few minutes she was behind the fall.

'Thee all reet?' Joe's voice penetrated the sound of tumbling water.

'Yes,' she shouted. 'But don't come up, there's barely room for me. We must have grown some.'

She saw Joe wave his acknowledgement. As she looked at him a tension came over her and she felt herself in the grip of doubt for he appeared only a misty figure, his customary solidity broken by the falling water. Was the waterfall trying to tell her something? Was it saying, this is not the man for you? She glanced round. There would be room for him. They could have shared this place again and yet she had told him not to come. Why? Had she done it unconsciously, wanting to keep some sort of barrier in place? Was she frightened to succumb to Joe and give him the answer he desired before the day she had set? Was the magic of this place trying to tell her something? Emma shuddered. She glanced back at Joe, but it was not him she saw standing there but a young man who reminded her of Mark, and the waterfall did not cast a veil over him. She started. Her mind was playing tricks. Was she seeing what she wanted to see? She closed her eyes and shook her head. When she opened them she saw she had been wrong. Joe awaited her. She scrambled back to him.

'It's time we were getting home,' she said sharply, and started off without another word.

Joe watched her for a moment with a puzzled frown. What had happened? Why this sudden change of mood? He sensed she was at odds with herself. But why? He deemed it wise not to pry and with a little run caught up with her. Their conversation was desultory. The sparkle had gone from their day.

Emma felt in her sleeve for her handkerchief. It was not there. She pushed her hand further. The handkerchief was missing. She stopped.

'Something the matter?' asked Joe.

'I've lost my handkerchief.' Emma's face showed her disappointment. 'It was the one thee gave me, the one trimmed with the beautiful lace. I'd hate to lose it.'

'When was thee last aware of it?'

'Just before I went behind the fall. I must have dropped it there.'

'I'll gan back and have a look,' said Joe, eager to seize on anything which might lighten her mood, and taking heart from the fact that she was concerned about losing the handkerchief he had given her. He started off.

'Thanks, Joe,' she called.

She had been waiting only a few minutes when she heard voices ahead and to the left. She was too far away to make out what they were saying but figured that they were on the track from Robin Hood's Bay. Curious to see who it would be, she moved stealthily forward until she had the ford in sight and then merged in with the trees and shrubs so she would not be seen.

The voices got louder. They were only in casual conversation. She heard the scrape of horses' hooves and knew that whoever it was was nearing the slope down to the stream where the ground became more stony. The figures came in sight, one man in the lead walking, the second on horseback leading two pack-horses. They moved into clearer view as they came down the slope. Emma stiffened. Her father and a pedlar. Then she recognised him – the pedlar who had called at Beck Farm with the curtain material that morning. Ben Thrower. Her eyes were drawn to the touch of colour on his saddle. Red, white and blue ribbons! Zac's sign. Her father must be taking him to the barn beyond Black Wood.

She watched them cross the stream, the Galloways sure-footed amongst the rocks and stones and climbing the bankside sturdily to pass over the ridge and out of her sight.

She was still crouched in the same place when she heard

Joe returning. 'Here I am,' she called, and stepped into the open.

'I found it.' Joe held up the handkerchief for her to see. He reached her and added, 'It was behind the fall as thee thought. I reckon we could both still get in there. Why did thee think we couldn't?'

Emma shrugged her shoulders. 'Just thought it was a bit small now for two adults.' She changed the conversation quickly. 'Thanks for going for it, Joe, I'm so grateful.'

'I'm pleased I found it,' he replied. As they walked on he wondered if Emma had deliberately kept him from going to their secret place when she was there.

As they neared Beck Farm Joe raised his arm and moved his fingers as if feeling the air.

Emma knew the signs. 'Well?' she said.

'I reckon, after the meal thy mother invited me to, I'll be finding my way home in a sea roak, and it'll be a thick one covering a lot of the moors.'

John followed the same procedure with Ben Thrower as he had done with Jim Harrison and Fergus Pinkney. He was pleased that more contraband was being moved from his barn. Once the panniers were loaded Ben was eager to be on his way.

'If thee won't stay the night, thee watch out, especially as thee isn't familiar with these moors,' said John as Ben climbed on his horse.

'Thanks for thy offer but I came on horseback so's I could get back to Pickering and Sue tonight. I'll be all right.' He raised his hand in salute and sent his mount forward with the two pack-horses following. John watched him for a while then turned for Beck Farm.

Ben kept to a good pace. He knew he had lingered longer in Baytown than he should and having to call at Beck Farm for the contraband had delayed him even more. He wanted to be home tonight and figured that he should be able to do it once he was on the trackway from Whitby to Pickering.

But Ben had not reckoned with the weather and the sea roak, peculiar to this part of the Yorkshire coast, which could hug the shoreline or roll far inland.

He felt the first dampness in the air with the onset of twilight, and as darkness began to enfold the vast bleakness of the moors the mist rolled across the heather. It moved in relentlessly from the direction of the sea. It swirled up the slopes, dipped into the valleys, filling them, and then climbing to the heights before spreading its frond-like fingers across the upland. They reached out as if feeling the way for the ghostly mass of mist behind them.

The fingers touched the horses' hooves, reached upwards, gliding over their fetlocks, billowing under their chests and swirling over their hind quarters. They dampened Ben's legs and rose to his thighs.

Uneasiness disturbed his mind. He did not really know these moors well enough to venture across them in the dark but had felt confident enough once he was on the main trackway. Now, with the mist rising and thickening behind him, his belief was being undermined. Fog could play all manner of tricks, confusing and upsetting a man's sense of direction. Ben urged his Galloways to more speed but, loaded as two of them were, he soon realised he would not be able to outrun the rolling mist.

It deepened and when he glanced back to see if the two pack-horses were all right he was startled to see only their heads. They appeared to be disembodied, as if they were only supported by a blanket of fog. The mist thickened, rose and swirled to embrace both him and his horses in a grey clinging shroud.

Ben checked his pace. He dared not ride with haste. It would be so easy to stray off the track and that could prove fatal. After a few minutes he stopped and slid from the saddle, deciding it would be safer to lead the animals on foot. He cursed his luck at being caught on the moorland heights in an enshrouding opaque fog on his first venture north from Pickering.

He walked on but within a short time his mind was fuddled by the eddying movement of the mesmerising mist. Where was he? Was he still on the right track? Had there been a fork which he had been unable to see and consequently was he on the wrong path? Was he moving in circles, going back on his path? Panic began to gnaw at him. These moors could prove treacherous. He could stumble, fall into a hollow, break a leg, unable to move, never be found. Why had he said he would be home that night? The desire to be back with Sue had clouded his judgement when he was behind the time he had set for his return. He should have stayed at Baytown or sought a resting place with John Dugdale.

Ben chided himself. It was no good dwelling on what might have been or what he should have done. He must keep moving on cautiously, hoping that the fog would lift and then at least he could orientate himself by the stars provided there were no clouds. He stepped forward. But was he right? In stopping had he lost his direction?

He went on. His steps, slow and deliberate, seemed to be moving into eternity.

He swore aloud at the fog, damning it to hell. As the sound of his voice was swallowed by the vapour a deep-throated chuckle came back mockingly. Ben stiffened. The mist was playing tricks! It was driving his imagination towards insanity. The fog cannot laugh and no one would be out on the moors on a night like this unless his name was Ben Thrower. But there it came again. If this was some real person, they were taking the situation lightly. He couldn't really believe that anyone was out here and that in all the vastness of the fogbound landscape he had run into them.

Ben swallowed hard, his head inclined, listening intently. The low laughter came again. Ben found himself shaking. He had heard of hobs and evil spirits which haunted the moors but he had always derided such tales. But now he was not so sure.

'Anyone there?' he called tentatively, his voice harsh with uncertainty.

No answer.

'Anyone there?' He projected his voice a little more.

He was greeted by another quiet laugh. Ben was about to call again when a huge figure emerged from the mist. Ben was so staggered by the size of the apparition that he recoiled. Stepping back, he lost sight of the shape in the swirling fog. Then it seemed to drift in and out of the mist like some unearthly manifestation.

'What . . .' The word was uttered with a touch of fear but before he could say any more the figure stepped forward and, though Ben had never seen anyone so tall and broad, emanating such power, he felt relief that this was no ghost, no hob or wizard, but a real solid man.

'Ma said I'd find someone in trouble on the moor.' The man's voice boomed through the fog.

'What?' Ben thought he couldn't be hearing right.

'Ma can sense these things,' replied the man. 'Lost, I reckon. Well, thee's safe now. I'll tak' thee home wi' me and thee can wait 'til daylight. She says the fog will be gone by then. I'm Dick Petch.' While he had been speaking, Dick had come forward.

'I'm reet glad to see thee,' Ben returned. 'And I'm grateful to thy mother for sensing I was lost.' The implications behind that statement suddenly hit him and when he linked it with Dick's information that his mother had said the fog would be gone by daylight, he began to feel a little uneasy. Had this woman sixth sense? Was she a witch? What other answer was there? 'Er . . . I . . .' he interrupted his own thoughts. 'I'm Ben Thrower.'

'Pedlar,' observed Dick, moving to the two pack-horses. He gave them a friendly pat on the neck and at the same time, so that Ben could not see him, took the weight of one of the panniers. He grunted to himself with satisfaction. The pannier was full. So, more than likely, were the others. Ben was coming from the coast so . . . 'Ganning home fra Whitby?' he added casually.

'Robin Hood's Bay.' Ben supplied the information automatically.

Dick gave a small half grin to himself. More contraband?

'Reet, then let's get out of this muck.' He took the reins of one of the horses and started off. Ben followed, panting as he matched his pace to Dick's. He must keep close. To lose contact could be disastrous. In a few minutes he was wondering how his saviour managed to keep up such a speed in this thick fog. He must know the tracks across the moors like the back of his hand. There was never any hesitation in his stride. It was uncanny. It was as if the fog did not exist and he could see his way clearly.

Ben could not keep track of time. It took all his concentration to keep up with Dick who did not speak another word. Ben was half expecting him to call out to draw his attention to some cottage, to a light which would signify they were nearing their destination, but no sound came and Ben was beginning to wonder where this hulk of a man was taking him when Dick stopped.

'Are we there?' asked Ben, mystified that there was nothing to see.

'Aye,' returned Dick. 'Come here. Leave the horses. They won't bolt.'

Ben threw the reins of his horse and that of the packhorse he had been leading over his saddle and, with the fog swirling around him, moved forward past the other Galloway to Dick.

'Aye, we's here,' said Dick when Ben joined him. As he was about to ask 'Where?' a rolling chuckle of satisfaction came from deep in Dick's chest. It sent a chill through Ben. He glanced sharply up and was stricken with terror at the fiery gleam of evil which glared down at him. He recoiled, stepping away from the terror which towered over him.

But there was no escape and his movement was helped by a push in the face from Dick's broad hand.

Ben staggered. He felt the ground turn soft beneath his feet. He lost his footing and tumbled backwards. The earth gave beneath him. He heard the squelch. Bog! The word seared through his brain. He flailed with his arms. He flung himself forward with an enormous effort, driven by an intense desire for self-preservation. His upper body left the sucking grip of the bog. His fingers closed on the edge of the path. Solid ground. It drove him to fight harder to survive. He looked up, hoping for help from Dick. There was pleading to be saved in his eyes and a cry for help on his lips. But when he saw the malevolent gleam of triumph on Dick's face he realised he was looking into the face of a monster who had found pleasure in doing this before.

Dick raised his foot and drove his heavy hobnailed boot hard on to Ben's fingers. The bones shattered. He screamed with pain. His grip slackened. Then all he was aware of was the same boot being drawn back and sweeping forward full force into his face. Ben's world exploded into oblivion. He pitched backwards into the bog which closed slowly around him.

Dick stood watching Ben sink, with the mist eddying across the bog drawing a curtain over a life's ending.

Dick turned and picked up the reins. 'Come on, my beauties,' he said in a quiet soothing voice. 'Ma'll be pleased with tonight's work.'

Chapter Eleven

For the tenth time Sue Thrower held the curtain back from the window and looked out, hoping that the fog, which had settled like a pall over Pickering with the coming of darkness, had cleared. With a sigh she let the curtain fall back into place. She wished Ben hadn't said he would be back tonight then she wouldn't have been anxious for his safety. She knew the moors could be treacherous for anyone unfamiliar with them even in the best conditions, but in the dark and blanketed with fog they could be a killer. She hoped that Ben had had the sense to wait in Robin Hood's Bay or find shelter if he had left before the fog came down.

She spent an uneasy night and sleep only came late. When she awoke she was relieved to find the fog clearing quickly and busied herself for Ben's homecoming.

When Emma came into the kitchen Amy was already having her bowl of frumenty and her mother was standing at the table cutting some home-made bread.

'I'm glad the fog's clearing,' she said as she went to the pan hanging on the reckon over the fire to spoon herself some warming breakfast. 'It makes the trip to market more enjoyable.' She came to the table where places were set for her father and brother who had not come back from seeing to the cows, and sat down opposite her sister.

'Amy can gan to market, thee can stay at home and help me make the curtains for thy room,' said Grace, laying down her knife and picking up a smaller one to butter the bread.

'Aw, Ma,' Emma started to protest.

'Now, does thee want those curtains or not?' Grace broke in sharply.

'Yes, please.'

'Well, let's get on with them today.'

Amy felt a flush of pleasure – a visit to Whitby with Joe and no one else to travel with them. 'Anything special thee wants in Whitby, Ma?' she asked.

'Don't think so, lass. Butter and eggs are all ready. There's nowt I want from shops.'

'Tell Meg I'll see her next week,' said Emma, glancing up at her sister.

'Any messages for Joe?' asked Amy, a twinkle in her eyes.

'No,' replied Emma with a touch of haughtiness. 'If I have any, I'll give them to him myself when he comes.'

The family breakfast had been finished half an hour when Joe arrived. Emma and Amy had cleared the pots and had washed up. John and Jay had left to do some hedging in the top field and Grace was getting on with her baking which she wanted finishing before she started on the curtains.

Hearing the clatter of hooves and the creaking of the trap, Amy took her long coat from the peg beside the door and shrugged herself into it.

'Hat,' said her mother.

'Not today, Ma,' she half pleaded. She wanted her hair free, tumbling to her shoulders. 'I've a hood on this coat.'

Grace smiled to herself. She recalled how, when she was Amy's age, she preferred not to wear a hat and had received many a scolding for not doing so until her mother became more vigilant and there was no escape. She had sworn then that if ever she had daughters she would not be too hard on them about wearing hats. 'All right, away with thee. Have a good day.'

'I will, Ma.' She flew across the kitchen, kissed her mother on the cheek and ran to the door, sweeping up the basket of butter as she went.

Grace chuckled and gave a little shake of her head. Amy was so full of life, never seemed to have a care in the world. Her easy, happy-go-lucky nature won her friends easily but Grace knew she could trust her youngest daughter to keep within the bounds of her upbringing.

Emma was already outside handing the basket of eggs up to Joe. 'Sorry, I'm not coming today,' she said.

His face filled with disappointment. 'Why not?'

'Curtains to make.'

'Couldn't they have waited another day?'

'Ma wants to get them done today, and they are for my room so I should help,' Emma explained.

By this time Amy was at the trap. 'Don't look so glum, Joe,' she trilled gaily, 'thee has me.' Her eyes sparkled teasingly as she handed him the basket of butter. Her mood was infectious.

'Aye, so I have,' he smiled.

Emma shot Amy a disapproving glance, feeling annoyed that she had lightened Joe's attitude so readily. Amy smiled back.

'Come on, let's away,' she said as she settled herself beside Joe.

He looked down at Emma. 'Sorry thee isn't coming,' he said. 'See thee when we get back.' He flicked the reins and sent the horse forward.

'Look after her, Joe.' The shout came from Grace who had come to the doorway.

'I will, Mrs Dugdale.' Joe raised his hand in acknowledgement.

'No need.' Amy's call was filled with laughter. 'I can do that myself.' She waved to her mother.

Emma walked slowly to the house, glancing every now and then at the trap rumbling away with the two figures side by side. She wished she had been going to Whitby.

'Much to sell today?' asked Amy opening the conversation.

'Usual,' replied Joe.

'Anything else to do in Whitby?'

'Not today. That's why I'd hoped Emma would be coming. I'd planned a walk on the cliffs.'

'I'll come with thee,' said Amy brightly. She shot him a sideways glance and saw his eyebrows rise and his lips purse with a slight nod of his head as if he approved the suggestion, but he said nothing.

During the few minutes they rode in silence Joe became very much aware of the girl sitting beside him. He sensed her energy, her vivacity and lively spirit. He had experienced them with Emma but in a more subdued way and wondered why that was so because the sisters were very much alike.

He knew Emma would make a good wife: dependable, thorough, one who would help him, keep a good home and raise a family with every consideration for their welfare. He reckoned Amy would be much more spirited in many things, that her happy-go-lucky nature would in some ways make life a little more uncertain. Her laughter would ring through the house with joy whereas Emma's would always be more restrained.

Joe startled himself with his thoughts of what life would be like with Amy as his wife and silently chastised himself. Wasn't he hoping in two weeks' time that Emma would be saying 'yes' to his proposal? He searched his mind for something to say, something mundane to bring himself back to reality. 'Are the hens laying well?' he asked.

'Aye,' replied Amy, and launched into chatter about the farm which took Joe, as she intended, into his favourite subject, for farming was his whole life.

As they talked Joe realised that Amy was very knowledgeable on the subject, more so than Emma who took only a mild interest in farming, sufficient as she felt befitted a farmer's daughter. Joe warmed to Amy's enthusiasm and realised her heart was in the land.

'I didn't know thee was so interested in farming,' he remarked.

'Oh, aye, I love it. Like nothing better than lambing time and calving time.' She inched nearer to him. 'I'll be satisfied with a farming life.'

'The way thee's talked, thee'll mak' some farmer a good wife.'

'Think so, Joe?' She glanced coyly at him.

'I know so,' he replied, giving her a wink. 'And a pretty one at that.'

Amy smiled to herself and flicked her long dark hair from inside her coat so that it tumbled in fetching disarray over her collar and down her back. She saw that it had not gone unnoticed and felt a little guilty that she should be flirting with him when her sister was likely to marry him, but then she dismissed the remorse as easily as it had come.

'Thank thee, kind sir.' She acknowledged his praise with a gracious inclination of her head.

'Emma isn't as keen on farming as thee,' observed Joe. 'Oh, she knows the jobs and can do them but she hasn't the same enthusiasm for it.'

'True,' replied Amy. 'But she'll make a good wife.' She felt obliged to make that statement to ease her conscience, but was careful not to say 'make thee a good wife' and wondered if Joe had noticed. 'I think she isn't as keen as I am on farming because of her closeness to Meg. She's seen a lot of Meg's way of life and I think she rather likes it.'

Joe said nothing, merely nodded acknowledgement of Amy's words. This was something he had not thought about. Maybe Emma wanted more than being just a farmer's wife. The life of a well-to-do merchant's family in Whitby was far removed from life on moorland farms, even on prosperous ones such as Beck and Drop Farms. Joe began to wonder, was this the reason Emma held back from saying 'yes' to him?

He was thoughtful as he manoeuvred his horse and trap through the crowds beginning to spill across the drawbridge in both directions as Whitby bustled with market-day life.

After handing over care of the horse to the stableman at the White Horse on Church Street, Joe and Amy took their baskets to the butter cross in the market square. The square was crossed by streams of people going about their work, or easing leisurely into the morning. The buzz of conversations, the calls of greeting and the cries of the farm girls and young men in town to sell their produce filled the air.

Joe found Amy a place at the foot of the cross and one for himself a few yards away. Regular customers, knowing their butter was good, spotted them and soon a brisk trade was taking place. It eased towards mid-morning and both Amy and Joe were pleased that the initial rush was over. They were able to relax and enjoy a jam sandwich which Grace had given them.

Amy was wiping her hands on the cloth which had covered the eggs when she caught sight of a uniform across the square. The bright red of the man's coat attracted her attention. It fitted well and accentuated the man's upright bearing. She saw he held himself with some assurance as he strolled among the people offering goods for sale. He carried an air of authority. In the same moment as she noticed the insignia proclaiming him an officer, she saw his face and recognised him as the lieutenant who had led the dragoons on their search of Beck Farm.

Resentment rose in her like bile. With animosity in her heart she watched him come nearer. He was looking in the baskets lying around the market cross. When he came to Amy's he glanced up at her.

'Not much left.' His remark froze as the light of recognition crossed his face. 'Ah, the lovely girl from Beck Farm,' he remarked.

Amy drew herself up and looked at him with disdain. 'I'm surprised thee remembers,' she said haughtily.

His rugged features softened with a knowing smile. 'I always remember people, part of my job to be observant, but who could forget a pretty face like yours?' He placed one foot on the step on which she was standing and, resting his hand on his thigh, leaned towards her. His bright eyes stared at her. She felt embarrassed under their gaze. 'Come to market every week?'

'Aye, but it's no business of thine,' she replied coldly.

'It could be,' he pointed out. 'We could meet, maybe take a glass of wine and . . .' He left the hint unspoken but his eyes carried his meaning.

Amy drew herself back with a look of disgust on her face. She shot a glance in Joe's direction and saw he was watching them.

Lieutenant Boston chuckled as he straightened up, his eyes narrowing. Suddenly he leaned forward again, thrusting his face close to hers. 'It might be worth your while, otherwise I might be tempted to search Beck Farm again.'

'Search all thee likes,' she returned loftily. 'Thee'll find nothing there. We ain't smugglers.'

Boston pursed his lips doubtfully. 'Your brother was keen to get home when he saw my trooper.'

'Thee scared the lad, that's all.'

'I wonder . . . but I could cease to wonder in exchange for some of your time.'

Amy stared at him with indignation and contempt but before she could reply Joe had pushed his way through the people around the cross. He had seen that Amy did not like the attention of this dragoon and, remembering his promise to her mother, did not hold back from interfering.

'Is he bothering thee, Amy?' he asked, the sharpness in his voice directed at Boston.

'And what is it to you?' demanded the lieutenant.

'She's with me,' returned Joe.

'But supposing she wants to be with me?'

'She'll not want to associate with the likes of thee.'

'And who might you be to be a judge of that?' Boston's

voice was harsh, his eyes ablaze at this annoying inter-ference.

Their voices had been raised. The people around had heard the exchanges and were now directing their attention to the disagreement.

'She's my girl!' Joe's eyes flared with fury. He knew he was courting real trouble but he was not going to stand by and see Amy harassed, he thought too much of her for that.

'Then I might just take her away from you,' grinned Boston.

'Like hell thee will!' snapped Joe. His temper broke under the supercilious look Boston gave him. His right arm swung with unbelievable speed and his fist caught Boston in the left eye.

The dragoon staggered backwards. People scattered. He kept to his feet and in one smooth movement drew his sword and crouched, pointing it at Joe. His eyes burned with hatred. No man did that to Henry Boston and got away with it. He could arrest the farmer, drag him before the authorities, but his cold reasoning, even in this tense moment, told him he would come out with a tarnished reputation which would not go down well with his superiors.

Joe drew himself up and met Boston's gaze unflinchingly, almost daring him to attack him. Joe knew from the gasp from the crowd when Boston drew his sword that he had their sympathy. There were plenty of witnesses as to what had happened. And he realised Boston knew it too. The lieutenant straightened and sheathed his sword. His lips were drawn tight, his eyes smouldered.

'I'll not forget this,' he hissed, and Joe recognised the threat behind the words. His gaze switched to Amy. Though she was shaking with thoughts of what might have happened to Joe, she did not flinch from his stare. 'Who knows what I might yet find at Beck Farm, and then you might be pleased of my goodwill.' He swung round and walked briskly away, smarting under the remarks he heard as a buzz of conversation broke out among the crowd.

'Come on, Amy, let's get out of here.' Joe took her baskets, sold her few remaining items cheaply to another vendor, picked up his baskets and led her to the White Horse.

She was too shaken to speak and Joe respected her feelings. By the time they reached the inn she had taken a grip on herself. Joe stored the baskets in his trap and turned to Amy. 'Still feel like ganning to thy aunt's or does thee want to gan home?'

'I'm all right now, Joe,' she said. 'We'll go to Aunt Matilda's and for that walk thee suggested. I was looking forward to it and no uncouth dragoon is going to spoil that.'

'Good,' smiled Joe, approving of her spirit.

He was about to start off when she restrained him with a light touch on his arm. He turned to her. 'Thanks, Joe, what thee did was brave. He might have killed thee. I'll never forget what thee did.' She pushed herself up on her toes and kissed him.

His arms came up and for one moment held her waist and she made no attempt to pull away.

'It was nothing,' he said, embarrassed by her praise but appreciating her action. He looked into her eyes and saw more there than thanks. 'I think we'd better get to thy aunt's.'

Their report on what had happened drew concern from her aunt and cousin Meg.

'I shall tell thy uncle and he'll see the dragoon is punished,' Matilda insisted, but when they pointed out that the lieutenant might be antagonised all the more if action was taken against him, she calmed down. 'All right, I'll leave thy uncle to take the wisest course but thee must promise if thee has any more trouble from him thee'll let Uncle Robert know.'

They calmed her with that promise but she still felt

indignation at his insinuations. 'Fancy him believing there could be smuggled goods at Beck Farm. What on earth was he thinking about? Nothing could be further from the truth. I know farms make ideal places to store contraband, and some farmers allow it, but to think our John and Grace could be involved . . . well!'

When Amy and Joe were leaving Meg sent messages to Emma hoping to see her next week and asking her to bring a sample of the curtain material with her if they did not meet before then.

They left the tranquillity of Bagdale with its imposing houses built by the well-to-do of Whitby and met the hustle and bustle of Baxtergate on their way to the bridge spanning the river. Housewives bustled into shops, momentarily halting the shopkeeper from shouting his wares; artisans went to buy timber from the raff-yards or hurried to their work at the block and mast-making yard. Here was the hustle of a thriving seaport as people went about their daily lives. Bare-footed boys raced from American Square and Laskill Square, escaping for a short while from the over-crowding to let their imaginations run on foreign parts as they viewed the ships tied to the quays along the river banks.

Concerned about the tight throng of people crossing the bridge, Joe took Amy's hand to guide her to Church Street. She felt safe at his touch. She saw him glare at a drunken sailor who called lecherously as she passed and once again revelled in the protectiveness Joe had displayed when he confronted Lieutenant Boston.

As they neared the White Horse Joe put the question, 'Still want to walk on the cliffs or would thee rather get home?'

'I'd like that walk.'

'Reet, then let's gan up the Church Stairs.'

Amy matched his stride as they wove their way among the crowds ebbing and flowing along Church Street. They reached the one hundred and ninety-nine steps which formed the Church Stairs, so named because they led to the parish church of St Mary squat on the cliff top close to the ruined abbey. Both religious edifices, beaten by the ocean winds, were landmarks for returning sailors, signs that their home port was in sight and they would soon be spared the wild capricious ways of the sea.

The climb was steep and Amy paused now and then to gaze back over the red roofs of the old town where the buildings were so packed that there seemed no room to escape. She wondered how people could live in such narrow and overcrowded garths and yards. Used to the open country, to life on a farm, it seemed impossible for people to live in such confined spaces. Even the more spacious side of the river in which her aunt, uncle and cousins had settled held no attraction for her. Farming would be her life and she wished it could be with the man who walked beside her, whom she knew had his heart set in the country and who would delight in combating the elements and nature's upheavals to earn a comfortable living from the land.

They reached the top of the steps where the path led through the churchyard. Gravestones, some greening with age, bore witness not only to lives spent in Whitby but to those taken early by the harsh, unrelenting sea. They passed the old church which, with the passing of time, had seen the panorama of life in marriages, births and deaths, and in joy and sorrow. They walked quietly, feeling that the hallowed ground and ancient stones required a respectful silence.

Once on the cliff edge they paused and gazed over the gently running sea. It lapped lazily at the cliffs far below, matching their tranquil mood.

'I love it up here,' said Amy, breathing deeply on the sharp, salty air.

'Thee prefers the sea to the country?' asked Joe as they started their walk along the cliffs.

'Oh, no!' Amy was quick to reassure him. She did not

want him to get a false impression. 'My heart and soul is with the countryside. I wouldn't swap life on the farm for anything in Whitby.'

'I sometimes get the impression that Emma likes Meg's way of life better,' he said wistfully. 'I'll have to see if I can combine some of it with Drop Farm after we are married.'

'I wouldn't want thee to if I was Emma,' said Amy. She stopped, and as he turned to her she reached up and kissed him on the lips. Involuntarily his hands came up to her waist. In the moment that he touched her she let her kiss linger. Then he stepped back, a look of embarrassed surprise on his face. She laughed lightly and her eyes were sparkling as she said, 'That's a second thank thee for looking after me today.'

'I did nothing,' spluttered Joe.

'Oh, thee did. That lieutenant could have turned nasty, so could that drunken sailor, and I have enjoyed my day with thee.'

Joe's mind was confused. He realised that he had enjoyed Amy's kiss. Until today he had only thought of her as Emma's younger sister but now she was much more than that. He had become aware of her as a desirable woman. He had the urge to reach out and take her in his arms again, to feel those gentle lips tremble under his own. He met her gaze and knew she would not protest if he did but he held back, drawn by the feelings he had for Emma, for the girl he hoped would soon say she would be his wife.

'And I've enjoyed having thee with me,' he said, 'but I think we'd better gan home.'

Amy made no protest. She wanted nothing to upset this day and she continued to enjoy the rest of the time with Joe.

Sue Thrower was anxious. The day had moved beyond noon and Ben still had not returned. Even if he had stayed the night somewhere she would have expected him to be here by now. He would know how anxious she would be especially when he had hoped to be home last night.

At three o'clock she could bear the anxiety no longer. She took her big woollen shawl, draped it over her head, left the house and hurried into Pickering. Within half an hour she had found Jim Harrison fishing Costa Beck.

'What's up, lass?' he asked when he saw the concern on her face.

'Ben's not back,' she replied, her brow furrowed with worry. 'He said he'd be back last night.'

'There was bad fog, that'll have delayed him.' Jim hoped he sounded reassuring.

'Aye, I know, but even if he'd stopped over he'd have been home by now,' pointed out Sue. 'Thee recommended him to gan to Whitby, told him where to gan. Tell me so I can look for him.'

'Nay, lass, thee can't gan raking across t'moors by thissen,' said Jim. 'I'm sure he's all reet. Maybe he'll be at home when thee gets back.'

'And if he isn't then I'm off to look for him. Now tell me where thee told him to gan.'

There was no mistaking the resolve in her voice but Jim felt he had to deter her somehow.

'Look, lass, those moors are wild and treacherous. They're no place for a woman to be on her own.'

Sue drew herself up. She fixed Jim with a look which told him she would not be put off. 'See here, Jim Harrison, I want to know and thee'd better tell me, 'cos I'm ganning whether thee does or not. It'll be easier if thee does, so out with it.'

Jim's lips tightened. 'All right. Thee's a stubborn lass, Sue Thrower. I told Ben to call at Robin Hood's Bay before ganning to Whitby. I reckoned he'd do a good trade there.'

'Good, then I'll start there.' Sue brightened. Armed with this knowledge, she felt sure she would find Ben. 'Thanks.' She started to turn away.

'Wait,' he halted her. 'I told him the folk at Beck Farm,

the Dugdales, were wanting some curtain material so if he took it he'd probably call there on his way to Robin Hood's Bay.'

'Reet,' said Sue, brightening even more at this specific news. 'Where's Beck Farm?'

Jim fished in his pocket and pulled out a stub of a pencil and a crumpled piece of paper which he smoothed on his thigh. 'Here, I'll draw thee a rough map.' As he did so he explained the drawing to her. 'But promise me one thing, lass, thee'll not leave 'til daybreak. The moors are no place to be at night.'

Sue nodded. As much as she wanted to be off she knew Jim's were wise words.

It was about midday when Sue knocked on the door of Beck Farm.

She had left Pickering at first light and had kept to an even pace, neither rushing nor loitering. She knew the best way to cover the miles and make them seem to pass quickly was to get into a steady stride. As anxious as she was about Ben, she enjoyed the fresh air and the wide open spaces, for the day was fine and white wispy clouds floated high against a bright blue sky. It was a day when all seemed well with the world, a day when she should have no worries. As she rapped on the door she hoped that in a few moments those worries would be dispelled.

The door was opened by Grace who was surprised to find a woman alone standing on her step. Even in the first glance she saw that this stranger was reasonably well-dressed; her cloak was simple and practical and beneath it was a plain brown fustian dress. Around her head she wore a matching shawl which came down over her shoulders. She was no beggar and she was not selling anything for all she carried was a bag slung across her right shoulder and hanging by her left side.

'Yes?' queried Grace.

'I'm sorry to bother thee,' returned Sue without hesitation, 'I'm Sue Thrower, wife of pedlar Ben Thrower. I'm told he was to call here on his way to Robin Hood's Bay. Can thee tell me if he did?'

'Aye, lass, he did. Got some fine curtain material from him.' Grace saw relief come to Sue's face. 'Why, something the matter?'

'He's not returned home.'

'And thee's walked all the way fra Pickering to look for him?'

'Aye.'

'Then come thee in. Thee must be ready for a rest and a cup of tea.' Grace liked Sue's frank open features and admired the spirit of a woman who, concerned about her husband, was not just going to sit down and wait.

'Thanks,' said Sue. 'It would be nice.'

Grace stepped to one side and Sue entered the house and immediately felt the warm, friendly atmosphere. She knew she was in a happy, family home.

'This is my husband, John.'

John, who was charging his pipe beside the fire, looked up, smiled and nodded.

'My daughters, Emma and Amy and son Jay.' With greetings exchanged Grace said, 'I said a cup of tea. Well, that can follow the rabbit stew.'

'Oh, but I couldn't,' said Sue.

'Then thee'll have to sit and watch us have it and that'll make thee feel all the more hungry,' smiled John. 'It's about ready. This,' he held up his pipe, 'is for afterwards.'

'Well, the good smell is making me hungry as it is,' laughed Sue.

'Then sit thee down, lass, between Emma and Amy there.'

Emma was already bringing an extra chair to the table and Amy was getting another knife and fork.

'Sue's trying to find her husband, Ben Thrower, the pedlar who brought the curtain material,' explained Grace as she ladled out the stew.

'I wasn't around when he called,' said John, without looking up from the bread he was cutting. So he did not see the astonished look which crossed Emma's face when he offered no information about seeing Ben later that day.

Words sprang to Emma's lips. Sue was seeking her husband, they should help her all they could. But she held back. To reveal that she had seen her father and Ben together would betray that he was withholding information. If that came out reasons would be demanded and the whole connection with the smugglers would be disclosed. Maybe Sue knew nothing of Ben's part in moving contraband, maybe it was better she did not know, and yet . . .

Emma's mind was troubled throughout the meal. She had taken to Sue. She found her a likeable person, open and friendly, someone who never appeared to have been a stranger. The feeling that Sue should know about that later meeting strengthened, especially when she asked if Ben had returned via Beck Farm and her father did not speak.

By the time Sue was leaving shortly after two, John and Jay had gone to check some sheep, Amy was starting to bake, so Emma offered to put Sue on the right road for Robin Hood's Bay.

Sue left the house, exchanging well wishes and thanks with Grace. The two young women fell into step and chatted gaily until the house was well out of sight. Emma stopped and when Sue turned to find out the reason she was surprised at the serious expression on Emma's face.

'Something the matter?' she asked.

Emma looked embarrassed. She glanced away from Sue and then back at her to find her watching her intently. 'There's something thee ought to know. Ben did return this way.'

'What!' Sue's eyes widened with astonishment. 'But I don't understand, no one said anything.' She was confused. She had been welcomed by the Dugdales, made to feel at home, she liked them, saw them as open, friendly people,

and yet they had been deceitful by withholding information. Something just didn't ring true.

'He didn't call at the house but I saw him,' explained
Emma.

'Why didn't thee say so?'

'Because I wasn't the only one who saw him.'

Sue's lips tightened. This was beginning to annoy her.
She was surprised at Emma. She had liked her from the
start, judged that she could be a true friend, and yet in this
instance she had held back. 'What's this all about, Emma?
I need to know. My husband comes on a journey he's never
been on before, he doesn't return. I'm worried sick. I'm
not told the truth. What's going on?' she demanded.

'Thee was told the truth,' persisted Emma. 'Thee just
wasn't told everything.'

Sue brushed aside Emma's explanation. 'Who else saw
Ben?' Her voice rose with a touch of anger.

Emma bit her lip as she hesitated to reveal her father's
role.

'Who?' she hissed.

'My father.'

'Why didn't he say so?' Anger flared in Sue's eyes. 'He'd
have let me gan on to Robin Hood's Bay when all the
time Ben might be lying somewhere on the moors injured,
needing help.'

Emma knew she must take hold of this situation quickly.
As she had been speaking she had made up her mind that
she would tell Sue everything. She was obviously a woman
who loved her husband very much and if he had gone
missing then she needed help. If his absence had anything
to do with the smuggling then it might affect her father.
Emma felt she needed an ally and in Sue she saw that
person. Whatever Sue found out might be of value to her
too.

'Calm down, Sue,' said Emma firmly. 'There's a lot of
explaining to do.'

'There certainly is, so get on with it,' she said harshly.

'Then let us continue to Baytown while we talk.'

'Maybe I don't want to be in Baytown as thee calls it.'

'I think thee will.'

'But Ben might be lying out there on the moors.'

'Did thee see any signs of his horses?'

'No.'

'Then, if he headed for Pickering and happened an accident, his horses must have been found and if they were then Ben most likely was.'

Sue nodded her agreement with this reasoning. 'But what does thee mean, *if* he headed for Pickering? He was coming home.'

'But supposing he was asked to go elsewhere?'

Sue shook her head. 'I just don't understand what thee's saying.'

'Then let's walk and I'll explain. But I must have thy promise that what I tell thee will be a secret between us until we see how things turn out.'

Though mystified and doubtful about making promises before knowing what she was letting herself in for, Sue realised that the only way to get more information was to agree. 'All right,' she said, 'I promise.'

She listened without interrupting as Emma unfolded her story about how she found out her father was involved with the smugglers of Baytown and how they planned to move contraband by pedlars, but she did not reveal the hiding place for the contraband. She told how she had seen Ben with her father and of the significance of the ribbons tied to the leading pack horse.

'So thee thinks Ben was recruited by the smugglers and that thy father was taking him to the contraband store?' said Sue when Emma had come to the end of the story.

'Aye. It looked like it.'

'Where could Ben have been delivering the goods that has delayed him getting home?'

'I have no idea.'

'Can't we ask thy father?'

'No.' Alarm rang in Emma's voice. 'He mustn't know that I'm aware he's doing this. Besides, I don't suppose he knows. All he'll be doing is providing a storage place for the contraband and making it available when a pedlar appears with ribbons tied to his lead horse. The pedlar's orders will have come from Zac Denby.'

'So I need to contact him to find out where Ben went to?'

'Aye. Thee'll find him in Baytown.'

'So that's why thee suggested we keep walking in this direction?'

'Aye. I knew once I'd told thee what I knew thee'd want to gan there.'

'Thee recognised me as a determined woman.' Sue smiled.

'That's reet.' Emma's face grew serious. 'But thee must be careful. The smugglers can be ruthless. If they think thee's a spy they'll not hesitate to get rid of thee.'

'I merely want to know about Ben.'

'Try and find out without letting them realise thee knows about the smuggling.'

'I will.'

'And please let me know what thee discovers. I'm concerned for my father. He's in danger from the authorities – thee knows what it means if he's caught – and at risk from the smugglers if things go wrong. That's what worries me about Ben not arriving home. If the goods were meant for Pickering, why hasn't he got there? If he has disappeared, does it endanger my father?'

Chapter Twelve

Zac paused at the top of the climb out of Bay. His gaze swept over the roof-tops and out over the bay to the cobles dotted across the water. They bobbed on the gentle undulations of the sea which reflected the blue of the sky. It was a good day for fishing and Zac wished he was out there with them, at one with the sea which he loved, but word had come that 'Armstrong's cow had calved' and he could do nothing but report to The Fox at Armstrong's Farm. He knew it would pay more in the long run than all the fish he could have caught, but on a day like this the sea had a strong pull.

He turned away from the view and as he broke into a quick pace he found himself wondering about the identity of The Fox. Someone from Whitby or from one of the estates close by? Obviously a man of influence with the right connections to be able to set up the running of contraband from the Continent and then its distribution once it had been brought ashore in Bay. A merchant maybe? Such a man would have the contacts abroad. Maybe there was more than one of them and The Fox was the spokesman or more probably the leader. A gang of merchants and local gentry would be able to set up the necessary organisation on both sides of the water and would know the movements of the anti-smugglers as he had witnessed in The Fox's knowledge about the coming of the dragoons.

Zac was inquisitive but as he had always known it was better not to pry. He realised to possess the knowledge of identity would be to throw his own life into greater danger so he curbed his curiosity.

He skirted the farmhouse near Stainsacre and made his

way to the cottage which he knew Sam Armstrong would have prepared in the usual manner. As he entered the cottage and closed the door behind him he sensed a presence. The Fox must be there already. He crossed the floor to the chair and sat down. The connecting door to the back room was open but as usual the chairs had been arranged so that he could not see who sat in conversation with him.

'Good day, Zac.' The voice was firm but Zac thought he sensed an edge to it.

'Good day,' he replied. 'Another consignment?'

'Yes. The vessel will be in the bay Sunday evening.' The information was given with a terseness not usual in The Fox.

Zac wondered if something had upset him, but that was no concern of his.

'Two days' time,' mused Zac, half to himself.

'Yes, nothing to upset that, is there?' There was a sharpness in the query.

'No, of course not,' shot back Zac quickly. 'Nothing like a holy day to run contraband ashore. Better the day better the deed.'

'Dragoons not causing any trouble?'

'No. They've been in Baytown, searched the Fisherman's Arms. Found nothing. It was a show of strength as it was to the farms they visited.'

'Watch them. I hear tell this Lieutenant Boston is a wily bird, experienced from the Romney Marshes.'

'He'll have a match to outwit a Yorkshireman,' chuckled Zac.

'Don't take him lightly.' The Fox's voice rasped with annoyance.

Now Zac did wonder what was the matter, for The Fox had always been so confident previously.

'Remember, he's got more men,' The Fox went on. 'The two who were stationed in Bay have been withdrawn, so he might try to put someone else in there. Beware of strangers.'

'I need no reminding,' replied Zac testily. He frowned. Was The Fox doubting his ability? He had shown no sign of it before, so why now?

'I hope not.'

Zac heard the chair in the back room scrape on the floor to be followed by a footstep.

'You sent contraband by four pedlars?' Though it was put as a question it contained information which shook Zac. How did The Fox know how many pedlars he had employed? He must have a spy somewhere, someone to keep a check on him. Maybe The Fox had done so only now, after a new distribution system, which had been Zac's idea, had been set up.

'Aye,' he replied, hiding his irritation.

The door was dragged wide with a suddenness which startled Zac. The unexpected movement made him jump. A tall, broad-shouldered figure loomed over him. There was fire in the eyes which met his. 'Then why did only two report to Ed Crosby at Saltersgate?' the voice boomed.

'Thee!' gasped Zac, his eyes widening with recognition.

'Yes, me!' The Fox leaned forward, putting his face close to Zac's. 'Keep this to yourself. If you don't, if you even so much as drop a hint as to the identity of The Fox, you'll be a dead man.'

The cold hostility in the voice made Zac shudder. He knew the lengths to which this man would go to preserve his identity and see that nothing jeopardised the lucrative trade he ran. So why had he revealed his identity now?

The Fox straightened, still keeping his penetrating gaze on Zac. 'Well, why did only two pedlars report to Crosby? Are you up to something?'

'Me? No. I know better than that.' Zac had pulled himself together after the initial shock of learning who The Fox was. His voice was strong. It did not prevaricate.

The Fox nodded and Zac was relieved to see he seemed convinced by his answer. 'I had to see for myself if you lied. I know from your reaction that you didn't.' He went into the back room and returned a moment later with his chair. He set it opposite Zac, sat down and drew a flask from his pocket. He unscrewed the cap which acted as a receptacle for the brandy he poured out. He filled the cap and handed the flask to Zac. They raised the brandy to each other and drank.

Zac smacked his lips. 'Drop o' good brandy, thee's got,' he said with a twinkle in his eye.

'It comes from foreign parts,' replied The Fox, his lips twitching with amusement. He leaned forward. 'Now, Zac, what about these missing pedlars?' His voice was more even.

'First I've heard. Know who called at Saltersgate?' Zac asked.

'Aye, Jim Harrison and Fergus Pinkney.'

Zac nodded thoughtfully. Luke Newell and Ben Thrower were the two pedlars who had not called at Saltersgate. In his mind they were marked men. No doubt they had seen an opportunity to line their own pockets. He'd make sure he'd trace them and then they'd reap a reward they wouldn't be expecting.

'Any ideas?' prompted The Fox.

'Leave it with me. I'll get this cleared up.'

'See that you do, especially with this consignment coming on Sunday.' Icy threat had returned to The Fox's voice and his eyes smouldered with a promise of trouble if things went wrong.

He finished his brandy, retrieved his flask from Zac and left the cottage.

As he walked back to Baytown, Zac's thoughts dwelt on his encounter with The Fox. He was amazed by his identity – a man respected by the whole neighbourhood, thought well of in Whitby, and a person of social standing. Yet he was a man whom Zac could see enjoying playing two roles: charming to the ladies, sociable to his friends, while behind the facade was a nimble-brained adventurer who revelled in running close to the law and flouting those who tried to curb the activities of the free traders. But he was also a man who found pleasure in wielding power to threaten, a ruthless sadist to whom life was cheap if it stood in his way.

He chuckled to himself. Knowing who The Fox was pleased him, but he realised that to reveal the truth to anyone would surely spell his end.

His thoughts turned to the missing contraband and he began to wonder if there was more to it than two men trying to make extra cash for themselves. They had collected contraband from Beck Farm, nothing had been moved from any other storage place in the same period, so could John Dugdale be in league with the two missing pedlars?

His thoughts were interrupted by a movement close to the cliff edge some way ahead. He stopped and sank to the ground, his eyes trained on the spot where he had detected movement. His mind, always alert for the unusual, was suspicious. Nothing. All was still. Had he imagined it? Or was someone trying to conceal himself? If so, why?

He crept forward cautiously to the top of a slight rise in the ground which would afford him a better view ahead. He lay still, his eyes scanning the grassy terrain. He was beginning to think he was mistaken when his attention was drawn to a hollow ahead but more to his left than the area on which he had been concentrating. The man he saw raise his head must have moved from right to left hidden by the hollow. Zac's attention became riveted, for the man, lying flat on his stomach, had propped himself on his elbows and was holding a spyglass to his right eye. Zac saw him swing his gaze across the sea, pausing now and again as if studying the cobles.

Zac grunted to himself. Preventive Man? Dragoon in disguise? Whatever, he no doubt was seeing if the cobles were 'sowing a crop', retrieving barrels of brandy from the seabed where they had been dropped from a ship. Well, he would be disappointed, there was no crop out there.

All he would see today were fishermen hauling in their catch.

Zac crept away to his right until he knew he could not be seen and then rose to his feet and hurried to the village.

He was greeted with friendly calls as he hurried down the main street until he came to a narrow alley on his left. He turned into it and stopped at the third cottage. His rap on the door was answered by a well-built man with a heavy-jowled face which made his eyes appear as two dark pin-pricks.

'Zac,' he greeted, running his hand through black curly hair.

'Tite, Joss in?' asked Zac.

'Aye.' Tite stepped to one side and allowed Zac to enter a two-roomed cottage which was roughly furnished and unkempt. Zac knew the brothers cared little what their abode looked like and when Joss, who was a match in size for his brother, tried to clear a chair of old clothes for him to sit down, he stopped him.

'I'm only here for a minute. I want a job done.'

'Aye, Zac, anything.'

Zac knew them as not of the sharpest intelligence but they were powerful men whose strength had often come in useful to him. He knew they could be trusted to carry out his instructions and say no more, for they liked money and he paid them well, throwing in a tub of brandy as well now and again.

He issued his instructions quickly and left the cottage.

The two men shrugged themselves into their jerkins, crammed woollen caps on their heads and left to climb to the top of the main street. There they cut away from the cliffs and headed away from Baytown before circling to approach the man they were seeking from behind. They were stealthy in their movements and froze close to the ground when they saw him. He was in the place described by Zac with his attention still concentrated on the cobles in the bay.

They watched for a few minutes then Tite tapped Joss on the arm. He indicated to his brother to go to the left while he went to the right. Joss nodded and moved away. Tite waited, keeping his eye on the stranger, until he saw Joss signal. Tite followed a slight dip which ran to the right and swung to meet the hollow from which the man was keeping his lookout. He paused before reaching the hollow and raised himself to see Joss positioned a few yards behind the man and slightly to his left. He knew Joss was ready. He raised his arm then stood up and called out, 'G'day, sir. What might thee be doing?'

Startled, the man twisted round. His mouth gaped when he saw the huge figure of Tite striding towards him. He had no time to answer for in that same moment Joss pounced. His full weight was behind the fist which struck the man on the side of the jaw. With his senses reeling he was unable to ward off the iron bar which Tite wielded. His skull shattered. The two brothers stood over the silent form, then glanced at each other and nodded their approval of a job well done.

Joss bent down and grabbed the front of the man's coat. He jerked him up and slung him over his shoulder as easily as he would a sack of corn. Tite picked up the spyglass which had fallen from the man's lifeless hand and followed his brother who was already striding towards the edge of the cliff.

Only the wind plucking gently at the three figures witnessed the macabre procession. The brothers paused at the edge of the cliff. The rock face dropped sheer to the sea, calm across the bay, beating gently at the base. The peaceful setting was at odds with the violence that had been done. Tite looked downwards, chuckled to himself then grinned at his brother and nodded. Joss smiled in satisfaction and then with one powerful jerk heaved the burden from his shoulder and saw it tumble over into space. The brothers watched it plummet down, hit the rocks far below and bounce off, as if suddenly filled with life, before plunging into the sea. For a brief moment they saw it reappear before the sea closed over it.

Tite and Joss looked at each other, grinned with satisfaction, slapped each other on the shoulder and turned to go.

Joss put out a hand and stopped his brother. Tite looked queryingly at him. Joss pointed to the spyglass which Tite still held. He glanced at it longingly. He could have such fun watching people through it. He looked at Joss who shook his head. Tite nodded. He turned to the cliff edge and hurled the spyglass far out. He watched it catch the sun as it twirled through the air. Then it lost its outward momentum and plunged downward to the sea. Tite watched the small splash then turned and matched his brother's stride. Joss was right. Obey Zac implicitly – get rid of all evidence.

Sue had a lot to think about as she walked to Robin Hood's Bay, and with Emma's words of warning that she could be courting danger in her mind, she tried to decide on her best course of action. She knew from Emma that the people of Baytown were a tight-knit community who would regard any stranger with suspicion until they knew otherwise. She could pretend to be a country lass coming to look for work, but realising this could raise suspicion in people's minds, decided to be open about her purpose in coming to Baytown.

When she reached the point where the track plunged down into the village she paused, for she had never seen houses and cottages packed so tightly together. There were areas of Pickering where they were crowded but here they seemed to be standing one on top of the other and appeared to be clinging to the cliff face as if their very existence depended on their ability to hold on. She expected it did, for they all looked in danger if there was a landslip.

Children stopped their play and eyed her with misgiving. Some ran into nearby houses, no doubt to tell their parents that a strange woman had come to Bay. Women at their front doors, or gossiping where the narrow alleys met the main street, eyed her with suspicion and curiosity. What was this young woman doing coming to Bay, and alone at that? She was a fine figure of a lass with a proud bearing and a determined set to her head, and though not what they would term pretty there was many a woman who would envy her her looks.

Heads came together in whispers after she had passed and a few male names were mentioned; the fishermen would give her a second look when they came ashore and there were those who could well be more persistent in their attentions.

Sue, sensing the appraisals which were being made, walked on, her mind anxious about Ben. Would she learn anything here? She would have to break through the hostile barriers of a close-knit community. Maybe it would all depend on Zac Denby if she could contact him. As she neared the bottom of the hill she could see the beach and beyond it the sea. She shivered, for what warmth had been transmitted from the sun was blocked by the buildings which cast their shadows across her path.

A pedlar was selling wares outside the Fisherman's Arms and Sue's heart beat a little faster. Maybe he knew Ben. She moved closer, mingling with the group of women who were examining his wares.

'Where's thee away to Will?' one woman asked.

'Back to Guisborough and then over to Yarm,' he replied. 'Soon as I've had some o' Nell's pie.' He inclined his head towards the Fisherman's Arms.

Sue's heart sank. This was not Ben's territory so it was most unlikely that they had ever met. Her lips tightened. Where should she begin? Should she come right out and ask for Zac Denby? Emma had indicated he was the head of the smugglers in Bay and if Ben was concerned with contraband then he would be the person to ask. But to enquire right out for Zac Denby might not be a wise thing to do. She only was half aware of the conversation going on but she must have been taking in the words for she suddenly found herself with a possible lead.

'Ah, thee pedlars are all t' same,' the woman was saying, 'must have some o' Nell's pies afore thee leaves Bay.'

Sue's mind raced. If Nell's pies had a reputation among pedlars maybe Ben had had some. Maybe this Nell, who-ever she was, had met Ben. Maybe she could put Sue in touch with Zac Denby. She edged her way away from the group around the pedlar. Her glance at the Fisherman's Arms was apprehensive for a moment, then she took a grip on her feelings and marched boldly through the front door.

She paused inside the door allowing herself to adjust to the gloom. Raucous sounds of drinking men came from a room to the right. She started forward and was halfway along the passage when a barmaid, carrying a tray of tank-ards foaming with ale, came from a room at the end of the corridor. She pulled up and stared at Sue, puzzled by the fact that a woman alone, a stranger, had ventured into the inn.

''Ere, what's thee want?' she queried suspiciously. 'This is no place for the likes o' thee. Nell runs a respectable inn.'

Sue smiled to herself. In the gloomy corridor the barmaid had not been able to assess her appearance properly and had jumped to the conclusion that she was there for only one purpose.

'And I'm respectable too, young lady,' said Sue with a vigour which left the girl in no doubt that she had jumped to the wrong conclusion.

'Oo, no one's ever called me a lady before,' she giggled.

'I'm here to see Nell,' said Sue.

'Wait a moment, let me get rid of these. Thee wait reet there.' She disappeared through the door on the right and a few moments later reappeared with an empty tray. 'Back in a tick.' She breezed by to the door at the end of the corridor.

A few moments later it reopened and Sue saw a well-built

woman whose rounded face seemed friendly though she looked at Sue with some curiosity.

'I'm Nell Randall, what does thee want with me?'

'I'm hoping thee might be able to help me,' replied Sue. 'I'm Sue Thrower. My husband Ben, a pedlar, came to Baytown a few days ago. He's not returned home so I've come looking for him.'

Nell raised her eyebrows. 'Why do thee think I know him?'

'Heard tell outside that pedlars like to have some of thy pie afore they set off home or to their next call.'

Nell chuckled. 'Aye, they do. And thee figures thy Ben may have had some?' Nell was keeping the conversation going while she assessed this stranger. She had never known wives come hunting their pedlar husbands before.

'Aye. It was his first time to Baytown. I reckon he'd try thy pies if he heard of them. He'd a hard ride back but he never made it.'

Nell nodded. 'Come through to kitchen, lass.' She turned and Sue followed her into a room which was warm with the heat from the ovens and filled with the aroma of home baking, stewing meat and ale.

'Sit thee down.' Nell indicated a chair beside the scrubbed wooden table which stood in the centre of the kitchen. 'Thee'll have some tea?'

'Thanks,' returned Sue as she sat down and slipped the shawl from around her head.

In the brighter kitchen Nell was able to make a better appraisal of the newcomer and she liked what she saw. She figured this person was genuine about her search. There was an honesty about her face and trustfulness deep in her brown eyes.

Nell busied herself with the teapot without speaking and Sue was content to wait. She did not want to upset the friendly atmosphere which she sensed developing.

'Thee's had a long walk from Pickering,' said Nell as she poured the tea.

'Pickering?' Sue seized on the word. 'So thee must have met Ben to know I've come from Pickering?'

Nell smiled at her sharpness and looked at her frankly. 'Aye. Ben was here and he did have some of my pie, but beyond that I know nothing. I know of no reason why he shouldn't have reached home.' She looked thoughtful for a moment. 'It came down foggy that night, I remember,' she added as if that might provide an answer for Ben's absence.

'Aye, it did,' agreed Sue, 'but that shouldn't have delayed him the next day.'

Nell pursed her lips and shook her head. 'I don't know.'

'Maybe Zac Denby can help,' said Sue.

Nell stiffened. For a fleeting moment suspicion crossed her face. 'Zac Denby?'

'Aye. I heard he has a lot of influence in Baytown.'

'Who told thee that?' asked Nell sharply.

Sue was surprised that the friendliness in Nell had vanished at the mention of Zac. She wondered why and realised she must be careful. She must not betray Emma's confidence. 'Must have heard it from another pedlar or it might have been Ben. He was recommended to come to Baytown so whoever did that might have mentioned Zac Denby.'

Nell poured herself a cup of tea and sat down opposite Sue. When strangers started asking about Zac she was always suspicious. She felt she must protect him. But this young woman seemed genuine in wanting news of her husband and maybe Zac might know something.

'He's out of the village at the moment but thee's welcome to stay here 'til he returns.'

'He'll come here?'

'Oh, aye, certain.'

'Thanks, I'll wait.'

Nell's mind had been racing. She must have a word with Zac before he met Sue. He needed preparing, needed time to weigh up the reasons behind this visit. There may be more to it than an enquiry for a missing husband. Ben had been a stranger and though outwardly he had seemed genuine he could just as easily be playing a double game and be working for the Preventive Men and Sue could easily be part of that, sent here on the pretext of seeking her missing husband, laying a trap into which Zac could walk.

'I don't know how long he'll be, may be late. Thee must be tired after the walk from Pickering, why not have a rest? There's a spare bedroom, you could use that,' suggested Nell. 'I'll wake thee when Zac arrives.'

'I don't want to be any trouble, but I am a little weary.' She was prepared to sit here until Zac arrived but realised that Nell probably wanted her out of the way so that she could have a word with him before they came face to face. It would be better to play along with her suggestion.

'It's no trouble. I'll show thee the room and bring thee up a piece of pie and some tea.'

About to say she had had a meal at Beck Farm, Sue held back. She must not reveal she had been there. 'Thanks, just a small piece.'

Nell took her upstairs and showed her into a room which though sparsely furnished with bed, chest of drawers and small table was comfortable. The bed was covered with a multi-coloured patchwork quilt. Nell turned it down at the head of the bed and Sue saw white sheets and invitingly soft-looking pillows. It would be nice to sink into what she expected to be a feather bed.

'Thee'll be all right here,' said Nell with a friendly smile.

'I'm sure I shall, thanks again.'

Nell was by the door. 'I'll be up with some food in a minute.'

When Sue tasted the pie she understood why the pedlars liked to partake of some before setting out on their journey from Baytown.

She did not linger over the food because the bed looked

so inviting. Once she was between the sheets, tiredness from the long walk took over and she was soon asleep.

Thankful to have Sue out of the way before Zac arrived, Nell busied herself around the kitchen while supervising the barmaid who was having a busy time.

When the back door opened she turned round from the kitchen range to see Zac closing the door behind him. Immediately she sensed something was wrong. His face was creased into a scowl.

'All go well, Zac?' she asked, for she was troubled by his attitude.

'Aye and nay,' he grunted as he placed his coat on a peg next to the door. He came across to the table. Nell filled a tankard with ale as she waited for him to go on. 'Next contraband comes on Sunday.'

'So what's wrong with that?' she asked as she placed the tankard in front of him.

'Nowt wi' that.' He scowled at his thoughts. 'Fox told me only two of the four pedlars I used called at Saltersgate. He thought I might be involved.'

'What?' gasped Nell. 'He couldn't think thee was double-crossing him?'

'He could and did, after all it was my idea to use pedlars, but I convinced him I knew nothing about their disappearance. I've got to find out what's happened to them.'

Nell's mind tried to evaluate the situation. She was glad she had got Sue out of the way before Zac had returned. Her story that her husband was missing was true but with all the suspicions that must be raging through Zac's mind, it could have been fatal for him to have been confronted with her immediately on his arrival. He would need to weigh up the situation carefully before he acted and with Sue out of the way he would have a chance to do so.

'So what does thee think could have happened to them?' she asked as she cut him some bread and cheese.

'Who knows?' he grunted. 'Lost on the moors? Maybe

so in Ben's case. It was foggy that night and it was his first time this way. Or did they see some way of making extra cash, selling the contraband for themselves?'

'If they did they wouldn't dare come this way again,' Nell pointed out, 'and they'd lose any further income from moving contraband.'

'Maybe,' said Zac, breaking a hunk of bread. 'And there's the possibility that they could be working for the authorities, finding out how we distribute the contraband so that the dragoons can move in.' He shook his head, took a bite of cheese and added, 'It's all very disturbing. So was seeing a man watching the cobles through a spyglass.'

'What?' Nell was shocked by the news. 'Where?'

'On the cliffs. Dragoon in disguise, I reckon. He's had an accident. Clever Lieutenant Boston will think his man's fallen from the cliff.'

Nell did not enquire further. She knew how Zac would have got rid of him.

His information was all the more disturbing with the knowledge that Ben's wife was upstairs, but she knew it was no good trying to dissuade Sue from meeting Zac. They would have to come face to face. It was no use putting off telling Zac about her.

'We have another problem on our hands,' she said as she sat down opposite him.

He glanced over the rim of his tankard. He put it down. 'Damn, not another,' he said as he wiped his hand across his wet lips. 'What is it?'

'Ben Thrower's wife is upstairs.'

'What?' Zac almost choked with surprise.

Nell explained why Sue was here and how she had asked to meet him.

'How did she know about me?' he asked, suspicion clouding his mind.

'Says she may have heard thy name from Ben or from another pedlar.'

Zac nodded. 'What's thy opinion?'

'I like her. She seems genuine. And now The Fox has corroborated her story that Ben is missing, I figure she is telling the truth.'

'Maybe,' muttered Zac. 'But they could be working together as spies.'

'Possibly,' agreed Nell. 'But we can easily keep her here on the pretext of trying to find Ben.'

'I bloody well want to find him!' Zac exploded. 'I want to know what happened to the contraband.'

'Reet,' said Nell calming him down. 'We can get her to help in this and by keeping her here we can see if she is working for the authorities.'

Zac looked thoughtful for a moment. 'Aye, thee's reet.'

'Thee talk to her first before thee makes up thy mind.'

'I will.' Zac returned to his cheese and bread.

Nell left the kitchen, went upstairs and woke Sue.

When Sue walked into the kitchen she was surprised by the shortness of the man sitting at the table. She had expected a much bulkier figure. But his lack of height did not detract from the strong air of authority she sensed emanating from him. She was startled by the ugly scar down his cheek and the black patch over his left eye but hid her feelings.

'This is Zac Denby,' said Nell, glancing at Sue. 'Zac, this is Sue Thrower, Ben Thrower's wife.'

Zac gave her a curt nod. 'What's thee want here?' he growled.

Sue would not be put off by his dismissive attitude. She met his one-eyed gaze without flinching. 'Ben has not returned home. I came to find him. I was told thee was a man of influence in Baytown so I thought thee might know something.'

'Why should I?' he snapped irritably.

Sue eyed him firmly. 'Look here, Zac Denby, thee appears to be in a bad mood but that's nowt to do with me. All I want is information about my husband so I'll thank thee to keep a civil tongue in thy head when talking to me and don't come any nonsense about not knowing Ben. Nell's told me he was here. Did thee meet him? Can thee tell me anything about what has happened to him?'

Zac's eye widened, anger flared. He glanced at Nell. Taken aback by Sue's outburst, she had stopped in the midst of pouring him a tankard of ale. No one, least of all a stranger, spoke to Zac like that and got away with it. His lips tightened. Fire burned in his eye. He glared his hostility at Sue. She held herself straight and met his anger with a solid determination not to wilt. Her eyes never blinked. Two strong personalities clashed silently.

With a suddenness which startled Nell, Zac's expression changed. He grinned and slapped his thigh as he sat down opposite Sue. 'I'll be darned, a lass with spirit. Ben Thrower doesn't know what a lucky man he is.' He chuckled deep in his throat. 'We've a reet one here, Nell,' he added as she relaxed and placed the foaming tankard in front of him. 'Thee's walked all the way from Pickering seeking thy man because he's not come home?' Sue nodded, still keeping her eyes firmly fixed on him. 'Well, thee's either daft or thee loves him deep.'

'I prefer to think it's the latter,' replied Sue coolly. She knew this man was weighing her up. She felt he knew something about Ben but was not prepared to say anything until he was sure what she really wanted. She would have to be careful.

He liked the look of this woman, had a sneaking admiration for her because she had not held him in awe. There was a determination about her which made him feel that he could trust her, but before doing so he wanted to know more about her. 'Tell me about thyself and Ben?'

'Not a great deal to tell,' replied Sue, knowing that she was still under his scrutiny. She was open with him, telling him how she had known Ben since schooldays, that they were happy in Pickering, Ben taking over the pedlar's trade from his father, how he had decided to make this trip to the coast after talking to a couple of pedlars who traded this way. 'This was his first time to Bay and he hasn't returned. I'm worried and I hope thee can tell me something.'

Zac pursed his lips thoughtfully as he rubbed his forefinger slowly up and down his scar as if it helped him to make a decision. How far could he trust this woman? She seemed genuine in her quest and after what he had just learned from The Fox her fear that something had happened to her husband could have a good foundation. If Ben was playing a double-cross then it seemed she knew nothing about it, nor about his involvement in smuggling otherwise she wouldn't be here. If he took her into his confidence she just might be able to help in finding out what had happened to Ben. He shot a glance at Nell and he saw her give an almost imperceptible nod. He realised she knew what he was thinking and was giving her approval of Sue.

Zac leaned forward, resting his arms on the table and looked hard at Sue. 'I've learned something today, just this afternoon in fact, but before I tell thee what I know, thee must swear that what I tell thee does not go beyond these four walls.' He gave a slight pause, letting his words sink in and adding impact to his follow up. 'If thee says anything about what I tell thee,' his voice had gone cold, 'thee won't live long.'

Sue felt her face drain of colour at the menace in Zac's tone and in his attitude. He was hunched as if he could leap upon her at any moment and drive a knife to her heart. What had Ben got mixed up in to produce this threatening attitude in the man across the table? Part of her told her she didn't want to know but her determination to find out what had happened to Ben was stronger. She nodded. 'All reet, I swear that what thee tells me will go no further.' She made her voice fill with sincerity so that Zac would not mistrust her.

He visibly relaxed. 'Reet. I run a smuggling gang here in Baytown.'

'Smuggling? Ben's got himself mixed up in smuggling?' she interrupted with a gasp, her eyebrows rising with surprise.

'Hear me out. Thee needs to know no more than that about the organisation. I needed a different way to transport the goods inland and had the idea of using pedlars and their pack-horses.'

'Thee recruited Ben?'

Zac nodded. 'Aye.'

'More fool him,' snapped Sue with annoyance.

'Hold on,' replied Zac sharply. 'I paid him well for a job with little risk.'

'Little risk?' She was contemptuous. 'Seems he ran into trouble the first time he did anything for thee.'

'Not necessarily,' said Zac.

'What is thee getting at?' she asked suspiciously.

'There's a chance that he was tempted by the value of the contraband.'

'Thee mean he's gone elsewhere to sell the goods for his own pocket?' Sue was incredulous at Zac's suggestion. She gave a little snort. 'Not my Ben. He's straight, and even though he's got himself mixed up with an illicit trade he'd be loyal, he'd not break a trust. Besides, he'd not go off without contacting me.'

Zac had been watching Sue's reactions carefully. He was satisfied that she knew nothing about her husband's disappearance unless she was a very good actress. Still it would be wisest to keep her in Baytown as Nell had suggested.

'I know nothing,' said Zac. 'Ben went on a job for me and that's the last I heard of him. More than that I'm not prepared to say. I could speculate but I won't. I think the best plan is for thee to stay here in Baytown and we'll see what we can find out.'

Sue was wondering just how much he knew. Was there more that he was not telling her? She realised that if she wanted to find out she would have to go along with his suggestion.

'Reet,' she agreed. 'All I ask is that if there's anything I can do to help solve this mystery, thee'll let me.'

'I will.'

'Thee'll need somewhere to stay,' put in Nell, pleased with the way Zac had handled the situation. 'Thee can have the room thee's just been using.'

'But I have little to pay thee with.'

'Thee can help out here. Maybe do some baking, serving customers.'

'Reet.' Sue nodded her appreciation with a smile. She was right where she wanted to be, in with Zac and Nell, and although she appeared to have won their trust she knew they would be keeping a watchful eye on her. The smugglers of Baytown did not accept strangers easily.

Chapter Thirteen

It was mid-morning the following day when Lieutenant Boston led his troop of dragoons into Baytown. He had instructed them to ride with a no-nonsense attitude. They needed to show strength and dominance, they had the authority and as such must make their mark. The Lieutenant was determined to do just that. He was seething with anger, had been ever since he had received the report from the relief who had been sent to take over from the man on the cliffs.

The relief had been puzzled when there was no one to meet him above Robin Hood's Bay, until his search took him to the edge of the precipitous drop and he saw the body far below.

The man could have fallen but Lieutenant Boston refused to believe that. In his own mind he felt sure that his spy had been dealt with by the smugglers in order to intimidate the dragoons.

Rumours were rife among his men when the news came in and he had had to exert all his authority to stop them. Though he realised he had little chance of proving the smugglers were behind the death, he knew that to ride in to Baytown in strength and confront Zac Denby would raise the morale of his troop and act as a warning to the smugglers.

Their approach had been noted and when the horsemen rode down the main street they could feel silent hostility from the watching townsfolk.

Boston rode straight in the saddle, his eyes everywhere, piercing, noting, watching for the slightest thing which would connect anyone with smuggling. But he rode more in hope than anticipation of success. He called a halt outside the Fisherman's Arms where news of their approach had brought the drinkers outside. He sat in the saddle for a moment, casting a contemptuous gaze over the group, then swung slowly to the ground. As he did so one of his troopers slid from his horse and took charge of the lieutenant's mount.

'Sergeant!' he called over his shoulder.

'Sir!' the soldier snapped smartly.

'Question that man.'

The sergeant called to two of his men who slipped from their horses. They grabbed the man whom the lieutenant had pointed out and, followed by the sergeant, bustled him across the street and into an alley.

Boston turned his attention back to the group from whom he sensed hostility. 'I want information. One of my men was found at the bottom of the cliffs.' He paused then added vehemently, 'Dead! Someone killed him and I want to know who.'

'How does thee know he didn't fall?' The voice came quietly but piercingly from Zac Denby who stepped from the doorway of the Fisherman's Arms.

The group parted and Zac strode through them to come face to face with Boston. Small though Zac was, even Boston felt that a powerful presence had come on the scene.

'I know my man better than that,' he scoffed.

'Accidents do happen,' returned Zac.

'They do,' he agreed. 'But I believe this was a contrived accident.'

'Think what thee like.'

Boston pushed his way past Zac and strode through the group whose murmurings did not go unnoticed. He paused in front of Nell and Sue who were standing in the doorway.

'What think you, Nell Randall?' he asked with a supercilious smirk as his eyes roved over her.

'I think thee's clutching at straws,' she replied haughtily.

'Maybe, but straws can sometimes be burnt to get the

truth.' He swung his gaze to Sue. 'Ah, a newcomer. I didn't see thee the last time I was here. What's your name?'

Sue knew this was a testing time for her. She realised that Zac would still be suspicious of her and of the reason why she was in Baytown. This confrontation between the lieutenant and herself could so easily have been set up to ingratiate her with the smugglers. She realised Zac was watching her carefully.

'Sue Thrower, and aye, I'm new here,' she replied, trying to match Nell's attitude and hoping no one could detect how nervous she was.

Boston stared at her for a moment then suddenly swung on his heels and strode back through the crowd with a quick pace.

Sue's lips tightened. She wished he had said more, wished she had been given the opportunity to convince Zac she was no spy. But it had not been so and she must still be wary, still find some way of impressing the smugglers.

Reaching the edge of the group, Boston shouted, 'Sergeant!'

'Sir!' The sergeant reappeared with his two men, pushing the man they had taken. He staggered forward at a half run to prevent himself falling.

The crowd gasped. The man's nose was bleeding, his cheek cut and his left eye was closing rapidly. He held his left side, wincing with pain. Two men hurried forward to support him.

'Learn anything, Sergeant?' rasped Boston.

'Nothing, sir.'

Boston swung round to find Zac glaring angrily at him, but before the smuggler could speak the lieutenant raised his voice. 'Let that be a lesson to you all. You'll get rough treatment if you step the wrong side of the law.'

'Thy law,' hissed Zac.

'Aye, my interpretation which the authorities will uphold.'

Zac glanced at the beaten man. 'Get him inside.' He

glared back at Boston, his face dark with anger. 'Thee do that to anyone in Baytown and thee does it to me – and I look after my own.' He swung round and hurried after the last of the crowd disappearing through the door of the Fisherman's Arms.

Boston sized up the situation quickly. When Zac went inside there would be no one on the street. He would dearly love to hear what went on inside the inn. At times like this, with tension running high, things were said, slips were made.

'Sergeant, cover for me. Make a pretence of getting ready to move off, but delay it somehow and keep anyone off the street until I get back.'

He slipped away and quickly but quietly made his way round the back of the inn. Making sure there was no one about, he approached the back window. Steadying himself against the wall, he took a quick glance into the kitchen. As he had expected the beaten man had been taken there. The helpers had been dispersed and only Zac, Nell and Sue were in the room. He held back as he saw Sue approach the sink beneath the window. He heard her pour some water from a ewer into a bowl. There was a moment's silence and then he heard a scrape as the window was opened slightly.

'We need a bit of air in here for him,' said Sue.

Boston smiled to himself. If Sue Thrower had been working for him she couldn't have done better.

'Damn Boston!' Zac spat the words with venom. 'I'd like to get *him* on the cliffs.'

'Thee'll have to watch that man. He's ganning to pursue his suspicions,' said Nell.

'Aye, but he'll get his comeuppance before I'm finished with him.'

'Now thee be careful, Zac,' warned Nell. 'Especially with Sunday coming up. Some more water, Sue, please.'

Boston figured he had spent long enough. He had gleaned something. Sunday had some significance. His mind was occupied with the possibilities as he hurried back to his troop. There he found the sergeant still maintaining an air of being busy.

'Any trouble, Sergeant?'

'None. A couple came out of the inn but they hurried away. They wouldn't be aware that you weren't here.'

'Good.' Lieutenant Boston was satisfied. Something was going to happen on Sunday, maybe running contraband. As he rode back to Whitby he made plans to keep an eye on Baytown that day.

'Ah, come in, my boy.' Edwin Roper, seated at his desk in the room he had set aside in his London home as his study, looked up from the paper on which he had been making notes when the door had opened. He laid down his pen and leaned back in his chair with a warm smile of welcome for his eldest son, Mark.

'You wanted to see me, sir,' said Mark closing the door behind him.

'Indeed,' replied Edwin, linking his hands contentedly across his ample stomach.

Life had been good to him. He maintained you always got out of life what you put in, and his hard work in building up a successful merchant business in Whitby had been amply rewarded. It had brought him the opportunity to expand the firm to London where he himself had taken charge leaving a capable manager, Silas Brent, to run the Whitby office. Eight years in London had seen, through his diligence and concentration, the growth of a thriving company, of which he was justly proud. Though his family had not settled easily at first, missing the north more than they had cared to admit, they came to terms with the new life, gave him their full support, and he saw to it that they were accepted by London society.

Edwin was proud of his two sons and two daughters, and especially of his eldest, Mark. He watched him through admiring eyes as he crossed the room. Tall – he touched an inch over six feet – well made, an athletic figure without an inch of fat. He moved lightly, holding himself erect, seeming to add to his height. His light brown hair held a tint of copper, something he got from his mother. He had a firm, rectangular jaw, which hinted at the determination behind a shrewd brain. His hazel eyes, evenly set, were alive, expressing a love of life and showing an alertness which would miss nothing. His brown coat was cut away at the waist, falling in two knee-length tails at the back. The low-cut dark blue waistcoat revealed a pale blue shirt and a precisely tied white neckerchief. His yellow ochre breeches ran into Naples yellow stockings with red Venetian knee-bands covering the joining, while highly polished black shoes were topped with bright steel buckles. He cut a fine figure as he walked towards his father.

No wonder he's in such demand on the London social scene, thought Edwin, and it's a wonder he hasn't found himself a wife for he never lacks female company whenever he attends concerts or visits a theatre. Invitations to house parties were ever forthcoming as matchmaking mothers tried to promote the eligibility of their daughters. Edwin wondered if Mark would miss this life. Would he also miss the clubs of which he was a member where he met companions of his own age and standing?

'Sit down, Mark.' Edwin indicated the chair on the opposite side of his desk. When his son was comfortable he went on. He knew Mark was one who loved directness, who preferred people to come straight to the point rather than talking around it. 'I want you to take over our business in Whitby.'

The words hit Mark like a thunderclap. 'Whitby?'

'Aye.'

'What about Silas?'

'He wants to resign as manager.'

Mark raised his eyebrows in surprise. 'Why?'

'His wife isn't well. He wants more time to devote to her. I received word by last week's London Packet from

Whitby. I replied saying I would make arrangements as quickly as possible.'

'You said nothing until now,' said Mark.

'I didn't want to until I had made my decision, which I did yesterday. I'd like you to take over. Now, my boy, I want your honest view. I don't want you to say yes just because I've asked you. It will be a big change from the life you've got used to here in London.'

'It will.' There was a touch of regret in Mark's voice but he quickly dispelled the doubt it had raised in his father's mind when he added, 'But I don't mind. Overseeing the Whitby branch will be a challenge.' He was pleased that his father considered him capable of doing the job.

'It's not just a matter of overseeing. I'm giving you full authority to expand as you see fit. I think there's every chance of doing so and we've got to keep ahead of our rivals.'

'I look forward to it. When do you want me to go?'

'I'll book you a passage on the ship for Whitby leaving Tuesday afternoon. You'll be in Whitby by Wednesday.'

'So soon?'

'Any objections?'

'No.' Mark shook his head. 'I have several appointments but none that are so important they can't be broken.'

'Good.'

'So Silas won't know I'm arriving on Wednesday?'

'No. My last word was that I'd find a replacement as soon as possible. He won't mind if you just walk in.'

'Right, I'll make arrangements for Tuesday.'

'Accommodation is one problem. I'm sorry we didn't keep our Whitby house.'

'I'll put up at one of the inns until I find somewhere.'

'Get a good property, we can afford it.'

Mark leaned back in his chair with a little catch of his breath. 'This is all so sudden. It's a new direction in my life.'

'Sorry to spring it on you. A new direction may not

be a bad thing, but will you miss the social life here in London?'

Mark gave a half laugh. 'In one way, yes, but on deeper consideration, no. There's something shallow about many aspects of it. Too many of the young men I know are just looking for a good time and chiefly on their father's money. I'm sure I can adjust to life in Whitby.'

'Good.' Edwin, pleased with his son's attitude, nodded his approval. As Mark rose to leave he stopped him. 'When I told your mother she naturally didn't want you to go, but she soon realised that it was a great opportunity for you. She's arranging a small dinner for tomorrow night as a farewell. A few of your friends and some of ours.'

'I'll go and thank her now,' said Mark, rising from his chair. 'And thank you, sir.'

The dinner had been a convivial affair with pleasant talk spiced with sufficient humour to make it a light-hearted occasion. The salmon had been followed by goose roasted with a currant pudding and served with sweet potatoes as well as Virginia potatoes, accompanied by carrots, peas and cabbage, with a speciality of lettuce and mint tossed in a little vinegar. Jellies of various colours along with a variety of sweetmeats were offered as adjuncts to the ever popular apple pie. Cheese accompanied a change in wine, a sweet Spanish wine consumed with the main meal now being replaced by port. After tea and cakes, a speciality of Mrs Roper's kitchen, the guests adjourned to the drawing room where Madeira malmsey was served with walnuts.

With their glasses charged, Edwin called for attention and announced that Mark was taking up a position as head of the firm in Whitby and would be leaving on the Tuesday sailing. After congratulations and commiserations were over, Sir William Bailey, Head of the Customs Board, drew Mark to one side.

'Looking forward to this move to Whitby?' he asked.

'Yes, sir, very much. It's a challenge and I like challenges,' replied Mark.

'I know you do,' smiled the tall man who, although good food and wine had begun to take effect around his middle, still showed signs of a once athletic body. 'I've watched your progress ever since your father came to London and we became friends through our interests in trade. You're a likeable young man, able to take care of himself, and from what I hear from your companions at fencing clubs no mean hand with a sword and rapier.'

'Sir, you flatter me,' said Mark, embarrassed by this praise.

'Not at all. And to go on, you have a shrewd and nimble brain, able to make swift decisions which more often than not are right.'

Mark eyed Sir William with a wry glance. 'All this praise must be leading up to something.'

Sir William chuckled. 'There, what did I tell you – a shrewd mind! Yes, you're right, I have a proposition to put to you.' He glanced around. 'But not here, I don't want to take up your time this evening. Come to my office tomorrow morning.'

'It's Sunday, sir,' Mark pointed out.

'I know, but I'll be there after the ten o'clock service. We can talk quietly without interruption.'

Mark, wondering what this was all about, agreed to meet Sir William at the appointed time.

'Good.' He beamed and raised his glass to their meeting. 'Now, don't let me keep you from your other guests. Oh, just one thing. This is just between ourselves. To anyone else, it has never taken place.'

As he moved away Mark watched him with curiosity. Why the mystery? What could the Head of Customs want with him?

The following morning Mark left his family outside church after the service on the pretext that he wanted to see some other friends before he left for Whitby.

He was dressed in the same clothes as he had worn the evening before for he had slept late and had had no time to seek out a change. The only departure from last night were his shoes for now he wore knee-length black boots and a top coat of vandyke brown, its shoulder cape edged with dark blue braid. He wore his low-crowned hat, with its brim curling up at the sides, at a slight angle, giving him a jaunty look.

He lost no time in reaching the office of Sir William Bailey where he was greeted heartily.

'Right on time, m'boy.'

'Believe in punctuality, sir.'

'One of your many attributes I've come to admire over the years,' said Sir William as he indicated a leather-upholstered chair to Mark. He himself sat down in a similar chair, the two having been drawn to face each other across the fireplace in which a fire crackled brightly. A small table holding a decanter of wine and two glasses had been placed conveniently to Sir William's chair and he proceeded to pour from the decanter.

Mark, wondering why he had been summoned here, accepted his glass with thanks and waited for his host to pick his up. As Sir William raised his glass his eyes met Mark's with a searching gaze, one which was looking for a reaction.

'To an association which I hope will be of benefit to us both,' he said.

Mark, his curiosity heightened even further, raised his glass in acknowledgement. He made no comment, knowing Sir William would reveal the reason for this meeting in his own time.

'I can see you are mystified as to why I asked you here, but before I put my proposition, or rather my request, to you, I must have your promise that whatever your answer nothing of what is said here will go beyond these four walls. Not even your father must know what I am about to put to you.'

Mark gave only a moment's hesitation before he said, 'You have my solemn word, sir.'

'Good.' Sir William seemed to relax more now he had that promise. 'Smuggling is rife on the Yorkshire coast. The efforts of the Preventive Men, the dragoons and revenue cutters, have met with very limited success. In fact, I am sorry to say, with no success in the Whitby area where Robin Hood's Bay seems to be the heart of the trade.' Sir William warmed to his subject. 'The smugglers there seem to run the whole community. To put it another way, all the village folk are willing accomplices or else are prepared to keep their mouths shut and regard the activities of the smugglers as legitimate trading. Robin Hood's Bay, Baytown or Bay as the locals call it, is isolated, only rough tracks lead out of the village, the main one, and that isn't very good, being to Whitby. But smuggling ways cover the wild moors stretching inland. We have recently increased the number of dragoons stationed at Whitby so that there is extra strength to patrol the Baytown area.'

'What has this to do with me?' asked Mark as Sir William took a sip of his wine.

'All in good time, m'boy. Let me give you the whole picture as I see it. We know the leader of the smugglers in Baytown is a man by the name of Zac Denby, but to prove it is impossible. The only way would be to catch him and his gang redhanded, but he's too wily. Seems to know a lot of what is happening among the forces ranged against him. But he isn't the person who concerns me.'

Mark raised his eyebrows in surprise. 'But I would have thought, catch him and the whole operation would be smashed?'

Sir William nodded. 'Probably for a while, but I believe that there are even shrewder brains behind the smugglers than Zac Denby's, and those are the people whom we want to catch – the organisers, the men who control everything from ordering the goods on the Continent, chiefly from

France, shipping them to England, and then distributing them once they've been landed.'

Mark gave a half smile of comprehension. 'And that's where you want me to come in? A spy for you to try to gain the knowledge you want, to get the men behind the smuggling gangs?'

'Right. There's a risk, a grave one, I'll not deny that,' replied Sir William. 'The smugglers are ruthless, show no mercy for anyone who crosses their path. We've had men try to turn informer but they've disappeared, never heard of again. We've tried planting men in Baytown but again they've disappeared. It's a dangerous role I'm asking you to play and I'll understand if you turn it down. I won't hold it against you. After all, you've your business to run. But I see it not only as a very useful cover but also as a means of getting to know local people and, ultimately, who might be the brains behind the smuggling.'

'You think there's more than one?'

Sir William shrugged his shoulders. 'I don't know. I do think there may well be a committee of sorts, but there may be one man in particular. We hear rumours that he or they are known as The Fox.'

Mark gave a little chuckle. 'A crafty animal to signify the craftiness of the smugglers.'

'Aye, and he's the man we want. Or men.'

'Any ideas?'

'None.' Sir William shook his head. 'Landed gentry, well-to-do farmer, merchant, parson . . . really anybody at all. But as I see it they must be in a position to organise, run and control a complex operation.' He leaned back in his chair. 'Well, there you have it.' His eyes were fixed on Mark. 'What do you say? Will you do it?'

He took a sip of his wine, his mind assessing the challenge. The adventure of it stirred him. As Sir William said he had a perfect cover and a position from which he would or could be in touch with all manner of people. It would add spice to his time in Whitby. 'Yes, sir, I'll do it.'

'Good man!' Sir William slapped his thigh with his free hand and raised his glass with the other. His face broke into a broad beam of satisfaction. 'Here's to success.' They both drank. As Sir William licked his lips his face resumed its serious expression. 'If ever the situation becomes untenable or threatening, you must pull out. I will understand. I want your promise on that.'

'Very well, I promise.'

'I'm throwing you into a dangerous situation. If anything terrible happened to you I could never face your parents and would never forgive myself.'

'Don't worry, sir. Nothing will happen to me. I can take care of myself.'

That same Sunday morning Lieutenant Boston mustered his troop as the eastern night paled with the rising sun and rode out of Whitby early on a trackway leading in the opposite direction to Robin Hood's Bay. He knew that eyes watched and had no doubt that word was passed quickly to the smuggling gangs along the coast.

On a lonely stretch of road he swung inland and made a wide circle to take him back to the coast between Baytown and Ravenscar. He had scouted the area previously for points from which he could advantageously keep watch on the village and now led his troop to a hollow in which the horses could be hidden. Leaving two men in charge of the mounts he led the other seven and the sergeant to a position nearer the edge of the cliffs.

He had no notion what to expect, maybe nothing, but intuition told him that the few words he had overheard were significant. It would be worth a long wait to smash the smuggling gang. Knowing his men could become restless if they were inactive in the field for long, he had brought along extra food and, as a special privilege, a bottle of wine per man. He was not going to have his men unhappy with their lot. Satisfied with their deployment they settled down to wait, unaware that their arrival had been observed.

'Where's Sue?' Zac demanded curtly when he came into the kitchen of the Fisherman's Arms.

Nell glanced up sharply from the frying pan she was tending at the fire. She knew the signs. Something had upset him and he had been dwelling on it during the night. 'Out. Said she'd try and find something out about Ben.'

'Where?' he snapped.

'How should I know?' replied Nell testily. 'What's biting thee?'

Zac scowled as he sat down at the table. 'Thee was careless yesterday. Struck me during the night.'

'Careless? What's thee mean, and what's that got to do with Sue?'

'Thee mentioned having to be extra careful on Sunday now that Boston was poking about.'

'Aye. And that's true.'

'Thee spoke in front of her.'

'So . . .' Nell stopped. She grasped what Zac was getting at. 'Thee doesn't trust her yet. Thee thinks she might be a spy and that she might jump to conclusions from what I said. It's unlikely.'

'Maybe, but thee knows how cautious we've got to be.' Zac frowned. 'She might be out there now passing on the information. To Boston maybe. Remember, he didn't question her as he might.'

Nell looked thoughtful for a moment then pulled a face as she shook her head. 'Nay, I think thee's wrong. I think Sue's genuine. Besides, from what I said no one could surmise that we're expecting contraband late this afternoon.'

'Maybe not, but give Boston a hint and he'll be around and I reckon he'll have the patience of Job if there's a chance of catching us. We'll see what she has to say when she returns, and if there's any doubt then . . .' He left his threat unsaid but drew his hand sharply across his throat. 'Now let's have that bacon, it smells good.'

He had almost finished his breakfast when Sue burst through the back door. She was breathing heavily, her faced flushed, hair windblown. She leaned her palms flat on the table. 'Thank goodness thee's here, Zac. I was afraid thee might have gone.'

Zac and Nell, regaining their composure after Sue's sudden appearance, were startled by the concern on her face.

'Here, sit down,' said Nell pushing a chair towards her.

Gulping for breath, trying to calm herself after her exertions, Sue nodded as she sat down.

'What's wrong?' Zac's cautious mind was toying with the idea that this might be play acting.

'The dragoons who were here the other day are on the cliffs,' she gasped. She swallowed hard and took another deep breath as she ran her fingers through her hair, trying to bring some sort of order from the havoc caused by her rush back to Baytown.

Zac and Nell exchanged a quick glance.

'Where?' he asked.

'Round the bay, between here and Ravenscar.'

'How was it thee saw them?' asked Zac. He pushed his plate away from him and leaned forward on the table, watching her intently.

'I'd been enquiring about Ben.'

'Where?' he queried sharply.

'Farms. Thought he might have had some goods left and tried to sell them on his way from Bay.'

'Had he?'

'No. No one had seen him.' There was despair in Sue's voice.

'The dragoons?' rapped Zac, bringing their attention back to the immediate problem.

'They left the horses in the charge of two men in a hollow and the rest went to a position nearer the cliff. They seemed to be settling down for a long wait as they looked to have plenty of food and wine.'

'Thee didn't speak with them?'

Sue's eyes sharpened to meet Zac's gaze. 'Does thee think I'd be here now if I had? Not after the way that lieutenant looked me up and down yesterday. I'd have been kept there for his entertainment.'

Nell poured a cup of tea. 'Here, drink this and then I'll get thee some breakfast.'

Sue glanced up at her. 'Thanks, but I'm not hungry.'

'Thee must have something,' replied Nell. Ignoring Sue's protests she went to the frying pan and dropped two rashers of bacon into the fat.

'Now,' went on Zac, still cautious, 'describe exactly where these men are.'

Sue did so as best she could, then concluded, 'I thought thee'd better know as soon as possible after what Nell said yesterday.'

Zac eyed her suspiciously. Nell turned from the fire. She could not see Sue's face, sitting as she was with her back to the fire, but she could see Zac's reaction when the answer came to his question, 'What was that?'

'Nell mentioned thee'd have to be extra careful on Sunday.'

'Aye, and does thee know why?' Zac's eyes narrowed.

'No.' Sue shook her head.

'Contraband. We're expecting a shipment late this afternoon.'

Sue gasped. 'And Boston is sat out there waiting?'

'Aye,' agreed Zac, his voice cold. 'But how did he get to know?'

His one dark eye pierced her very soul. His scar seemed to flame and accentuate the black patch over his left eye. He looked evil as he leaned forward even more. There was no mistaking the accusation.

Sue recoiled, pressing back in her chair, but at the same time anger welled in her.

'Thee think I told him? How could I? I was here all night.'

'How do I know? Thee could easily have slipped out and gone to Whitby.'

'Thee's a vivid imagination,' snapped Sue. 'And why the hell would I be telling thee he's on the cliff if I'd set him up there?'

'A cover. Besides, how else could he have known?'

Sue's lips tightened. She searched her brain for some answer. 'Overheard thee?' she suggested.

Zac snorted with contempt.

'He could have done,' put in Nell quickly. 'The window was open.'

'Aye, it was,' put in Sue to back up the statement. 'I opened it.' Immediately the words were out she knew she had erred.

Zac's face darkened. 'Very conveniently,' he sneered. He looked at Nell as he pushed himself from the table. 'Don't let her out of thy sight, not for one second. I'm ganning to check this out.'

Sue started to protest but Zac took no notice as he hurried out of the back door. Sue swung round in her chair and gave Nell a helpless, pleading look. 'I swear I don't know how Boston could have got hold of the information except through that window, and I didn't open it because I knew he'd be there. How could I? I'd never even seen him before yesterday.'

Nell came to her and put a comforting hand on her shoulder. 'We don't know that for certain,' she said quietly.

Sue looked up at her in surprise. 'I hadn't!' Tears welled in her eyes.

'I believe thee, lass. But in this game thee's got to trust no one. Zac's always suspicious until he knows otherwise. The stakes are high, the penalties unspeakable. Thee must see his point of view.'

Sue nodded silently then said, 'Truly I only came to find Ben.'

*   *   *

206

Zac hurried up King Street to a cottage at the lower end of Chapel Street. His sharp rap on the door was answered by a little girl of eleven, who peered up at him, squinting against the light.

'Is tha dad in, lass?' he asked with a smile.

The girl had not flinched on seeing the scar and patch. She was used to seeing Zac Denby around Baytown and he had called at the house many times to see her father.

She ran back into the cottage, shouting, 'Pa! Pa! Mr Denby wants thee.'

A moment later Pete Bray appeared, his face holding a query for he had not expected to see Zac until shortly before the contraband was due.

'Trouble, Pete, get tha jacket.'

Without a query he turned, grabbed a woollen cap from a peg close to the door, crammed it on his head, lifted down a thick, waist-length jacket and slipped into it as he stepped outside. He swung the door shut and fell into step beside Zac.

'I'm told Boston and his dragoons are on the cliffs,' said Zac as they walked towards King Street.

'Hell. Where?'

'Round the bay.' Zac went on to impart the information he had got from Sue. 'I want thee to gan and check it out. Report to me at Nell's as soon as possible.'

As soon as Sue's information was confirmed, Zac and Pete hurried to find Tom Fewster.

'Tom, dragoons are on the cliffs between here and Ravenscar. Thee's on duty as signalman. I want thee to get over to Ravenscar now and when the ship is sighted give the signal to hold off. Seven o'clock, when it's dark, signal her in.'

Zac left Tom to get some warm clothes and some food to take with him to the lookout point the smugglers had devised below the top of the Ravenscar cliffs. From there they could watch the contraband ships approach and make any necessary adjustments to the procedure by a series of specially designed signals. Zac knew Tom to be competent and reliable. He was certain that the ship would be held up and would appear in the bay at seven.

Zac and Pete went quickly through Baytown alerting the gang of the change. The cobles would not be needed until seven and the men would assemble at the Fisherman's Arms half an hour before that. He despatched messengers to the nearby farms where the contraband would be stored to alert them to the changes and sent a special instruction to John Dugdale to be in Black Wood from seven-thirty onwards.

Back at the Fisherman's Arms Zac pondered how to divert the dragoons when the goods were run ashore. 'We have the cover of darkness but there'll be lights, and as much as we shield them Boston is sure to see something and take action.'

'Can we work fast enough to dispose of the goods before the dragoons get here?' Pete suggested.

Zac screwed his face up with doubt. 'No, this cargo's a big one and some of it has to be dispersed inland to the farms.'

'Run his horses off,' proffered Nell. 'That would leave him on foot and give us more time.'

'But not enough time,' said Zac.

Sue turned from the stone sink. 'Can thee run the contraband ashore anywhere else?'

Zac scowled and she read it as a sign that she should not be interfering. She realised that she had been allowed to remain so that she would know Zac's plans. She had no doubt that she would be given the opportunity to let Boston know and if he acted on them she would be in trouble.

'No,' replied Nell, attempting to dispel some of the tension Zac was creating. 'We have run contraband ashore at Boggle Hole but that's nearer the dragoons' position so we can't use it tonight.'

'There's only one thing for it – a fight,' said Zac. 'Pete, see the men are well armed when they report.'

Sue shot a glance at Nell. She saw concern cloud her face.

'Zac, that's risky,' Nell protested.

'Aye, it is, lass, but we'll be more than a match for them. We have the advantage of surprise. They don't know that we know they are there.' Zac chuckled to himself at the thought of outwitting and outfighting Boston and his dragoons. He pushed himself up from the table. 'Let's go, Pete, we've a bit more preparation to do than usual.'

'Will thee run their horses off?' asked Nell. 'It'll delay their attack for a short while.'

'Aye, we'll do that, it will give us a bit longer, but the timing will have to be just right.'

Nell sighed as the door closed behind the two men. She shook her head slowly. 'I don't like it when it comes to a fight, but what must be must be.'

By the time the hour came for the smugglers to gather at the Fisherman's Arms, Zac and Pete had almost doubled their complement of trusted men. Although many were not directly concerned with the smuggling, Zac knew he could count on their loyalty. He deployed them in ambush positions along the routes Boston could lead his dragoons to Bay. He had also sent two men to run off the horses with strict instructions that they do so just before seven.

As that hour approached he gave the order to move out to the men assembled in the Fisherman's Arms. They needed no further instructions. Each knew his specific job. They had been warned about the presence of the dragoons and were prepared for the necessary action when it came.

As he stepped outside Zac glanced upwards. The sky was overcast, dimming the tell-tale moonlight. He felt some measure of protection.

With few whispered words, the smugglers launched their cobles into the gently running sea, unshipped their muffled oars and headed out into the bay.

High on the cliffs at Ravenscar, in a small gully, two

flashes signalled to a ship lying off-shore. Within a matter of moments she was underway. She sailed past the headland and, halfway across the bay, hove-to. The crew not engaged in the manoeuvre were already preparing to unload the cargo of contraband. They knew that the delay until darkness could mean that there were government forces, in one form or another, lurking about.

The cobles came alongside and the transfer of the contraband started.

On shore Zac waited anxiously. He had warned his men to work quickly. He wanted as much contraband out of sight as possible before the dragoons arrived. In the Fisherman's Arms Nell and Sue were restless. They felt frustrated at not being able to do anything to help the smugglers, Nell because of the dangers in a fight and Sue because she wanted to wipe Zac's suspicions from his mind. They spoke little, each lost in her own thoughts.

'A decoy!' Sue, her eyes wide with excitement, looked up from her mug of chocolate. 'That's it. We'll lure the dragoons away. If their horses have been scattered they'll have to pursue us on foot and so we can keep them away longer, possibly until Zac's got rid of all the goods.'

'But how?' asked Nell, puzzled at Sue's enthusiasm for a scheme she herself couldn't see working.

'Baytown sends fish by pack-horses to Pickering?' Sue put a known fact as a question.

'Aye,' agreed Nell.

'And very often the women take them?'

'Aye.'

'And the horses are kept here?'

'Aye.'

'Then let's get the women to take a pack-horse train out of Baytown. When we get so far we can reveal our presence with lanterns.'

'Boston will see them and think it's the smugglers getting the goods inland and hopefully he'll follow.' Nell had seen the possibilities and warmed to the idea.

'Better still if he can find fish when he reaches us,' suggested Sue.

'Come on,' urged Nell, grabbing a shawl and throwing it round her shoulders. 'Beth Gill's our lass. She looks after the shipments of fish to Pickering.'

Within a few minutes they were confronting Beth with the proposition. It was almost seven. Beth's nimble brain seized on the idea. 'Anything to put one over on those bastards.' She was a big woman, broad-backed and full-breasted. Her arms, thick through handling boxes and panniers of fish, were matched by the width of her thighs and the strength in her legs. She was out of her chair immediately and surprised Sue with her nimble movement. 'We were leaving with today's catch early morning. Just means we start sooner. Nell, rouse the other women.' Her voice was rough and sharp. She took in Sue with one assessing glance. 'Don't know thee, lass, but let's away and start getting the horses ready.'

'Sue Thrower.' Nell made the introduction as they left the house but Beth gave no indication that she had heard. They strode up the hill, Nell leaving the other two to go on when they reached the first alley.

Soon ten women were converging on two buildings at the top of the hill. They found the pack-horses almost all ready to be loaded. Beth had worked hard enough for two and Sue, bewildered for a minute or two, soon caught on to what was required. She was glad when the other women appeared and she could take a moment to catch her breath.

'How much fish have we got next door?' Nell asked.

'Enough,' called Beth as she led the way to collect the panniers.

With each woman knowing what to do they worked fast without mishap, while Nell and Sue sought out six lanterns which were stored at one end of the fish-house.

'Everyone ready?' called Beth. 'Thee and Sue coming?' she added when she had everyone's assent.

'So far,' said Nell. 'We must see if this ruse works.'

The pack-horse train left Baytown with Beth setting a brisk pace. She knew it was essential for them to appear to be moving from the beach area as soon as possible.

'Where are these bloody dragoons?' she asked.

Nell quickly explained the position as described by Sue.

Beth grunted, her mind picturing the lay of the land so familiar to her. 'Reet, a little further and we swing to the right. That'll start to take us inland. Half a mile on we light the lanterns. They should be visible from the place thee described.'

Lieutenant Boston stirred. It had been a long day. The men had become restless with inactivity and had to seek comfort in food and wine, especially when the daylight faded into night and an extra chill came into the air. The sergeant's suggestion that nothing was going to happen and that they would be better off going back to Whitby was curtly rejected.

'I sense something's going on. Contraband can be run ashore at night.'

'The men are weary of this waiting.'

'So am I,' retorted Boston, 'but enduring hardship makes a good soldier.'

'They're getting drowsy. Maybe we should let 'em sleep, sir.'

Feeling drowsy himself, Boston conceded to that idea and, after putting one man on watch, made a rota for the others.

Lieutenant Boston turned over. He pulled at his coat for extra warmth but something resisted him. His mind sharpened out of the haze. Someone was shaking him. A voice said: 'Sir. Sir!' with an urgency which brought reality tumbling back. He sat up.

'What is it?' he snapped.

'A ship, sir.'

Boston scrambled to his feet and moved with his dragoon

to a position from which to view the bay. Sure enough he could make out the form of a vessel against the dark sea.

'How long's she been there?' he asked.

'Just come, sir.' The dragoon wasn't going to let on that he did not know for he must have been asleep when she came round the Ravenscar headland.

'Seen anything else?'

'No, sir, it's too damned dark.'

Boston peered at the sea. One moment he could have sworn he saw a boat, the next nothing. He turned his attention to the beach and ran his eye round to Baytown. Were they movements he could see? Or was the dark playing tricks with him?

His lips set in a tight line. What did it matter? There was a ship out there. She could have just anchored for the night, but why do so? The sea was reasonably calm, there was no need for a ship to seek shelter. He'd gamble she was a smuggler. Contraband from the Continent bound through Baytown for the cellars of gentry, the hidey holes of farms, the wine cellars of the well-to-do, silks and lace for ladies' wardrobes and tobacco for the parson's jars. Boston's eyes narrowed. Well, this was one consignment that wasn't going to reach its destinations, and with it he'd take Zac Denby redhanded.

'Rouse the men,' he ordered sharply, and the two men proceeded to wake them without ceremony. Protesting at the kicks and shouts, men came reluctantly out of their sleep and stumbled after their officer and his sergeant to the hollow where they had left the horses.

Boston drew to a sudden halt at the top of the rise and stared in disbelief. No horses. What the hell had happened? Where were the guards? He was about to order a search when a groan drifted through the darkness.

'Over here, sir.' A dragoon had detected movement in the direction from which the sound had come.

A few strides took them to two men, holding their heads and struggling to sit up.

'What happened?' demanded Boston angrily as he guessed at the truth.

'Dunno, sir,' slurred one of them. 'We was sitting here minding the horses when — bang! My head exploded. That's all I know.'

'Damned fools!' stormed Boston. Rage swept over him when he realised the smugglers had outwitted him. Somehow they had known he was there and had scattered the horses to delay him getting to Baytown. Maybe there was still time . . .

'Get them on their feet,' he snapped. 'And every man keep up with me.'

He started out but they had gone less than a hundred yards when his sergeant called out, 'Sir, over there.'

The troop came to a halt and stared in the direction indicated by the sergeant.

A light had appeared from behind a rise in the land. It was moving. Another one, then another, and another until there were six moving inland at a steady pace.

'Got 'em.' Boston chuckled with delight. 'That's a smuggler's pony train. I reckon Zac Denby thought that without our horses we wouldn't give pursuit. Well, he thought wrong. Come on, men.'

He set off in the direction of the lights. He figured it wouldn't be long before he caught them up but had not reckoned on the roughness of the terrain and the number of hedges which blocked their path. They had covered over five miles before they even glimpsed a horse and knew for sure that it was a pack-horse train. His shout for the smugglers to halt went unheeded; in fact it only served to quicken the movement of the horses, so that it was another two miles before the dragoons caught up with the train and were able to halt it.

Expecting resistance at any moment, the dragoons, muskets at the ready, moved warily as they covered the smugglers, but the cloaked figures stood by the horses without giving a sign of retaliation. Boston drew his pistol, grabbed a lantern and approached the leader. This wasn't Zac Denby as he had hoped. This person was much bigger. But what matter? He had caught some of the gang with contraband and that was a start to what he saw as his breakup of the Baytown smugglers. When he hauled this lot up before the magistrates in Whitby there would be thirteen fewer smugglers operating out of Baytown. Thirteen! If he was a superstitious man he'd think that an unlucky number, but now he saw it as just the opposite.

'What the hell has thee stopped us for?' demanded the leader.

Boston was startled. Were his ears playing tricks with him? He raised the lantern higher, shoved his pistol back into his waistband and pushed the hood from the face. He stared for a moment. A female! Then he gathered his composure. Why shouldn't the smugglers recruit their wives and sweethearts? He'd been told that Baytown was a community which was all for one and one for all.

'Smuggling,' he rapped.

'Smuggling?' Beth gave a derisive laugh. 'We're innocent fishwives taking fish to Pickering.'

'Trying to put me off,' mocked Boston. 'Well, we shall see. We know contraband's been run ashore from a ship in the bay tonight.'

'Then thee knows more than I do,' mocked Beth, a note of challenge in her voice.

'Check them, Sergeant!'

'Sir!' The sergeant acknowledged the order then snapped: 'Move it!'

The dragoons quickly revealed that all the cloaked figures were women.

'Now the panniers.'

As the soldiers opened them there was no mistaking what they contained but Boston was not going to let it rest at that.

'The fish might be a cover. Check them thoroughly,' he ordered.

His men moaned and cursed as they went about the unpleasant task of scrummaging amongst the fish. Some, to make the job less unpleasant, tipped the contents of the panniers on the ground, ignoring the protests of the women.

By the time the sergeant reported that the panniers were carrying only fish, Boston was seething. He had found nothing, had lost his horses, though no doubt they would be recovered, had been outsmarted by the smugglers and found nothing incriminating. He had been made to look a fool and now faced a walk back to Whitby with his troop smelling of fish.

Ignoring the show of protest still coming from the women at the destruction of their load, he ordered his men to form up for the march to Whitby. They shuffled into order with some reluctance. A day spent on the cliffs watching for smuggling activity and then chasing an elusive target at night had not improved their tempers.

As they walked away, a shambles of a troop, with Boston knowing it was useless to try to smarten them up, the women gathered together chuckling at the success of their venture.

'Sorry about the fish, Beth,' Nell apologised.

'Think nothing of it,' she laughed. 'It was worth it to see that lieutenant's face. He was so sure he'd caught smugglers with the goods.'

'Let's give thee a hand to salvage what we can,' Nell offered, looking at the fish strewn on the ground.

'Forget it. Let the birds have it. The loss is nothing. It was worth it to help Zac.'

'He'll see thee reet,' Nell assured her. 'Mind if we get back to report to him?'

'Off with thee,' said Beth, with a wave of her hand.

Nell and Sue hurried away, feeling pleased with the way things had gone.

When they arrived at the Fisherman's Arms they noted that the cobles were all drawn up on the beach and that

Baytown seemed to have settled down from its night's activities.

'Where the hell have thee been?' snapped Zac when they appeared in the kitchen.

'Did the dragoons turn up? Was there a fight?' Nell returned question for question.

'No, there wasn't. We saw nothing of them,' he replied sharply, annoyed that she hadn't answered his question.

'Then thank Sue,' said Nell.

Zac glanced at her then back at Nell. The grin on her face was beginning to irritate him. 'What the hell is thee talking about?'

'She suggested we use the fishwives as a decoy.' Nell went on to tell him all that had happened. By the end of her story he was laughing.

He looked at Sue. 'Well, lass, seems I misjudged thee. Welcome to Bay.'

Chapter Fourteen

'Emma, Joe's here,' Grace called to her daughter.

'Coming, Ma.'

Emma hurried into the kitchen, swinging her cloak around her shoulders as she did so. 'Just the two baskets?' she asked as she picked up her bonnet and placed it neatly on her head, tying its ribbons under her chin.

'Aye. Give Aunt Matilda my love. Tell her I hope to make a visit before too long.'

'I will, Ma.' Emma made to pick up the two baskets but Amy swept one up into her hands.

'I'll carry one out for thee,' she said brightly. With that she was outside and hurrying down the path. She reached the trap on which Joe was waiting patiently before Emma had left the house. 'Good day, Joe. How's thee this morn?'

'Well, thank thee.' He gave Amy a warm smile and almost added: 'All the better for seeing thee,' but he bit the words back as being unseemly.

'Sorry we won't be able to walk on the cliffs today,' said Amy with a teasing twinkle in her eyes.

Joe's reaction was lost as Emma emerged from the house and his eyes went to her. She handed him the basket and climbed on to the trap beside him. Joe passed her a rug which she laid across her knees. They called their goodbyes as he sent the horse forward.

The sharpness in the air heightened when Joe put the animal into a trot. Emma shuffled closer to him as if seeking a little more warmth. Joe leaned across and tucked the rug around her.

'Thee comfortable, luv?' he asked.

'Yes, thanks.' She nodded with a half smile of appreciation for his concern.

'Would thee like the collar up?' He started to turn up the collar of her cloak.

'It's all right, thanks,' she returned.

'But I'm sure it will help to stop the breeze around thy neck.' He went on adjusting the collar.

Emma squirmed her shoulders with irritation. 'Oh do stop fussing, Joe. I can do it when I want it up.'

'Sorry,' he apologised, showing some surprise at her reaction. 'I'm only concerned for thee. I just want to look after thee.'

Emma felt guilty at her petulant reaction when she noted the touch of hurt in his voice. 'Sorry, Joe.' She laid a hand gently on his arm. 'I know thee means well. Thanks.'

'It's more than meaning well, lass.' He turned towards her. 'I love thee, want nothing better than to look after thee for the rest of my life. Marry me, Emma. I know we will be happy.'

'I promised thee an answer, it will be a week today, and thee promised not to press me.'

'But what's a man to do when he feels like I do?'

Emma gave a slight smile. 'Be patient. I'll give thee an answer in a week's time.' She slipped her arm through his, knowing that he would draw some assurance from the gesture that her answer could be 'yes'.

Emma knew her man, for that was exactly how Joe interpreted her action. With a deep sigh of satisfaction he settled more comfortably on the seat. In a week his life would take on a different aspect. There would be the wedding to think about and arrange, and the whole future would take on a new meaning for him. The girl he had grown up with, whom he had taught the ways of the countryside, would be his. He would do everything to make her happy and would aim to bring to their home some of the luxuries she had seen on her visits to her aunt's. Life would be good.

Emma bit her lip. She could almost sense what he was

thinking and somehow she felt smothered by it. But surely that would pass? Should she say 'yes' to him now?

She glanced out of the corner of her eye at him. A contented smile had settled on his face. Should she turn that contentment into rapture? She knew she could if only she would say that one word. She sensed life with Joe would be good and that she would probably grow to love him in the way that he loved her, so why did she hesitate? Would the situation be any different a week from now? She could not see her feelings alter in that short space of time. Everything would be as it had always been so why not say 'yes' now?

She shifted in her seat and half turned to him. She licked her lips as if in preparation to speak, as if trying to summon the courage to do so. She started. If that was what she was doing then this was not the time to give Joe his answer. But in seven days she must.

She settled herself and concentrated her thoughts on seeing Meg.

The cousins were overjoyed to see each other again. With all her produce sold and Joe having business to do which would occupy him until four o'clock, Emma was free to spend the time after lunch with Meg.

The day had brightened considerably but still with a nip in the air so the two girls decided to go for an invigorating walk by the quays on the west bank of the river and then along the stone pier.

Cloaked against the sharp breeze, they hurried out of Bagdale, past the bridge to the east side, and threaded their way through the flow of people about their work or idling their time watching others, fishermen unloading their catch, housewives buying fish for their suppers, boat repairers doing minor jobs on boats at their moorings, men patching sails, and labourers fetching a new set of ropes from the ropery. The life of the busy port flowed around them. Orders were yelled, prices were shouted, curses were flung, remarks were made, shrieks of laughter were caught by the breeze and underneath them all was the constant buzz of conversation, while superimposed were the cries of the seagulls as they glided gracefully on the air currents.

Emma was contented. She loved visiting her relations in Bagdale, enjoyed walking with Meg and feeling part of Whitby life. Any cares that she had drained away when she was here; she was able to thrust them to the back of her mind and ignore them, just as now her mind was blank to her father's connection with the smugglers, to Sue Thrower's problems, and to the decision which would face her in seven days.

But when they walked along the quay she kept getting reminders of smuggling for they caught snatches of conversations as they headed towards the pier. Whitby still buzzed with stories and rumours of Sunday's events at Baytown.

It was no secret that the dragoons had been seen walking into Whitby, dishevelled and disgruntled, smelling of fish. Tales soon circulated as to how they had lost their horses. Jokes about their attempt to arrest Baytown fishwives did nothing to improve their tempers. Feelings ran high as Whitby folk laughed about and enjoyed the outwitting of the government's forces.

With their horses recovered, Boston had led his men on a search of Baytown and the surrounding farms, but even that brought sneers and derision for they found nothing. All it brought was more hostility to them for they showed no respect for property in their search. Emma told Meg how they had searched the farm thoroughly, leaving behind a trail of broken furniture and shattered tools, but did not reveal the anxiety she had felt in case they discovered the secret of the old barn.

Instead she threw off the despondency on hearing Whitby talk and chatted gaily as they walked, stopping every now and then to watch some boat fussing across the river or a coble tying up with its latest catch. As they moved out along the pier they pulled their cloaks more tightly around them to combat the breeze which strengthened as they passed beyond the protecting cliffs.

They were halfway along the pier when Meg stopped. 'Look.' She pointed to a vessel beating its way towards Whitby. 'The London Packet. Let's stay here, we'll get a good view of her as she comes into the river.'

They strolled up and down, watching the ship come nearer and nearer. Men went aloft, furling sails as ordered by the captain until she carried just sufficient canvas for her to make her approach. One minute she seemed to be standing off, the next rushing towards the narrow entrance between the piers. Emma held her breath. She thought the London Packet must crash into the pier. But then she was there, gliding from the sea to the river. Sailors swarmed to their tasks to bring the vessel successfully to her berth beyond the bridge. Several passengers were on the deck and Emma's eyes swept over them as the ship moved past. A middle-aged gentleman and lady, presumably his wife, stood by the far rail, he pointing something out to her. A group of young men were laughing and chattering among themselves, no doubt anticipating the life to which they were returning or to which they were coming anew. A smartly dressed young woman with two small children holding her hands, one of them a little boy who jumped up and down excitedly, seemed to be looking anxiously ahead as if longing to see someone she knew. A tall young man, elegantly attired in a finely cut top coat, carrying a walking-stick and holding his hat in his hand, no doubt to save it from being blown away, who had had his attention riveted on the east side of the river, turned and spoke to her. She inclined her head and followed his gaze as he turned his attention back to the east cliff and the abbey.

Emma's heart skipped a beat. In that brief moment when the man's face had been turned her way she thought she recognised him.

'Mark. Mark Roper!' she whispered. It was more to herself than for anyone else but Meg caught the words.

'What? Where?' she gasped.

Emma started. For a moment her mind had wandered from reality. She had briefly entered a dream world from which Meg's words brought her tumbling back. 'That man, next to the woman with the children. I thought . . .'

'But he's looking the other way. Thee can't see his face,' Meg pointed out.

'But he turned and spoke to the woman and briefly I saw his face.'

'Even so, he's too far away for you to be positive. It's wishful thinking, Emma. Thee's getting too close to giving Joe an answer and it's befuddling thy brain into trying to make a schoolgirl's dreaming come true. Besides, how on earth could thee recognise Mark Roper after all these years, he'd be so changed from boy to man?'

'Then let's gan to the quay where she'll tie up and see the passengers disembark.'

Meg shook her head. 'Never make it. We've too far to walk, have to cross the bridge, and that'll be raised so we'd have to wait. Passengers will be ashore before we could get there.' Meg smiled sympathetically. 'Sorry, Emma.'

She shrugged her shoulders, resigned to accept Meg's remarks as the truth. 'I must have been reacting subconsciously to the fact that I nearly said "yes" to Joe on our way to Whitby this morning.'

'Thee what?' Meg gasped, her eyes widening.

'I almost did, but something held me back. Maybe that's why I thought that man was Mark.'

'As I said, wishful thinking.'

'Yes, I suppose thee's right.'

'Let's go home. Thee can have some tea before thee sets off for Beck Farm.'

'Like to come to a small party on Saturday evening, Emma?' Matilda Dugdale made the invitation as she breezed into the room where the two girls were having a cup of tea and toasted teacakes. She knew how much

Emma loved coming to the house in Bagdale and being included in such occasions.

'Er . . . yes . . . thanks, Aunty,' spluttered Emma, surprised at this sudden invitation.

'Party, Mother? What's all this about?' asked Meg. 'You've not said anything before.'

'Just arranged it,' cried Matilda, heading for the door again. 'Met Sabina Brent. She hasn't been too well of late so Silas is retiring as manager of Roper's. Thought I'd give them a little farewell party.'

'A wonderful idea. Who's coming?' cried Meg.

'Haven't decided yet. Just going to make a list.'

'Can we help?' asked Emma.

'Come on then. We'll use Father's study.'

When Mark Roper left the London Packet he carried one leather bag in which he had brought the private possessions he wanted with him in Whitby and one change of clothes for he had decided to travel light and obtain everything else he needed in Whitby.

He had enjoyed the voyage and as the ship approached Whitby had spent his time on deck reviving memories of the town from his schooldays. He was surprised that he felt he was coming home. True, he had been born here, but with going to boarding school in York and then moving to London it would have been no surprise had he felt that he was arriving in an unfamiliar place. Yet now, as he walked towards the drawbridge, it seemed as if he had hardly been away.

Though Whitby life hustled and bustled around him and smoke curled from the chimneys, crammed close on the east side, it was nothing to the smoke which hung like a pall over London where life moved day and night without a pause. Mark already felt relaxed and knew he was going to like it here.

He crossed the bridge and turned into Baxtergate. If his memory served him correctly here he would find the Angel, the principal inn in the town, the meeting place of merchants, ship owners and sea captains, the place where Whitby society met and held their dinners, public or private. Here he would book a room for an indefinite period until he could find a house and have it prepared to his liking.

He made his reservation under the name of Mr Smith with an attentive clerk, was shown his room which met with his approval, freshened up and left the inn for the offices of his father's firm.

He entered the building, knocked on a door and entered a room he remembered from a boy. It had not changed one bit except that there were now four desks instead of two at which four young men were busy with ledgers and documents. A youth rose from a stool beside a small desk which occupied one corner, near the counter which ran the full width of the room.

'Yes, sir?' he queried with a bright smile.

'Is Mr Brent in?'

'Yes, sir.'

'I would like to see him if I may.'

'Yes, sir. Who shall I say wants to see him?'

'Mr Mark Roper.'

'Yes . . .' The words died on his lips. His eyes widened. His jaw dropped. 'Mr Mark Roper?'

All four clerks looked up from their work and turned to stare incredulously at the newcomer.

'Yes.'

The youth took a deep breath, lifted a panel in the counter and scuttled out of the room.

Mark smiled at the clerks and as one they all turned back to their ledgers and documents.

A moment later the door burst open and the youth gasped, 'This way, Mr Roper, this way.'

Mark followed him across the passage to a door which was already open and at which a smiling Silas Brent stood waiting to greet him.

'Welcome, Master Roper, welcome indeed.' He held out his hand and shook Mark's firmly then glanced beyond him. 'All right, Tommy, that will be all.'

'Yes, sir.' The clerk rushed away back to the office where Mark guessed there would be speculation about the arrival of the owner's son.

'It's a pleasure to see you, Master Mark,' said Silas. 'Oh, I'm sorry, but you see I've always remembered you as Master Mark. Now . . .' He seemed to be getting flustered by his explanation so Mark stopped him.

'Silas, I'm Mark to you – well, maybe except in front of the staff. Wouldn't want them to think they can be as familiar. But you are an old and trusted employee, a friend, so please call me Mark.'

'Very well. You're here to appoint a new manager?' asked Silas.

'No. I *am* the new manager.'

The unexpected announcement took Silas completely by surprise. 'You've come to be manager?' he gasped.

'Yes.' Mark smiled. 'I have been in the business in London, you know.'

'Oh, I didn't mean you weren't capable,' spluttered Silas, his face reddening with embarrassment. 'Your father gave no indication it would be you, merely said he would make an appointment as soon as possible.'

'I know. I'm sorry. When he decided to send me I saw no point in hanging around in London and I was booked on the next ship, so you see a letter and I would have arrived together. Besides, we thought you wanted to be relieved of your post quickly?'

'Yes, and I'm grateful for the prompt action. My wife is not well.'

'We were all sorry to hear that. I hope it's not serious?'

'She's up and about but she does need more care and attention.'

Mark nodded. 'When do you want to leave?'

'That's up to you.'

'Should we say a week today? That'll give me time to settle in and for you to give me an insight into the business here.'

'Very well. That will suit me. Are you sure you don't want me to stay on any longer?'

'No. Should there be any queries, I can contact you.'

'Any time, any time,' said Silas, feeling relieved that he might still be of use to the firm with which he had spent all of his working life.

'Just one thing, Silas. I'd like the fact that I am here kept a secret, at least for two or three days. Just want to get the feel of Whitby again without being known. I don't think anyone will associate me with the boy who left seven years ago – more than that if you take in the time I spent at boarding school in York.'

'I understand. We'd better instruct the staff.'

'I'll do that when you introduce me.'

'Accommodation?'

'I've got a room at the Angel, booked under a false name, so there'll be no rumours spreading.'

'You should be very comfortable there.'

'What I want, Silas, is a house. So if you know of any . . .'

He smiled. 'Well, isn't that a coincidence. What about your old house?'

'You mean the one we had in Bagdale?' A tone of excitement had come to Mark's voice.

'The very one. The people who bought it from your father, you may remember, were getting on in years. Well, he's died and she has gone to live with her daughter in York. The house is for sale. Mind you, it has been neglected over the last few years so it will need a bit of renovation.'

'Never mind that,' said Mark. 'I would love to move back into my old home. Can you buy it as an asset of the firm? That way you can do it right away and I needn't be involved at the outset.'

When Mark left the office he was highly satisfied with

the way things had gone. He had arranged the next meeting with Silas for Friday and looked forward to spending the rest of the day and tomorrow reacquainting himself with Whitby.

'Right, Silas, here I am ready to be shown the firm's business in Whitby.' Mark was eager to get to grips with the work when he arrived at the office on Friday.

'I cleared my things out yesterday, the desk is yours.' Silas motioned to the seat behind the large oak desk which was situated so that the light would come over Mark's left shoulder from the window which overlooked the harbour.

'I didn't want you to rush,' said Mark.

'I believe in getting on with things,' returned Silas. 'After all, this office is now yours. But before I get down to showing you what's what there are two things to clear up.' He picked up two keys from the desk. 'The keys to your new home.'

'You completed the deal?' Mark showed his delight by the pleasure in his voice.

'Almost. Everything has been agreed but there are some documents still to be signed. The firm will own the house. I've made an entry in the books accordingly. They are there for your perusal.' He indicated two ledgers open on the desk.

'Thanks, Silas. You certainly worked fast.'

'Didn't want anyone to get there first.'

'And what was the other thing?' queried Mark.

'Matilda Dugdale, wife of Robert Dugdale, firm of Dugdale and Sons, one of the biggest merchants in Whitby, is giving a party tomorrow evening, Saturday, to mark my retirement. Apparently she bumped into my wife on Wednesday and Sabina happened to say I was retiring but didn't know when there would be a new manager to take over. Mrs Dugdale is impulsive and there and then said she would give a dinner for me.'

'Good,' said Mark. 'I've no doubt you've always had a

228

good relationship with the Dugdales so it's what you deserve. It's something I should be doing, but having just arrived . . .'

'Think nothing of it,' protested Silas. 'Your father has been more than generous with bonuses over the years.'

'Well, I will arrange something later on.'

'I would like to make a suggestion if I may?' Silas went on. Mark made a sign of approval. 'Let me take you as a guest. I can arrange it with Mrs Dugdale.'

'Oh, I couldn't intrude.' Mark shook his head.

'I think this would be the ideal occasion to break the news that you are to be the new manager of Roper's and to introduce you as such.'

Mark thoughtfully rubbed his chin. 'I see your point, and you could be right. It could be a good opportunity to meet our rivals.'

'Rivals in a friendly way.'

'Of course. Arrange it if you can.' Mark gave a little smile. 'But keep my name a secret. Just say the new manager has been appointed and could you bring him along.'

'Leave it to me. You will arrive completely unknown.'

'I remember the family, was at school with some of them before I went to York. They'll get a surprise to see me back in Whitby . . .'

On Saturday morning Beck Farm was in a turmoil. There was no containing Emma and Amy as they got ready for the party. Jay couldn't see what all the fuss was about as he helped his father finish repairing the furniture damaged by the dragoons.

John worked quietly, thankful that his womenfolk were happy. He had experienced anxiety at the dragoons' visit. He had kept his protest at their intrusion mild, fearing that anything stronger would provoke them into a deeper search. He was thankful when they rode away without mentioning the old barn. Furniture could be repaired without trouble; discovery of the contraband would shatter their lives.

'Amy, thee still at that iron?' cried Emma in despair as she whirled into the kitchen carrying a dress.

'Got it too hot, had to wait for it cooling,' replied Amy as she gave the back of her dress one more sweep of the iron. She replaced it in front of the fire to reheat, picked up the second one which had been standing on the hearth close to the red coals, and tested its smoothing surface by spitting on it. The saliva sizzled and ran off the metal. 'Just right this time. Shan't be long.'

'Hurry it up or we won't be ready when Joe comes.'

Their mother laughed. 'Thee's plenty of time, Emma.'

'Oh, Ma, we'll never be ready.'

'Never's a long time,' said Grace, folding a second night-gown. 'Here, thee'll need these.'

Emma took one. 'Thanks, Ma, but Amy can look after her own.'

'Got everything else?'

'All on my bed. Just got my bag to pack when I've ironed my dress.' She looked despairingly at her sister. 'Do hurry.'

Amy gave a teasing smile and went on ironing.

Emma stormed over to her. 'Thee's being deliberately slow just to annoy me. Come on, give me that iron.'

'There thou is,' laughed Amy, putting the iron back in front of the fire. 'Don't get so worked up.' She swept her dress from the ironing stand and held it up in admiration, picturing herself coming down the curving staircase at her aunt's. It was of pale blue silk flaring slightly from the waist, its straightness broken at three stages with lace frills. From the tight waist it rose to a cape-like covering of the shoulders. The sleeves, puffed to the elbows, came in tight at the wrists.

Grace smiled to herself when she caught her daughter admiring the dress. 'Thee'll look reet bonny,' she commented.

'Think so, Ma?'

'I know so. Careful how thee packs it. Want me to do it?'

'Would thee, Ma, please? I want it to look its best when I unpack it at Aunt Matilda's.'

Mother and daughter went upstairs, leaving Emma ironing her dress.

The excitement continued until shortly after two o'clock when Joe arrived with the horse and trap. Even then last-minute checks had to be made to be certain that they had got everything they wanted for their stay.

'Come on, get off with thee,' Grace tried to hustle her daughters.

'Oh, I don't know whether I packed a clean kerchief,' cried Emma. 'I'll get another.' She flew out of the kitchen.

Grace shook her head in amusement. 'Come on, Amy, get thee to the trap then thee won't be to wait for.'

Amy grabbed her bag, gave her father a kiss, and with a 'goodbye' for Jay ran out of the house.

Joe was standing by the trap, and as he took Amy's bag, she said, 'Hope thee'll like my dress, Joe.'

'New one?' he asked lightly.

'Especially for thee.' Her eyes twinkled with a teasing amusement but behind them he read a touch of seriousness.

'Amy.' Although he was roused by the flirtation he put a note of reproachfulness in his voice.

All further badinage between them was stopped by Emma's, 'Hello, Joe.'

'Hello, Emma. Thee looks very smart, but what better delight is there in this bag?' he asked, taking it from her. As he swung it into the trap his glance caught Amy watching him. Her eyes smouldered with envy of the compliment he had paid to her sister.

'Ah, thee'll have to wait and see,' smiled Emma as he helped her into the trap. Joe climbed in, seated himself and picked up the reins.

Goodbyes were shouted and he sent the horse on the track to Whitby.

*   *   *

Amy, who was sharing a room with Emma, made sure she was ready before her sister. She knew that some of the guests had arrived and that Joe was already downstairs. As she came into the large drawing room, Meg came to meet her.

Chairs had been rearranged so as to leave a suitable open space in the centre of the room and yet still provide seating for those who wanted it without feeling they were away from the flow of guests and conversation. A table along one wall held decanters and glasses which were being looked after by two maids, both identical in long black dresses with white aprons and small mob caps. A fire danced merrily in the grate, adding its own sense of life to the room which was pleasantly decorated with a soft lemon-coloured paper. Several seascapes hung on the walls, one particularly attractive of whalers sailing into Whitby.

'That's a pretty dress,' observed Meg as she greeted her cousin.

'Thank thee,' replied Amy with a generous smile. 'And so is yours.'

Joe, who was at the table receiving a glass of sherry from one of the maids, spotted her arrival and took another glass. He came over to her. 'Amy?' he said offering her the glass.

'Thanks, Joe,' she replied pertly. 'Well, does thee like the dress?' she added, recalling the hope she had expressed when they left Beck Farm.

'Admirable,' he replied, his eyes swinging over her. 'And it makes thee as pretty as a picture.'

'Aren't I always, Joe?' she asked coyly.

'Aye, thee is, lass.'

The flirtatiousness in Amy's eyes and in her attitude was not lost on Meg. She was sure Joe was flattered by it.

'Come and meet some of the guests,' she put in quickly to divert their attention to other matters for Emma's sake. They moved further into the room just as one of the two maids attending to the guests as they arrived announced from the doorway, 'Mr Edward Beaumont.'

Robert Dugdale detached himself from the three men to whom he was talking and crossed the room quickly to greet the new arrival.

'Edward, so pleased thee could come,' he said with a genuine pleasure.

'I'm honoured to be asked.'

Robert raised his hands in a gesture which parried the compliment and indicated that the honour was reciprocated.

'I thought it a good idea after our conversation last week when thee told me thee was looking for some sound firms in which to invest. This evening thee will meet people who might be interested.'

One of the maids came forward with a glass of sherry on a silver tray which the newcomer accepted with a graceful inclination of the head.

Although conversations continued he knew all eyes were on him. He was a big man, broad-shouldered, and his height of two inches over six feet accentuated his narrow waist. His close-fitting clothes revealed an athletic figure of a man who cared about his physical appearance. He wore a coat of Prussian blue which flared from the waist and was trimmed with yellow buttons. Beneath it was a short red waistcoat which showed off the pure white cravat tied neatly at his neck. The red Venetian braid which decorated the upper part of his breeches of Venetian yellow matched the colour of his waistcoat perfectly. His black shoes were highly polished and decorated with silver buckles. He commanded attention and knew so.

At twenty-six he held an air of authority, of someone used to giving orders, someone who demanded respect. His dark brown eyes had an intent, concentrated look, giving the impression that you had all his attention while you knew that he was missing nothing that was happening around him. His hair matched the colour of his eyes and its slight wave in the front and at the temples added attractiveness to the handsome Roman nose over a well-defined mouth and shapely chin. He moved with an aristocratic grace which did not detract from his masculinity.

Matilda fluttered forward to meet their guest, and after the formalities were over Robert turned to Meg.

'My daughter Meg, her cousin Amy, and Joe Wade whom we expect will soon be marrying my other niece, Emma. She will be with us in a few minutes.'

As Robert and Matilda took Edward on to meet the other guests, Meg stared at him.

'Isn't he strikingly handsome?' she whispered in an aside to Amy. 'I've occasionally seen him around in Whitby but I didn't realise he was so good-looking.'

'Thee's smitten,' teased Amy. 'I'd rather have someone like Joe,' she added, tucking her arm through his.

This action only served to bring Meg back to her purpose of introducing Amy and Joe to the other guests but before she could do so she spotted Emma standing in the doorway. With some relief, Meg excused herself and went to meet her.

Joe saw Emma too and would have gone to her, but Amy tightened her grip on his arm and held him there.

He glanced questioningly at her but received only a smile in reply.

'Emma.' Meg greeted her with a smile of admiration. 'That dress is delightful.'

'Thank thee,' replied Emma. 'Hope Joe likes it.'

'Let's go and see what he says.'

Amy let go of Joe's arm when she saw her sister approaching, but only after she knew that Emma had seen the gesture. Joe knew she had seen Amy unlink arms and blushed when he noticed Emma's querying glance.

'Well, Joe, how do thee like it?' she asked.

He gulped. 'Beautiful.'

He admired the dress of pale violet silk which dropped

elegantly from the waist in neat pleats with the front panel a cascade of lace ovals trimmed with narrow puffs of dark violet ribbon. This ribbon ran above the waist to sweep round the neckline, with the upper part of the dress giving way to a flurry of lace which was repeated at the end of the elbow-length drop sleeves.

'Thank thee.' She smiled her acknowledgement with a gracious inclination of her head. 'Everyone here?' she asked as she took a glass of sherry and glanced around the room where people were circulating and Robert was continuing to introduce Edward Beaumont to his guests.

Everyone knew Edward Beaumont as the son of sixty-year-old Cornelius Beaumont, owner of the Ruswarp estates, extending for ten miles on either side of the River Esk and stretching upstream for over eight miles. He owned and worked land through tenant farmers as far as Hawsker and had built a fine country house, Thorpe Hall, on the south bank of the river. They knew that Edward, as an only child, had been doted on and spoiled by his father ever since his mother's death when he was seven, leaving him with a streak of selfishness which was not always apparent.

Robert introduced him to three men deep in earnest conversation.

'Gentlemen, Edward Beaumont. Edward, Joshua Clements, merchant, who specialises in the import of wines and spirits.'

'Ah, a man of my taste. It's a pleasure to meet you, sir.' He added the latter word in deference to an older man. 'I have enjoyed some of your imports. This one of them?' He held his glass up to the light, admiring the gold colour of the sherry. 'An admirable wine, Robert.' He cast a glance at his host. 'It's a trade I could get very interested in,' he said with a wicked twinkle in his eyes.

'Emmott Riley, son of Gerald Riley, timber merchants. Emmott just about runs the business.'

Edward saw a man of about his own age, well-built with

shrewd eyes. 'You could be interested in any timber I have to sell?' he asked.

'Aye, I could that. Thee has some fine standings just out of Hawsker,' replied Emmott, ever one to seize an opportunity whenever it arose.

'We'll arrange a meeting.' Edward chuckled. 'Do a good deal, gentlemen, and I'll have some more money looking for an investment.'

'Then here's a likely man to get you interested,' said Robert. 'Petch Chapman, looking to expand his whaling trade.'

'A risky business?' commented Edward.

'Yes, but the rewards are high. We're coming to a boom time in the whaling business, I'm sure of it,' replied Petch.

'We might talk sometime.'

'I would be delighted.'

Robert excused them and moved Edward on to two more guests whose wives had left them to their discussions while they were admiring Matilda's dress.

'No need for introductions here,' smiled Robert.

'None at all,' agreed Edward. 'Jeremy, Hugh, I didn't know you were well acquainted with Robert?'

His remarks were addressed to two men in their late-thirties who owned estates upstream from those of the Beaumonts, Jeremy Hardcastle on the north bank and Hugh Lomas on the south. With their common interest in the land they knew each other well.

'Oh, we've had dealings with Robert over the years. Most efficient and obliging merchant in Whitby,' said Jeremy. Hugh nodded his approval.

'What about Roper's?' asked Edward.

'Pretty close, pretty close,' said Hugh.

'Silas Brent has done a good job since Edwin Roper took off to London. That was a shrewd move, and Silas was quick to use it to expand the firm in Whitby. I've every respect for him and am delighted to give this little farewell party.'

'I wonder who's taking over?' mused Jeremy.

'We shall know this evening. Apparently the new man has just been appointed and Silas requested that he might bring him to meet us this evening.'

'A splendid idea,' agreed Hugh. 'Who is he?'

'Silas wouldn't say.'

'Ah, a mystery man,' said Edward. 'I like mysteries.'

Catching a signal from his wife, Robert moved away.

Meg and her elder brother were chatting to Emma, while Joe had joined her younger brother who was entertaining Amy and four more young people from Whitby who all knew the Brents from their friendship with their only son who, aged eighteen, had drowned in the harbour trying to save a small girl. It was a tragedy from which his mother had never really recovered and was the cause of her present illness.

Robert and Matilda had tried to keep a balance between ages so that no one would feel overpowered and they were happy with the way people began to mingle as they awaited the arrival of the guest of honour.

'We must introduce Edward to the ladies he doesn't know,' said Matilda when Robert joined her.

'Of course,' he agreed, and a few moments later Edward was turning his charm on the five wives who had now grouped together.

As Matilda and Robert crossed the room towards the young ones, one of the maids came from the hall. She paused in the doorway and announced, 'Mr and Mrs Silas Brent.' There was a pause during which Matilda fussed towards the new arrivals, a smile of welcome on her face. She was followed by Robert who held out his arms in greeting.

Then the pause was broken. 'And Mr Mark Roper!'

Chapter Fifteen

For a moment, with her attention still directed on her cousins Meg and Simon, the words did not register with Emma. Then they struck like an arrow piercing her mind. She went numb. Colour drained from her face. She stared unbelievingly at the young man who stood in the doorway. Her eyes misted over. She sensed herself shaking. Her stomach knotted as this impossible event seemed about to take place.

Astounded by the announcement, Meg glanced at her cousin and was startled by her ashen appearance. She leaned close to her and whispered, 'Thee all right?'

Her words brought Emma sharply back to reality. Mark Roper was here. She must get a grip on herself. Joe must not see her reaction. She nodded and whispered back, 'Yes.' She bit her lips and rubbed her cheeks, bringing colour back before anyone else could notice. The buzz of conversation went on around her, but though she made polite noises her attention was on Mark.

He was so handsome, with such lively eyes. His well-fitting clothes showed the lithe figure of a man who was proud of his appearance. He had an air of confidence, of someone comfortable in any situation. He gave the air of being master of his own destiny. A flicker of light touched his hair, accentuating the copper tint, drawing a small gasp of admiration from her. She saw no one else. He was the only person in the room for her, and though she tried to devote some attention to her cousins it was almost impossible.

She watched him as Robert introduced him to other guests. Here was the man she had dreamed about and her racing heart told her that in person he was no disappointment. She could feel him sweeping her into his arms and those full lips taking hers.

Her mind jolted. Mark might be married. That woman on the ship, those children . . . Oh, no! Don't let it be!

A flutter of excitement ran through her. Her uncle was bringing Mark this way. In a moment he would be here.

'Now, Mark, I wonder if you remember my daughter Meg, my son Simon and my niece Emma?'

'Indeed I do,' he replied with a smile, and then greeted each in turn.

Emma felt her heart lurch. The sound of his voice caressed her, sending shivers up and down her spine.

She wanted to say she'd have known him anywhere, that she had kept an image of him in her heart ever since their schooldays which had changed with the passing years. Yes, she would have known him, but he was even more handsome in the flesh. Her mind was awhirl. She wanted to ask him so much.

'Look after Mark,' said Robert. 'I want a word with Beaumont before we dine.' He moved away to find Edward.

'Are you pleased to be back in Whitby? It must be a big change from London?' Simon asked.

'I'm delighted to be back. London is so busy and crowded.'

'Please excuse us,' put in Meg quickly. 'Simon and I have something to see to before the meal.' She grabbed his arm and bustled him away.

'We've nothing . . .' he started as they headed for the door.

'We have. Just come,' she cut in with a low insistent voice.

Simon knew better than to protest or question his sister's motives.

* * *

'Emma Dugdale,' Mark said slowly as if he was savouring her name on his lips. His eyes consumed her. 'That little schoolgirl has grown into a beautiful young woman.' He bowed slightly as he paid the compliment but his eyes never left hers.

He had often thought about the girl with whom he walked to Bagdale after leaving their tutor and could recall day visits to Beck Farm during holidays. He had wondered what had happened to her, thinking that she might have married her other friend, Joe Wade, and become a farmer's wife with children. Instinctively he glanced at her left hand – no ring. This desirable young woman, who had aroused deep feelings in him even in these few minutes, was not even engaged.

He looked back at her eyes, pools of brown shimmering in the light, dragging him into their depths. He was fascinated by their vitality, and the fact that they revealed her pleasure at seeing him thrilled him.

'Ah, Emma.' Joe's voice cleaved the unspoken understanding which was growing between them.

Emma's lips formed a tight smile but her mind cursed his intrusion. Why did he have to come just now?

Mark noticed the brief flash of annoyance and drew some satisfaction from it. It was a look which Joe missed for he had turned to Mark.

'Mark Roper.' He held out a friendly hand. 'I'm Joe Wade.'

'I remember you,' he replied politely.

Before they could indulge in any further conversation, dinner was announced.

Joe held out his arm to Emma. She could do nothing but take it. She glanced at Mark with an apologetic look. His eyes smouldered. Could Joe be a serious rival?

Meg had returned to the room and much to her chagrin had seen Joe come between Emma and Mark. She glided quickly across the floor and said, 'Mark, please?'

He smiled and held out his arm. 'A pleasure,' he said graciously, and escorted her to the dining room.

Emma, who found she was sitting opposite Joe, was delighted when she saw that the card on her left, written in neat flowing copperplate, announced that this place was reserved for Mark Roper. She caught Meg's glance and knew what she had been up to when she had left with Simon.

Conversation flowed between the guests as they enjoyed oysters, Yorkshire pudding with succulent gravy, roast beef, and a speciality for the occasion, roast swan with chawdron sauce.

Although there were a thousand and one things she wanted to know about Mark, Emma steadied her thoughts with the more mundane by asking, 'Where are thee staying?'

'I've a room at the Angel, but Silas told me our old home in Bagdale was for sale so I got him to purchase it for me. It needs some renovation so I'll stay at the Angel until it's done.'

'How exciting moving back into the family home! I remember it well. I missed visiting when thee went to St Peter's in York, and even more so after thee had gone to London. Is the house still the same?'

'Come and see for yourself. Are you staying here tonight?'

'Yes.'

'How about tomorrow? I'll call for you.'

'Let me see if it's all right with my aunt first.'

'Very well. I hope it will be. You can see what you think to my ideas and advise me on decoration.'

Emma's heart was racing. Tomorrow she could be alone with Mark. Oh, her aunt must say yes! And already her mind was reaching beyond tomorrow.

As he was having a word with Edward across the table Mark caught the word 'smugglers' from someone else. He glanced in the direction of the speaker and saw that it was Jeremy Hardcastle. Maybe this was an opportunity to learn something. For all he knew these respectable people around this table, enjoying a convivial meal together, could be behind the notorious smuggling gangs. He decided to play ignorant.

'Smugglers, you say? Is there much smuggling along the Yorkshire coast?' he called out.

All eyes turned in his direction and then back to Jeremy.

'Yes. Enough to trouble the government and have them send in extra dragoons to the area.'

'Hasn't done much good,' put in Emmot Riley. 'I hear one was found dead at the bottom of the cliffs north of Robin Hood's Bay.'

'Aye, and there was a reet ganning on down there last Sunday,' added Petch. He went on to relate the happenings when Mark expressed his curiosity.

Laughter rang round the room at the end of his story.

'Time the government really did stamp it out,' Joshua Clements said soberly.

'Oh, come on, Joshua,' Edward boomed, leaning back on his chair. 'You've benefited from it one way or another.'

'Sir!' Joshua looked indignant.

Edward chuckled. 'Don't tell me you haven't taken smuggled wines and spirits and sold them at normal prices and so made more profit?'

Joshua huffed and puffed with irritation.

'He's got thee there, Joshua,' teased Hugh Lomas. 'But don't take it to heart, we'll all admit to buying smuggled goods at one time or another. How many of these dresses have passed through smugglers' hands?' He smiled and added, 'Don't look shocked, dear ladies. Maybe you don't know it, but were they presents from your husband, and did you ask where he obtained the material? Oh, we're all as guilty as each other, but who cares so long as no one is caught? Smugglers? No, not at all. Free traders? Yes, with a rightful place in the commerce of this country.'

Mark was surprised by this general approval of smuggling. Could Hugh Lomas have more than an outside interest in it? He decided to take the subject further. 'Everything must be highly organised, even from as far away as the Continent.'

He was hoping that Hugh might take up his point but it was Edward who did so and so diverted Mark's line of probing.

'It couldn't operate if it wasn't. You'll be tempted by cheap goods once you've settled in.'

Mark glanced at Silas and saw an almost imperceptible shake of his head and knew that the retiring manager had never touched smuggled goods.

'We'll see,' was all he said, and let the matter drop. He did not want to appear too curious.

He turned to Emma and saw a little frown of concern creasing her forehead as if some thought was troubling her. He sought to regain the light-hearted conversation of a few moments ago when, in a joking tone, he asked, 'And is your dress made of smuggled goods?'

The question reverberated in her mind, underlining the troubling thoughts which had taken hold of her when Mark first mentioned the smugglers. All the worry over her father had returned to mar the pleasure of the evening. Now Mark was making it worse. She fought down a desire to cry and run away. Instead she drew on her inner strength to hide her real feelings and replied tersely, 'No, indeed it is not.'

'And what about the others?' he asked in an off-hand tone as he attempted to lighten a situation which had disturbed her.

'Who knows?' She gave a little shrug of her shoulders.

'And they won't tell.' Mark steered the conversation to other channels and saw Emma's cloud of concern disappear. He wondered what had disturbed her but had no thought of posing the question for he did not want to upset her.

After the meal, when the guests had returned to the drawing room, Emma sought out her aunt and drew her to one side.

'Aunt Matilda, may I stay over until Wednesday?' she asked.

'Of course, my dear. But what about thy mother, won't she be expecting thee home?'

'It'll be all right. Amy can tell her I stayed on, and Joe can pick me up on Wednesday when he comes to market.'

'Very well, if thee think it will be all right.'

'Thanks, Aunt.' Her eyes dazzling with delight, she sought the first opportunity to tell Mark.

Breakfast in the Dugdale house was a casual affair taken between seven-thirty and nine. The family then went about their own affairs, but today being Sunday they would all go together to the service at ten o'clock.

Emma was pleased that Amy was the only person in the dining room when she came for her breakfast. As she helped herself from the bowl of frumenty standing on the sideboard with a jug of milk beside it, she said casually, 'I'm staying until Wednesday.'

'What!' Amy looked up in surprise, pausing with her fork halfway to her mouth. 'What will Ma say?'

'Thee can tell her Aunt Matilda had no objections, and Joe can pick me up on Wednesday.'

'What made thee change thy mind?' Amy wasn't really bothered. She realised she would have time alone with Joe today and on Wednesday for, without Emma at home, she would have to bring the butter and eggs to market.

'Thought I'd like to spend time with Meg.'

'And maybe see Mark Roper again? He was very attentive to thee,' chaffed Amy.

'Talking over old times, that's all.'

''Morning, Joe.' Amy was first to greet him as he walked into the dining room and stopped beside the table to make his morning greeting to the sisters. 'Thee'll have to be content with me on our ride home.'

'What's thee mean?' His puzzled glance shot from one to the other.

'I'm staying until Wednesday,' explained Emma. 'Thee can pick me up then.'

Joe frowned and a look of disappointment clouded his features. 'What brought this about?' he asked.

'She says she wants to spend some time with Meg but I think she wants to see Mark Roper again,' Amy informed him with a sly glint in her eyes.

Emma shot her a withering look and Amy knew she was near the truth although her sister had denied it.

'Is that reet?' demanded Joe, his face darkening with annoyance.

'No,' returned Emma. 'Thee knows Meg and I like being together.' The words sounded so lame that she thought Joe must realise Amy was right.

'Thee can't stay,' he snapped harshly. 'Thy ma will be needing thee back, and if she doesn't, I do.'

'I don't care,' she asserted. 'I'm staying. Ma will have Amy, and I'll see thee on Wednesday.'

Joe's lips tightened in exasperation. His eyes flashed with displeasure. He knew how stubborn Emma could be when she had her mind set. 'All right, have it thy way. I can't make thee come home. But don't forget Wednesday's importance.'

'I won't,' she replied sharply.

Emma saw the questioning look come to Amy's face at the mention of Wednesday being important. She knew her sister would love to know the reason but before she could air her curiosity Meg arrived for breakfast and announced excitedly that Edward Beaumont was taking her riding this afternoon.

With the service over and polite exchanges made with the vicar, the family walked back to Bagdale where at one o'clock they took a light lunch.

Joe and Amy left at two, and half an hour later an excited Meg, dressed for riding, was ready when Edward Beaumont called.

As she left in his carriage, Matilda turned to her niece. 'And what about thee? I think Meg should have stayed.'

'Oh, no, I wouldn't want to spoil her day,' Emma hastened to reassure her. 'Besides, Mark Roper is calling for me.'

Her aunt raised her eyebrows. 'Is he indeed?'

Momentarily alarm appeared on Emma's face. 'It is all right, isn't it, Aunt? He wants some advice about furniture and decorations for the house he's bought, just along here in Bagdale. I'm sorry, I should have asked thee first.'

'Maybe thee should,' returned Matilda, feigning sternness. Then her face creased into smiles. 'Of course it's all right. Thee's old enough to make up thy own mind. Maybe your ma wouldn't approve, but thee knows thy Aunt Matilda.'

Relief had swept over Emma. Her eyes shone brightly, a fact not lost on Matilda, but she made no comment. Her niece was obviously more than looking forward to this meeting.

Mark arrived at three o'clock and paid his polite respects to Emma's aunt and uncle before escorting her further along Bagdale to the house which had once been his home.

'Will thy wife like living in Whitby?' Emma asked tentatively as they walked down the garden path.

'I'm not married,' he replied.

'The lady and children on the ship? I thought . . .'

Mark laughed. 'Just fellow passengers. So you saw me arrive?'

'Meg and I were a long way off and I only caught a brief glimpse of thy face, so I wasn't sure.'

'And of course you weren't expecting to see me.'

Emma hardly heard his words for her mind was joyously seizing on the fact that he was not married.

'Have thee no apprehension about returning to thy former home?' she asked as they approached the door of number twelve.

'Not with you by my side,' he returned. The softness of

his voice sent a shiver through her, and a shaft of pure longing to be always close to him. 'I'm grateful to you for coming.'

'Nothing would have kept me away,' she replied huskily.

As he opened the door Emma could hardly believe she was beside the person whom she had thought about so often, who had captured her heart and held it throughout the years.

They stepped inside.

Cobwebs clung to the slim glazing bars of wood in the tall window halfway up the curving staircase. A thin film of dust covered the handrail supported by a wrought-iron balustrade. The bare walls cried out for some paintings and the open space for furniture. As she remembered it this hall always had a welcoming atmosphere and seemed to enfold the visitor in the warmth of a close and loving family. It could soon regain that atmosphere, she sensed.

'There's one room I must see first.' There was excitement in his voice as he took her hand and hurried to the stairs.

In that touch both felt a sense of union, an empathy that had never been broken. Their fingers entwined in an unspoken vow that they wanted to be together.

Mark stopped at the third door around the landing. He turned the knob and pushed, allowing the door to swing open of its own accord.

Though she had never been up here, Emma intuitively knew that this had been his room.

'Thine?' she whispered, as if breaking the silence and his memories was a sacrilege.

He nodded. 'Welcome to my world.'

They stepped into the room. Silent and bare though it was, she could picture it, a bed here, a chest of drawers there, a table, a chair. And everywhere a boy's treasures: papers, pencils, pieces of wood carved into animals, marbles, a model of a ship, and all the other magical things which transformed a boy's world into a wondrous place.

He untwined his fingers from hers and crossed to a wooden seat set into the wall beneath the window. He raised the hinged seat and gave a little cry of satisfaction. 'It's still here.' He glanced round and held his breath. The light from the window seemed to be directed in one shaft on to Emma, illuminating her in such a way that it drew out an ethereal beauty. Her copper-coloured hair, peeping from under her small bonnet, glinted in the light, her brown eyes shone with happiness, and her face was radiant with pleasure. She stood erect, holding herself with an assurance which seemed to be drawn from beyond herself.

Mark waited. He did not want to break the picture. The schoolgirl of memory had grown into a beautiful young woman. He watched, etching what he was seeing on his mind to be stored and recalled far into the future.

Emma raised her arm and swept a strand of unruly hair back under the rim of her bonnet with long supple fingers. The gesture was graceful but, even as it was added to Mark's memory, it had broken the spell.

'Emma, come here,' he said quietly. 'See.' He pointed to some marks on the underside of the raised seat.

She bent so that she could see them better. She saw one word, roughly carved but nevertheless clear: EMMA.

'Thee carved that?' She looked at him kneeling by her side.

'Yes. The day before we left for London. I knew none of my family would see it. The contents had been emptied two or three days before. And I hoped the new owners would not remove it if they saw it.'

'Thee thought of me when thee was leaving?' Tears of joy dimmed her eyes.

'I realise now I must have loved you even then.'

'I loved thee too.' Her voice was scarcely above a whisper but he caught her words.

He took her hand and stood up.

A moment's silence in which two loves became one stretched between them and sealed their future.

'Nothing must separate us again,' he said slowly, looking deep into her eyes.

His lips met hers gently with a tenderness which revealed his love.

Her heart sang in ecstasy and her mind raced with joy at the thought of a future with Mark.

'You ride well. You have a good seat.' Edward Beaumont shouted his compliments against the wind during their exhilarating ride.

Meg laughed loudly and tossed her head provocatively, delighted that her ability had surprised him.

He had a reputation as a hard rider, but Meg reckoned that, as well-bred and gentle as she might seem in Whitby, she could match him on a horse. She had done a lot of riding, her father indulging her wishes from an early age, but her path had never crossed that of Edward Beaumont and when he had asked her to go riding she had looked forward to surprising him with her skill.

She had recognised his horse as somewhat lively and admired the way he handled it, using his broad strong hands with the gentlest of touches on the reins, and his thighs to the right effect. She could see his strength through his riding breeches which were tight at the thighs and over his calves until they ran into calf-length black leather boots. She admired the way he was at one with the animal, man and beast moving in unison with nothing marring the flow.

They had left Thorpe Hall, crossed the river and climbed the west cliff, and were now heading for Sandsend, a tiny hamlet which nestled where a cutting split the land and a stream tumbled towards the sands and sea. They galloped headlong to their goal where they paused before putting their horses to the slope beyond the hamlet. The land climbed steeply with precipitous cliffs forming on their right.

The ground flattened and Edward turned towards the

cliff edge. He stopped and swung from the saddle in one smooth movement. 'A rest,' he called.

'If thee wishes,' agreed Meg.

Edward came to her. She slipped her foot from the stirrup and, with his hands guiding her, slid to the ground. He let his hands linger momentarily round her waist even when she was standing.

She took a deep breath and said with satisfaction, 'I enjoyed that.' It broke the spell and he released her.

They left the horses free to champ at the grass and sat down close to the cliff edge. The sun shone from a blue sky dotted with fluffy white clouds. The air was sharp but not cold in the warming sun. The endless sea was calm with tiny waves hardly able to break on the beach which stretched its golden sands to Whitby.

'Then we must do it again,' said Edward.

'I'd like that.'

'I'll tell you what, why not on Tuesday morning? And after the ride you can dine with me at Thorpe Hall.'

'That would be delightful,' replied Meg. 'I'll look forward to it.'

'So will I,' he replied.

Their eyes met and held each other, his heavy with admiration, hers inviting. She lay back on the ground with a contented sigh as she gazed at the vast canopy of blue. He rolled over, looking down on her. She focused her eyes on him. He came slowly to her, his eyes never leaving hers. His lips closed on hers. A tremor ran through her body. Her arms came round his neck and held him as she matched him kiss for kiss. Passion blossomed and held out a promise for Tuesday.

There was shared excitement as the cousins got ready for dinner that evening, talking about the day's events.

'I'm seeing him again on Tuesday,' Meg informed Emma after telling her about the ride and singing Edward's praises as a horseman. 'Now thee,' she pressed as she slipped a petticoat over her head.

Emma, sitting on the bed pulling up her stockings, replied with new joy in her eyes: 'Meg, he loves me.'

'Then thee's got thy wish,' she said excitedly. She gave her cousin a hug but then looked worried. 'But what about Joe?'

Chapter Sixteen

Sue was a heroine in Baytown. Her outwitting of Boston was not only audacious but pleased everyone. A fight had been averted in which husbands and sweethearts might otherwise have been killed.

She was glad that she was no longer the object of suspicion and sullen glances, but instead received smiles and greetings. The women would stop and talk, and the men were not averse to passing a word with a pretty woman.

While she enjoyed this newfound friendliness, worry about Ben still gnawed at her mind. No word had been received about the missing pedlars, and with each day her anxiety grew, fearing for Ben's safety and dreading the possibility that she would never see him again.

But after the near run-in with the dragoons Zac was content to lie low for a while. He deemed it wisest to allow Bay to settle down to its normal pattern of life, and made no attempt to move the contraband. He was wary. He would not be panicked by the two strangers who came into the village one day, stayed the night and left the following morning. They were known to have left their beds and roamed through the streets and alleys at night. Zac had them watched and was prepared to use the knife but knew that would only bring Boston roaring into Bay, determined to arrest someone on the flimsiest pretext. He let them go. Nor did he interfere with the watchers he knew were on the cliffs. There was no incriminating activity for them to see.

It annoyed him therefore when, summoned by The Fox to Armstrong's Farm, he was ordered to start disposing of the contraband. 'Goods in storage bring no money,' The Fox reproved.

After these sharp words Zac returned to the Fisherman's Arms in a black mood which even the attentions of Nell and Sue did little to dispel.

'I've a good mind to move it all by pony-train and risk the attention of the dragoons,' he snapped with irritation.

Sue's heart sank. If that happened all hope of tracing Ben would be thrown back. 'If thee does, thee'll maybe lose the chance of finding out what happened to the missing pedlars,' she urged.

Zac eyed her knowingly. 'And thee wants to find out what happened to Ben?' He nodded. 'Thee's reet. I'll continue to move the contraband from Beck Farm by pedlars.'

When Emma woke that Monday morning, the day after seeing Mark, she was not in the best of moods but her displeasure was directed at herself. She had gone to sleep elated by their declarations of love for each other, but had spent a fitful night for Joe kept haunting her dreams.

As she dressed she realised that the young man with whom she had shared much of her life was going to be hurt. She wished she could avoid that, but there would be no escaping what she had to say when they met on Wednesday.

'Want to talk about it?' asked Meg when they were alone after breakfast.

'About what?' returned Emma.

'Thee's at sorts with thyself. Even Mama noticed it. She gave me one or two glances at breakfast.'

Emma's lips tightened, annoyed that her indisposition had been obvious. She glanced wryly at her cousin. 'I don't want to hurt Joe.'

'Thee's not having doubts about Mark?' asked Meg.

'No.' Emma's reply was emphatic enough to convince her cousin.

'Then there's only one thing to do — be straight with Joe. He deserves that.'

*   *   *

Meg's remarks were in the back of Emma's mind when she and Mark climbed to the top of the west cliff. They paused to regain their breath and gaze back over the town. Below them new buildings spread upwards from the older dwellings at the foot of the west cliff. The fine houses were occupied by the merchants, ship owners, ships' captains and the better off. The river was busy with shipping and most of the quays were occupied by ships which linked Whitby with all parts of the known world. The crowded houses on the east bank climbed on top of each other reaching for the sky. Smoke curled from the chimneys laying a haze across the red roofs. Overlooking them all like two watchful sentinels were the old parish church of St Mary and the ruined abbey.

'Just as I remembered it,' said Mark.

'Not a bit like London?'

He laughed. 'Not at all. Well, maybe the smoke and the overcrowded conditions across the river, but even those are not to be compared with London – vastly bigger and more squalid.'

'Ah, but not the parts thee was used to.'

They started to stroll along the cliff top.

'No. We lived in an elegant house in spacious surroundings in Russell Square, not too far from green fields and open country.'

'Does thee miss it?'

They had walked beyond the town. The open cliff top stretched before them bathed in sunshine which sparkled on a tranquil sea. Here was peace, undisturbed by another soul. They were alone in their own world.

'Yes, I miss it, of course I do, and I expect I shall for a time. It's been my life for several years. I also miss my family and my friends there. But that will pass. Besides, I have you.'

He stopped and turned her to him, gazing down at her with eyes filled with an overwhelming love which he saw was returned. She reached up, sliding her arms round his neck as he bent to kiss her. Their lips touched, sending tremors through them, speaking of a desire which must be fulfilled. They sank into the grass together.

'Oh, Emma, I love you so much.' His words came hoarsely, heralding the deep passion stirring within him.

'And I love thee,' she murmured seductively. Her lips sought his with a hunger which threatened to overwhelm them.

Mark's brain pounded with a desire to take her. Lost in the passion of their kiss, Emma was unaware that his hands moved to the buttons of her dress. He fingered the first, then stopped. He wanted her so much, but taking her here, driven by lust, could mar their whole future. It could compromise their love, damaging it beyond repair. That he did not want. He cared for her too much to jeopardise, by one rash act, the love which had lain dormant all these years, unrecognised, until it had been brought to full bloom by meeting her again. He raised his hand to caress her cheek as he returned her kisses.

They walked the cliff, lost in love, joyous in mutual under-standing, with the future promising unending bliss. They laughed, they talked, they recalled the past and planned the future frivolously and outrageously.

But even in her euphoria, Emma was touched by a feeling of guilt. She frowned with annoyance that such a feeling could intrude on her jubilation, but it was there, and she could not deny it. In two days' time she must destroy Joe's dream.

Mark saw the shadow crossing her face. 'Something wrong?'

'Not really.'

He was not convinced. Her bright, breezy tone had been hiding something. 'There is,' he insisted. 'Tell me. A trouble shared is a trouble halved.'

Emma bit her lip and looked at him with eyes which pleaded with him to understand as she said, 'It's Joe.'

'What about him?' For a brief moment a touch of dread clutched at his heart.

'He expects me to marry him.' Emma saw no point in holding back the truth. She expected Mark to be strong enough to hear it.

'You aren't engaged? You don't wear a ring.'

'No.'

'Then why should you be troubled? You're free and it's me you love.'

'I've spent so much time with him. We're such good friends.'

'No more than that?'

'Not on my part, but Joe says he loves me and has constantly asked me to marry him.'

'You've never said yes?'

Emma was gratified by the alarm in his voice. 'No,' she replied, and saw relief sweep over him. 'But he asked me again recently and I promised him an answer on Wednesday.'

'You must say no,' Mark urged, fearing a change of mind.

'I will. It's thee I love.' She paused, a catch in her voice. 'But I don't want to hurt him. He's such a dear friend and I don't want to lose his friendship.'

Mark's forehead creased into a troubled frown. He wanted to ease her troubles, shoulder them for her, but there was no easy way to do it. 'Can I help?'

She shook her head. 'No. I must face him myself.'

'And when you do, remember me. Remember I love you, that I want you. No one, certainly not Joe, must ever come between us.' His eyes blazed with resolve, convincing her of his love. His arms came round her, drawing her close. His kiss defied her to find love elsewhere.

Joe rammed his spade into the side of the ditch and broke the overgrown soil away. He glanced back. He had done about a hundred yards. He jumped down into the ditch and started shovelling the earth and grass from the channel. His face was set grimly as he flung the debris on to the bank side. Ditching was just the right job for the mood he was in. He could work off his pent up feelings through sheer physical effort.

He was grieved that Emma had chosen to stay in Whitby rather than return home with him. No doubt Mark Roper had something to do with her decision; she had paid him a lot of attention at the party and he had reciprocated.

Jealous? Joe stabbed his spade into the ground. No, he wasn't jealous. Oh, hell, too damned right he was jealous! He couldn't get the picture of Emma and Mark out of his mind – or not until he was aware that Amy had crept insidiously into his mind. He smiled to himself as he thought of her attempts to cheer him up on the ride back to Beck Farm. He had made little response and now cursed himself for being such an oaf. How could he have been so morose and ungracious to the vivacious girl who had linked her arm with his as if it was the natural thing to do? His mind dwelt on her flirtatious ways and enjoyed dwelling on them.

The two girls had haunted his dreams that night, both pretty and tempting in different ways. He had seen Emma as reliable, a good wife, but one who could never share his enthusiasm for the land and the farm. This niggled at him. Then Amy would sweep into his dream like the west wind. She tackled life head-on, loving every minute spent on the land. Then, with thoughts of Emma, Amy's bright image would disappear.

He tossed and turned in his sleep, was not in the best of moods at breakfast and decided to do some ditching, a job by which he could purge his mind of last night's dream and the doubts it had brought. Why should he have doubts? After all he was expecting an unequivocal 'yes' from Emma on Wednesday.

*   *   *

The ride had been exhilarating. They had ridden along the Esk valley at a gentle pace during which Meg's conversation matched Edward's for liveliness and local gossip.

He admired not only her good looks and vivacity but also her intellect. She was unlike many of the young women he had charmed, for they were empty-headed with little talk. Meg fascinated him with her love of life and adventurous spirit. As they turned their horses out of the valley he hung slightly behind her. His eyes narrowed as they rested on her and he wondered what it would be like to take this woman and bend her to his will. He promised himself he would find out.

When they reached the level ground above the valley, Meg sent a shrill laugh over her shoulder. 'Race thee,' she cried, and sent her horse into an earth-jarring gallop.

Edward responded and bent low on his horse as he pursued her, seeing in the chase a challenge which would go far beyond this ride.

Hooves thundered. Laughter was torn away on the wind. Cries for greater speed urged their mounts on to stronger effort. He reached her and moved slightly ahead. She allowed it and matched her pace to his so that she could admire the movement of his body and the strength of his thighs. She approved of the long supple fingers which caressed the reins with just the right pressure to control the pounding power beneath him. She wondered what it would be like to feel those fingers touching her, running smoothly over her skin. Some day she would know.

They had ridden across country to Sandsend, then along the beach, allowing the sea to lap around the horses' hooves before turning inland to skirt Whitby and cross the Esk to Thorpe Hall.

As they pulled into the cobbled yard bounded by stables, storerooms and servants' quarters, with a passageway to the main house, two grooms appeared to take charge of the mounts.

'None too soon,' observed Edward as the first huge drops

of rain started from the dark clouds which had been moving steadily towards the coast.

He took her hand and they ran to the passage at the end of which he pushed open a door and held it while she passed through to a flight of stairs leading upwards. At the top he opened another door and they entered the main hall. To the right was the glass-panelled front door with a small glass vestibule giving on to a stone terrace from which two flights of steps ran down to ground level. Meg paused to look out of the large window beside the door.

Even though rain was slanting hard across the landscape she could not help herself from remarking, 'What a lovely view.'

The grounds in front of the house sloped gently to the river. The grass was well cut and the space was dotted with fine trees, oak and chestnut. The river did a slight turn as if embracing the house and those who lived there. Across the river, wooded slopes climbed gently to farmland.

'Better when it's not raining,' remarked Edward. 'I'll show you to a room where you can change.'

He turned towards the wide heavy oak staircase which turned twice before reaching the upper floor. On one wall was an ornate marble fireplace with a family coat-of-arms adorning the chimney breast. Two oak settles stood at right angles to the fireplace with a small oak table between them, matching the dark panelling.

'That leads to several withdrawing rooms,' said Edward, indicating the door to the right of the fireplace. 'And that,' he nodded towards the door close to the foot of the stairs, 'to the dining room.'

He started up the stairs with Meg close behind him. At the top he turned on to a landing and went to the third door along. He pushed it open and said, 'I think you'll be all right here.'

'I'm sure I shall,' replied Meg, her eyes appraising the small but cosy room into which she had been shown.

'I think you'll find everything you want. Come down when you are ready. I'll be in the dining room.'

'Very well. And thank thee, Edward.' Her eyes showed her appreciation when they met his.

He inclined his head in acknowledgement and closed the door.

Hugging herself with pleasure, Meg surveyed her surroundings. The single bed was covered with a spread of delicate lacework. Beside it stood a small oak table, and on the other side a chair with an elaborately carved back. Beside one wall there was a small dressing table with a covered stool in front. A mirror was fastened to the wall and on the table were two china bowls, a silver-backed brush and a hand mirror.

She crossed to a door and looked into a small room with a high window, the light from which revealed a table holding a basin and a ewer filled with water. Beside it was an open china bowl with a perforated inner sleeve on which a piece of soap had been left for her use. Towels hung from a rack on one wall and all the other necessities for her comfort were at her disposal.

She went to the valise containing her dress which had been placed on the windowseat which filled the space of the tall bow window. She paused and looked out. She realised she was overlooking the gardens at the back of the house. She stood still, for the aura they cast seemed to hold her in a spell. The area behind the house as far as she could see, for the rain hid the far distance, was laid out in an elaborate maze of high hedges surrounding small grass parterres, cunningly linked one to another. She started. There were figures in some of them, a single person in each, never more than one. She concentrated her gaze, wondering who they could be. No one moved. She closed her eyes and looked again. They were still there.

She bit her lip in exasperation as she realised they were life-sized statues. She stared, drawn to them by the weird fascination of seeing them lashed by the driving rain. It thickened, obscuring them. She shivered and turned away.

'Ah, Meg, my dear.' Edward rose from his chair at one end of the long table as she walked into the dining room. He came to meet her with arms outstretched. 'Welcome to my home. I trust you are refreshed?'

'I am, thank thee,' smiled Meg, as she took his hand.

He led her to a seat on his right hand and held the chair as she sat down. She took in the high-ceilinged room with its large fireplace with carved wooden mantelpiece which rose to the height of the wall. The oak panelling came shoulder high with dark green paper covering the rest of the wall. The ceiling was white, taking away some of the sombreness of the room. There were two high windows on one wall and a third on another, which on a better day than this would allow the room to be flooded with brightness. The long table at which they sat occupied the centre of the room, while several small ones were situated against the walls, some of them set with bowls, servers and spoons.

Meg noticed that there were no more place settings. 'Thy father not dining with us?'

'He's away.'

She hid her surprise. 'But thee seemed to indicate to Mama when thee asked if I could stay to lunch, that he would be here.'

Edward's lips twitched with amusement. 'Do you think she would have allowed you to dine, and not only dine but to bring a change of clothes, if she had known my father wouldn't be here? She'd regard him as a chaperon.'

Meg feigned shock. 'Edward, what are you planning? I think I'd better leave.'

He leaned back in his chair, eyes flashing with satisfaction for he recognised interest in Meg's attitude.

'And miss the pleasure of this sumptuous meal?'

As if on cue a door opened and a footman carrying a

steaming bowl of soup came in. An appetising aroma wafted across the room. 'Well, it would be unkind to leave after all the trouble thee has taken,' she said teasingly.

The soup was followed by a succulent leg of pork and a game pie with accompanying vegetables and potatoes. A fruit compôte and jellies preceded the cheese course. The appropriate wines not only delighted Meg's palate but relaxed her.

When they left the dining room Edward took her hand and led her towards the stairs. She stopped and looked at him coyly.

'What about the servants?'

'They are discreet.'

'When will thy father be back?' Convention demanded she put the questions. She should resist the rising desire to know this man more intimately but felt irresistibly drawn to him. His manner charmed, his good looks attracted, but it was the mystery which lay behind the façade which fascinated her. There was a sense of power and an underlying ruthlessness to which she felt drawn. She felt flattered by the brooding desire in his eyes and knew in her heart that, despite propriety, she would not resist any suggestion he might make.

'We have plenty of time,' he replied.

'I should go home,' she returned.

Edward's eyebrows lowered, their dark brown colour seeming to intensify the penetrating gaze he directed at her. 'Home, when another world awaits you?'

'We shouldn't. What would folk think?'

'Oh, damn convention!' he snapped. 'I don't care a fig for it. Besides, who'll know?' A wry smile touched his mouth and his voice softened. 'I think you are as curious about me as I am about you, so there's only one way to find out.' His grip on her hand tightened as if he wouldn't let her escape. He started towards the stairs again. This time she did not stop.

They went up the stairs together and he led her into a

room which was three times as big as the one in which she had changed.

'Thy room?' she asked as he closed the door.

'Yes.'

She sensed in his voice tension charged with desire and sexuality. He turned her to him and his lips met hers with a hunger which would not be satisfied until his desires were fulfilled. She matched him kiss for kiss, trembling as the need for him set her body tingling with desire. His arms crushed her to him. She leaned back against them, arching her body to mould temptingly to his as he bent to prolong the kiss.

They broke away, each knowing what the other wanted. They watched each other as they undressed, he eagerly, she provocatively. Naked, he swept her in his arms and carried her to the bed.

Meg was in a state of high elation when Edward drove her home. She knew she had not been the first, for she had heard rumours of Edward Beaumont's reputation, but what did that matter? She was the one who satisfied him now and she would see that it remained that way for she was determined to marry him.

'Are you prepared for tomorrow?' Mark put the question as he and Emma strolled on the east cliff beyond the abbey.

'As right as I'll ever be,' she replied with a note of regret at what she would have to do. 'Oh, I wish our wonderful love didn't have to hurt someone.' Her eyes were damp.

He stopped and kissed them. 'Dry those tears,' he whispered. 'There's nothing we can do to prevent hurting Joe. I wish there was, but I'll not give you up.'

'I don't want thee to. I love thee too much. Thee were the only one in my dreams last night. Thee drove all fear of telling Joe out of my mind. It was only with daylight that the thought of facing him came back to haunt me.'

He looked seriously at her. 'Would you like me to tell him?'

'No! No!' Emma was quick to object. 'It really would hurt him if I dared not face him. He would feel I had no affection for him and I do want him to remain my friend.'

He kissed her lightly.

'Oh, Mark, hold me tight.'

He responded to her plea, enfolding her in his arms. He hugged her tight, seeking to give her strength for the ordeal which faced her tomorrow.

Sue quickened her pace when she reached the outskirts of Whitby. She had left Baytown with the sun just marking the eastern horizon, seizing on the chance remark by Nell that she wanted some extra butter and eggs. Sue wanted to see Emma and, knowing that she came to market most Wednesdays, hoped she would be there today.

She came down on the east side of the river where the quays were already imparting a sense of liveliness to the new day. She hurried along Church Street until she came to the market-place where girls and young women from outlying farms were taking up their places and displaying their wares, some of them starting to trade with housewives wanting to beat the throng of folk who would gather as morning wore on.

Her eyes swept over the scene quickly but there was no one she knew. On pretext of examining goods on offer, she bided her time.

Ten minutes later she saw Emma come into the market-place and was surprised to see that she carried no basket. As Emma crossed the square, looking about her, Sue edged nearer.

'Hello, Emma,' she said when she was only a few feet away.

'Sue! What brings thee here?' She smiled pleasantly, pleased to see her again.

'Came to see thee. I took a chance thee'd be here. Thee's no basket?'

'I've been in Whitby since the weekend. Going home today. Came to find Amy but she isn't here yet.' She looked curiously at Sue. 'But what do thee want with me?'

Sue did not answer immediately but edged Emma away to a quieter corner of the market-place. Her face was serious when she spoke in a low voice, glancing round to see that they could not be overheard. 'I'm no nearer finding out what happened to Ben.'

The desperate tone of Sue's voice was not lost on Emma. 'But what can I do?'

'The last contact Ben had was with thy father – something he's not willing to admit. And Ben isn't the only pedlar to have gone missing after leaving thy farm . . .' She saw a touch of hostility shadow Emma's eyes and added quickly, 'I'm not suggesting thy father had anything to do with it, but Zac is going to start using pedlars again and I wanted to ask thee to keep alert for anything thee might see or overhear which might help in tracing Ben.'

Emma could not deny the plea in Sue's voice. Through her concern about her father's connection with the smugglers, she knew how desperate Sue must be. Not knowing what had happened to her husband who had disappeared without trace must be causing her all sorts of anxieties. 'I'll see if I can learn anything, but I can't promise.'

'Thanks,' replied Sue. 'But be careful.'

'And thee.' Emma spotted Amy and Joe arriving and the two friends went to meet them.

After the greetings were over, Amy said, 'Thanks for coming to help, Emma, but there's no need for thee to stay. I can manage. Joe and I will be at Aunt Matilda's for lunch as usual.'

Emma grasped the chance to leave. She did not want to be around Joe all morning, and it gave her the opportunity to postpone the moment she was not looking forward to.

Amy wondered as she watched her go. Her sister had not been full of enthusiasm when greeting Joe. A constraint, which only a sister could have noticed, had been there. But Joe's welcome had been warm. Could their two different attitudes have something to do with what Joe had mentioned as their day of importance?

The squeak of leather and the sound of voices brought Grace Dugdale hurrying from the farm to greet her daughters.

'Staying to tea, Joe?' she called.

'No thanks, Mrs Dugdale, but I'd like Emma to ride with me a little way, if thee don't mind?'

'Of course,' smiled Grace. 'Let's away in, Amy.' Mother and daughter hurried into the house.

Joe was about to flick the reins when Emma stopped him. 'Wait, Joe.'

He looked at her in surprise. 'But thee knows what thee promised today?'

'Aye, I do,' she replied quietly. She looked down at her hands, fingers linked in her lap, and felt the colour drain from her face.

'But I can't take thy answer here, not in front of the house,' he protested.

She looked up sharply. 'Why not, Joe?' she demanded.

'Well, it'll be embarrassing.'

'Why will it?' Her eyes blazed with indignation.

'Thy ma and Amy might be looking. I pictured us being on our own when thee said yes.'

'When I say yes?' So Joe took it as a foregone conclusion. He had taken their deep friendship as a certain indication of romance and marriage just as everyone else had done. The tenderness which had passed between her and Mark when they saw those carved letters flashed into her mind. 'I'm sorry, Joe, the answer is no.'

He looked astounded, as if he could not comprehend

what she had said. He fought to find words but only spluttered until he was able to gasp, 'What?'

'I said no. I'm sorry but that's my answer. I don't want to hurt thee, please try to understand.' Emma's voice was low.

He gulped. The unexpected had shocked him. 'But why?'

'I don't love thee,' she said quietly.

'But why?' he insisted vehemently.

'Oh, Joe, how can I explain? I like thee a lot. We shared so much together when we were growing up and people expected us to marry someday. I think in some ways we expected the same, but I began to realise I didn't love thee as a wife should.'

His thoughts had been racing, trying to put his own reasons to her decision as she had been speaking. 'These few days in Whitby, that was it?' His dejection smouldered into anger. 'It was him, wasn't it? Mark Roper? Thee fussed about him at that party. What's happened while thee's been in Whitby?' He grasped her arms as if he was about to try to shake an answer out of her.

'Nothing.'

'Thee saw him?'

Emma nodded. 'Yes.'

He pushed her arms away in disgust. He looked at her with contempt, all reason gone from his mind. 'And thee say nothing happened? It must have done to make thee change thy mind!'

'It didn't, Joe, it didn't. Please don't think that of me. I don't want our friendship to be destroyed.' Tears filled her eyes.

The pleading look she gave him calmed him. 'Does he love thee?'

'Yes.'

'Does thee love him?'

'I've loved him since we were at school.'

'A schoolgirl infatuation! But now, what about now?'

'I still do.'

Joe's lips tightened. He looked away in exasperation as he tried to make sense of what was happening to his world.

She reached out and placed a hand on his arm. 'Please forgive me, Joe.' She jumped down from the cart and, with tears streaming down her face, ran into the house. She flew past her mother and Amy and ran up the stairs to her room.

'What's that about?' gasped Grace.

Amy shrugged her shoulders. She had seen most of the exchange between Emma and Joe from the window. As she had watched, the significance of Joe's remark that Wednesday was of importance dawned on her. 'I would say that Emma has just turned down Joe's proposal of marriage.'

'What?' Grace was astounded. 'Never! She wouldn't! They've been ... Everybody expects...' she spluttered without finishing her sentences.

'She would and I think she has,' replied Amy.

'But why?'

'Mark Roper's back in Whitby.'

Chapter Seventeen

Following a week of anxiety over her decision, Emma woke the following Wednesday wondering what to do. It was market day and Joe would be driving to Whitby as usual. How could she face him? She knew she had hurt him deeply. What would his attitude be now? Maybe she could get out of going, maybe Amy could go. But she wanted to visit Whitby and see Mark again.

During the past week the Dugdales and the Wades had come to terms with the fact that their daughter and son would not marry. The expected union of the two families had been shattered by Emma's surprise decision. Her mother and father had talked to her, pointing out all the advantages there would be in marrying Joe, but they met with stubborn resistance. They had no answer to her declared love for Mark and her insistence that he loved her just as deeply. Being the understanding and liberal-minded people they were, her father and mother did not insist on marriage to Joe as many a parent would have done, for they took the view that their daughter's happiness was paramount.

'Ma, can Amy go to market?' she asked.

The request was not unexpected and Grace, knowing how her daughter must be feeling, agreed. Amy did not comment though secretly she was delighted for it meant she would have Joe to herself and could assess his attitude, seeing just how devastated he was by Emma's decision.

The sisters were in their bedrooms when Amy heard the trap approaching from the direction of Drop Farm. She opened her window to lean out and call to Joe but checked the words when she saw he was not driving the trap. She spun from the window and, realising Emma wanted to see Mark, raced to her room, startling her sister with her sudden entrance.

'Emma!' cried Amy excitedly. 'It isn't Joe, it's his pa. Thee can gan to Whitby.'

Emma's eyes brightened momentarily but dulled again with doubt about what David Wade's attitude to her might be.

'Don't look like that,' chided Amy. 'I know thee wants to gan to Whitby to see Mark and I know it might have been awkward riding with Joe, but this is his pa. The Wades have accepted thy decision and they aren't people to hold grudges.'

Emma brightened. 'Maybe thee's right, and I would so love to see Mark again.'

'Then gan instead of me. I don't mind.'

Emma needed no further persuasion. She grabbed her bonnet and cloak and raced downstairs with Amy following her.

'What's to gan, Ma?' asked Emma as she burst into the kitchen.

Her mother who was peeling some potatoes looked up in surprise. 'Thee's changed thy mind?'

'Joe isn't driving the trap, it's his father,' explained Amy.

Grace nodded her understanding. 'Two baskets there on the table.'

Emma needed no more instructions. She grabbed them and was waiting by the track when David Wade pulled up. He took the baskets and helped her on to the seat. He shouted cheerful greetings to Grace who had come to the door and then flicked the reins, setting the horse into motion.

Emma was silent for a few minutes then tentatively put the question, 'How's Joe, Mr Wade?' She glanced out of the corner of her eye to try to catch his reaction and was relieved to see satisfaction that she had mentioned his son.

'He's all right, lass, thank thee.' He turned his gaze on

her and let her see that he held nothing against her. 'Hurt, but he'll get ower it.'

'I didn't want to hurt him,' cried Emma, her face troubled.

'I know that, lass. Better to find out now rather than later that marriage for thee two was not reet. I'm grateful for that. I've pointed it out to him and he understands. There's other fish in the sea.'

'I do hope he finds someone worthy of him. I think a lot about him and I hope we'll always be friends.'

David smiled and patted her hand. 'I'm sure you shall. Now don't worry about it any more.'

'Ma, I've finished the bedrooms,' said Amy as she came into the kitchen. 'Mind if I gan for a walk?'

'Off with thee, lass, it's a nice day. It'll do thee good.'

Amy needed no second telling. She swung her cloak round her and as she stepped outside flicked up the hood.

Grace smiled to herself as she watched her daughter from the window. She had a good idea where Amy would be going.

She called to Bess who was lying near the gate. The sheepdog pricked up her ears and jumped to her feet. Wagging her tail, she waited for Amy.

'Want a run?' There was an excited lilt in her voice.

Bess ran round her and then bounded ahead as Amy turned along the track to Drop Farm. She walked at a brisk step, enjoying the impact of space with the land running to distant horizons. White clouds like gossamer scarves trailed high in the sky filtering the sun and where they were absent the rays came to earth to roam the moorland tops and delve into the dales. Amy was happy. This was her country and she loved to let her gaze skip across the landscape then fasten for a moment on a grouse or soar with a curlew uttering its plaintive cry. Here she felt free and could let her heart take wing.

'Hello, Amy,' Kate Wade called from the door of Drop

Farm. She had seen her coming as she was mixing herself a cup of chocolate. 'Out for a walk?'

'Yes. It's a grand day.'

'Aye, it is that. Make the most of it before winter sets in. Come on in. Have some chocolate before thee gans on.'

'Thank thee, Mrs Wade, that would be nice.'

Amy told Bess to wait and the dog sat down beside the door, only moving to wag her tail when Kate brought her out a bowl of water.

A quarter of an hour later, Amy came from the house having enjoyed the refreshment and the chat, and, having gleaned that Joe was hedging in Colton field, walked in that direction.

Reaching the gate she saw him busy at the far side. She opened the gate and called Bess to heel. Amy did not want her racing ahead to Joe just yet. As she walked towards him she admired the ease with which he wielded the slasher, laying and trimming the hedge to his will. This was no wild chopping and cutting with no rhythm to the action, it was a smooth flow of arm and shoulder, an artistic weaving of branches, obtaining the maximum impact for the least effort. She cast an appraising eye on the section he had done and then let her eyes slide back to the man who had made the hedge a work of art.

His presence seemed at one with his surroundings. He was no intruder. The power he exerted with his body was not alien to the wind and sun for they too shaped the land with their strength. He was in his element and his affinity with nature was a source of pleasure to him. Amy found herself wanting to share it all.

She was halfway across the field when she whispered, 'Go, Bess, go.'

In an instant the dog was stretched in a full run towards Joe. She was still a hundred yards from him when he became aware of the movement. He looked up. Recognising Bess immediately, he threw his gaze beyond her to the figure striding towards him. For one fleeting fraction of a second his mind said 'Emma' but almost immediately reason took over, jolted by recognition. Amy.

He wiped the back of his hand across his forehead. Disappointment? No. If there had been any in that one fleeting moment it was gone, replaced by relief, not knowing how he would have handled seeing Emma again. He stretched, dropped the slasher and flexed his fingers. 'Amy. Nice to see thee,' he called with a smile.

'Hello, Joe,' she said quietly, without masking her joy at seeing him.

'Not gone to market?'

'No. Emma's gone instead.' Amy squirmed inside, chiding herself for mentioning her sister, for she detected pain in Joe's eyes at the mention of the name, but in the same moment she saw it was gone, leaving behind a warm twinkle.

'Then good luck to her,' he said.

'Thee bears no grudge?' she asked with curiosity.

Joe shrugged his shoulders. 'What's the point? Oh, I did at first. It hurt and I was angry, but I realised that would get me nowhere. Besides, how could I stay angry with her forever? We've shared a lot together, as thee knows, and that counts for something, always will. Our families have been close friends, even before we were born. Something like this should not come between us. Maybe it's all for the best. Emma would have made me a good wife but her heart isn't really in farming.' He looked wistful. 'I hope she finds what she wants.'

Amy's lips made a tight firm line of understanding as she nodded. 'And I hope thee does. Thee's a good man, Joe Wade.'

He smiled wanly. 'Maybe I could be better.'

'Thee's just right as far as I can see.'

'Walking far?' he asked.

'Couple of miles or so.'

'Mind if I come along?' He cast his eye at the hedge.

'The rest can wait for another day. I've only had Ma and Pa to talk to this last week, it'll do me good to have someone like thee to talk with.'

'Of course I don't mind, Joe. It will make a change for me too.'

He picked up his woollen jacket and shrugged himself into it. His eyes caught his haversack. 'How about walking over to the coast? I've got some sandwiches and cake for my dinner. We can share them.'

She saw the hope in his eyes and replied with excited approval. 'Right, Joe, let's go.'

As they walked their conversation ranged widely, on friends and relations, on Drop Farm and Beck Farm, on the countryside and farming. Whatever misgivings Joe might still have had about his break-up with Emma, vanished in the effervescence of the girl at his side. Her appetite for life was catching and he responded as she helped him throw off his last remnants of self-pity. His father had been right, there was life after Emma, there were other fish in the sea – and maybe one not so far away.

Even as the thought crossed his mind he was wary. Was he turning to the first girl who came along? But he had known Amy all her life. She had grown into a fine young woman, seeming even more so today. Gone was the impish chit who saw it as her duty to flirt with her sister's boyfriend. There had been no sign of her today. In her place there was a more serious woman, one he had never suspected lurked beneath the surface of the light-hearted youngster whose flirtations he had enjoyed. But that cheerful girl was still there, mingling with the more responsible woman of whom he was now aware.

They shared the food Joe had brought while sitting on the cliffs looking out over a gentle sea which matched their mood. Afterwards they walked back to Beck Farm where Joe was welcomed by Grace, who waved aside Amy's apologies for missing lunch. She did not want to spoil what, from their demeanour, had obviously been a pleasant time together. She was pleased that Joe and Amy at least were still friends.

Emma bubbled with excitement at the prospect of seeing Mark again, though outwardly she kept an appearance of decorum while riding to Whitby.

Having arranged to meet Mr Wade at three o'clock, she sold her goods quickly, even dropping her price to do so, and was at the offices of Roper and Sons by mid-morning. Her request to see Mr Mark Roper raised some questioning glances from the clerks but she was quickly ushered into his office once her presence had been made known to him.

'Emma, I'm so pleased to see you.' He rose quickly from behind his desk and came to greet her. He took her in his arms and kissed her. 'I've missed you so. It's been a long week. I was wondering if you would be coming to market today, and how Joe had taken your refusal. You did turn him down, didn't you?'

Emma laughed merrily as she leaned back in his arms and looked into his eyes, clouded with misplaced doubt. 'Don't look so worried. Yes, I did.'

Mark felt all the apprehension he had harboured during the past week drain from him.

'Poor Joe,' Emma went on. 'He took it bad, but from what his father said – he brought me to Whitby today – he's getting over it now.'

Mark's elation spilt over and he swept her into a passionate kiss. 'Oh, I love you, Emma Dugdale, love you so much.' He hugged her tightly. 'Will you marry me?'

'Oh yes. Yes. Yes.' Joy sang in her heart. Nothing could mar her happiness now.

'Come on, thee must tell me all,' enthused Meg after she had greeted her cousin with mounting excitement. She led the way into the drawing room. 'Ma's out so we can have a real good natter.'

Emma grinned at Meg's exhilaration for she could see that her cousin was not only interested in her news but was longing to tell her something.

They sat down on the sofa half turned towards each other.

'Well, who's first?' said Emma.

'Thee of course. I've hardly been able to contain myself this past week. I've been dying to know what happened last Wednesday.'

'I said no.'

'And?' prompted Meg.

Emma paused, heightening the moment. Her eyes shone with tantalising brightness as she saw her cousin hanging on her every word. 'Mark's asked me to marry him. Only a few minutes ago. Thee's the first to know.'

Meg's eyes widened with delight, her face shone with happiness for the cousin she loved so dearly. She hugged her. 'Oh, I'm so happy for thee. When will the wedding be?'

Emma laughed. 'We haven't talked about that. Mark has only just come to Whitby. There's his home to see to, his business to run. We'll wait awhile. Maybe some time next year, next summer. We'll see. Now what about thee? What's happened to thee this week? I can see thee's bursting with news.'

'Oh, it's been so exciting.' The words came fast, bubbling with elation. 'I've seen Edward every day.' Emma raised her eyebrows in surprise but made no comment as her cousin rushed on: 'We've been riding four days. I've had lunch at Thorpe Hall on three occasions, and I've met his father – a nice old man, I think he took to me. And Edward asked me to be his partner at a dinner given by Hugh Lomas. I'm sure he likes me, sure of it!'

Emma laughed, amused by Meg's enthusiasm, but she knew that it had not just been his handsome looks or his charm that had attracted her to Edward. There must have been something much deeper between them, and she suddenly dared not think how far that might already have taken them.

With everything ready for the contraband to be moved, Zac awaited the right moment. It came when Peter Bray hurried into the Fisherman's Arms by the backdoor.

'Boston's men have gone,' he announced.

Zac, who was sitting at the table holding a tankard of ale, looked at him with surprise and doubt. 'The watchers on the cliffs?' he asked.

'Aye. They must have left last night. I kept watch for a while then I had Tite and Joss scour the cliff top, but there was no sign of anyone.'

'Thee can move the contraband,' put in Nell.

Zac rubbed his chin thoughtfully. 'I don't know. Could be some trick of Boston's.'

'Look, thee's got to get the goods out of Baytown soon,' went on Nell. 'If there are no watchers on the cliffs, then thee's got a start.'

'Reet.' Zac, his mind made up, slapped the table. 'If they don't return tomorrow and the weather's reet, we'll use the pony-train tomorrow night. Pete, get Tite and Joss to patrol the cliffs tomorrow all the time until we move out. They report anything the least suspicious.' Pete nodded. 'And we'll move with an armed escort.'

'Thee still thinks there could be trouble?' said Nell.

'I don't trust Boston. He could be up to something. But in any case, there's never been so many dragoons in the region so we've got to be cautious and have sufficient men to protect the train.'

'The ghost to ride?' queried Pete.

'Aye. Scare the local folk so they stay indoors, and those that ain't scared know what it means so they'll keep out of sight. They can't betray what their eyes don't see.'

By that evening the whole of Baytown was alerted to the operation and preparations were underway the next morning with contraband being moved from the hiding places to the panniers, ready to be loaded on to ponies in the early-evening. Reports were channelled to Zac at the Fisherman's Arms from where he co-ordinated the whole operation with precise timing. Men were sent out to scout the main track to Saltersgate for the presence of dragoons. The escorts for the pony-train were briefed and their arms checked. Pleased that the word from Tite and Joss was good, Zac was relaxing when Nell came from the bar room to inform him that the pedlar Fergus Pinkney had just come in.

'Good, couldn't be better. Bring him through here, Nell,' Zac enthused.

When Fergus came into the kitchen, carrying his tankard of ale, Zac indicated a seat across the table from him. 'Good to see thee, Fergus. Willing to move some more goods?'

'Aye. If there's brass in it for me, I'll do owt.'

'Like some pie?' Nell asked.

'Please, lass, I'm starving.'

Nell bustled away to the range.

'Thee willing to move it tonight?' asked Zac.

Fergus looked at him with surprise. 'I've just got in from Whitby. Thought I'd stay the night and return to Pickering tomorrow.'

Zac screwed up his face with doubt. 'Got to be tonight.'

'Supposing I hadn't come?' asked Fergus. He put the question as a protest at having to leave tonight.

'One of my men would have had to do it but it would be trickier for him, he wouldn't know the moors like thee. They hold no fear for thee, thee could get through to Pickering even in the dark.' Zac offered his words as praise and as challenge. He wanted Fergus to call on John Dugdale tonight. Considering the disappearing pedlars, Zac had realised that they had all picked up their contraband late in the day. Those who had collected it early had not encountered any trouble.

'Oh, aye, I know the moors like the back of my hand.

I'll get through all reet.' Fergus glanced slyly at Zac. 'Extra for night work?' He shot Nell a glance as she placed a plate of hot meat pie in front of him.

'This time, yes. I'm robbing thee of a night's rest. But I want thee to report anything unusual to me.'

'Something bothering thee?' Fergus forked potato into his mouth.

Zac was wary. He wondered if Fergus knew that some pedlars had gone missing. 'Just that some contraband moved by pedlars has not got through.'

Fergus nodded. He wondered if Ben Thrower had been recruited by Zac, and if so had it anything to do with his disappearance. And he wondered what had happened to Sue after she had said she would look for her husband. But he did not pursue the matter for he was wily enough to know that the less he knew about the smuggling the better, and the safer his life would be.

'Reet, I'll go tonight.'

'Good.'

With the bargain sealed, he fell to enjoying his pie and ale.

He was almost finished when the back door opened. He glanced up and was startled when he saw Sue. This was the last place he had expected to see her, walking into a smuggler's den as if she was familiar with them all.

Sue got a shock when she saw Fergus. For one moment she thought the best thing was to pretend she did not know him but, deciding otherwise, she was open with her greeting. 'Hello, Fergus. It's good to see thee.'

He ran his tongue round his teeth, saw Zac glance at him with curiosity. 'Knew Sue and her husband Ben back in Pickering.'

'Thee knows Ben's gone missing?' put in Zac.

'Aye. And Tom Oakroyd and Luke Newell. Their families are reet upset. Sent search parties on to t' moors but saw no signs of them.' He turned to Sue. 'Thee learned anything?'

'Not yet.' She shook her head. 'I sought help from Zac and I've made lots of enquiries but so far found nothing.'

Fergus heard the despair in her voice. 'I'm sorry,' he said.

Her fingers played nervously with the edge of her shawl. She drew a deep breath and turned to Zac. 'Beth Gill sends her good wishes.'

He nodded. He knew the ponies were ready.

Allan Cliff kept his horse to a steady pace as he headed for Whitby on his way back from Pickering. It had been a mission he had enjoyed for it had meant an escape from discipline and uniform. Lieutenant Boston had despatched him in civilian clothes to see if he could pick up any leads as to the disposal of contraband in Pickering. Now after two days he was returning with a negative report.

People were close, reluctant to talk to a stranger even if his questions seemed innocuous, but he had been pleased with the break from Whitby. He had been late leaving the market town on the south side of the moors but was not worried about the gathering dusk. The clear sky would prolong the light and would enable him to reach the Esk valley before total darkness took over.

With visibility good, the moorland afforded him a wide horizon, though without the brightness of daylight, detail was not sharp. Rather he saw the countryside as blocks of varying intensity of dark, giving way to the lighter sky.

He eased himself in the saddle and relaxed for there was no need to hurry back to the discipline and harsh words of his superior officer whom he knew would be none too pleased that he had discovered nothing. He hummed quietly to himself, content to allow the horse its own gentle pace.

A few minutes later the sudden restlessness of the horse startled him. The animal stiffened, hesitated, as if unsure of itself.

'Steady, steady.' Allan Cliff spoke soothingly but it

brought no reaction. 'What's the matter? What's upset thee?' He cast his eyes around, seeking some reason for this nervousness in his mount.

Nothing. Then it appeared from the ground some two hundred yards away across the moor. The ghostly white of horse and rider streaked out of a hollow at full gallop, but there was no sound of hooves tearing at the ground. Only a faint beating reached Allan's ears as his eyes widened in horror. The ghostly figure was heading straight for him!

His horse shied away. He fought to keep it under control and turned it on to the moor, heading off at a tangent away from the apparition. He dropped into a depression. Out of sight of the spectre, he slid from the saddle and, holding the reins, calmed his horse with soft words and soothing hands. He could still feel the tension in the animal but it responded to him.

His nerves were taut, his heart racing as he waited. Then the phantom was there, riding across the rim of the hollow with a glance neither to right nor left. The horse was stretched in gallop, its mane and tail streaming with the unearthly wind it created on this still night. Its hot breath, vaporised on the sharp air, trailed as if from nostrils afire. The figure crouched low, a white cloak billowing behind, hood drawn up so that no face was visible. Allan stared in frozen dread – was the rider headless?

His horse shuddered. In spite of the terror which gripped him, Allan automatically patted the animal's neck. Then the apparition was gone, the almost silent beating of its hooves quickly fading.

He led his horse to the ridge above the hollow to see the ghost, sharp against the black background, still heading across the moor. He saw it turn, disappear below a rise to reappear again silhouetted against the horizon. It headed towards the main track across the wasteland.

'Let's get out of here.' There was an urgent note in Allan's voice as he swung into the saddle. The ghost rider might turn this way once it reached the track and he certainly did not want to be around if it did. The horse sensed his urgency and was into a gallop almost before he was ready.

Low in the saddle, he glanced back over his shoulder. He caught a glimpse of white now on the main track between Whitby and Pickering, still some distance away, but could have sworn it had turned in his direction. The sooner he was off the moor the better.

Five minutes later, it was with some relief that, as he started to drop away from the moor to the more fertile land, he saw the darker mass of a cottage, the occupants of which eked a precarious living from a few sheep and potatoes. He was out of the saddle almost before the horse had stopped.

His desperate pounding on the door did not provoke an immediate answer. He glanced over his shoulder in the direction from which he had come. He had dropped below the edge of the moor and could see nothing as he stared into the silent darkness. But was the spectre at this very moment galloping towards the rim of the moor? Would it appear in an instant, pointing a finger at a human who had dared to gaze upon it? Allan pounded the door once more.

He heard a bolt drawn back. 'Hurry, hurry,' he called, his tone charged with fright.

The door eased ajar.

'Let me in, let me in,' he cried at the white face which peered at him.

'What's thee want?' The voice came deep from within the man's chest and was filled with suspicion.

'A ghost, a ghost out on the moor!'

Immediately the door was thrown open. A huge hand grabbed Allan's coat and dragged him inside. He stumbled as the hand released him and only prevented himself from falling by grabbing the back of a chair. The door crashed shut behind him and the bolt shot home.

Allan turned to see a big man, broad-shouldered and giving the impression of strength, but hunched a little as if he had the yoke of trouble on his shoulders. His head was big and block-like, his hair cropped almost bald.

'Ghost, thee says?' the man asked gruffly, a tremor of fear in his voice.

Allan heard a gasp behind him. He half turned and saw from the light of two candles a woman, equally as shabbily dressed as the man, sitting to one side of a fireplace in which peat sent smoke curling upwards. Three children, obviously frightened by his hammering on the door and by the word 'ghost', clung to their mother's skirt.

'Yes,' said Allan. 'Horse and rider.'

The man grunted. 'Seen it afore?'

'No,' he replied. 'I'm a stranger in these parts. Just on my way to Whitby.'

'Smugglers abroad.' The scared croak came from the woman.

'Smugglers?' Allan's attention was captured. Although he had been scared to his core, the fact that he didn't believe in ghosts had begun to reassert itself. He had started to look for a logical reason for what he had seen. Maybe this was it.

'Aye.' The man glowered from beneath bushy eyebrows. 'It's the ghost of Jonas Marten. Allus appears just afore smugglers of Baytown move contraband.'

'Why should that be? Had he dealings with the smugglers?'

'Don't know. I'll tell thee, I wouldn't set foot outside nights the ghost rides.'

'Why not?'

'Anyone foolhardy enough to be out and caught by the smugglers . . .' He left the consequence unspoken but drew his hand across his throat.

Allan swallowed hard and bit his lips nervously. He must get to Whitby. He had information here which could put him in good odour with Boston and make up for his failure to glean information in Pickering. 'I'm expected in Whitby tonight. Will I be safe to go on?' he asked.

'Thee wouldn't get me out,' replied the man, twitching his hands nervously. 'But thee on a horse might be all reet. Which way was the ghost ganning?'

'That way.' Allan pointed in the direction.

'Get off now and thee should be all right. But ride like the wind!'

'Then I'll be on my way,' said Allan, stepping towards the door. 'And thank you for the shelter and advice.' He turned and nodded to the woman and her children. The man opened the door and as Allan passed through he pressed a coin into his hand. The man grunted his thanks and as soon as Allan was outside, shut and bolted the door.

Allan lost no time in getting into the saddle and setting the animal at a gallop to Whitby.

Reaching the town, his information was soon imparted to Boston who swelled with excitement at the news.

'You've done well. I'll not forget this. Now rouse the sergeant and the men.'

Within twenty minutes Lieutenant Boston, his sergeant and nine dragoons were climbing out of the valley of the Esk on the moorland track to Pickering.

The sharp rap on the back door of Beck Farm startled the Dugdale family who were just about to sit down for their evening meal.

They glanced questioningly at each other. Who could it be calling at this time as the last remnants of light from the setting sun were fading? The sky was clear so total darkness would not come soon but few people were abroad at this time unless on some nefarious exploit.

John rose from his chair and went to the door. 'Fergus Pinkney, what's thee doing here so late?'

The reply was lost to the rest of the family then they heard John speak again.

'If thee's bent on crossing the moors tonight, thee'd better come in and partake of some refreshments with us.'

'That's mighty kind of thee, John,' replied Fergus as he stepped into the room. He made his greetings to the rest of the family then added, 'It will surely fortify me for what I reckon's ganning to be a cold journey, but I have to be in Pickering tonight.'

Emma was puzzled. Pedlars never called at this time of day. Maybe Fergus was just looking for sustenance before his night's journey, but he could so easily have brought some from wherever he had been. She reckoned he was here for one thing only and that, when he left the farmhouse, he would be visiting the lonely barn with her father.

She excused herself and left the room by the back door. Making a pretence of going to the privy across the yard, she went quickly to Fergus's pony and there saw the coloured ribbons tied to the saddle. She was right. Contraband would be moved this night.

It came as no surprise to her when Fergus declared he must leave as soon as the meal was finished and her father took his coat from the peg, saying he would accompany the pedlar to the edge of the moor.

Lieutenant Boston checked the pace of his troop once they had reached the land above the Esk. He sent out two riders as scouts and was elated when they returned ten minutes later to report that a pony-train was crossing the moor and would reach the main track probably about two miles ahead.

'How many?' he asked.

'Didn't go too close once we'd identified it as a pony train.'

'Certain it wasn't the fish wives?' asked Boston cautiously. He didn't want to be made a fool of again.

'Men's voices,' came the reply.

'How many of them?'

'Don't know. Daren't go any closer.'

'Doesn't matter. We'll have surprise on our side.' He set the troop in motion.

Two miles further on, a track from the coast joined the main track in a small valley cutting across the moor. Boston quickly assessed the situation and saw it as an ideal place for an ambush. Accordingly, leaving one man in charge of the horses, hidden from sight by a twist in the terrain, he deployed the remainder along either side of the valley and posted his sergeant to the top of the ridge as lookout.

Ten minutes later he scurried back to report that he could hear the smugglers in the distance approaching the head of the valley where it ran out on the moorland plateau.

Boston checked his men quickly. With swords drawn, they had used what cover they could to hide their presence. He issued his final orders quietly and returned to his position from which he would have an overall view of the smugglers as they came down the valley. Tension gripped the dragoons. Though they had all seen action against smugglers in the south, there was never a moment when action was imminent that their nerves were not taut. Though the night was chilly they were warm with nervous sweat. Individuals seized odd moments to wipe their clammy hands on their tunics and adjust their grip on their swords.

They became edgy when they heard the first sound of horses and men slipping from the moor and starting down the valley. Some licked dry lips in apprehension, others bit them as the tension which immediately precedes violent action gripped them.

Boston counted them as the first pony drew level with him. Ten of them. One man with each. One man in front, no doubt checking the way, and one in the rear acting as guard. Boston smiled to himself. Numbers fairly even and he had the element of surprise. Tonight he would smash the Baytown smugglers!

Elation gripped him, he wanted to be at them but waited,

watching for the right moment to spring his surprise. Now? A moment longer? He glanced quickly along the terrain. The train was positioned between himself and the last dragoon down the valley. Now!

Boston sprang to his feet. 'Halt!' he yelled. 'You're under arrest!'

His shout was a signal to his men to show themselves. As one they rose from the heather and started down the slopes on either side of the valley. The suddenness of their appearance brought momentary confusion to the smugglers, but before the troopers reached them they had drawn their cutlasses and prepared to meet violence with violence. Ponies twisted and turned in the confusion caused by the yells and shouts of the troopers as they charged down the slopes.

A sudden volley of pistol shots from above followed by chilling yells as men attacked from behind brought terror to their hearts. They were trapped between two gangs of smugglers! Boston had a grip on the situation in an instant. He knew the smugglers would show no mercy, but would slaughter his whole troop without compunction. Though folk would know who had done it, no one would be able to prove a thing. None of the smugglers here tonight would talk. To go down fighting would achieve nothing while to run would mean they could live to remain a thorn in the side of Zac Denby and his gang. It hurt Boston to think he had been outwitted by that man again. Zac had been shrewd enough to provide an escort and place it away from the pony-train.

'Retreat! Retreat!' He bawled his order as loud as he could to be heard above the yells and the clash of steel where combat had already taken place.

Troopers still on the slope scrambled along the incline towards the spot where the horses had been left. Those in conflict ducked and weaved, thrust and parried, all the time retreating, seeking a moment when they could break off the engagement and run. They knew it was every man for himself in this situation and each was determined to survive. With the odds stacked so heavily against them they knew their officer did not expect any daring deeds of valour for, in his determination to smash the smuggling ring, dead heroes in one individual engagement meant nothing.

As soon as each man reached his horse he was into the saddle and away. No one was expected to wait. They were not required to form ranks and ride out as a troop. Some men holding back to help a friend soon realised it was not necessary, for the smugglers were not pressing their pursuit with any enthusiasm. They were content to have broken up the ambush and saw a greater need to assemble the pony-train again. They knew with such numbers opposed to them the troopers would not attack a second time. Several shots were fired after the retreating dragoons as reminders of what they could expect if they contemplated another attack.

That was the furthest thing from Lieutenant Boston's mind. His men were scattered, and even if he could muster them again they would still be heavily outnumbered. It was an angry man who rode back to Whitby.

Fergus Pinkney halted his two ponies and listened intently. Had he heard a shout somewhere to his right across the darkened moor? It had been a considerable distance away but he felt sure . . . Shots! Repeated. Yells. Cries. Pandemonium. A fight. Fergus stiffened with anxiety. Dragoons and smugglers? It must be. It could be no one else. He cursed. This was no place to be with contraband in the panniers strapped to his ponies. He could only be thankful that he had chosen to take this narrow, less used track to save time. But now he was in a dilemma. With troopers about he was in danger. He shuddered at the thought of deportation or worse.

He must get off the moor. Forget reaching Pickering tonight. Better be safe and arrive in the market town tomorrow. He'd seek shelter with the Petches on Deadman's Howe. They'd not betray him if the hated dragoons called. Ignoring the sounds of combat across the moor, he hurried on to the safety he thought existed in the lonely cottage.

Dick Petch chuckled as he walked away from the bog. He had watched the water swirl and the mud suck at the unconscious form of Fergus Pinkney until it swallowed another victim in its dark depths.

More goods to sell, and valuable ones at that. Brandy, tobacco, lace and silks to add to those already stored in the barn. Whoever had decided to send contraband by pedlars had done the Petches a good turn.

As he went to the fire to warm his hands, his mother looked up with a satisfied cackle. 'Another helped on his way to a new life.'

'Aye, Ma. He went down reet nice like,' grinned Dick.

Eliza nodded her approval. 'Phoebe!'

Her daughter came from the kitchen where she had been preparing some soup.

'I've been thinking, we'd better get rid of all that stuff in the barn. Dick, thee can take it to Yarm tomorrow, the horses as well. It should all fetch a pretty penny. Keep a little for ourselves, thee can see to that, Phoebe, and the rest can go.' With her instructions given, she leaned back in her chair. 'That soup ganning to be long?' she barked.

Phoebe said nothing but hurried away to the kitchen to keep her mother in a good mood.

Dick was thinking of his trip. He wouldn't be returning astride the horse they had had for three years. He liked the look of the one which had belonged to the pedlar who had called himself Ben Thrower. It was strong and sturdy, and ever since Ben had had no further need of it Dick had given it extra care. He nodded and pursed his lips. That would be the horse on which he would return from Yarm.

Chapter Eighteen

Amy stopped and narrowed her eyes against the distance. She was still some way from Beck Farm but her sharp eyesight had picked out a rider beyond the farm on the track from Whitby.

On the pretext of going for a walk again she had visited Joe at work in the same field where she had seen him two days before. He had seemed genuinely pleased to see her again and she detected that it was more than just politeness because she was Emma's sister, someone he had known all his life. She was delighted but realised that she must not rush any expression of deeper affection for him. Though he appeared to have come to terms with Emma's rejection of his proposal, he must still be hurting. She had left him lightheartedly for he had suggested that they spend the day in Whitby together on Saturday. In two days' time she would be with him again.

Even at this distance Amy thought she recognised the rider. A few yards more and she had her suspicions confirmed. She hurried her pace and then, raising her skirts a little and with Bess bounding along beside her, broke into a run. She startled her mother and father when she burst into the house.

'Mark Roper's coming!' she cried. 'Where's Emma?'

Taken aback by the sudden intrusion her mother could only gasp, 'She's upstairs.' As Amy shot through the kitchen, Grace stared after her in amazement and then glanced at her husband with raised eyebrows.

John grinned, amused by their reaction to the simple fact that Mark Roper was coming.

'Emma, Emma!' called Amy as she raced upstairs. She

flung open the door of Emma's bedroom to find her on her knees in front of an open drawer. Emma looked up, wondering what all the excitement was about.

'Mark's coming,' panted Amy.

'What?' gasped Emma. She slammed the drawer shut and scrambled to her feet.

'Saw him, way down the track,' explained Amy.

Emma ran to the window, raised it and leaned out so that she could see the track from Whitby. A rider! Mark! 'Oh, my goodness,' she gulped as she let the window drop and turned back into the room. With quick strokes she smoothed her dress. 'Amy, am I all right? Oh, I should have had a smarter dress on, not this everyday old thing.'

Amy laughed at Emma's confusion. 'Thee's perfectly all right. It's thee he's interested in, not thy dress.' Becoming a little impatient with all the fuss, she added, 'Thee hasn't time to change. He'll have to take thee as thee is,' and started for the door.

Emma took one last look in the mirror, nipped her cheeks for more colour, and hurried after her sister.

'Ma, Mark's on his way,' she cried as she entered the kitchen.

'I know, I know,' replied Grace with amused tolerance. 'Amy didn't dash through here without telling us. Now just calm thyself.' She read in her daughter's agitation the love she felt for Mark Roper.

'Will I do, Ma?' pressed Emma.

'Thee's reet, lass, just reet.'

'Will I, Pa?'

'Thy mother says so.' John smiled at the commotion and added quietly to himself, 'Women!' He shook his head as if he would never understand the ways of the opposite sex.

Emma could hardly keep still. Somehow it had been different in Whitby. There she had had him to herself, the time had been theirs. But now she felt like someone whose young man was calling at her home and would meet her mother and father for the first time. Only when she heard the clop of hooves did she get a grip on herself, though her heart was still fluttering. She must appear calm, just as she had in Whitby.

The horse stopped. Footsteps approached the front door.

When no one else rose to answer the knock, Grace hurried from the kitchen.

'Good day, Mrs Dugdale.' The young man removed his hat when she opened the door. His smile was friendly. 'Remember me? Mark Roper?'

'I do,' returned Grace. She had already summed up her first impressions: a likeable, polite, handsome young man with a warm, open countenance and a soft pleasant voice. 'Though thee were but a schoolboy when I last saw thee. Come in with thee.'

Mark stepped into the house and paused as she closed the door. He glanced around. 'Just the same, just as I remember it,' he said.

The affectionate tone pleased Grace. 'Thee remembers it?' she asked with some surprise. 'But thee only came a few times.'

'Ah, but I remember the warmth and friendliness of this house. It has always stuck in my memory.' Grace had moved towards the door which led to the withdrawing room, one which the Dugdales only used for special occasions, but she stopped when Mark added, 'I especially remember your kitchen and the good smells it held – new baked bread and those jam pasties you used to make, a real treat for a schoolboy. Is it still the same?'

Grace smiled, flattered by his recollections. 'Like to see?'

'I would,' he replied. 'It will bring back happy memories.' He was pleased he had diverted Mrs Dugdale from the formalities attached to using the best room. He wanted no ceremony.

Grace opened the door to the kitchen.

'Hello, Emma, Amy.' He greeted them in turn with a smile and an inclination of his head. 'And good day to you, sir.' He crossed the floor to John who was rising from his chair.

John held out his hand and felt a firm, friendly grip. 'Pleased to see thee, Mark. Thee'll have seen a bit of life since thee was last here?'

'Indeed I have, but I've been nowhere I like as well as Whitby.'

'Make some tea, Amy, please,' said Grace. 'Emma, some jam pasties. Mark's just reminded me how much he used to like them.'

Emma rose from her chair and went to the pantry, a small shelved room off the north side of the kitchen. Grace followed her to get some fruit cake.

'Mother, did thee have to bring him into the kitchen?' asked Emma in an agitated whisper, as if she was put out by the fact that her mother had not shown him to the best room.

'He asked,' replied her mother sharply. 'Apparently he likes the homely atmosphere.' She turned on her heel without waiting for Emma's comment.

Mark spent an hour at ease with the family, enjoying his pasties and cake, chatting about his return to Whitby and how his family were faring in London. Eased by his relaxed attitude, Emma enjoyed his visit and was tolerant of her brother's outburst when he tore into the kitchen with a couple of rabbits.

'It's time I was out of your way,' said Mark eventually, 'but before I go I have two requests to make of you, Mr and Mrs Dugdale. May I have your permission to marry Emma?'

There was a moment's silence as if each was waiting for the other to speak. Emma's heart skipped a beat. Surely they would not object?

Grace glanced at her husband who was slowly filling his pipe. He pursed his lips thoughtfully for a moment, then looking up said, 'Aye, lad, thee has it.'

Excitement coursed through Emma. She jumped from

her chair and flung her arms round her father's neck. 'Oh, Pa, thank thee.' She kissed him on the cheek as he shrank back from the open display of affection even though he liked it. She turned to her mother who was reassured by the radiant look on her daughter's face. 'Thanks, Ma.' And Emma kissed her. As she turned, Amy gave her a joyous hug while secretly thanking Mark for returning to Whitby.

'The second request?' prompted John, after Mark's thanks had been expressed in a handshake for him and a kiss for Grace.

'Would you allow me to take Emma to the theatre tomorrow evening and accompany me to a dinner on Sunday evening at Hugh Lomas's? Meg is going to be there,' he added by way of reassurance.

John glanced at his wife and saw her almost imperceptible nod. 'Well, it's up to Emma. As far as her mother and I are concerned, she's at liberty to accept thy invitation.' He smiled to himself when he saw relief cross his daughter's face.

'Thank you for your permission,' said Mark. He looked at Emma with a hopeful smile. 'Would you like to accompany me, Emma?'

'Oh, yes, thank thee.' There was laughter in her eyes. 'I would love to. What are we going to see?'

'*The Beggar's Opera*, a humorous play with sprightly songs by John Gay. I've heard it's good fun.'

'We'll have to arrange for Emma to stay at her aunt's,' put in Grace. 'Then thee can see she's back here on Monday morning.'

'I will, Mrs Dugdale,' Mark reassured her.

'Oh, Ma, thanks,' enthused Emma. She shot Mark a glance to assess his reaction and saw pleasure in his eyes. 'But how can we let Aunt Matilda know?'

'If you write a note to Mrs Dugdale, I will be glad to deliver it,' he suggested.

When Grace had written the letter, Emma accompanied him to his horse.

'Oh, Mark, I'm so happy,' she said.

'So am I.' He kissed her, not lingeringly but with a fervour which revealed the depth of his love. 'I look forward to the weekend.'

During the interval of *The Beggar's Opera*, when Emma and Mark were in conversation, they were interrupted by a deep voice. 'Well, if it isn't one of the charming ladies from Beck Farm.'

Emma scowled as she turned and saw Lieutenant Boston, but knew she must be polite. Arrayed in his best uniform he made a dashing figure. His demeanour was friendly, as if he had never caused the Dugdales any trouble. 'Good evening,' she greeted him coldly. She turned to Mark who was eyeing the soldier with quizzical interest. 'Mark, this is Lieutenant Boston. Lieutenant, Mark Roper.'

The two men greeted each other politely as if each was assessing the other's relationship with Emma.

Mark felt some easing of his attitude when Boston smiled and said to Emma, 'And how's that charming sister of yours?'

'None the better for thee asking,' she retorted.

Boston hid his chagrin at the answer by a hearty laugh. 'Well said, Miss Dugdale. I don't suppose she is, but please remember me to her. Tell her I might even call on her.'

'I rather think it would be a waste of time, Lieutenant. She is friendly with Joe Wade.'

A momentary flash of annoyance crossed the soldier's face at the reminder of his encounter with Joe. He leaned forward and lowered his voice as if speaking in confidence. 'Ah, but there's nothing like a bit of rivalry to bring out the best in me.' He straightened and turned to Mark, changing the subject. 'Mark Roper? You've come to Whitby to run your father's firm after the resignation of Silas Brent.'

'You're well informed,' replied Mark, without disguising his surprise.

Boston grinned. 'Have to be when you're trying to stamp out smuggling. You need to follow all possible leads.'

'Heard tell you had a run in with the smugglers on Thursday night?' observed Mark.

'We did. Unfortunately we were outnumbered but I gained valuable information. I know that the last contraband run ashore was a big consignment, it couldn't all be on the pony-train we encountered. I reckon there's a lot in hidey holes in outlying farms.' He cast a pointed glance at Emma. 'But I'll find it, you can be sure of that. I'm determined to smash this smuggling ring one way or another.'

'That's a fine attitude,' complimented Mark. 'They are a scourge in the government's side.'

'Wouldn't be if folks didn't encourage them, especially merchants wanting better profits.' Boston was watching Mark closely.

His eyes glinted at the inference. 'You can't lay anything at our door.' The snap in his voice had the ring of steel.

Boston raised his hands in apology. 'I'm sorry, I wasn't meaning you.'

'Shouldn't you be looking for the brains behind the smugglers? There must be someone who organises the whole operation.'

'That's not my job,' returned the lieutenant. 'But the authorities either aren't bothered or they're afraid of what they might unearth and who they might have to bring to justice. But I reckon if I can smash the smuggling gangs, the operation will fold up. Maybe that's what the authorities want and then they can avoid prosecuting their own kind.' He stopped and turned to Emma. 'Oh, Miss Dugdale, I apologise for this conversation. It must be boring to you with no cause to be interested in smuggling.'

Emma was already churning inside. The talk of smuggling had upset her, recalling as it did her father's involvement. Here she was, with this secret, talking to two men who had just professed their antagonism to contraband runners and dealers. She felt faint.

'Emma, are you all right?' asked Mark, troubled by the pallor of her face.

Lieutenant Boston frowned, 'I'm sorry if the talk of smuggling has upset you.'

She was aware of him watching her intently, and was thankful that before she could reply the resumption of the play was announced.

Boston bowed gracefully to her and nodded to Mark.

'An interesting conversation,' he commented, 'maybe we could continue it some time. You know where my office is?'

Boston made no remark but moved away, wondering at Emma's reaction to the conversation.

'Why do thee want to have anything to do with him?' she whispered to Mark with agitated annoyance as they walked back to their seats.

'I think we should all do what we can to stamp out smuggling. Being a merchant I might be able to help if I offered to deal in smuggled goods. With Boston's knowledge, of course.'

Emma was shocked by Mark's suggestion and saw that it might have threatening implications for her father. She made only a pretence of enjoying the rest of the play for her mind was too preoccupied with the conversation between the two men.

Matilda Dugdale gave up trying to calm her daughter and niece as they got ready for the evening.

'Well, how do we look?' cried Meg as she and Emma turned to show off their dresses.

Meg had chosen a dress of cream silk with a flower pattern in red, yellow and green, which opened narrowly down the front to reveal a green silk petticoat. The three-quarter sleeves were trimmed with lace and came gently off the shoulders. Emma had brought her brown watered silk dress figured with twisting stems of wild roses. Her petticoat was of white quilted silk and gave way to a pale blue bodice over which the neckline of her dress plunged v-shaped.

They made a kaleidoscope of colour as they spun round, dazzling Matilda with their exuberance.

'You look right bonny,' she said admiringly.

Since the party she had given for Silas Brent she had seen her daughter all aglow, revelling in the attention she was receiving from Edward Beaumont. Meg was obviously happy in love and Matilda felt that it must be reciprocated, otherwise a handsome young man of Beaumont's standing would not continue to pay her such attention.

Edward was the first to call and whisked Meg away, saying he wanted a word with Hugh Lomas before the other guests arrived. Ten minutes later Mark called for Emma and, after paying his compliments to Mr and Mrs Dugdale, escorted her to the horse and carriage he had hired for the evening.

When he had seen that she was comfortable, with a rug tucked round her against the sharp air, he set the horse into a steady trot. Cocooned in the warmth of her cloak and rug, sitting close to Mark, she felt cared for and protected. They chatted conversationally and she felt caressed by the softness in his voice. Moonlight lit the track beside the winding river until they turned between large stone pillars surmounted with stone carvings of owls. The way to the house wound beneath large oaks until they came out into a lawned space circled by the carriage way which swept up to the front of the house.

A footman was waiting to escort them indoors while a groom took the reins and drove their carriage to the back of the house.

When they stepped through the door Emma found herself in a high square hall. To the left, stairs climbed upwards, turning right to reach the landing on the upper storey. Close to the bottom of the stairs a door stood open, giving a view of a long dining room in which a table was finely laid out for a meal. A maid dressed in a long black dress with white apron and white cap came to meet them, and she and the footman took their coats and hats. A second maid escorted them to a door on the right and as she opened it voices and laughter met them.

Seeing the door open, Hugh Lomas excused himself from the two guests to whom he was talking. 'Ah, Roper, my dear fellow, so glad you could come.' He smiled broadly and turned to Emma, welcoming her with a little bow. 'And you too, Miss Dugdale. Welcome to my humble home both of you.'

She inclined her head in greeting.

'It is good of you to invite us,' replied Mark.

'Ah, we must make newcomers to Whitby welcome,' returned Hugh. 'Come meet my other guests, though of course you already know Edward Beaumont and Emma's cousin. We are only a small party tonight.'

He introduced them to the six other guests and they all enjoyed a glass of Madeira until they were called to dine.

They enjoyed a sumptuous meal of beef reared on the Lomas estates and game caught in the woods, supported by a variety of vegetables and potatoes. Sweetmeats and cheese aplenty were being enjoyed with a piquant accompanying wine when Lomas purposely mentioned the smugglers.

'I believe the dragoons were outdone by the Baytown smugglers again on Thursday night,' he said with a smile, recalling what he had heard.

A chuckle ran round the table.

'A large consignment, I'm told,' commented Edward.

'Any silks or lace for us ladies?' asked one of them.

'How should I know?' replied Edward with a shrug of his shoulders.

'You seem to know most things,' she answered with a twitch of her lips.

'Silks, eh?' Edward glanced at her husband. 'I see Sheila's after more dresses, Miles. Have to keep a hand in your pocket.'

'The dragoons will never stamp it out. Zac Denby's too wily for them. Besides, too many people benefit from smuggling to turn traitor and help the authorities,' commented one of the guests. He looked across the table at Mark. 'Do you trade in smuggled goods?'

'That's a loaded question,' replied Mark, pretending to be taken aback by its directness.

'It is,' boomed Edward with a deep-throated laugh. 'But you needn't worry, no one here's going to give you away. We've all benefited in some way from smuggling. We wouldn't want to see anyone suffer who might be able to supply us.'

Mark took the point and nodded. He eyed his questioner. 'Your answer, sir, is that I haven't as yet but I might be tempted by the extra profit when I've had more time to look into the matter.' He was beginning to see a way in which he could gain confidences which might lead him to the mastermind behind the smuggling, whose identity he would then be able to pass on to Sir William Bailey.

'If ever you do, I might be interested in making an investment with you, if it's financial backing you need to acquire the contraband,' said Edward, shrewdly watching Mark's reaction.

'I'll remember that,' he replied. 'Emma and I were at the theatre last night, and got into conversation with Lieutenant Boston.' He saw he had everyone's attention as he went on: 'I remarked on Thursday night's escapade and he wasn't put out by it, or at least didn't show it. He said that although he had come away empty-handed, he had gained valuable information.'

'What was that?' The question came just a little too sharply from Edward Beaumont but it was Hugh Lomas who was leaning on the table watching him intently, as if hanging on to every word.

'He said the contraband which was run ashore was a big load and it could not all be on the pony-train he attacked the other night. So he reckons there must be a large amount still hidden in the farms around the district.'

Lomas screwed up his face thoughtfully as he nodded. Beaumont leaned back in his chair and made no comment.

'It looks as if he will scour the district again,' put in Miles.

'I hope he doesn't!' cried Emma with some alarm in her voice.

'Have you been troubled, m'dear?' Lomas threw up his arms in horror at the thought.

'Oh, yes. More than once, and it isn't a very pleasant experience. He's an abominable man. I feel certain he'll come again.'

'I'm sure you have nothing to fear,' returned Edward pleasantly. 'Unless, of course, your father has something to hide?'

He glanced round the table as he made this final remark and received knowing nods from the guests.

'My father couldn't be involved,' protested Emma, hoping that she lied convincingly.

'Who can tell? But I'm sure he isn't,' said Lomas, making light of the situation.

'Mark, I'm puzzled,' said Emma as they rode back to Whitby. 'Thee talks one way to Boston and differently tonight. Are thee really thinking about getting involved in handling contraband?'

He gave a little laugh. 'In this matter it depends who I'm talking to.'

'Would thee pass on any knowledge to Boston? Thee indicated to him that thee thought smuggling ought to be stamped out.'

'Just a way of talking to him,' replied Mark, trying to pass off her questioning yet wondering if he should reveal to her the trust Sir William Bailey had placed in him. However, he decided against doing so. It would do her no good to know and might even endanger her. 'After all, I wouldn't want him nosing around too much if I decided to handle contraband. I've come to the conclusion that it seems to be the done thing, that most people acquire smuggled goods for their own use, so . . .

He left the sentence unfinished then added: 'But there's no need for you to worry about it.' He changed the conversation by remarking on the splendid meal they had had and said that he must give a dinner in return once he was settled into his house in Bagdale. 'And I hope you will help me with it, when I do?'

'Of course, I'll be delighted,' replied Emma, but she had been only half listening to him. Her thoughts had been preoccupied with her father's part in the smuggling. She feared Boston's insinuations meant that he suspected there was contraband at Beck Farm even though he had not found it. She was tempted to confide in Mark, to ask his help, but what could he do? And she still wasn't sure of his real attitude to smuggling.

It was ten o'clock in the morning when Zac hurried out of Baytown. He had received an urgent call via Sam Armstrong that The Fox wanted to see him at the usual meeting place at eleven. The urgency of the message had left no doubt in his mind that something was troubling The Fox. Zac made good time, never pausing once, so bent was he on not being late.

When he arrived at the farm there was no one about. He went to the cottage and found that he had arrived before The Fox. Nothing had been arranged for the meeting: there was no necessity now that Zac knew The Fox's identity. He walked round the bare cottage and finally sat down on one of the two chairs.

Five minutes later he was on his feet when he heard the back door open and someone cross the other room. The adjoining door was flung open furiously and The Fox stormed in. His face was clouded with anger. He seemed to tower over Zac, but the smuggler was tough and would not be easily intimidated.

'Fergus Pinkney did not reach Pickering!' The Fox thundered. 'That's another pedlar and his contraband gone missing. What the hell's going on, and what's thee doing about it?' His eyes blazed with fury.

'Pinkney missing?' Zac was incredulous. 'Not another one?'

'Yes,' snarled The Fox. 'This is losing us too much money. Someone's playing a fast game, and you'd better find out who soon or you're in trouble.'

The threat needled Zac. Defiant words sprang to his lips but he held back. He knew how ruthless this man could be. He had influence in high places and would sell his own if it benefited him, but Zac feared more the contacts he had with rogues and thugs who would murder a man at his say so and for the coins it could bring.

'Look, it's been bothering me as much as thee...' started Zac.

'No, not as much as me,' snapped The Fox. 'I'm losing, you aren't. You've still been paid for your part in the organisation.'

'And rightly so. We got the pack-horse train through safely on Thursday night,' Zac pointed out.

'That was good work, I have to admit. You outsmarted the dragoons. But have you any thoughts about what is happening to the contraband you move by pedlars?'

'Those who have vanished have all passed through Beck Farm.'

'Beck Farm? The Dugdale place?'

'Aye.'

'Been using it long?'

'No.'

'Looks as though Dugdale is up to no good.' The Fox's lips tightened. 'And I know the dragoons are more than interested in Beck Farm. They've been giving him a hard time and are likely to do so again.' He paused thoughtfully then added, 'I think you'd better get rid of Mr Dugdale.'

'But we can't be certain . . .'

Zac's point was cut short. 'Get rid of him, he might talk.' The Fox's voice held a cold finality.

Chapter Nineteen

Nell turned from the pan she was stirring on the fire and knew immediately from the scowl on Zac's face that his interview with The Fox had not gone well.

'Trouble?' she asked as she placed her spoon on the table and went to a cupboard from which she took a glass and a bottle of brandy.

'Aye,' grunted Zac, peeling off his jacket and hanging it on a peg beside the door.

'Then get this inside thee afore thee tells me,' said Nell, handing him the glass into which she had poured a good measure of the liquid.

'Don't think thee should know,' mumbled Zac, pulling out a chair from under the table and sitting down. He reached for the glass.

'Now, Zac, we've held no secrets where smuggling's concerned,' said Nell sharply.

He wiped the back of his hand across his lips and looked up at her. She saw hesitation still lingering in his eyes.

'Thee's found out who The Fox is?' A tremor of excitement had come to her voice.

'No, lass,' he lied. This was one secret he would not dare to divulge to her. 'He wants John Dugdale killed!'

Nell's eyes widened as she sank on to a chair opposite Zac.

'Thee knows contraband moved by pedlars from Beck Farm has gone missing?' he went on. 'He says it can't be tolerated any longer. Dugdale could be behind it and The Fox can't risk having a traitor in the chain. He also fears that there will be extra dragoon activity directed at Beck Farm and Dugdale might talk under pressure.'

'But is there sufficient proof?'

Zac shrugged his shoulders. 'The Fox won't wait for that. He sees the possibility that Dugdale is involved, or if not might turn King's evidence, and that's good enough for him.'

'Then thee'll have to do it,' returned Nell.

'Aye,' said Zac. He drained his glass and reached for the bottle.

'When? How?'

'Soon. I'll have to take the opportunity when it arises.'

Sue made her way down the main street after visiting Beth Gill. Her heart was heavy. She had hoped Beth, knowing the moorland tracks from taking fish to Pickering, might be able to help. But all she had been able to say was that the moors were treacherous and to stray from known paths could prove fatal. Ben could have been lost in a gully or sucked down by a bog. Sue felt numb at the thought that she might never see him again, and every day that passed made that seem more likely. Maybe she should return to Pickering, but to do so would mean losing all the contacts she had made, and she needed to know what had happened to him, even if it meant learning the worst.

By the time she reached the Fisherman's Arms she had made up her mind to remain in Robin Hood's Bay throughout the winter and continue her search which so far had come to naught.

As she approached the back door she was aware that it was ajar, had not caught on its sneck when the last person had used it. Voices engaged in earnest discussion reached her. She slowed her steps. Under normal circumstances she would have abhorred eavesdropping but her situation was not normal and there was something about the tone of these voices that made her stop and listen.

A chill touched her heart and made her draw breath sharply when she realised she was overhearing Emma's father being condemned to death.

She could not let this happen to the girl who had befriended her when she had come looking for Ben. Sue knew she ran a risk by informing Emma, that Zac would show no mercy if he found out she had forewarned the Dugdales, but she could not stand by and let it happen. Besides if it did she might lose a vital link in finding out what had happened to Ben, for John Dugdale could have been the last person to see him alive.

She turned and hurried quietly away from the Fisherman's Arms.

Emma glanced up from the pots she was washing. She stopped, her attention caught by the figure striding purposefully down the long slope of the hill from the moors.

'Sue,' she whispered to herself. 'And she seems to be in a hurry.' Emma rubbed her wet hands on her hessian apron, flung it on to a chair and grabbed her shawl. She was alone. Her mother and Amy had gone to Drop Farm and her father and Jay were out in the fields. But she would not await Sue's arrival for she had read an urgency in the stride, as if Sue was set on a matter of importance. She hurried to meet her friend.

'Emma, thank goodness thee's here!' panted Sue, trying to catch her breath as she spoke.

'What is it?' Emma revealed her own concern as she read the anxiety in Sue's expression.

'Thy father's in danger.' Sue clutched at Emma's sleeve as she bent to draw air into her aching lungs. There was alarm in her eyes as she straightened up.

'What's thee mean?' A shiver of foreboding assailed Emma.

Sue gulped another breath. 'I overheard Zac talking. He thinks thy father is behind the pedlars' disappearance.'

'Pedlars?'

'Aye. More than Ben have never reached their destination, and Beck Farm was the last place they all called,' explained Sue. 'Zac suspects thy father knows something about them. He's been ordered to kill him.'

'What?' The words were drumming in her mind, threatening to overwhelm her. Emma felt bile rise in her throat and her face drained to an ashen white. 'Who would do that?' She managed to get the question out in a strangled gasp.

Sue shook her head. 'There's someone from whom Zac takes his orders, who it is I don't know. But that's not the point. Thy father must be warned.'

Dread hung cold and heavy in her mind. This was what her father's brief excursion into the world of smuggling had led them to! The smugglers were ruthless and unless her father escaped they would wreak their revenge. Their family would be devastated, their lives in ruins. Where could he go? And if he escaped, what could the future hold for them all? Emma saw her whole world shattered.

'Emma!' Sue shook her arm, rousing her from the apathy which threatened to swamp her.

She started. She must do something. Her father must be warned and then they must plan to get him away. She glanced sharply at Sue. 'When is it likely to happen?'

'I don't know. I don't think they'll come and drag thy father out and kill him. It will be done subtly, so he should take care at all times.'

'Sue, thanks. I'll go and find him now. He's in Hawthorne field. Come with me?'

Sue could not disregard the plea in Emma's voice.

They soon found her father working on the ditch at the bottom of the field while Jay stood near the far end.

John straightened when he heard someone coming and was pleased for the excuse to take a rest from his hard work. He was surprised to see Emma and the pedlar's wife. 'Good day, Mrs Thrower.' He glanced at his daughter. 'Emma what brings thee out here?' He had noted the anxiety on her face and it troubled him.

'Pa, Sue has brought news which thee should hear,' she explained.

He looked questioningly at Sue. What could she know which would be of interest to him?

'Mr Dugdale, thy life is in danger from the smugglers.'

The statement hit John like a thunderclap but he kept his composure. 'Smugglers? Why should they be interested in me?'

'Father, I know all about thy association with them.' The words came cold and matter-of-fact from Emma. John knew there was no point in denying it.

'How?' he asked quietly. In his expression, even in that one word, there was relief. The burden which had lain heavily on him was now shared.

Emma quickly related her story and told how Sue was drawn into it and had decided to go to Baytown. Sue told of her experiences there and how she had the confidence of Zac and had heard the threat against John Dugdale.

When they had finished John looked at his daughter with a troubled frown. 'I'm sorry to have brought this on thee, lass.'

'The missing men, Pa?' Though she felt sure what the answer would be, she had to hear it from her father's lips.

'I know nothing about them,' he replied firmly. 'I never heard any more after they left here.'

'Then go and tell Zac that,' urged Emma.

'Wouldn't be any use,' said Sue. 'They assess the facts they have, make a judgement, act on it and ask questions afterwards. Zac's had his orders and he'll carry them out.'

John's lips tightened. He knew she was right. He was a marked man. 'We'll have to discuss this with the whole family, and thy ma and Amy won't be back until this evening.'

'But we must do something, Pa!' cried Emma.

'We shall, we shall,' said John, trying to calm the panic he could sense in his daughter.

'Let me seek help from Mark,' she said.

'What could he do?' queried her father.

'Maybe offer help if we went to London.'

John made no comment on what he saw as an absurdity. What would he, a farmer born and bred, do in London? What would his family do? Instead he said, 'But that would mean he would know of my involvement with smuggling.'

'He's more than a friend. He'll soon be one of the family. I'd trust him to keep our secret.'

John could see from her manner that there would be no denying her. Besides she might be right. Someone outside the situation might see a solution which they could not. 'All right,' he agreed. 'Thee'll ride into Whitby, then thee can be back by the time thy ma returns.'

'Right, Pa.' She felt the tension ease with the decision, to be replaced by elation at being able to do something which might save her father. She turned to Sue. 'Thanks for what thee's done.' She reached out and pressed her arm as an expression of gratitude.

Sue smiled. 'I wish I could do more. Maybe it's best if I get back to Baytown. I could be more use there. If I hear anything else, I'll get word to thee.'

John expressed his thanks and she turned to head for Baytown.

Emma dismounted outside the Roper office, called to a passing urchin and handed him a coin to take care of her horse until she returned. Delighted, the boy took the reins and watched admiringly as Emma went into the building. She was relieved when her knock on the door was answered immediately.

Mark smiled with pleasure when he saw her and rose from his desk to come to meet her. His smile turned to a look of concern when he saw the worry which clouded her usually cheerful features.

'Something wrong?' he asked with solicitude as he took her hands.

'Oh, Mark, there's trouble and I need thy advice,' she cried, her voice shaky with worry.

'Come and sit down,' he said gently, and led her to a chair. 'Take your time and tell me what it's all about.'

Emma composed herself as he pulled up another chair beside her. This situation obviously did not warrant the formality of his returning to his chair behind the desk. Emma needed to be calmed and he could achieve that with closer contact.

She drew strength from the kindness in his eyes and knew she had been right to come to him. She sighed deeply as if gathering strength to tell her story.

Mark listened to her intently, resisting any temptation to interrupt. His mind reeled when she revealed her father's connection with the smugglers. How could he cope with the dilemma which faced him? He had sworn to help Sir William, but now he was faced with the task of protecting the father of the girl he loved. To inform Boston of what he had been told would condemn Emma's father to arrest or worse. Mark would shatter Emma's dream and faith, would lose the girl he wanted to marry.

It was a thoughtful young man, anxiously searching for an answer, who heard her desperate cry: 'Oh, Mark, what are we to do?'

He made no immediate reply but rose from his chair, crossed to a wall cupboard, took out a decanter and wine glasses. He poured the Madeira thoughtfully, then turned and handed a glass to her. 'Drink this, you've had an anxious time.'

She took it without a word. The look in her eyes plucked at his heart. He wanted desperately to fold her in his arms and wipe away all her cares so that when he released her there would be no worries left. He sat down and met her hopeful gaze. Should he tell her of the second reason he was in Whitby? He was on the point of doing so when he decided it would serve no purpose. Her father was not the person he wanted. John Dugdale was only a very small part of the operation, and might not lead Mark to the person or persons he sought.

'We've got to get your father away where the smugglers won't find him.' His voice was firm and positive.

'I thought maybe thee could help if we went to London?' Emma put the suggestion tentatively.

Mark shook his head slowly. 'I don't think that would be any good. London isn't for the likes of your father. Although mine would help, I'm afraid yours would wither away with melancholia. He's a countryman, the city would kill him as it would you all. There's no life for any of you there. Besides, I want you here with me.'

A little of the despondency ebbed from her. She had feared that he might want to disassociate himself from her when he knew her father was involved in an illicit trade.

'No,' he went on, 'London isn't the answer, but going away could be. Supposing your father went away where the smugglers couldn't reach him? By the time he returned the mystery of the missing contraband might have been resolved and your father's innocence proved.'

A new light came to Emma's eyes. Mark was offering practical help. She hugged herself. She knew she had been right to come to him. 'Where would he go?' she asked as she placed her empty glass on his desk.

'I could arrange for him to be taken on a merchant ship, a month's voyage – time for things to be sorted out here.'

A great joy surged through her as the idea took hold. This certainly could be the answer to their problems. She jumped from her chair, unable to hold back her joy, and flung her arms round his neck and hugged him tightly. 'Oh, Mark, that's a wonderful idea. Pa must agree. When could he leave? The sooner the better.'

'There's a ship sailing tomorrow afternoon, carrying Roper goods. I'll see the captain. He and Silas are old friends. He'll take a passenger if I ask him.'

'Will he have to know why?'

'No. I'll tell him your father needs sea air for a chest complaint.'

Some of the gloom lifted from Emma. 'I'm so grateful for thy help. I'm so glad I had thee to turn to.'

'Let me go and see the captain now. His ship lies at the east quay. I'll not be long.'

Once the door had closed, Emma's mind started filling with doubts. What if the captain refused? How else could they get her father away? Could he ever escape from the smugglers? What if Zac discovered that he had been warned by Sue? She had risked so much and her life wouldn't be worth a penny then.

Emma jumped from her chair and started pacing the room, her restless fingers plucking at the end of her sleeves. What was taking Mark so long? Surely he should have been able to fix a passage for her father by now?

Dread was uppermost in her mind, raising the worst possible thoughts, when Mark hurried in.

'It's all arranged,' he cried eagerly.

Anxiety was lifted from her troubled mind. 'Oh, Mark, that means so much to me!'

'Your father must be on board by ten in the morning.'

'He will be.'

'What about the farm while he's away?'

'Oh, we'll manage. Not so much to do in winter.'

'Good. There's nothing else you want me to do?'

'Just be here when I need thee.'

'I will.'

'John, I think Emma's right, Mark's suggestion is a good one.' Grace emphasised her approval. She had been shocked at the news when she and Amy had returned from Drop Farm. She was afraid of the consequences should the smugglers strike, but drew on her iron-like strength to hide her true fears from her family. She had to be strong for them.

Young Jay, a little bewildered by it all, was reassured by

the attitude of his elders and strengthened his determination to do whatever was asked of him. Amy was staggered by what Emma and her father had revealed. She was numb at the thought of her father being involved in such a nefarious trade, though as the reason for it bit through her shock, she sympathised with him.

'But that means leaving thee with the farm to look after,' John protested.

'Better that than have thee dead,' replied Grace. 'As Mark said to Emma, the answer to the missing contraband may be found by the time thee returns. We'll manage the farm. Winter's coming, there'll be less to do. Jay's a good lad.'

'Joe will help where necessary,' put in Amy.

'That means he'll have to know why I've gone,' pointed out John. 'And the less people know the better.'

'All right, we'll ask him only if we really need to,' said Grace, knowing how much her husband would want to hide his predicament from the neighbours. 'If we have to, I know he'll be discreet.'

'We can trust him, Pa,' urged Amy.

'All right, it's agreed.' John made his voice firm and hopeful.

Any more discussion was stopped by a loud, determined knocking on the door.

The family cast anxious glances at each other. Jay looked at his father, trying to draw reassurance that this was not the smugglers. Grace bit her lip, hiding a tremor of alarm, wishing she had been here earlier so that John could have been away by now. Dread filled Amy. Did this mean there was no escape for her father? Emma felt drained, had her warning come too late? John hesitated, regaining control of himself.

The sharp rap came again. John pushed himself to his feet, whispered, 'Keep calm, act naturally,' and went to the door.

He hid his surprise when he saw Lieutenant Boston and

two dragoons. He had not heard horses approaching. When he glanced beyond the three men he saw the reason why. A third dragoon stood with the horses a short distance along the track. Lieutenant Boston had wanted to employ an element of surprise. Maybe he had even searched the outbuildings before coming to the house. Was this just a routine visit or had he some evidence which had aroused his suspicions? John knew he must be wary.

'Thee again. What does thee want this time?' John tried to keep the animosity out of his voice.

Boston's bearing was hostile, his voice cold as he rapped out his order, 'Search it!'

The two dragoons pushed roughly past John before giving him a chance to get out of the way.

Strong words of protest sprang to his lips but he held them back, saying instead, 'Thee's done this before and found nothing. Thee's still on a fool's errand. There's no contraband here.'

Boston ignored the remark as he strode into the house, his eyes watching for a reaction from the family.

'Ah, all the Dugdales here. Nice and cosy. Deciding what to do with the brandy?'

Grace was watching the two men rummaging through her cupboards and drawers, not caring how they upset them. She wanted to rush forward and stop them or at least protest about the mess they were making, but she held her temper under control. She would gain nothing if she let it get out of hand.

Boston's hand thrust out and grabbed Jay by the shirt front. He wrenched him forward and, bending down, shoved his face close to Jay. 'Where is it, boy?' he hissed. His eyes burnt with a menacing fire. Jay tried to hold back but there was no escaping the malevolent face.

'I . . . I . . .' he gulped, his eyes wide with fright.

'Leave the boy alone.' John's voice held hostility.

'Frightened he'll betray thee?' rapped Boston over his shoulder. 'Talk, boy.' He jerked on Jay's shirt.

He stiffened himself. 'I . . . I don't know what thee's talking about.'

Boston thrust him sharply away. Jay staggered backwards and would have fallen had not Emma grabbed him.

She glared at Boston who saw defiance in her stance. His eyes narrowed as he stepped close to her. 'Where's the silk for pretty dresses?' he asked sharply, hoping to catch some flicker of concern.

'We buy all our cloth from pedlars or in Whitby,' she answered coldly. 'Isn't that right, Ma?' she added to divert her mother's attention from the search and to calm the agitation she could see rising in her. It was an agitation which, if it rose unchecked, could spill over and innocently betray them.

'Er, yes,' replied Grace. The threat had been broken. 'Smuggled silks would never taint my hands.' She looked at Boston with disdain.

'Not even to make that beautiful dress your daughter had on at the theatre?' sneered Boston disbelievingly.

'Not even that,' she said haughtily.

'Nor this lace?' Boston had moved in front of Amy. His hands fingered her collar then slid over her small firm breasts. He felt her shudder and grinned at her.

Her lips tightened and her face clouded with a hatred which dared him to go further.

He was tempted, but he was here for another purpose. He met her look and laughed loudly. Suddenly he swung round on John and shot a question at him, hoping to catch him off guard. 'Know Zac Denby?'

'I know of him,' replied John calmly. Wits had to be kept sharp and he hoped the others were up to it. 'Don't know him personally.'

'Denby visit here?' He rapped the query at Grace.

'No.'

The two dragoons finished their search and reported that nothing had been found.

'Right, the rest of the house,' ordered Boston.

'Oh, no,' cried Grace, remembering the destruction of the previous visit.

As sharp as lightning, Boston was on to her. 'There's one way to stop it, Mrs Dugdale. Tell us where the contraband is.' Grace flinched.

Her family watched her with a mounting tension. They knew how upset she had been before. To have to face it again might break her resistance.

'There is none,' put in John quickly to bolster his wife's defiance. 'Why does thee think I'm involved?'

The query diverted Boston's attention and the officer turned to him.

'Denby needs more places to hide contraband than he has in Baytown and he needs to disperse the goods, so he gets sympathetic farmers who like the extra income to provide hiding places. Beck Farm is ideally situated.'

'Maybe it is but I'd have to be a willing ally and that I ain't.' John put all the conviction he could into his words. He met Boston's gaze unwaveringly.

The officer stared back at him for a moment, dropped his eyes and yelled, 'Get back here!' The two dragoons hurried into the kitchen. 'We're leaving.' His men left the house wondering at the sudden change of plan. Boston paused at the door. He turned and surveyed the family, hoping that he still might catch a hint which would condemn them, but all he saw were impassive faces gazing at him. 'I'll catch you farmers yet.' He breathed heavily with a determination not to be taken lightly and swung out of the house, leaving the door wide open.

The tension in the room dropped as the Dugdales relaxed, thanking God they had been spared the upheaval of Boston's last visit but still knowing they were not done with him.

The following morning Zac was up before first light. He wanted to be watching Beck Farm early to seize the first opportunity to carry out The Fox's orders. Maybe the chance would come if Dugdale went out into the fields to work or on to the moors to tend his sheep.

He spoke little as he had his breakfast and then prepared for his vigil. He armed himself with knife, pistol and musket so that he was prepared for any eventuality.

Dawn was breaking as he left a Baytown still enfolded in sleep. His steps were swift and with Beck Farm in sight he searched out an advantageous position from which he could see the house and the track to Whitby. He could move from here without attracting attention and could be sure of John's movements before making his own. He drew his short jacket closer around him against the morning chill, took a swig from his brandy flask and settled down to wait.

The eastern sky was paling to a new day when Lieutenant Boston mustered his men. His orders were brief as he instructed them to bring in five farmers for questioning. Relying on an instinct which had been bred in the Essex marshes, he figured these men allowed their farms to be used by the smugglers of Baytown. He had been unable to prove anything against them, his searches of their farms had produced no evidence, so now he was hoping that he could play one off against the other. For ease of bringing in the farmers and expediency in carrying out their task he ordered the operation to be carried out on foot, each man being armed with sword, pistol and a musket.

The sergeant and two men were dispatched to bring in John Dugdale.

'I've packed all thee'll need,' said Grace. 'Now get thy breakfast and be off with thee. The sooner thee's safe in that ship, the better I'll like it.'

As her father sat down at the table, Emma forked some sizzling bacon from the pan on to his plate and followed it with two fried eggs. Amy sliced some bread and Jay poured him a mug of tea.

'Thee's all very attentive this morning,' he said lightly with a grin.

'Don't know when we'll do it again,' said Emma, a catch in her voice.

'Soon, I hope,' replied her father.

'How long will thee be gone, Pa?' asked Jay as he put down the teapot.

'About a month, son,' said John between mouthfuls, 'and thee's the man in the family 'til I get back, so look after thy ma and sisters.'

Jay's chest seemed to swell. Assuming a man's responsibility he said firmly, 'I will, Pa, I will.'

John was pleased to see a shadow of a smile touch Grace's lips at her son's attitude. He knew how churned up with worry she had been last night.

'Don't fret about the farm, Pa,' put in Amy. 'I'll get Joe's help if we can't manage.'

'And I'll see if I can find out anything about the missing pedlars,' said Emma, 'then thee'll be cleared with Zac Denby.'

John looked up from the bacon he was cutting. His face was serious as he fixed his eyes on her. 'Thee be careful, lass. The smugglers can be ruthless folk.'

'I will, Pa. I'll seek Mark's help if I need to.'

The early sun gave off little warmth and the autumn chill still touched the valley as Grace helped John into his coat. There were tears in everyone's eyes as he made his goodbyes, giving his children a loving hug and a kiss. He held his wife tightly in an extra embrace, let his kiss linger and whispered, 'I love thee.'

He swung his bag over his shoulder as he strode away from the house along the track to Whitby. He paused at the rise, turned and waved and then was gone from sight.

Zac Denby stiffened. The door at Beck Farm had opened. His gaze scanned the distance. Dugdale! With a bag and dressed as if leaving. The family at the door. Final words.

Goodbyes. Dugdale certainly wasn't going to work. What was afoot? Did it matter? This might present the chance he wanted.

Zac watched. Dugdale left the farm by the track to Whitby. Zac saw him pause, look back and wave, then walk on with a determined step. He glanced back at the farm. The family filed back into the house and closed the door.

Zac scrambled to his feet, picked up his musket and, making sure he would not be seen from the house, paralleled the track taken by John. Once he had him in sight Zac matched his pace although he had the rougher terrain to negotiate. He kept searching the way ahead looking for a vantage point from which to complete his mission.

Engrossed in his own thoughts, John was not immediately aware of the three figures approaching from Whitby. Then he stopped. Dragoons! Were they going to Beck Farm? They were on the right track. Should he turn back to be with his family? But there was something about their manner and the fact that they were on foot and carried muskets which disturbed him. He had a premonition that it was not the family they were interested in, but that he was the object of their presence.

Confirmation came when he heard a yell directed at him and the men quickened their pace. He glanced round desperately. If he headed across the moor he might just have a chance to escape, for he knew the terrain and they were strangers.

He turned to his right and headed across the stunted heather, floundering and stumbling on the rough tufts but keeping to a good pace. He saw the three men leave the track in an attempt to cut him off. John pressed on, ignoring their yells for him to stop. He moved faster. If he could lose them and get to Whitby they would have no inkling as to where he had gone.

*　　*　　*

320

Zac was travelling in a long dip parallel to John's track, pausing now and again to check on his quarry. Half a mile ahead the dip swung closer to the direction Dugdale was taking and he resolved to carry out the killing there. He would be unseen and the body could lie on the moors undiscovered for some time.

He stopped in mid-stride. Shouts. Someone else on the moor. His mind filled with vexation. Was he going to be thwarted in his objective?

He dropped to his knees and crawled up the slight rise to seek the reason. He saw John cutting across the moor towards the dip pursued by three men whom Zac immediately identified as dragoons. He cursed to himself. What the hell were they doing here and why were they pursuing the farmer? Dugdale with a pack heading for Whitby – had he known the dragoons were coming and was trying to make an escape? Had the missing pedlars been taken by Lieutenant Boston and were being linked with John Dugdale whom he wanted for questioning? Zac's mind investigated the wildest possibilities until he pulled it up short. No matter what this scene was all about he was here for one purpose – to carry out The Fox's orders to kill Dugdale. Better to get him now before he was made to talk. Maybe the opportunity would soon present itself but the dragoons must not see him.

He crouched in the heather assessing the situation quickly. Dugdale would reach the dip less than a hundred yards from where Zac lay. He would make a perfect target as he topped the rise. Zac eyed the dragoons. The sergeant and two men were making good progress, in fact he estimated they had gained a few yards on Dugdale. John stumbled and fell and the gap closed even more before he was on his feet again.

He neared the rise. Zac saw the dragoons stop. The sergeant raised his musket to his shoulder. He yelled for his quarry to stop. John ran on, climbing the slight rise. The sergeant fired. The shot, meant to deter, boomed across the moorland, but John ignored the warning.

'Prepare to fire!' The sergeant's order rang out.

The two dragoons dropped on one knee and levelled their muskets.

Zac saw his chance. He put his own musket to his shoulder. He drew John into his sights and followed him, all the time listening intently. Still Zac waited. Dugdale was almost at the top of the rise.

'Fire!'

Zac squeezed the trigger and almost simultaneously heard other shots mingling with his.

John jerked, staggered, pitched forward and lay still. Zac knew he had carried out The Fox's order. He slid away through the heather, seeking the protection of a small hollow a few yards across the moor. There he lay prone, watching for the appearance of the dragoons.

A few moments later they appeared, breathing heavily with the exertion and shock of seeing Dugdale fall after their shots. Their chests heaving, they stared down at the body. The sergeant kicked it.

'Dead all right.' he grunted. He looked at his two underlings, his face dark with anger. 'What the bloody hell were you two doing? There'll be hell to pay for this.'

Disbelief creased their faces. 'I aimed in the air,' cried one, wanting to exonerate himself from all blame.

'So did I,' the other hastened to add.

The sergeant looked round. 'Then you didn't bloody well aim high enough,' he rapped. 'This damned rise must have brought him into the line of fire.'

'What do we do now?' wailed the first man as he pictured the lieutenant's wrath thundering down on them.

'Only one thing to do,' spat the sergeant. 'Take the body back to Beck Farm and report an accident to Boston.'

'But . . .'

The protestation was cut short. 'You suggesting we try to cover this up? Don't be a bloody fool. The truth would be sure to come out and then we'd be in deeper trouble. I'll try to cover it as an accident with Boston.'

The other two men muttered their thanks.

'Right, you two carry him, I'll bring his pack.'

A few moments later the little procession moved off in the direction of Beck Farm. Zac waited until he was sure he would not be seen and then made off in the direction of Baytown, safe in the knowledge that the dragoons would be seen as the killers of Dugdale, accidental or otherwise.

'Ma, I'm ganning to see if there's any rabbits,' Jay called as he went to the door.

'All right,' approved Grace, pleased that Jay, even with his father just gone, wanted to be active. It would keep his mind from dwelling on the revelations which must have stunned him. She pursed her lips thoughtfully as she watched him go. Maybe youngsters could cope better than adults imagined. Her mind turned to John and she hoped he would soon be sailing out of Whitby.

Once out of sight of the house Jay turned up the long slope to the moors. Maybe he could catch one more glimpse of his pa. He would miss him, miss helping him with the hedges and ditches, checking on the sheep, bringing them off the high ground for the winter; and through those hard months he would miss helping him repair tools and check that the barns and buildings would stand up to the harsh weather.

The crack of distant shots caught his ears. His step faltered. Strange, who could be shooting on the moors at this time? He quickened his pace, his sturdy legs driving at the soft turf. Reaching the top of the slope he stopped and let his eyes adjust to the distance. He could make out three figures in a group but there was no sign of his father. He wished his eyesight was as sharp as Amy's, she might have been able to identify the men even at this distance. He saw them bend and straighten as if they had lifted something. A sack? It seemed to weigh heavy between two of them. What were they doing? Curious, he watched them head across the moor towards the Whitby track but they did not turn in the direction of the town as he expected, instead they headed in the direction which would bring them past Beck Farm.

He concentrated his gaze on them. It flicked to the third man who was carrying something over his shoulder. A bag. It was familiar. His pa's! Jay's eyes shot back to the two men with the sack. Sack? That was no sack. Two arms flopped in time with the men's steps. Jay's mind turned over with shock. His pa's bag. They must be carrying his pa! He had heard shots . . .

'Oh, no!' The words were drawn out in a sad cry of disbelief and despair. He turned and ran, his stride lengthening with the slope towards the farmhouse.

'Ma! Ma!'

Grace looked up from the baking she had started doing to take her mind off John's departure. A chill gripped her for she had recognised alarm in Jay's cries. Something was wrong. She glanced at Emma who was stoking the fire to get the side oven hot for the baking. She saw that her daughter too had sensed trouble in the shouts.

'Ma, Jay's in trouble.' Amy sensed it too.

As one, all three headed for the door, Grace wiping her hands on her apron. Emma flung it open and they stepped outside. They saw Jay hurtling down the slope so fast that his feet seemed barely to touch the ground. They knew there was trouble and rushed forward to meet him.

'Ma! Ma!' He slid to a halt, gasping for breath. His eyes were wide with fear of the unknown, for he was not certain of the significance of the news he was bringing. 'It's Pa,' he gulped. 'Or I think it is.'

Grace grabbed him by the shoulders. 'What's happened, Jay?' she cried. She wished she could read his mind.

'Two men are carrying him. Dragoons, I think. There were shots.' The words tumbled out as he strove to catch his breath.

Alarm chilled Grace. Her face drained of all colour. She

released her grip on her son and stepped past him to hurry up the slope. Shots? Her mind was numb. John must have been hurt. She must be with him. She was oblivious to everything else. Emma and Amy, their minds full of thoughts of what they might find, were but a step behind her with Jay panting alongside them.

Three figures appeared against the skyline. Grace stopped in her tracks, her whole world frozen by what the cortège could mean. Her children stood beside her. Emma, dread clawing at her heart, slipped her hand into her mother's as much for her own comfort as to comfort. Amy stared disbelievingly as the procession started towards them. That unwieldy bundle carried by the two dragoons couldn't be her father. She sensed Jay shudder and her arm came round his shoulders as if to protect him from the truth.

They stood, frozen in time, until the full implication of what she was seeing became clear to Grace. 'John!' His name rang from her throat and she started to run. The terror in her heart erupted when she yelled his name again. Then she was beside him, unwilling to believe what was evident to her eyes. 'John, John!' she cried as she dropped to her knees and reached her arm across him, willing him to respond to her touch. But his head lolled to one side when the dragoons laid him on the ground. With tears streaming down her cheeks, Grace touched his face, hoping there would be some response, but there was none. Sobs racked her body as she stared at the man who only a short time ago had been so much alive.

Emma and Amy, with silent tears flowing freely, drew close to her. The shock of the truth had numbed all feeling. After a few moments, when the fact that her father was dead had registered on her mind, Amy slipped her arm through her mother's, hoping that in some small way she would draw support from it. Emma just stared at the face which would never smile at her again. Her father lay there like some moorland bird struck down by the hunter. A life finished by one shot, a life which should have gone on much longer, bringing joy to the people who loved him. Ended. Why? Anger at this waste when he'd had so much more to give welled inside her and boiled over.

She looked up, her eyes ablaze. 'Why did thee kill him?' she snarled. She was trembling with the after-effects of shock and her fury embraced the three men.

'Ma'am, it was an accident,' muttered the sergeant who had laid her father's pack on the ground.

'Accident? What does thee mean, accident?' she snapped disbelievingly.

'We were sent to take him into Whitby for questioning. He made off across the moor when he saw us. We shouted for him to stop but he didn't. We fired warning shots as we had been instructed if there was any attempt to make off. I'll swear they were only meant to be a warning but something went wrong. We didn't mean to kill him.'

The two troopers muttered their agreement.

As much as she was raging inside, what could she say to these men? If they had really meant to kill him, would they have brought him to Beck Farm? Would they be admitting to the killing? Wouldn't they have just left the body on the moor with no one the wiser as to who had done the shooting? There was the ring of truth about the explanation.

'Did Lieutenant Boston order thee to arrest my father?' she asked.

'Yes, ma'am. And we'll have to face his fury. He's lost a man he wanted to interrogate.'

Grace looked up. Though she still wept she had regained control of herself. No matter how much she hurt she knew she must be strong for her children. 'Will thee take him to the house?' she asked in a sad whisper.

'Yes, ma'am.'

As the mournful procession wound its way silently down the slope, Emma was stunned by the sight of her father's body but her mind kept recalling what she had just heard.

These dragoons had been ordered to detain her father and take him in for questioning. Why, when Boston had visited them only yesterday? Emma was puzzled. What had made him want to question her father again? These men had been told to stop him. Stop him from doing what? Had Boston known he was leaving? But how could he? Only the family knew he was going.

Only the family – and Mark!

Emma felt numb, as if all life had been drained from her. Mark had betrayed them! She had thought she could trust him. She had divulged a secret which she had thought would be safe with him. Instead he had used it to help Boston in his fight against the smugglers. But what had he gained? Nothing. Her father was dead. Now he could not be interrogated, Boston could not learn anything.

Mark's treachery had been for nought. She shuddered. All the time he had been pretending to arrange her father's escape, he had been planning to use it for his capture. But it had gone drastically wrong.

Tears filled her eyes again but now they were tears for a love betrayed and destroyed so soon after its blooming.

Chapter Twenty

'Emma, someone is going to have to go into Whitby to tell thy uncle and aunt.' Grace's weeping had stopped after she had left the bedroom where her husband's body lay. Alone, outside the door, she had paused and stiffened her resolve to be strong for her family before going down to the kitchen where her children, still in a state of shock, were making some pretence at being busy.

'Yes, Ma,' replied Emma. 'Do thee want me to drive thee in the trap?'

'I'd rather stay here with thy pa.' Though she knew it sounded strange, it seemed a natural thing to say and want to do. 'I'll be all right,' she added, seeing concern come to her daughter's face. 'I'll have Amy and Jay.'

With Jay's help, Emma soon had the horse saddled, and when she had changed she left for Whitby.

After about a mile she came out of the bewildered daze which had gripped her ever since she had seen those men carrying her father's body and had realised that only one person could have informed the dragoons that he was leaving. Every action since then seemed to have been carried out as if reality was playing tricks on her. But now, with the sharp air tingling on her face, the real world impinged on her and her mind concentrated keenly on the events which had shattered her family.

As bruised as she was, she fought the desire to shut out the horrors and focused her mind on events, seeking some way to release Mark from blame. She could find none. It was only after she had exhausted every possibility, coming each time to the fact that Mark must have betrayed her father, that her anger at him began to deepen and lay a relentless hold on her mind.

As she left her aunt and uncle trying to come to terms with the tragic news, her fury at Mark rose to the surface. She had not mentioned her father's connections with the smuggling nor her suspicions regarding Mark to them, but now, with her mind still dwelling on him, she decided to confront him before returning home.

She flung open the door of his office without knocking, not caring if anyone was with him.

His look of annoyance at the sudden intrusion vanished when he saw Emma, only to be replaced by one of alarm and bewilderment at the sight of the smouldering anger darkening her pale face.

'Why?' she demanded in a voice which would brook no nonsense.

'Why what?' he asked, his eyes widening with surprise.

'Why did thee do it?'

'Do what?' He rose from his chair and started to come from behind his desk, all the time looking at her with eyes pleading for an answer.

'Betray my father.'

'What are you talking about?' He stood beside her and took her arm. 'You are obviously upset about something. Do sit down and calm yourself.'

She shook herself free and stepped away from him. 'I don't want to sit down. I don't want to be in this room with a traitor any longer than I can help.' Her eyes were cold and hostile.

This was a different Emma to the one with whom he had shared pleasant days since his return to Whitby and he was beginning to feel annoyed. 'Betrayal, traitor . . . I don't like to hear you accuse me like this.' Irritation had crept into his voice though he kept his words cool.

Emma drew herself up. 'My father was shot by the dragoons who had been sent to stop him leaving. Only the

329

family and thee knew he was going to seek a passage out of Whitby – a passage thee had arranged!'

For a moment Mark was thunderstruck by the news. 'Your father . . . dead?'

'Aye, thanks to thee.'

'But I know nothing about it,' he protested.

'That's exactly what I expected thee to say,' she sneered.

'I did *not* tell the dragoons,' replied Mark quietly but firmly, trying to will Emma to believe him.

'No one in the family did and that only leaves thee who knew he was going.' She bit her lip, holding back the tears which threatened as she felt all the love she had nurtured for Mark dying. 'I hate thee for what thee has done, and I'll never marry thee now.'

He reeled from her words as if he had been struck in the face. He reached out as if to fend off blows and stop her accusations. 'I didn't . . .'

'I don't believe thee!' Her eyes blazed with fury born in the depths of hate.

His denials were lost as she swung round and left his office, slamming the door shut behind her.

'What will thee do, Grace?' Robert asked when the family had sombrely settled themselves with a cup of tea in the withdrawing room of the house in Bagdale.

The burial of John in the churchyard high on Whitby's cliffs had conformed to all the usual ritual. The family gave strength to one another in this time of deep sadness. Sympathy had been profuse from those attending the funeral but when Mark came to offer his condolences he met only cold aloofness. Saddened, and wondering how he could prove his innocence, he hurried from the churchyard.

Now, with the front door closing on the last of the mourners who had come to the house, Robert approached the subject of the future.

'I'm not sure yet,' Grace replied. 'The farm was John's life. I'd like to keep it going for his sake.'

'It will be hard,' put in Matilda. 'Why don't thee come and live in Whitby, be near us?'

Grace gave her sister-in-law a wan smile. 'That would be very nice, but I do have to earn a living. There's the family to think of. We have a roof over our heads now. The landlord is sympathetic and willing to let us stay there so long as the land is not neglected.'

'Can thee work it?' asked Robert doubtfully.

'That's something I will have to consider carefully. The children, well . . . Emma and Amy are young women now. They are supportive and want to stay. Amy and Jay are the two interested in farming, Emma not so much, but thee knows her – she'll give of her best no matter what she undertakes.'

'Well, I'm afraid neither I nor my sons can offer anything in the way of practical help, we're not farmers, but if there's anything else I can do, please don't hesitate to come to me.'

'Thanks, Robert, and thee, Matilda. It is a comfort to know thee are here.'

Three days later when Emma came out of the cow byre carrying two pails of milk, Joe was just turning into the yard. He hurried to her.

'Let me take them, they're heavy.' He took them from her hands.

'Thanks, Joe.'

'How is thee?' he asked, aware of the strain and worry the family must be facing.

'All right,' she replied. 'Trying to believe it still. We miss Pa.'

'Of course thee does and will do for a long time,' he said sympathetically. 'How's the farm work?'

'We're managing now but I don't know how we'll do when spring comes, bringing more work.'

'Aye, it will that,' he agreed. 'That's what I've come to see thy ma about.'

Beside him now, feeling the gentleness and understanding in him, pangs of regret stabbed at Emma's heart. Wouldn't it have been better to have submerged her dreams of Mark in the love Joe had offered her? She would have had a dependable man for her husband and an assured life, but she had thrown it all away. She had destroyed his love for her and he had turned to Amy who had seized the chance when it came her way. Hadn't Meg warned her? Now she had no one.

She opened the door to the kitchen and let Joe enter.

'Hello, Mrs Dugdale,' he said as he placed the pails on the stone slab near the door.

'Hello, Joe,' Grace replied brightly. She was pleased to have a visitor, especially someone who would divert Amy's introspection.

'Hello, Amy, Jay.'

They returned his greeting, Amy with a welcoming smile. She had seen him briefly after the funeral and had been hoping that she would see him again before long.

'Emma tells me thee's managing the farm at the moment but are worried about the spring.'

'Aye, lad, I am. We'll miss John's pair of hands as well as his planning, though Amy's good at that, knowing what there is to do. But I don't know whether we'll manage the physical side. If only Jay had been a couple of years older.'

'I'll do it, Ma,' he said staunchly. He was determined. Hadn't his pa told him he was the man of the house when he was away?

Grace gave a wan, understanding smile but knew Jay couldn't cope with all the hard physical work at his age. She sighed. 'We'll see, but it could be that we'll have to give it up.'

'We can't do that, Ma!' cried Amy. 'Thee knows how Pa had his heart set on buying this place. We must do it for his sake.'

'If only we could,' said Grace wistfully, knowing how much she would like to achieve her husband's dream.

'Thee could borrow from Uncle Robert?' suggested Amy.

Grace shook her head. 'No, that would be breaking faith with thy father. He knew he could do that but he wouldn't, he was too independent. He wanted to achieve it on his own. He had seen his brother make good and wanted to do the same.'

'Then we'll do it between us.' All eyes turned on Joe, surprised by this unexpected statement. 'Knowing how much thee all want to stay here, I came with a proposition and my father approves.' He hesitated and glanced round them all.

Grace was aware that he was serious but she also saw the light of excitement in his eyes. 'Sit down, Joe,' she said, prepared to listen to any suggestion which might help them retain Beck Farm.

The rest of the family, wondering what Joe had to say, came and sat round the table.

'Well, thee's going to need help so Pa has agreed that I should come and work here as necessary. Sometimes it may be only half a day, other times it may be two or three or even a week.'

'But what about thy work at Drop Farm?' queried Grace.

'Pa's been thinking of taking on a hired hand. Now he's decided to do it, it will allow me to come here.'

'Payment? How could we pay thee?'

'No need,' replied Joe, then added with a smile, 'maybe a slice or two of thy curd pies, but it will be payment enough to see Amy every time I'm here.' He glanced at her with a twinkle in his eyes and saw her blush.

Amy avoided her mother's glance, thinking she would give nothing away about her feelings for Joe, but there is no fooling mothers and Grace had long suspected that her younger daughter was in love.

'Very well, Joe. Maybe we can do what John wanted,' agreed Grace. 'Thank thee, and please thank thy father.'

'We'll do it. We did it at Drop Farm so we'll do it here and make the future secure for us all. I've come to realise how fond I am of Amy and I don't want to lose her because she has to leave here. We both love farming, Drop Farm will be ours one day, and . . .'

Amy's mind reeled. Ours? Had the word just slipped out or did Joe mean it? 'Ours?' she gasped. 'Is thee proposing, Joe Wade?'

Joe stared at her, then realised what he had said. His face coloured but a chuckle broke through his lips. 'I suppose I have, but I'll ask thee again when thee comes out of mourning.'

Amy gulped and looked at her mother. A smile crossed Grace's face but before she could make any comment Jay cried out excitedly, 'Then we'll have two farms between us.'

'Aye, lad, we will,' grinned Joe. 'Maybe thee'll marry and have this one,' he added teasingly, knowing it would embarrass Jay. 'And we'll be able to take our bairns to visit Aunty Emma Roper in Whitby.'

Emma stiffened to hear the idea put so lightly, for Joe, like other folk, knew only that John Dugdale had been accidentally shot by dragoons.

Emma was quiet. She felt relief at Joe's suggestion but the mention of relationships struck at her heart. The future might look well for the farm but hers looked bleak, though Joe did not know it – an old maid living with her brother and his family.

That night she cried herself to sleep with the words drumming in her mind: 'Why, Mark? Oh, why did thee do it?'

Two days later when Joe, Jay and Amy had gone to bring the sheep off the moors for winter, Grace took the opportunity of bringing up the question of the contraband with Emma.

'I want it off the farm as soon as possible. Thy father would never tell me where it was hidden. He said it was better if only one of us knew, but from what thee said about following him, thee knows.' She held up her hand to stop the words Emma was about to utter. 'I don't want to know where it is but I do want it removed.'

'That'll mean contacting Zac Denby,' Emma pointed out. 'Thee wants me to do that?'

'Aye, lass, if thee will. But thee will have to be careful. It means ganning into Baytown, and they aren't all that friendly to outsiders. Thee could be walking into trouble when thee reveals to Denby that thee knows where the contraband is.'

'I'll take care, Ma.'

'Then be off with thee while the others are busy. The sooner this is sorted out the better. We're sure to get a visit from the dragoons again and I don't want them coming across the contraband.'

'I don't believe they'd ever find it,' returned Emma.

'There's always the chance, so it's better gone.'

Curious and suspicious glances were cast in Emma's direction as she walked through Baytown. They made her feel uncomfortable and unwanted, but she held herself erect and kept up a determined step. She kept her shawl tight around her head even though the houses offered protection against the wind, whose full strength she had felt as she crossed the moor.

Halfway down the hill she stopped in front of two middle-aged women who were standing on a doorstep gossiping and speculating about the young woman, a stranger in Baytown.

'Can thee tell me where I can find Zac Denby?' she asked pleasantly.

The two women exchanged a quick glance and Emma sensed them draw together as if for protection.

'I have a message for him. It's important,' offered Emma by way of explanation.

Their second glance at each other carried with it signs of acquiescence. This young woman seemed genuine. If it

335

was important, they knew better than to delay the message reaching Zac while they conducted enquiries about this newcomer.

'Try the Fisherman's Arms, bottom of the hill,' said one of them as she retied her hessian apron. The other nodded her agreement.

'Thanks,' said Emma with a smile, and left them pondering about her.

Fishermen idling beside two cobles drawn up from the beach at the bottom of the hill eyed her with curiosity as she entered the inn.

She found herself in a dingy corridor with shouts and laughter coming from a room on her right. Just as she reached the door it was flung open and the noise thrust at her. A man staggered out of the room, almost colliding with her. He pulled up sharply, surprised by what he had found in the corridor.

He leered at her as she pressed against the wall in an endeavour to get away from his beer-smelling breath as he peered closely at her. 'Looking for me?' he asked suggestively.

'No. Zac Denby. Can thee tell me if he is here?' Emma tried to sound unworried by his attentions.

The man hesitated but in that brief moment she saw him glance at a door further along the corridor. It was shut and the man seemed to draw courage from that fact. He leaned closer to her. 'And if I tell thee, do I get a favour?' He placed one hand against the wall close to her shoulder and the other reached out to fondle her. She shrank from him and in one quick movement dipped under his outstretched arm and stepped quickly towards the closed door. Glancing over her shoulder, she heard the man give a grunt of contempt and saw him turn and stagger back into the room.

She rapped sharply on the door and was relieved when she heard the sharp command, 'Come in,' even though it was in a female voice.

She opened the door and was met by a delicious smell

of stewing meat and home made bread. The curiosity on the face of the well-built woman who stood beside the table, arms up to the elbows with flour, still lingered even when she gave a welcoming smile. There was no mistaking the man who sat at the table, a tankard in front of him. The patch over his left eye would have betrayed him but Emma knew him for the man she had seen with her father in Black Wood and at the old barn. She was face to face with Zac Denby who now regarded her with interest touched with hostility.

'Mr Zac Denby?' she asked tentatively as if she did not know the man in front of her.

A chuckle came from deep in his throat and his one eye lit up with amusement. 'It's a long, long time since I was called Mister.' He straightened and looked hard at her. 'Aye, I'm Zac Denby, what's thee want of me?'

Emma glanced at the woman and back at Zac, hesitating to answer his question.

'Thee can speak in front of Nell,' boomed Zac.

Emma nodded.

'Sit down, lass.' Nell's tone was friendly and she put Emma more at ease when she offered her a cup of chocolate which Emma gratefully accepted.

'Well, what is it?' asked Zac.

'I'm Emma Dugdale, John Dugdale's eldest daughter.'

'Sorry to hear about thy pa,' he offered. 'Nasty business. Uncalled for from what I hear.'

'Aye, it was.' Emma was amazed at the gall of the man, sitting here calmly condemning the dragoons, yet if it hadn't been for them he could well have carried out the killing. Contempt burned in her but she kept an iron control on her feelings. Nothing must alarm Denby. 'I'm here,' she went on, 'because I know of the contraband and where it is hidden.' She saw a spark of surprise touch Zac's face but then it was gone.

His one eye narrowed. It was no use denying the contraband's existence. Dugdale must have taken at least one member of the family into his confidence. 'Anyone else know where it is?'

'No.' She surprised him when she added, 'I followed Pa and thee one night.'

'Oh, did thee now? Maybe thee learned more than's good for thee.' There was no mistaking the threat behind the words.

Emma stiffened but met his gaze unflinchingly. Though she felt nervous inside, she kept a level voice as she said, 'Don't threaten me, Zac Denby. If anything happens to me, my family has a letter which will go straight to the authorities, telling them what I know.'

Zac grunted as he leaned back on his chair.

'Thee move that contraband and we'll forget thee ever used Beck Farm. That way my father's name will not be connected with the smugglers.'

Zac looked thoughtful as he said, 'Thee's a determined lass.'

'Aye. I want my way and I'll get it.' She fixed him with a look which would brook no nonsense.

'Thee could make a pretty penny if thee lets us gan on using the hiding place on Beck Farm. It's so good . . .'

'No!' The word came like a pistol shot, leaving Zac in no doubt that no matter what he said, this young woman would not see things his way. 'I want that contraband removed as soon as possible.'

Zac's lips tightened, his face grew grim. 'Very well, but it may be spring before we can move it.'

'What? Leave it there all winter?'

'Might have to. Thee'll have heard about our run in with the dragoons?' Emma nodded. 'Well, I can't use another pony-train for a while. The dragoons will be keeping a watch, just the same as I reckon they'll be keeping an extra watch on Beck Farm if they were suspicious of thy father. I've got to use pedlars to move the contraband from there and it ain't always easy to find someone I can trust. Besides, in winter the pedlars won't be coming.'

338

Emma took a sip of her chocolate.

'Zac's right, lass,' put in Nell to strengthen his argument. 'With the dragoons becoming so active, it's wise to lay low for a while.'

'If I can I'll move some before spring,' promised Zac. 'But if I think it better not to it'll have to wait. It's such a good hiding place, as thee knows. Nobody'll find it, not even the nosy Lieutenant Boston.'

Emma realised there was nothing she could do about it. She couldn't force Zac to move the illicit goods immediately and so accepted his word that he would do so as soon as possible.

She was agreeing when the back door opened and Sue came in. She showed surprise at seeing Emma. 'Miss Dugdale, nice to see thee again.' She removed her shawl and hung it on a peg.

Emma was quick to realise that the use of the address 'Miss Dugdale' was a warning that they should appear no more than acquaintances. 'And thee, Mrs Thrower,' she said.

'Thee two know each other?' Zac cast a glance at them both.

'We met when I called at Beck Farm to enquire the way to Baytown when I came looking for Ben,' Sue explained.

'Have thee heard anything of him?' asked Emma.

'No.' Sue shook her head. 'It seems he's completely disappeared. I had thought of going back to Pickering but I changed my mind. If I'm going to learn anything I think I must search the area where he was last seen.'

'I wish thee success,' said Emma. She drained her cup and stood up. 'Well, I think that concludes our business, Mr Denby. I expect to hear from thee as soon as possible.'

Ten minutes after Emma had left the Fisherman's Arms, Sue made an excuse to go out again. Careful not to be seen, once she had left the village she took the track she knew Emma would have followed. They were halfway to

Beck Farm when Sue caught her first sight of her friend and was able to call to attract her attention.

Emma heard the shouts and when she saw it was Sue she waited.

'I was surprised to see thee with Zac,' she said, gulping air after her strenuous efforts to catch up. 'I don't know what it was about but please be careful in thy dealings with him. He can be a dangerous man.'

'Thanks for the warning, I'll be careful.'

'Sorry about thy father.' She laid a comforting hand on Emma's arm.

'Thanks. It'll take some time to get used to not having Pa around, and it still hurts to think he was betrayed by Mark Roper.'

'Betrayed?' Sue looked puzzled.

'The dragoons were coming to arrest him. They must have been told he was leaving. Only the family and Mark knew that. It was Mark who planned it all, getting Pa a passage on a ship that very morning when the dragoons turned up. Only he could have told them.'

'Oh, I'm so sorry.' Sue bit her lip and remorse showed on her face. 'Maybe if I hadn't warned thee about Zac . . .'

'Thee did right,' cut in Emma to exonerate her friend from any blame. 'If my pa had got away all could have been well, but there was someone determined he shouldn't escape.'

'I hear the dragoons say it was an accident?' said Sue.

'Aye. It seems likely. They wouldn't shoot to kill if they wanted Pa for questioning.'

Sue looked thoughtful. 'Early that morning Zac left Baytown armed with a musket. I didn't know it until it was too late to warn thee.'

Emma looked curiously at her. 'Is thee saying Zac could have shot Pa?' She shook her head. 'No, it couldn't have been. The dragoons have admitted it. Besides, no one else was seen on the moor.'

'Well, if the dragoons have said they did it . . . But Zac is a wily bird. And thee be careful about dealing with him.'

'I will. I came to see him about moving the contraband from the farm. We want nothing more to do with it.'

'And is he?' There was a touch of distress in Sue's voice.

'Aye, but it may not be until spring. He says it'll have to be moved by pedlars and as thee knows winter will curtail their activities. He doesn't want to do anything immediately because the dragoons are more active.'

A look of relief came over Sue's face. 'Thank goodness. Pedlars moving the contraband from Beck Farm are the one lead I have which might tell me what happened to Ben.'

'Thee be careful,' said Emma, showing concern for her friend's safety.

'Emma, thee can gan to market today. Amy wants to see to getting the sheep on to turnips.'

'But doesn't Amy want to go with Joe?' asked Emma.

'Aye, I'd like to,' called Amy as she was tying her boots, 'but the sheep have to be seen to. Joe understands.'

'It'll do thee good, make a change. Thee'll see Meg. So away and get ready,' urged Grace. She had seen that John's death had weighed heavily on her daughter and that the betrayal by Mark had left a deep scar. To get away from the farm for a few hours, and especially seeing Meg, might help to take her mind off the recent traumas.

'Comfortable?' asked Joe shortly after they had set off at a steady pace.

'Yes, thanks,' she replied, realising he was the same thoughtful Joe as he had always been. She had been a fool to direct her love elsewhere.

'I'll not come to thy aunt's, thee'll have family matters to discuss and I'll be in the way.'

'No, thee won't, Joe.'

'Thee wants time with Meg. Besides, I have some things

to see to in Whitby so I'll call for thee about half-past three.'

They rode in an uneasy silence for a while until Emma broke it. 'I hope thee and Amy will be happy.' She kept regret that she was not in Amy's place out of her voice.

Joe glanced at her, grateful for her understanding and that she bore him no ill-will. 'Thanks. Maybe things have turned out for the best. Thy refusal to marry me made me see how much I cared for Amy. And thee's found Mark.'

His words pierced her heart. Mark! If only Joe knew, but Emma would say nothing. To do so would be to reveal her father's connection with the smugglers and knowing Joe's strong views about illicit traders, she realised any connection between them and the Dugdales might destroy his feelings for Amy.

By the time they reached Whitby, Emma's thoughts had turned to her conversation with Sue and her observation that Zac, armed, had left Baytown early on the morning of her father's death. She did not see how he could be implicated but maybe another word with Boston, even though she disliked the man, might elicit fresh information.

Since the day of his confrontation with Emma, Mark had constantly asked himself questions, trying to get into perspective John Dugdale's involvement in the smuggling, the missing pedlars, Zac's threat and the shooting. He searched for answers in his anxiety to clear himself in Emma's eyes. He pondered as to whether Zac had taken it upon himself to condemn John, or whether the order for the assassination had come from higher authority. He thought the latter most likely but proving it would be difficult, especially as the dragoons had accepted responsibility for John's death. And what of the contraband at Beck Farm? When Emma had revealed the facts about her father he had hoped it might lead him to the man he sought but now that tenuous link had gone unless Zac persuaded the Dugdales to continue working for him.

With these thoughts in mind Mark made his way to the market square where he hoped he might see Emma if she had brought produce to the market.

He weaved his way through the crowds crossing the bridge and turned into Sandgate where the buildings on either side seemed as if their upper storeys were trying to meet and form a tunnel to the market place. Here there was activity as the vendors tried to catch the attention of potential buyers in the crowd which worked around in a seemingly unending milling movement. Mark threaded his way towards the steps of the small Town Hall, only slightly bigger than a tolbooth, a name by which it was sometimes known, where folk from the country displayed their market produce and where Mark hoped he might see Emma. He searched for her face over the heads of the crowd and was more than pleased when he saw her standing at one corner.

He pushed a little harder to get through the mass of people but held back a step when he saw she was dealing with a customer. He stepped forward when the transaction was finished and as she straightened from her basket he said in a quiet, friendly tone, 'Hello, Emma.'

Her expression changed abruptly. Her face darkened and she felt her flesh tingle with contempt. 'What do thee want?' she asked without any attempt to disguise the disdain in her voice.

'I'd like to talk. There are things which must be put right between us.' His eyes searched for a chink in her armour but found none.

'We have nothing to say to each other after what thee did,' she replied haughtily.

'Please, Emma, give me a chance to explain,' he pleaded.

'I'm busy,' she returned curtly.

'I'll buy the lot then you won't be,' he urged.

'Don't be ridiculous,' she snapped.

'But I need to talk to you.'

She was about to open her mouth to object when she felt a gentle grip on her shoulder. She glanced round to see

Joe, who had been selling his eggs at the opposite corner of the Town Hall.

He nodded at Mark with a smile. 'Hello,' he greeted, and then turned his eyes on Emma. 'I've sold everything. If thee wants to gan off with Mark I'll sell the rest of thy butter and eggs and meet thee this afternoon as arranged.'

'But . . .' she began, then realised that to refuse the offer would mean offering an explanation to Joe.

'There you are then,' put in Mark quickly. 'You can't refuse that offer.'

Emma was caught. She nodded to Joe and stepped down to join Mark. They left the market-place for Church Street and walked towards the Church Stairs.

He touched her arm lightly to guide her through the stream of people going about their everyday business. He drew hope from the fact that she did not pull away, but she viewed it as only a helpful gesture.

Once they were clear of the immediate crowds he said, 'Emma, I did not betray your father. I don't know why the dragoons were coming at that time.'

'To stop him,' she replied coldly. 'They must have known when he was leaving and only thee could have told them.'

'I didn't. Believe me, Emma, I wouldn't have had thee hurt for the world.' He put all his sincerity into his voice. His eyes pleaded with her to believe him.

Her heart skipped a beat when she saw the vulnerable look on his face. There was a genuine frankness in his eyes as they searched for her reaction and pleaded for her trust. She wanted to believe him but the evidence was against him. How else could the dragoons have known about her father? They had accepted blame for the killing. The information from Sue that Zac had been on the moor crept into her mind. Could Zac . . . ? Impossible. Should she mention it to Mark? Part of her wanted to and yet another part warned her against it for he would be sure to seize on it to prove his innocence and she wanted no more deceit, no more lies.

344

'So thee says, but what else can I believe?'

'I know it looks bad for me, but I'm telling you the truth. Look, I want to help. If the contraband is still hidden at Beck Farm let me help you get rid of it, then you will be clear of any hold the smugglers may have on you.'

Emma stiffened. What was Mark up to? Accept his help and she would have to tell him where the contraband was hidden, a place Boston had never been able to find. Tell Mark and how easy it would be for him to inform the Lieutenant. Her family could end up under arrest. Boston could lay a trap for Zac, and Sue's only likely chance of finding out what happened to Ben would be gone.

'Trying to get more information for Lieutenant Boston?' snapped Emma contemptuously.

'No,' cried Mark, alarmed at her wrong interpretation of his offer. 'I only . . .'

'Thee don't fool me.' As she stared at him, this handsome man whose return to Whitby had caused her love to blossom, she felt her eyes filling with tears. She glared her hatred and hostility at him. 'I never want to see thee again,' she screamed, turned and ran.

He took two steps after her, reached out as if he would prevent her leaving, but stopped. He shook his head in despair. What could he do to make her see he was telling the truth?

Emma saw one or two curious glances cast in her direction as she reached a point where there were more people. She slowed to a walk and turned into a narrow thoroughfare which led to a small section of the harbour. Reaching the end she stood staring into the water, trying to compose her thoughts and feelings. She was hurt deeply. Mark had tried to use her again. Her life lay shattered.

As she walked back to Church Street with her feelings under control she remembered that on her way to Whitby she had resolved to visit Boston. Was it still worth it? As she pondered the question she realised she had turned in the direction of the Custom House, where Boston had been

345

given an office with access from the outside, independent of the entrance to the rest of the building.

Emma hesitated and then started forward again. She had nothing to lose by having a word with him. She was still about fifty yards from the Custom House when she saw Mark hurrying towards the building with a determined step. She stopped and watched him. A cold hand gripped at her heart when she saw him enter Boston's office. She remembered Mark's remarks at the theatre. He must be helping Boston. She had been right. He had been trying to get information from her to pass on to the officer.

Emma waited, watchful for Mark's leaving. After ten minutes he left the building and went along Sandgate in the direction of the bridge. When he passed from her sight she went to Boston's office.

'Ah, Miss Dugdale, a pleasure to see you.' Boston jumped to his feet when she came in. 'Do sit down.'

'I'll stand, thank thee,' she returned coldly.

'As you wish. What can I do for you?'

'My father's killing. Thee accepts thy men were responsible?'

'Yes, but it was an accident. My men fired warning shots. Unfortunately one of them aimed too low. It is regrettable and I'm sorry.'

'Why was thee coming for my father?'

'I wanted to ask him a few more questions.'

'Why couldn't thee have done that at the farm?'

'I had my reasons and they are no business of yours,' replied Boston irritably. He was getting annoyed at being questioned by a slip of a woman.

'How did thee know he was leaving?'

Boston held up his hands. 'No more questions,' he snapped. 'You are seeking answers which don't concern you.'

'The visitor thee's just had – what did he want?' Emma

shot the question hoping to catch Boston off his guard but he was too crafty.

'What goes on in this room is private. If you want to know you'll have to ask him, Mark Roper's a friend of yours. Now, no more questions, you must leave.'

Emma bit her lip, holding in check the frustration she was experiencing. She knew it was useless to prolong the confrontation. She glared at him, swung round with a haughty swish and stormed from the office.

She had gained no further knowledge except that in Boston's refusal to speak she had read a sign of Mark's guilt.

Chapter Twenty-One

Shattered by the further evidence against Mark, Emma made her way to the bridge. She was oblivious to the people around her. Her body felt numb, her mind in a daze. Deep down she had held a hope that she had been wrong about Mark, even though she couldn't see how. Now that hope had been completely destroyed.

As she came from the protection of the buildings on to the bridge, the breeze stung her cheeks and the cry of the seagulls challenged her senses. She became aware that she had automatically headed for her aunt's. She needed to get control of herself before she arrived. Halfway across the bridge she paused to gaze along the river towards the sea. She breathed deep on the salty air and, with the feel of it inside her, settled herself down.

If she was the least bit agitated Meg would sense it, their relationship was so close, and with an explanation would come the revelation about her father.

But she need not have worried for when she arrived at the house in Bagdale she immediately knew that her cousin was just bursting to tell her something and that her own excitement was overriding all other thoughts.

Meg ushered her into the withdrawing room almost before Emma had taken off her coat and hat.

'I was just dying for thee to get here before ma comes back,' cried Meg, her whole body quivering with the information she was eager to impart.

'Why? What is it?' Emma asked earnestly as she was swept into her cousin's enthusiasm.

'I'm going to have a baby!'

Emma gasped. Her eagerness to hear Meg's news

vanished and her expression changed to one of concern. 'But, Meg . . .'

'Don't look so troubled, Emma. I'm not. Be happy for me. Please?'

The initial shock which held Emma in stiff disapproval was tempered by Meg's joy so that she could not but feel happy for the cousin she loved so dearly. She hoped everything would go smoothly for her. If not then Meg's problems could be more serious than hers.

'Oh, Meg, if thee's happy so am I.' She gave her arm an affectionate squeeze. 'When is it due?'

'It's early days yet,' said Meg as they sat down on the sofa, still holding hands. 'Thee's the first to know.'

'Aunt Matilda doesn't know?' Emma's eyes widened with surprise.

'Not yet. Nor does Edward but he will later today. We are dining with his father. Oh, I hope he'll be as pleased as I am.'

Concern touched Emma's face as she asked, 'And how is he going to take the news? What if he doesn't want to marry thee?'

'Oh, don't say that,' protested Meg with a troubled frown. 'I'm sure he will. He must!' In her mind she willed him to. The frown vanished. Her eyes brightened. 'Oh, I love him so. He's so thoughtful, kind and considerate. He's exciting, interesting and so full of life. And I know his father will be thrilled. He's dropped hints about Edward having a son and heir. He's a nice old man and I know he likes me.'

'Then I'm so pleased for thee,' enthused Emma, 'and I'm sure Edward will be. Thee'll certainly want for nothing marrying into the Beaumonts.'

'Nor will thee with Mark Roper when the time comes,' said Meg. 'Oh, we'll both be so happy.' She smiled and, leaning forward, hugged her cousin.

Even in her happiness for Meg the words hurt, but she would say nothing to spoil her cousin's gaiety.

* * *

'Will thee stop, Edward, please?' asked Meg as he turned the horse and trap between the stone pillars of the gateway to Thorpe Hall.

He looked at her with curiosity, wondering at the unusual request. 'Why? Something wrong?' he asked with concern.

'No.' She smiled, laying a reassuring hand on his arm.

He pulled the horse to a halt. The air was still, the afternoon breeze having faded with the approach of evening. The trees, many of their leaves lying carpet-like along the drive to the house, intertwined their branches into an unmoving canopy.

The pale light softened his features, making him more handsome. Meg's heart raced faster.

'What is it?' he prompted when he detected a slight hesitation.

She met the enquiring look in his dark brown eyes. 'Edward, I'm going to have a baby.'

The silence lay heavy for a moment until it was broken by a curt query. 'Mine?'

Meg was shocked by the question. She was startled, almost frightened, but did not give way to the anxiety which welled up in her mind. 'Of course. I've been with no one else. It's thee I love.'

Edward had tensed with her announcement. His mind whirled this way and that. Hell! He wanted no brat messing up his life. He didn't want tying down. The girl would want him to marry her. Well, why not? He knew she loved him. Physically they were good together, she better than some others he had taken to bed, and she was attractive, a pretty lass with a good brain. She had poise and was a good mixer. She'd make a good wife. Maybe he did love her. Whatever, he needn't be tied down if he married her, there was still a life to live. Besides, marriage might make it even better. Hadn't his father always said he would make him a settlement once he married a girl he approved of?

He knew his father liked Meg and she had been sensible enough to see that he did.

His initial horror softened, a new light came to his eyes. 'I didn't mean anything by it, love. It was just the surprise.' He leaned towards her, taking her hands gently in his. 'I'm pleased.'

'Are thee truly?' Meg's brow furrowed with doubt and she looked earnestly for a reassuring answer.

'I am.' He ran his fingers gently across her forehead. She relaxed at his touch. 'There,' he smiled, 'I've wiped the worry away from your brow.' He bent and kissed each eyelid gently. 'And I've banished it from your eyes.'

She looked at him with adoration. 'Oh, Edward, I do love thee so,' she whispered.

He met the look which had set his whole being yearning for her. 'And I you.' His kiss moved quickly into passion and power as he took her into his strong arms, crushing her yielding body to him.

He felt a new exhilaration when he picked up the reins and sent the horse along the drive towards the house. 'We've something to tell Father tonight,' he said with a chuckle. 'Not the baby,' he added quickly. 'That must wait until after the wedding.'

'No one will know until the right time,' agreed Meg.

'And so the wedding must be soon,' he added decisively.

'As soon as thee wishes.' She sighed with contentment and slid closer to him, snuggling into the arms he held out to her.

Mark spent an uneasy day. He was annoyed that he had been unable to persuade Emma that he was innocent of her accusation, and his enquiries with Lieutenant Boston had gained him no more knowledge than that the dragoons accepted responsibility for what they saw as an accident. Boston had stated that there was nothing more to be said, he could not allow his men to be questioned by a civilian, he had done all the questioning that was necessary and that was the end of the matter.

Mark had been almost on the point of revealing that he was working for Sir William Bailey, head of the Customs Board, and demanding the right to question the dragoons, but he figured Boston's influence over his men would be too powerful for him to wheedle any more information out of them. Besides he deemed it advisable to keep his role as an undercover agent still a secret. He wanted no possible leak to become a warning to the brains behind the illicit trading.

By the end of the day, recalling the smuggling talk at the party at the Dugdales, he decided that his best lead might be to approach Hugh Lomas.

Accordingly the next day he rode out to the Lomas residence in the Esk valley.

As he halted his horse beside the six steps leading to the imposing colonnaded entrance, the front door opened and Hugh Lomas strode out. He was an impressive figure dressed in a dark magenta tail-coat with frilly cravat tied neatly at the throat, topping a white shirt, and tight brown breeches which ran into brown calf-length boots.

'Greetings, Mark Roper, what brings you out here this chilly morn?' His voice boomed amiably.

'A word with thee, sir, if I may encroach on your time?'

'Certainly. Come in.' He drew a deep breath and then yelled at the top of his voice. 'Oliver! Oliver!'

There was a scurry of feet from the archway to the left of the house which Mark judged led to the stables. A boy of about fifteen raced into view. 'Sir! Coming, sir!' he shouted.

'Good lad,' laughed Lomas. 'Take care of this gentleman's horse.'

'Yes, sir.' He glanced at Mark as he took the reins.

Mark smiled. He fished in his pocket, then flicked a coin in the air which Oliver caught with a sweep of his hand. His face lit up, his eyes widened. 'Thank thee, sir, thank thee.' He started to lead the animal away.

'See you take good care of it,' called Lomas. He grinned at Mark. 'He's a good lad, place wouldn't run without him. Now what can I do for you?'

Mark walked up the steps. Hugh opened the door and stood back to allow Mark to enter the house.

They came into a square, high-ceilinged hall with an imposing stairway, heavily balustraded beside the left-hand wall. The little furniture around the hall was of excellent quality and, when Hugh took him into a room on the right, Mark saw that it too spoke of money.

'Welcome to my study,' said Hugh with a smile.

A large desk stood across one corner with the light coming from the left from a tall window which looked out on to a well-kept, walled garden to which access could easily be gained from a door beside the window, making it almost a private extension to the study. The rest of the room was comfortably furnished around the focal point of the fireplace with its ornate mantelpiece, and was in no way dominated by the desk as a symbol of work. Fine paintings hung on the walls and a long oak sideboard was set with decanters and fine glassware.

'A glass of Madeira before we talk?' offered Hugh. He crossed the room to pour the wine. He returned with two glasses, proffering one to Mark with a friendly smile. 'Do sit down.' He indicated a wing chair to one side of the fireplace and took the opposite one himself. He raised his glass. 'To you, Mark, may this visit be the first of many.'

Mark raised his glass. 'Thanks, and the best of health to you.'

He was struck by the atmosphere of wealth and he wondered if any of the finances to furnish this house so elegantly, to run it and work the estate, had come from smuggled goods. Indeed, could the man sitting before him be the person the authorities wanted to unmask?

'Well, what can I do for you?' asked Hugh, leaning back in his chair, his gaze concentrated on Mark, weighing him up.

He had liked what he had seen at the Dugdale party but now he could assess him more closely and get on good terms with him. He had always found it wise to have a good relationship with Whitby's merchants, especially those who conducted foreign trade. He figured Mark would have a shrewd business brain, otherwise his father would not have entrusted him with the Whitby branch of the firm when Silas Brent retired.

'I've had time to settle into the business and I hope to open up one or two new ventures. I recalled your talk of the smuggling trade and how most people benefited from it and reckoned I might be foolish to turn a blind eye to the money I could make if I became involved.'

'You're seeking my advice?' queried Hugh.

'You appeared to be sympathetic towards the smugglers so . . .'

'Sympathetic merely from a selfish point of view because I would miss my cheap brandy and gin and the lace for my lady if smuggling was wiped out,' interrupted Hugh. 'Approve? Ah, we shouldn't approve illicit trading even though these people see themselves as pursuing a legitimate business as free traders.' He chuckled at the niceties of his phrasing. 'So what is it you're after?' He sipped his wine and watched Mark closely over the rim of his glass.

He was aware of the scrutiny and again wondered if he was sitting with the man whose brains organised the whole operation.

'Well, I see two things.' Mark leaned forward as he warmed to his subject. 'First I can deal in smuggled goods and make a nice profit.'

'True,' agreed Hugh. 'But you would have to be careful you didn't encroach on other merchants doing the same thing.'

'That I wouldn't do. I'm running a business in an important port so I see it would be advantageous to have my own ship and Whitby is noted for its shipbuilding. I could then ship the goods to London and make more profit than

I could restricting my operation to Whitby. And that leads to my second point – with a ship I could run contraband to Whitby or unload it off Baytown.'

'You've certainly been doing some thinking and those ideas could work. But why are you telling me all this? Aren't you frightened that I might tell the authorities?'

Mark gave a wry smile. 'If I'd thought that, I wouldn't have told you. After you expressed your views at the party I felt fairly certain I was on safe ground talking to you.'

Hugh chuckled. 'You're a shrewd judge, Mark Roper. I'll not betray you. In fact, if you want any financing for this enterprise, I'll back you.' He paused then added, 'But I don't think you've made the point you've come about. Your propositions mean nothing to me, they would only mean something to someone in authority . . .' His voice trailed away. He stared at Mark. As the realisation dawned on him, he started to laugh. It began as a low noise in his throat but was soon a full guffaw. 'You thought I was the brains behind the smuggling,' he gasped, and shook his head. 'Well, I'm not.'

Mark hid his disappointment and cursed himself for letting his imagination cloud his judgement.

'If you're not, then who is?' he asked.

Hugh shook his head. 'I don't know.' He saw a look of doubt come over Mark's face. 'It's true.' He made his voice firm to reassure Mark he was being straight with him. 'Whoever runs the smuggling, it's the best kept secret in these parts.'

'How do I get in touch with him?'

'You'll never be able to contact him face to face. Who can? Who does? No one knows. You've told me you're interested, I'll pass on that information to my contact and the word will go on from there. How and by whom, I don't know. If The Fox – that's how folk know him, because he's so wily – if he's interested in you, he'll have someone contact you.'

'But there must be someone, the final contact, who knows who he is.'

'True, I suppose, though you never know. He may have a system of receiving and relaying messages which precludes personal contact,' Hugh pointed out.

Mark nodded. 'But surely, with a proposition as important as mine, The Fox, as you call him, would want to discuss it in detail.'

'Who am I to know the workings of his mind?' He spread his hands in a gesture of resigned acceptance. He leaned forward, his face serious as he looked hard at Mark. 'A word of warning. Don't you ever try to find out who he is. You could end up dead. The smugglers are ruthless and The Fox will do anything to preserve the secret of his identity. There's a lot of money at stake. You can be part of it if The Fox approves and as long as you are content to play your part without questions. Now, with that warning, do you want me to pass the word along? If not I can assure you that nothing that has passed between us will ever come out.'

Mark had listened intently. He knew if he let his ideas go forward he would be walking a very thin tightrope which could easily break. If ever the true reasons behind his propositions came out he would be dead, but he owed it to Sir William Bailey to try to unmask The Fox. Besides, it could lead to his proving the truth to Emma.

'I'll be in,' said Mark firmly.

Hugh chuckled. 'Only if The Fox says so. I'll pass the word. You'll be contacted sometime.' He rose and recharged their glasses then raised his. 'To good profits and lace for my lady.'

A week later, sitting in his office, Mark puzzled over a piece of paper on which was written, 'Armstrong's farm three o'clock tomorrow'. It had just been brought to him by one of his clerks who had received it from an urchin as he was returning to the office.

Mark could not figure out who had sent such a strange message for he had no knowledge of anyone called Armstrong, let alone where his farm was. He soon gained the information from his staff that the farm lay between Whitby and Baytown but it still meant nothing to him. He examined the writing again. It was ill-formed, an uneducated hand. If this was a message from The Fox it certainly hadn't come directly from him. His only way of solving the matter was to keep the appointment.

So it was that the next afternoon, armed with pistol and rapier, Mark left Whitby on horseback.

The day was dry but dull with only the occasional shaft of sunlight breaking through the clouds to pass over the landscape and be gone. Rain had threatened from the west all day but when the clouds reached the coast they came to nothing. But Mark had little time to consider the weather for his thoughts were on the mysterious summons.

He topped a rise and pulled his horse to a halt. The farm he judged to be the one he wanted lay close to the bottom of the long slope. He sat still, eyes probing the buildings and the surrounding land. He was puzzled. There was no sign of life. From this distance it looked as if the place was deserted, yet the house, its neighbour, which bore the resemblance of a cottage, and the rest of the buildings appeared to be in a state of good repair. Yet nothing stirred, no human, no animal.

Mark felt uneasy. The unease which had settled on his mind was suddenly broken by the plaintive cry of a curlew in lonely flight. He started, took a grip on his feelings and set the horse at a walking pace down the slope.

He directed his gaze on the buildings but saw no one, not even when he circled to the front. He sat for a moment looking around him. The area was tidy, the buildings cared for, so it seemed strange that they lacked life. Puzzled, he slid from the saddle and, looking about him, walked to the house. The only answer he received to his knock was a fading sound in the depths of the building. He went tentatively to the windows, looked in and was puzzled even further. The rooms looked lived in yet there was no sign of anyone. If this was where he should be at three o'clock, why was there no one at home?

He turned away and started towards the cottage but seeing no curtains at the windows changed direction to the buildings across the cobbled yard. Mark's lips tightened in exasperation when he looked inside. There were no horses in the stable, no cows in the byre.

Mark swung on his heel and hurried outside. Why had he been brought here? Why was there no one to meet him? His temper was rising. He would examine the cottage and if that gave him no clues he would leave.

He lifted the sneck on the door and pushed it open. He hesitated as it swung back with a squeak and he inclined his head, listening. With the fading of the sound an unsettling hush seemed to descend on the cottage. He stepped into a room which ran the length of the building. The flagged floor was well swept. The only pieces of furniture were two chairs facing each other in the middle of the room. A door in the opposite wall was closed. Mark opened it. He looked into what had been a kitchen but was now bare of anything resembling a work room.

Exasperated at having been lured on a fool's errand, he swung round determined to leave. He pulled up sharply, startled by the sight of a small man leaning against the outside doorpost observing him from one eye, the other being covered by a black patch.

Mark's hand automatically went to the hilt of his rapier. 'Who are you?' he snapped.

The man straightened. He was not as small as he had first appeared but even so Mark judged him to be about five and a half feet. He saw it as no sign of weakness for there was power in his body and the bearing of a man who would stand no nonsense. Mark also detected a ruthless streak in him, a man who would not pull back from the worst crime if it would further his cause. Could this be

The Fox? For one moment Mark considered it possible but there was something about the man which suggested otherwise. He was clothed as a fisherman and did not carry that aura of gentlemanly authority which Mark deemed necessary to the brains behind the organisation. There was a shrewd crafty air about him and Mark immediately got the impression that this man had been observing him ever since he had arrived at the farm.

'Zac Denby,' came the clipped answer.

Mark was surprised. He had not expected the head of the Baytown smugglers to be the contact. So this was the notorious Zac Denby. Mark knew he would have to be wary in his dealings with this man. He knew of his reputation and realised he was not a man to be trifled with. He also realised that Zac must have a high standing with whoever ran the whole operation for he was vital to its final success. Maybe he could use Zac to gain the information he wanted but he would have to exercise the utmost caution.

'Pleased to know you,' replied Mark, relaxing into affability.

'Is thee?' Zac gave him a wry crooked grin as he came into the room. 'If we have to talk we may as well sit down.' He eyed Mark as he did so. 'Before we start, what passes between us in this room goes no further.' There was no mistaking what the consequences would be if it did so.

'I'm no fool,' replied Mark, an edge to his voice. 'I have a lot to lose if it did. And don't you forget, that works both ways.' He was determined to show that he was not intimidated by the reputation of this man.

Zac stiffened. His one eye flared with annoyance at the implication behind the words, but before his retort was uttered Mark went on.

'We aren't here to parry words, let's get down to business.'

'Right. Thee have some propositions to put to me?' Zac listened intently while Mark explained. 'The ship could be most useful,' he agreed. 'But thee'll understand that when it's used for smuggling it will be under strict orders which must be followed to the letter and it'll have to have a trustworthy crew.'

'It's not my idea to supply the crew, only when it's used for a legitimate trading voyage. When it's used for smuggling, you or your superior, whoever he may be, will have to hire the crew.'

Zac pursed his lips doubtfully but said, 'Might be a good idea, but we shall see. I'll pass on thy message.'

'I'd rather do it myself.' Mark shot the remark quickly, hoping he might catch Zac momentarily off guard, but the smuggler was alert.

'Can't be done,' he replied, and added before Mark could ask why, 'When will the ship be ready?'

'Late spring. The keel's just been laid.'

'That will be soon enough. With winter coming there'll be no smuggling. Difficult to get the goods inland, cut off as we will be by snow. If thee's wanting to deal with contraband we might be able to arrange something before then.' Zac stood up, signifying that there was nothing more to be said. 'I'll make my report and thee'll be contacted again.'

That same day the Dugdale house in Bagdale was full of excitement as plans for Meg's wedding were pushed ahead.

With Edward's father delighted by the prospect of his son's marriage and Meg's parents more than pleased that she would be marrying into a local wealthy family, a New Year's Day wedding was agreed upon to comply with the wishes of the young couple.

Matilda's time was full and would be until the important day was over. She had determined that nothing but the best was good enough for her daughter who would be marrying a Beaumont. Today she fussed around, advising and hinting, as Meg, Emma and Amy chose the material and the design for the bridesmaids' dresses. After all the chatter and excited laughter that had gone on for three hours they were ready for the tea and cakes which were served at three o'clock.

'I have the invitations,' said Matilda as she poured the tea. 'Would thee like to take Joe's, Amy?'

'Certainly, Aunt,' she replied. 'It will give me an excuse to go and see him.'

'And thee, Emma, does thee know if Mark has moved into his house yet? There's been deliveries of furniture but I don't know whether he's moved yet.'

'I wouldn't know, Aunt,' she answered in a flat tone.

Matilda raised a quizzical eyebrow and glanced at her daughter. Meg gave a slight shake of her head. She knew nothing and was as surprised as her mother at Emma's attitude.

'But I thought thee and Mark . . .'

'We don't see each other any more,' cut in Emma.

Matilda realised it was better to pursue the matter no further so she let the subject drop.

Meg was concerned for her cousin. She was dying to know what had happened to crush the dreams Emma had held for years, but the opportunity to question her in private never arose before it was time for the sisters to leave.

As they closed the door after seeing them off, Matilda turned to her daughter. 'Do thee think I should send the invitation to Mark in view of what Emma said? After all we were inviting him for her sake?'

'I think we should. I'm sure it's only been a lovers' tiff. Maybe I can get them together again at the wedding.'

Zac quickened his pace. He did not want to be late for his next appointment with Mark.

At his last meeting with The Fox, it had been suggested that they test how genuine Mark Roper was in his desire to handle contraband.

Accordingly Zac had drawn up a note stating a time and date for a meeting at Armstrong's Farm. Sue wrote the note so that the handwriting differed from the previous one written by Nell.

Arriving at the farm he made straight for the cottage and only had a few minutes to wait before he heard the clop of an approaching horse.

'Good day, Zac,' greeted Mark as he came into the room and saw him sitting on one of the chairs. Zac nodded. 'What do you want this time?'

'Sit thee down and take a swig of that.' Zac handed him a flask.

Mark took it, sat down and removed the top of the flask. The aroma of brandy swept over him like some enticing goddess. He nodded his approval with a smile, raised the flask to his mouth and drank. He licked his lips with relish as he passed it back to the smuggler. 'A top class brandy,' he commented.

Zac grinned. 'Thee knows brandy.' He approved Mark's judgement. 'We handle only the best through Baytown.'

'I could do a good trade with that in London,' said Mark eagerly.

'How many tubs could thee handle?' queried Zac.

'A tub?' Mark looked thoughtful as if considering. 'Four gallons. Well, I could start with a hundred.'

Zac raised his eyebrow. 'As many as that?' There was a shadow of doubt in his voice.

'I reckon I could dispose of that number,' confirmed Mark without hesitation.

'Thee knows the risks?' warned Zac. 'Especially running them into London.'

'I know my port authorities,' replied Mark firmly.

Zac shrugged his shoulders. 'That's up to thee. Once the brandy is on board thy ship, it's thy responsibility.' He eyed Mark closely as he went on: 'If thee's caught don't try to implicate any of us at Baytown, or The Fox. Thee'll be a dead man wherever thee are.' The cold threat in his voice left Mark in no doubt that he was playing a dangerous game.

'You have some brandy for me?'

'Not a shipment. We're looking ahead to spring. There are arrangements to be made. But I can let thee have a tub for thy own use.'

'Please,' replied Mark.

'Reet, be here same time tomorrow. I'll have it for thee.'

'I can collect,' suggested Mark quickly.

Zac gave a short laugh. 'And let thee know our hiding places?' He shook his head. 'It'll be here for thee.'

'What about some lace?' asked Mark, thinking he might be able to use it to sweeten Emma's attitude.

'Aye.' Zac gave a sly grin. 'Who's the lucky lady?'

'None of your business.' Mark smiled wryly. 'If you have secrets, so have I.'

As soon as Zac reached Bay he sought out Sue. 'I gathered the other day that thee and Emma Dugdale are friendly?'

She was immediately on her guard. 'Not friends, only acquaintances.'

'Well,' Zac gesticulated with his hands, 'thee knows each other. Thee could call at Beck Farm again?'

'Aye, I could. Why?'

'I want thee to take a message to Emma and tell her I will be in Black Wood this evening half an hour before sundown to collect some contraband.'

Sue knew better than to question further. Reaching for her coat and shawl she merely said, 'I'll gan reet away.'

Emma entered Black Wood with caution. Grace had insisted that Jay accompany her and now Emma was glad she had done so. Though it was still light, darkness would come soon as clouds obscured the sun. The wood added its own gloom and Jay moved a little nearer his sister as they moved among the trees.

'Where will he be?' he asked in a whisper as if his normal voice would rouse unearthly beings.

'We'll go where I saw him meet Pa,' replied Emma, matching her intonation to his.

They moved forward slowly, looking about them. The sudden snap of a twig startled them. They stopped, eyes trying to pierce the fading light, until they realised that it had been Jay who had stepped on the twig.

'About here,' said Emma in a low voice when she had estimated they were near the spot where she had seen her father and Zac Denby meet.

They waited. A chill came to the air. Jay shivered.

'Cold?' his sister asked.

She accepted his nod though she suspected he had shivered more with uneasiness and apprehension than with cold.

'Tuck thy scarf in,' she suggested.

Jay pulled it more tightly around his neck and was tucking it into the front of his jacket when he was startled by a voice.

'What the devil's he doing here?' The words were snapped harshly.

Emma started. They both swung round to find Zac standing about three yards behind them. They were shaken by the fact that they had not heard a sound, nothing to indicate that he was near until he had spoken.

Jay's eyes widened with amazement. He swallowed hard and took a firm grip on his feelings. He was here to protect his sister and protect her he would, even against this sturdy man with one eye.

Emma was glad that her mother had insisted on Jay's coming for she felt some comfort in his presence. She forced herself to face Zac with confidence.

'Company for me,' she replied firmly.

Zac grunted. 'He stays here until we get back.'

'He does not!' Emma's eyes flared defiance.

'He's not seeing where the contraband is hidden,' rapped Zac, irritated that someone should challenge his authority, and a woman at that.

'I'll tell him, if thee doesn't take him along.'

Zac's lips set in a tight line. 'I could have just come and taken what I wanted but I played fair with thee because it's worth money to thee and I'd hoped thee would continue to let us use the barn.'

'And I did right by thee by not telling Lieutenant Boston where the contraband was hidden.' She eyed him unflinchingly. 'Now, let's get on with the job thee came to do.'

Zac hesitated. His one eye glared at Jay sending a shiver down his spine. 'Keep thy mouth shut about what thee's going to see, or else . . .' Zac left the threat unspoken but gave it clear meaning as he drew his hand sharply across his throat.

Jay shuddered with fright.

Emma put an arm round his shoulders. 'No need to scare the boy,' she snapped, glowering at the smuggler.

Jay drew himself up. 'I ain't scared, Emma.' He felt her hand tap his shoulder comfortingly. 'Truly I'm not.' He drew deep on his courage and said to Zac, 'Well, are we going or not!'

Reaching the edge of the wood Zac indicated to them to stop. He carefully surveyed the intervening ground and the area around the barn. Satisfied that there was no one about, he signalled to them to move forward.

They crossed the field to the barn quickly and once inside the tumble-down building paused for breath. Jay's eyes widened with amazement when he watched Zac uncover the entrance to the underground room. He had played here on summer nights and had never known of its existence. Zac found the hidden lantern, lit it and held it so that all could see their way down the steps.

Once at the bottom, he held it high. It sent light dancing around the room which was more like a cavern. Jay stood transfixed by the sight of tubs, barrels, chests, boxes and bales stacked around the room.

'When will thee get all this taken away?' she asked, her gaze moving incredulously across the contraband.

'I told thee, lass, we can't start moving it before the winter snows have gone. All I want now is a couple of tubs of brandy and some lace.'

As he was speaking he had been uncoiling a rope which he had brought with him. He selected two tubs and arranged the rope over his shoulders so that it held one tub across his chest perfectly balanced with the second one across his back. He tested them for comfort and then, from the bales, selected a role of lace.

'Fine stuff,' he commented, glancing at Emma. Maybe he could bribe her into allowing him to keep using the barn.

She stepped forward so that she could see it more clearly. He moved the lantern. Its glow picked out the intricacies of the delicate work.

'Beautiful,' she murmured, as she fingered the intertwining threads and drew her hands across the unusual pattern where mice were intertwined with oak leaves.

'For a special customer,' said Zac as he rerolled the piece he had opened out for her to see. 'Thee could have some if I could go on using this place?'

'No,' she replied unwaveringly. 'I want nothing more to do with smuggling. Look what happened to my father.'

Zac made no reply. He tucked the lace under his arm and they left the room.

Jay helped him cover the entrance so that it could not be seen.

'Thanks, lad,' he said. 'Wouldn't have been easy with these tubs on.' He eyed Jay with a more friendly look. 'And remember, not a word to anyone, *Anyone*, about what thee's seen tonight.'

'No, sir.'

'Not even Ma or Amy,' added Emma.

'I won't,' confirmed Jay with determination.

'Reet, then away home with thee,' said Zac. 'Thanks, lass,' he added. 'I'll contact thee again about the rest of the contraband.' He turned and fell into a steady stride towards Black Wood. Emma and Jay cut across the fields for Beck Farm.

Mark Roper collected the brandy and lace from Armstrong's Farm and returned to Whitby with the tub carefully disguised in a large bag. Once they were safely hidden in his house in Bagdale, he went down the road to the Dugdales'. His knock was answered by a maid.

'I would like to see Miss Meg Dugdale, if you please,' he requested amiably. 'Is she at home?'

'Yes, sir. I'll see if she is receiving visitors.' The maid smiled politely. 'Whom shall I say is calling?' She put the question as she had been taught even though she recognised the caller.

'Mr Mark Roper.'

'Yes, sir. Please step inside.' She held the door while Mark entered the hall. She stood by the open door and bobbed a little curtsey when Mark passed her with a word of thanks.

'Mark, how delightful to see thee.' Meg, hearing his arrival, came to meet him with outstretched hands.

He took them in his as a greeting and bowed to her.

'Do sit down. Will thee take tea?' She had gone to the bell-pull beside the fireplace.

Mark raised his hand. 'No, thank you. It is very kind but I only have a few minutes.' Meg smiled and went to a chair on the opposite side of the fire to him. She looked at him, wondering as to the purpose of his visit.

'Meg, I need your help.' She noted a touch of pleading in his voice.

'If I can,' she agreed.

'You may know that Emma and I have had a little difference?'

'I suspected something,' replied Meg. 'Emma and I are close, we share most things, but whatever happened between thee she has kept to herself. A lover's tiff?'

'Call it that if you like. As Emma has not confided in you, I must respect her wish.'

'Quite right,' replied Meg, though she was a little disappointed that she had learned no more.

'I want to patch things up with her as soon as I can. I have a present for her which I hope will do that. I don't want to take it out to Beck Farm, so I wondered when she was next likely to visit you and if I could come here to see her?'

Meg liked being part of a conspiracy. Besides, wasn't this just ideal? Get them together now and then firm the relationship at the wedding. 'Easily arranged,' she agreed, a note of intrigue in her manner. 'Emma is due here tomorrow at half-past eleven, she's coming about the bridesmaids' dresses. Come about twenty-past, then thee can see her before we take up her time.'

'Thanks, Meg, I'll be here. I'm so grateful to you.'

'Only too pleased to help. We must patch up the quarrel between thee and look forward to another wedding.' The teasing twinkle in her eye showed she revelled in the role of matchmaker.

The following morning Meg guided Mark into the same room, saying, 'I'll show Emma into here when she arrives. I've briefed Ma and everyone that they must keep out of here until after thee's gone.'

'Thanks, Meg.'

'Oh, don't thank me.' She waved a dismissive hand. 'Just do it by making up with Emma.' She eyed the roll in his hand with curiosity but saw that she was not going to be told what it was. 'Thee must excuse me, I've a lot to do, but I'll see Emma comes in here as soon as she arrives.'

The next ten minutes were an eternity to Mark. He paced the floor, fidgeted with the roll, looked at the paintings on the wall but didn't really see them, and tried to come to terms with the empty feeling in the pit of his stomach. He chided himself for being so nervous but that did not help.

He swung round to face the door when he heard voices in the hall.

'Meg, I hope I'm on time.'

Emma! His heart beat faster.

'Of course thee are.'

He imagined Emma taking off her coat and hat.

'We'll be in here.'

Meg was as good as her word.

The door opened. Meg gave Mark a quick knowing look, then stood to one side to let Emma enter the room.

She came in, all smiles. They vanished when she saw Mark. She turned sharply on Meg but the door was already closing. Annoyance clouded her face as she swung back to face him.

'What are thee doing here?' Hostility sharpened her tone.

'It was the only way I knew of seeing you on neutral ground.'

'Thee dragged Meg into this. What did thee tell her?' demanded Emma haughtily.

'I told her nothing. She thinks it's some minor tiff. She's keen to see us on friendly terms again and was willing to help me.' He looked hard at her, searching for a chink in her antagonism. 'Please, Emma. I don't want this rift.'

'It's of thy making.'

'Believe me, I did nothing.' He held out the roll. 'A peace offering. Let's start again.' As he spoke he allowed some of the lace to unroll.

It caught her eye. Immediately she was taken by the exquisite work, but then she froze when she saw the unusual motif – mice intertwined with oak leaves!

Chapter Twenty-Two

Emma stared disbelievingly at the lace. She felt numb, mesmerised by the sight of it. Her eyes came slowly to Mark but she could not interpret his look of anticipation, of hope that he had made the move towards friendship and beyond.

His half smile faded to be replaced by an expression of bewilderment, for her eyes were cold and condemning. 'What is it?' he asked, his voice low as if to speak too loudly would bring catastrophic results.

She gave a half cry of uncertain meaning and, with tears flowing profusely, ran from the room, leaving the door wide open.

Meg, who was coming down the stairs, stopped and stared in disbelief at her cousin who ran past her. She hesitated and half turned to see Emma run into her bedroom, slamming the door behind her. Meg hurried down the stairs and reached the front room just as a bewildered Mark came out.

'What happened?' she asked.

'I don't know,' sighed Mark. 'She was put out because you had been involved, but I had hoped that we could resolve our differences. I brought this lace as a peace offering. She looked at it, then turned and ran.' He threw up his hands in despair. 'Why, I don't know. What must I do to win her back?'

Meg eyed him shrewdly. 'Thee loves her?'

'Truly.'

'And I know she really loves thee. Whatever has come between thee must be destroyed. What is it, Mark? Can't thee tell me? I may be able to help.'

He hesitated. He was almost on the point of telling Meg

but drew back. 'If Emma tells thee, then I'll speak too. Until then I must respect her wishes and say nothing.'

Meg nodded her understanding, admiring his loyalty to her cousin who, for some reason, seemed to want to have nothing more to do with the person she had held secretly in her heart since schooldays. 'I'll see what I can do.'

When Mark had left, Meg hurried up the stairs to her bedroom where she found Emma sprawled on the bed weeping into the pillow. Meg sat down gently beside her and laid a comforting hand on Emma's shoulder.

'What's the matter, love?' she asked softly.

'That man, that cruel man!' cried Emma. 'Why did thee bring him here?'

'Come.' Meg exerted a slight pressure on Emma's shoulder. 'Come here.' She took her cousin into the comfort of her arms and let her cry. 'Hush now, if he's as bad as that he's not worth crying over,' she said when she felt the worst of the tears were over.

Emma sniffed. Her mind had dwelt on the shock of seeing the lace. Zac must have given it to Mark, so he must be working with the smugglers. Sue had said the smugglers were going to kill her father. Had they been behind the killing, working through Mark's information to try to lay the blame on the dragoons? If so, it had worked and Mark had been the betrayer. Whichever way she looked at it, she could not get away from this last condemning fact.

'But I think thee still love him,' went on Meg.

Emma straightened quickly, staring indignantly at her cousin with reddened eyes. 'How could I after what he's done?'

'Talking about it might help,' Meg suggested.

'Oh, I can't, not even to thee.' She sank against Meg and sobbed until the tears ran dry.

New Year's Day dawned bright but with an invigorating sharpness to the air. The snow which had come the previous week had been light and had almost disappeared from Whitby, though on the moors, where the falls had been heavier, it still lay deep.

Emma had thrown off the hurt, determined to get on with life. She was swept into the excitement generated in the bride-to-be's home and shrugged off the feeling that she was being left behind by her cousin and by Amy. Though she saw herself turning into an old maid and some-times let tears fall in the silence of her room, she hid her feelings and put on the appearance of happiness for the sake of her cousin.

The wedding took place in the parish church on the cliff top and gaiety, after the solemn vows, swept through the party afterwards. Matilda, who was determined that her daughter should have only the best, had revelled in organis-ing a sumptuous reception in the imposing setting of Thorpe Hall which, along with his staff, Edward's father had been only too delighted to put at her disposal. He took pleasure in lending the female touch to such an event, something he had missed since the death of his wife whose parties had been the highlight of Whitby's social scene.

Cornelius was content. At last his son had found a girl whom he reckoned was good for him. He had taken to Meg at their first meeting and had been pleased that the relationship had developed this far, for he saw that she would be good for Edward. She was a sensible, level-headed girl whom he was sure would have a calming effect on Edward's impetuosity. He had grown out of the wild escapades of his youth but occasionally that wild streak would surface and it troubled Cornelius when it did. Now, with a wife to consider, his son would settle down and run the estate with all the efficiency of his undoubtedly keen mind.

Mark hoped that the wedding might afford him the opportunity to seek an explanation from Emma as to why the sight of the lace had upset her. He had tried to reason it out but could only come to the conclusion that it was associated with smuggling and that the sight of it had reminded her of her father and his untimely death, for which she blamed him. His one brief word with her, when he arrived at the reception, received a curt, cold 'Hello,' and a hostile look, before she turned to greet the next guest. Throughout the rest of the day he tried to get her attention but she always managed to avoid him.

Emma tried to ignore his presence, tried to shut him out of her mind and forget what might have been. There were times when to be so near Mark and not acknowledge him hurt almost beyond endurance.

He sought out Hugh Lomas and, under the pretence of what to outsiders would appear a casual conversation, thanked him for putting him in touch with the smugglers.

'Your proposals have been accepted?' queried Hugh as he nodded a smile at a passing acquaintance.

'No,' replied Mark as he glanced round the room, wondering if the person behind the smuggling was here. He could well be and nobody would know. 'Just a couple of items for myself.'

'Ah, enjoying the fruits of the free traders, like us all?' chuckled Hugh.

'That's all very well, but I'd like to know where I stand. Is there no way I can see The Fox? I believe . . .'

Lomas held up his hand to stop the request. 'Impossible. The Fox won't deal with you direct. You'll have been told what is to happen, and I don't want to know, so just be patient and do whatever is asked when you are contacted. Believe me, it is the best and the safest way for everyone. Have no doubt your proposals, and you, will be under close scrutiny.'

Hoping his enquiry might have raised some response, Mark kept an eye on Lomas and noted to whom he spoke in anything like earnest conversation through the rest of the time at Thorpe Hall. His curiosity was roused when he saw Lomas and Edward Beaumont leave the gathering and disappear through a door at the far end of the hall. Did Lomas know more than he was letting on? Could

Edward be The Fox? Though that seemed unlikely, the Beaumonts being such a respectable and highly thought of family in these parts, Mark was prepared to keep an open mind. Anything was possible. The chance of investigating further was spoiled when one of Whitby's leading ship-owners engaged him in conversation. He kept his eye on the door and saw the two friends emerge five minutes later when Edward went to rejoin his bride.

Guests started departing in the early evening, leaving the Hall to the newlyweds. Edward had decided that, as it was winter, they would not take their honeymoon until the better weather. Meg did not mind. It would be some time before she would be ready to travel. Besides she would be happy with Edward anywhere, and wasn't their future home a good place to start their life together? This had been a happy day so far and only one thing would make it more so – to lie in Edward's arms overpowered by love.

She wished her dear cousin was as happy as she. Her attempts to bring Emma and Mark together had failed but she would not give up. That would be made easier by Edward's invitation to Emma to visit Meg whenever she wished. He knew how close the cousins were and Emma's visits could prove a pleasant diversion for his wife.

She thanked him for the wonderful day and for being so considerate as she lay in his arms, their passion sated.

'And I thank you for being so kind and considerate to my father,' said Edward, turning over to gaze into her eyes.

'Oh, that's easy, he's such a kind old man,' replied Meg, sliding her arms around his neck.

'I know he likes you. Please continue being nice to him.'

'Of course I will, thee knows that.' She kissed away the worried frown which marked his brow.

'It can be important to us,' he said.

'How do thee mean?'

'Well, Father has kept a strict hold on the money he allows me to run the estate and for my own personal use. I was a bit wild in my youth and he didn't want the money wasting. Although he's making me a further allowance now we are married, I am still restricted.'

'Thee wants thy father to make more money available?'

'Yes. He likes you and sees you as a steadying influence on me.'

'But there's nothing to steady,' laughed Meg, surprised that Edward was hinting at another side to himself that she had not seen.

'Ah, Father doesn't see it that way. But with you beside me I think he will make an even bigger allowance, especially when he knows about the baby and sees it as a son and heir.' Edward's eyes brightened. 'If I had that money I could make a lot more. Then I could buy diamonds for your hands, rubies for your ears, pearls for your neck. I could make you rich beyond your dreams. You nor your son would want for nothing.' His eyes had taken on an almost fanatical look. 'I could expand my ideas, hiring more ships to . . .' He stopped.

'To do what?' prompted Meg.

'Never you mind,' he laughed.

'But I'd like to know,' she insisted, her curiosity roused.

'That's my secret and there's no need for you to bother your pretty little head about it,' he said quietly, and before she could say any more he met her lips with a kiss which flooded into passion, driving all queries from her mind.

Winter took a firm grip on the moors. Heavy snowfalls cut off communication with Whitby. The town's only contact with the outside world was by sea, and at times that was tenuous because of the storms which this year seemed to be more frequent and more ferocious than usual.

Beck Farm lay in deep snow. Jay and Emma kept paths cleared to the byre, stable and sheepfold so that the daily tasks of seeing to the animals could be carried out. Joe struggled to the farm once a week and sometimes twice to make sure they were all right. On these occasions he and Amy always found an excuse to slip away to barn or byre.

Emma envied them their pleasure. The first week of the heavy snow, Joe brought them a pig which his father had killed, and Grace and her daughters were kept busy salting down the bacon, making pork pies, curing the hams and rending the fat for lard. Milk was turned into butter and Grace's baking kept them in with bread, pies and cakes.

Time was filled by cleaning out cupboards, scrubbing floors and tidying the house right through. Grace pointed out that this was a good opportunity to do it for come the thaw there would be much to do on the farm. Besides she knew it was best to keep her family busy; that way there was no time for brooding.

Mark, in his attempt to forget Emma, was pleased that the moorland snow prevented her from coming to Whitby. He thought it would be 'out of sight, out of mind' but it was not so. Emma haunted him, and the desire to vindicate himself strengthened. He craved further contact with the smugglers, but with the bad weather he knew he might have to wait until the spring. He trifled with the idea of going to Baytown and confronting Zac again but realised that it could lead to his connection being severed completely. He must curb his impatience, and to do so threw himself wholeheartedly into running the business and overseeing the renovation of the house in Bagdale.

When he walked into it, on completion, the house felt too big and oppressed him with a feeling of loneliness. He had hoped that at this moment Emma would have been sharing it with him, that there would have been laughter and joy here. Instead he was left with the problem of proving his innocence. He thought about it daily but could find no answer.

Inactivity because of the weather brought the matter of John Dugdale's death back into Lieutenant Boston's mind. Folk had accepted the idea of an accidental death and he had agreed that it seemed the only explanation, but something niggled at him. He knew his men were good shots, he had seen to that through meticulous and constant training. To think that one of them, in firing a warning shot above a man's head, should aim so low as to kill him seemed preposterous. But there had been no one else on the moor. Or had there? The thought began to intrigue him. If there had been someone else on the moor, how had they carried out the killing without another shot being heard? He called the three troopers in again.

'Tell me what happened on the moor the day when John Dugdale was killed,' he ordered when they were standing before him.

'But we've told you,' they protested.

'Tell me again.'

They went through their story. Boston could find no flaw in it. All their versions tallied.

'You saw no one else on the moor?'

'No.'

'Heard no one?'

'No.'

'Didn't hear another shot?'

'No.'

'Your shots didn't sound any different?'

The men looked thoughtful. This was a question they had not been asked before.

One of them started to shake his head slowly. 'No.' He drew the word out slowly. Another nodded his agreement.

Boston looked enquiringly at the sergeant, who had fired the first shot. 'Well?' he prompted.

He frowned. 'I'm not sure. I'd fired first, so was listening when these two fired. Maybe the noise was louder than expected.'

Boston leaned forward on his desk, drawn by the implications if the sergeant was right. 'You mean there could have been another shot?' He was cautious with his query.

The sergeant screwed up his face with doubt. 'Well, there might have been but I couldn't swear to it. It could have been my imagination.'

Boston knew it was no good pressing this too hard. Instead he pursued another form of questioning. 'You were directly behind Dugdale?'

'Yes, sir. Like we said before.'

Boston nodded and looked thoughtful for a moment. 'So if you had hit him, it would have been in the back or the back of the head?'

'I suppose so, sir,' the men agreed.

'You carried the body to Beck Farm. Did you notice where the wound was?' He watched them carefully as he put the question.

The men did not answer immediately as they tried to visualise the scene. Then they glanced at each other, amazement changing their expressions in such a way that Boston knew that what was coming could not have been made up. 'Sir, he had been hit in the right side,' said the sergeant.

'You're sure.'

'Certain.' They all agreed.

'Think again, did Dugdale turn at all?'

'No, sir. His back was to us. He was running away from us.'

'So even if you had accidentally fired low, you couldn't possibly have hit him in his right side?'

'Impossible.'

Boston straightened with satisfaction. So someone else had been on the moor that morning. Someone who had set out to kill Dugdale, someone who had been watching his movements. 'Describe exactly what happened,' he ordered.

'I fired the first shot,' replied the sergeant. 'Dugdale didn't stop. I ordered my men to prepare to fire. They did so. I yelled, "Fire." They did. Dugdale fell.'

'You gave the command with your usual vigour?'

'Habit, sir.'

'Then someone else could have heard your order and acted on it at the same time as these two.'

'I suppose so, sir.'

Boston was elated. Had Dugdale known someone wished him dead? He had been carrying a pack and had been heading for Whitby until he spotted the dragoons. Had he been trying to escape his assassin? But who would want to kill an ordinary farmer – unless he was mixed up in some nefarious trade? When the snows were gone, he would visit Beck Farm again.

He leaned back in his chair. 'What has passed between us just now, keep to yourselves. No word of this must get out until I say so. But I think I can safely say you did not kill John Dugdale.'

When the men had left, Boston gave the situation a lot of thought. Unable to see a reason behind Dugdale's murder, unless he had been involved in smuggling and had fallen foul of Zac Denby, he recalled Mark Roper's visit and request to know more about the way the farmer had been killed. He had refused him information beyond the fact that the dragoons took full responsibility for an accidental killing. Now he wondered if there had been more behind the enquiry. He knew Mark was sweet on Dugdale's daughter. Was he questioning on her behalf? Could they know more than he? If so, would it pay to reveal his theory to Roper in exchange for learning what he might know?

Boston pondered the question carefully. With a decision made, he pushed himself from his chair, shrugged himself into his greatcoat, put on his hat and stepped out into the wild weather.

A cold wind was blowing from the sea and people hurried about their business, eager to get indoors as soon as possible. He lost no time in reaching the Roper offices and his request to see Mark was immediately agreed to.

Mark was curious. What did Boston want with him? He greeted him amiably and asked him to sit down. He took his own place behind his desk and looked questioningly at the officer. 'What can I do for you?'

'It may be a question of what I can do for you, or more probably what we can do for each other.'

Mark raised his eyebrows. 'Sounds intriguing.' He leaned back in his chair ready to listen.

'I recalled our conversation at the theatre when you agreed with me that smuggling should be stamped out.' Mark nodded. 'And remembering your visit to my office when you enquired about the shooting of John Dugdale, I began to wonder if you thought the two might be connected, and if, being a friend of his daughter, you might know something I should?' Boston paused.

'Why should I think the two might be connected? You admitted your men had accidentally shot Dugdale. I accepted that. Has something happened to make you change your mind?' said Mark cautiously.

Boston did not answer the question but said instead, 'Through your friendship with Dugdale's daughter, do you know of any reason why he should have been leaving Beck Farm, maybe even leaving Whitby?'

'What makes you think he might have been leaving Whitby, let alone Beck Farm?'

'He was carrying a pack. A substantial one, my men said. And why did he try to avoid them if he was not thinking of leaving? I think he was, but why? Do you know?'

Mark's mind was racing. Boston obviously had some theory, or maybe even facts, about John's death. They might be useful to him in his search for the person behind the smuggling. But to answer the question would be to disclose John's involvement. It could also lead the dragoons to the contraband at Beck Farm and the subsequent arrest of the family. Mark faced a dilemma.

'Well?' urged Boston. 'Do I read in your hesitation that you do know something?'

Deny or divulge? If he told, how much should he reveal?

Maybe they could help each other. Mark studied the officer thoughtfully for a moment, then said, 'I have some facts which may be of interest to you.' His remark was full of caution.

'Then you do know something?' said Boston eagerly.

'Perhaps, but I can only judge if it is useful after I have heard what you have to say. And I must have your promise on oath that what passes between us from now on will not go beyond these four walls.'

'Very well,' replied Boston. 'I would want it that way too.'

Mark nodded his agreement. 'Whatever you say is safe with me.'

'Nothing shall be divulged unless we both say so?'

'Agreed.'

Mark listened intently as Boston expounded his theory as to what had happened on the moor and why he believed that another person was there, even though he was not seen. Excitement coursed through Mark when he heard about the position of the wound. This information could exonerate him in Emma's eyes. By the time Boston had finished Mark had decided to reveal everything to him.

'Before I say anything, I want your promise again about certain aspects.'

'What are they?'

'That publicly John Dugdale's death remains an accident.'

'You're shielding the killer?' snapped Boston irritably.

'No,' replied Mark firmly. 'Protecting John's reputation. You can have the killer if we find proof.'

'Very well.'

'And certain people whom I name will have no charges brought against them.'

'That could be misdirecting justice.'

'I think not, as you will see.' He saw Boston hesitate doubtfully so added, 'You will lose nothing by giving me your word. If you don't, then I won't talk.'

'All right, I agree.'

'Good. First of all I have to tell you that although I am here to run the Whitby branch of the family business, I am also working for Sir William Bailey.'

For a moment Boston disbelieved him but realised Mark had no reason to lie. 'Head of the Customs Board?' he gasped.

'Yes. He's a friend of the family and when he knew I was coming to Whitby asked me to see if I could find out who was the brains behind the gang in this area.'

'A risky business for a civilian. You'd be a dead man if the smugglers found out. Have you discovered who their leader is?'

'No, just some ideas. Right, the next thing is that the information I am about to give you came to me because I was friendly with Emma Dugdale and she was desperate for help.'

Boston's interest quickened.

'Unknown to her father, she had witnessed a meeting between him and Zac Denby in which he became involved with the smugglers, and later she saw the contraband hidden.'

'I knew it! I was damned right!' Boston slapped his thigh, his face full of satisfaction. 'Where is it? I searched that farm inside out and never found anything.'

'I don't know,' replied Mark, and saw disbelief shadow the soldier's face. 'It's true, I don't.'

'Then why was Emma seeking your help?'

'Because her father's life had been threatened by Zac Denby.'

'How did she know that?' There was doubt in Boston's mind. 'That would mean someone in the know had told her and the smugglers are so close-knit . . .' He let his voice trail away with misgiving.

'A certain Sue Thrower, whose husband was a pedlar from Pickering, came to find the reason why her husband had not returned home. Emma befriended her and was able

382

to tell her that her husband had picked up contraband from Beck Farm on his return journey. Sue got in with the smugglers and when she heard Zac had been ordered to kill Dugdale because he was suspected of cheating them, she just had to let Emma know. Emma came to me for help, revealed all this to me, and I advised her to tell her father and arranged for him to go on a sea voyage for a month. Hopefully, by the time he'd returned, proof that he had not been lining his own pocket would have been found.'

'So he was leaving for Whitby?' mused Boston. 'He panicked when he saw my troopers and ran. And the other person on the moor was Zac Denby!'

'We've no proof that it was he, only that there was another person there.'

'True, but I'd stake my life on it that Zac Denby fired the fatal shot.'

'And so would I.'

'I'll take him in for questioning. I'll break him down!'

'No!' rapped Mark harshly. 'I want Zac free. He might just lead me to the man I seek.'

'But . . .'

'You don't arrest him,' cut in Mark sharply. 'I need every possible lead I can get and he's one of them.'

Boston screwed up his face with regret. 'All right,' he mumbled. 'What do you intend to do?'

'The first thing is to clear my name.'

'Clear your name?'

'Yes. Apart from the Dugdale family I was the only one to know that John was leaving. After our conversation at the theatre and the fact that Emma saw me going to your office, she assumed that I had betrayed her father. Now you can tell her the truth.'

Chapter Twenty-Three

It was early-February when the cold relented a little and the first signs of a thaw were seen.

Though Mark knew that snow still lay deep on the moors, reports that some of the tracks were passable with care took him to Boston's office.

'We'll try again tomorrow,' he informed the officer.

'This will be the fifth attempt we've made to get through to Beck Farm,' Boston pointed out.

'I know, I know,' replied Mark, not pleased to be reminded of their failures. He had known at the time that the attempts might come to nothing but was anxious to clear his name with the Dugdales and to persuade Emma to resume their relationship. 'This time the reports are good.'

The following morning the two men left Whitby on horseback. As they climbed away from the town the snow became thicker but presented no problem until they reached the moorland heights.

The thaw had taken some of the snow and the tops of track markers had become visible again. The sturdy animals thrust their way through the drifts, taking it in turns to lead so as to ease the task of parting the snow. It was slow progress, and once Boston suggested that they turn back, but Mark would have none of it.

'We'll make it,' he insisted. He could no longer bear the suspense of having information which would clear him and not being able to reach Emma.

Grace glanced out of the window. She had eyed the white landscape so many times during the last few weeks, wishing

384

that the snow would go and something like normality would return to Beck Farm.

Today she started. The familiar view was marred, the whiteness broken by two smudges of dark. She rubbed at the window, trying to make the picture clearer. Riders. Two men on horseback. Who? It wasn't Joe who had kept faithful to his visits, in spite of the struggle it must have been to penetrate the white wilderness. Why were these two strangers on the moor? Why coming here? Her thoughts were broken by the sight of the uniform. 'Boston,' she hissed. 'Will he never give up?' But who was the other man? She concentrated her gaze on him. 'Emma!' she yelled over her shoulder.

Startled by the alarm in her mother's voice, Emma came running into the kitchen.

'What is it, Ma?'

'Look!' Grace remained staring out of the window.

Emma reached her mother's side just as Amy and Jay burst into the kitchen.

'What's wrong?' cried Amy, her face full of concern.

'Mark!' Emma gasped. What had brought him to Beck Farm in this weather? 'Boston! Oh, no!' If she needed any further proof of Mark's guilt then here it was – riding with Lieutenant Boston to Beck Farm. Indignation rose in her. How dare he after what he had done?

The family watched the two riders reach the gate, swing off their horses and come to the house along the path which had been cleared by Jay.

Before they reached the door, Grace had it open. She held herself erect, a defiant air about her. 'What d' thee want?' she said, her manner hostile.

'Good day, Mrs Dugdale,' said Mark.

'It's not good for seeing the likes of thee two,' she snapped.

'Please, may we come in? We have something important to say to you and all your family,' said Mark gently, ignoring her remark.

'Come to hound us again, no doubt.'

'No, ma'am,' put in Boston. 'Far from it. We have some news which we know will be of interest to you.'

Remembering his previous visits, Grace eyed the man with suspicion.

Her three children had come alongside her. Mark's heart missed a beat when he saw Emma. She was as lovely as he remembered her, but when her eyes met his they were cold.

'Maybe we'd better hear what they have to say, Ma. It must be important to bring them all this way in such snow.' It was Amy who made the suggestion.

Grace hesitated then said, 'Very well, come in with thee.' There was no real welcome in her voice as she stepped aside. 'Well?' she asked as she turned after shutting the door.

'We have news about your husband's death,' said Boston. 'First of all, I did not know he was leaving. I sent my men out early to fetch him in for questioning, just as I had done with several other farmers. I was hoping to play one man off against the other to learn the whereabouts of contraband.'

The words were thundering in Emma's mind. Boston did not know her father was leaving! If that was true . . .

She glanced at Mark and saw that he was watching her intently. There was hope in his eyes and a longing for her to believe what she was hearing. She looked at Boston. 'Thee did not know Pa was leaving?'

'I did not, Miss Emma.'

There was something about his tone that confirmed he was telling the truth, but still she said, 'Thee swears it?'

'I do.'

Emma's mind reeled. She had accused Mark wrongly. He had not informed Boston that her father was leaving. But there was the lace. He must have got it from Zac Denby. Had he betrayed her father to the smugglers to gain their confidence?

'I've told Lieutenant Boston all that happened leading to Mr Dugdale's regrettable death.'

Alarm crossed the faces of all the family. Emma was incredulous. Why was Mark doing this to them? Words of condemnation sprang to her lips but before she could utter them, he was speaking again.

'But I have his word that he will take no action against you, and that he will let the official verdict on Mr Dugdale's death remain "accidental" so that his name will not be connected with the smugglers.'

Relief showed on their faces but Grace was curious also. 'Thee says remain "accidental death". Well, wasn't it?'

Mark glanced at Boston and nodded. The lieutenant explained his theory. When he had finished, he added, 'When I put this to Mark he told me of the smuggler's threat. It would seem that Zac Denby or his delegate shot your husband, but I would think it was Denby himself.'

'Sue overheard Zac telling Nell that he had been ordered to kill Pa,' said Emma.

'So somebody higher up authorised it?' mused Mark.

'I hope thee's ganning to arrest Denby?' snapped Emma viciously. She wanted retribution for her father's death.

'There is no proof that he did it,' Mark pointed out. He saw rebuttals spring to the family's lips, and held up his hand to stop them, at the same time saying, 'There isn't. He'd be free almost before the lieutenant took him in. Besides, I don't want him arrested.'

'Thee what?' gasped Emma with surprised indignation. 'What has it to do with thee?'

Grace stared aghast but Mark went on: 'I'm working for Sir William Bailey, Head of Customs, in an attempt to uncover the real brains behind the operation and I hope that I may get a lead through Denby. That's why I want him to remain free, at least for the time being.'

'Thee agrees with this?' Grace directed her question at Boston.

'Yes.'

Emma's eyes softened as she looked at Mark. 'Why didn't thee tell me before?'

'You might have been in danger if I had. It was better no one knew until the appropriate time.'

She looked thoughtful. 'Leaving him free might also help Sue solve the disappearance of her husband.'

'You had better warn her to be extremely cautious,' Boston pointed out. 'She'll get no mercy from the smugglers if she is found out.'

'I will at the first opportunity,' replied Emma. She turned to Mark. Her features softened. 'Oh, I'm so sorry that I accused thee.' Her eyes were filling with tears, pleading forgiveness.

He came to her. 'There's nothing to be sorry about,' he said gently.

'Oh, but there is,' she cried.

'It was understandable.'

'Am I forgiven?' she implored him.

'If you need forgiving, then you are.'

'And us too,' put in Grace. 'We misjudged thee.'

Suspicion had been lifted. Emma's heart sang with joy and she knew she would be impatient until the day she could ride to join Mark in Whitby.

The thaw continued, albeit slowly. A 'cold thaw' the locals called it. Emma eagerly watched for signs that a journey to Whitby would be possible. That day came a fortnight later when Joe, knowing of her intentions, brought the news that the main track was passable and that he would escort her to it.

'Away with thee, lass.' Grace smiled at Emma's enthusiasm as she rushed around to get ready. 'Thy aunt will give thee a bed for a few days. But watch the weather. Remember the snows can come back even though the days are lengthening.'

'I will, Ma.'

'Give her and all the family our love,' said Grace. 'And

remember us to Mark,' she added with a twinkle in her eye.

'And I must see Meg. I'm dying to know how she's enjoying being mistress of Thorpe Hall.'

The snow eased considerably as she dropped off the moors into the Esk Valley, and in Whitby there was little lying about as the salt air had been a deterrent.

Her aunt gave her an enthusiastic welcome and expressed delight at having her for a few days. 'I miss Meg,' she explained, 'especially as my family's all men now, so I'm pleased to have some feminine company in the house.' Her face broadened into an even wider smile as she took pleasure in announcing that Meg was going to have a baby.

Emma feigned surprise, hiding the knowledge that she already knew. 'Oh, I must see her as soon as possible. I'll ride out there tomorrow morning.' First she must see Mark.

Once she had settled in, she left the house and hurried to the Roper offices.

'I was hoping you would come soon.' Mark greeted her with obvious pleasure as he came from behind his desk. He took her hands in his and, leaning forward, kissed her. He would have drawn away but Emma held him close and returned his kiss.

'How long are you here for?' he asked when their lips parted.

'Three or four days.'

'Splendid. I want to make up for the time we lost and be with you as much as possible.'

'Oh, Mark, so do I.'

'Now come, you must see the house.'

He put on his great coat, fitting at the waist and flaring almost to ankle-length. The wide lapels swept round to the large collar which would afford ample protection against a snarling wind. He cut a striking figure and Emma was proud to be walking beside him to Bagdale.

She gasped in amazed delight as she stepped into the house. The hall had been decorated in white and yellow, giving it a sunny atmosphere even on a dull day, and creating the effect that the stairway was floating on air. It was tastefully furnished with no more pieces than were necessary to create a warm welcoming appearance.

'It's beautiful,' said Emma, her eyes expressing her appreciation.

She found the same care had been taken throughout the house and noticed that Mark had incorporated her suggestions. She was flattered that he had done so.

'With care and good taste thee has made a beautiful home,' she commented when they had returned to the withdrawing room.

'I'm pleased with it,' he commented. 'When I first walked in, after the work was finished and the furniture in place, it felt lonely, with a chill about it. Something was missing – the warmth of love. Today that warmth returned. I felt it as soon as you crossed the threshold. You brought love to it. The house needs you, Emma, just as I do. Please say you'll marry me?' He took her hands in his and looked intently into her eyes.

She met his gaze with tenderness. 'I will,' she whispered. Her mind was dancing with the joy she had thought had been dashed from her forever.

Mark enfolded her in his arms and kissed her longingly.

When she broke the news to her aunt, Matilda was so excited. 'Another wedding in the family soon,' she cried, giving her niece an enthusiastic hug. 'Thee will have as grand a wedding as Meg, I'll see to that. Tell your mother she need have no worries.' She paused, sudden alarm masking her face for a moment in case she had assumed too much. 'The wedding will be in Whitby, of course?'

Emma laughed at her aunt's reaction. 'Of course it will.'

Matilda sighed with relief. 'Well then, we'll . . .'

Amused by her aunt's familiar spur of the moment approach and eagerness to take on the organisation, Emma calmed the situation. 'Aunt, we haven't fixed a date, we have no wedding plans at the moment, we haven't discussed it. Mark's only just proposed to me again.'

Matilda gave a wave of her hand. 'Then thee must get thinking about it, my dear. The sooner the better. Don't want a handsome man like Mark to slip away from thee.' She started for the door. 'Think carefully about what I say,' she called over her shoulder.

Laughing to herself and shaking her head at her aunt's almost overpowering fervour, Emma went to her room with her heart soaring at the joyful prospect of becoming Mark's wife.

The next day dawned bright but cold, with a breeze blowing from the sea. The sun was beginning to give out a little warmth, something which was only noticeable when sheltered from the wind. People on the bridge felt the blast as it swept up the river and hurried to find shelter among the buildings crowding on either side of the water.

Emma dressed in warm clothes for the ride to Thorpe Hall which she knew she would find both enjoyable and exhilarating.

As she turned into the long carriageway which swept to the house a mile away, she felt a new surge of excitement, anticipating her meeting with her cousin, receiving her news and imparting her own.

The door was answered by a maid who said she would see if Mrs Beaumont was available. As she waited, Emma surveyed the hall. The woodwork was magnificent but it was dark and oppressive. The staircase looked so solid that it seemed to weigh heavily on the hall. She found herself comparing it with the light, welcoming atmosphere of Mark's home.

Her thoughts were broken by the rustle of silk and Meg appeared, rushing towards her, arms held out in welcome.

'Emma, Emma! Oh, I am so glad to see thee. It's been too long.' Her eyes were bright, her smile joyous.

The pleasure of seeing her cousin swept through Emma.

'It has, far too long, but what could we do with the weather as it's been?'

They hugged each other in the rapture of reunion.

'Well, never mind, we're together now. We've lots to talk about.' Meg turned to the maid who had waited discreetly near the staircase. 'Mary, take Miss Dugdale's coat and hat.' Once this had been done she said, 'Come, we'll go in here.' She led the way through a door on the right and into a room in which the oak furniture and half-panelling were of the highest quality but which, with the dark green wallpaper, cast a gloomy atmosphere which even the two tall windows and the fire did little to lighten.

'How is thee? Thee looks radiant,' said Meg as she closed the door.

There was a huge smile on Emma's face as she turned to her cousin. 'Oh, life is so good. Yesterday Mark asked me to marry him.'

Meg's eyes widened with surprise and delight. 'Thee's made it up?'

'Yes, everything's all right. It was just a misunderstanding.'

'Oh, I'm so pleased. I hope thee'll be very happy.' She clasped her cousin to her and kissed her on the cheek. 'Sit down and tell me all that's been happening.'

As they sat down on the sofa, Emma said, 'First, what about thee? Is thee well? Baby?'

'Yes, I'm well. Everything seems to be as it should be.'

A little bell of concern rang at the back of Emma's mind. Her immediate sparkle had dimmed as Meg spoke, as if something had come to mind that she did not wish to recall.

'And Edward? How is he?'

'He's well. Out on the estate.'

'How is he taking to the idea of a baby?'

In her hesitation, accompanied by a shadow which fleetingly crossed Meg's face, Emma detected sadness and sensed a change. This was not the happy-go-lucky Meg she had once known. Was the responsibility of marriage too much for her? Was she finding being mistress of Thorpe Hall a burden now she was carrying a baby? Or was it something more than that? Emma had no more time to speculate for Meg was speaking.

'He doesn't mind being a father,' she answered weakly.

'Doesn't mind? He should be overjoyed,' replied Emma indignantly, and eyed her cousin critically. Her face had become serious which emphasised a slightly drawn look. It had been temporarily banished in the joy of seeing Emma, but had now returned.

'Something wrong?' Emma put the question gently.

Again Meg hesitated, biting her lip as she did so. She met her cousin's gaze and saw there kindness and understanding. It broke down the barrier that she had been erecting, a wall to hide her feelings from those who pry. Emma was someone special. They had shared so much throughout their lives.

'Oh, I'm so glad thee's here. I've wanted someone to talk to.'

Emma read a plea for help in her tone, the plea of someone who was not sure where to turn. 'Why? Is something the matter?' she asked anxiously.

'Oh, I don't know, maybe it's me, maybe I let my imagination run away with me.' Meg paused as if gathering her thoughts. She drove the look of anxiety from her face. 'No, it's not my imagination. Edward doesn't give me the attention he used to do before we were married.'

'In what way?' asked Emma.

'It was little things at first, trivial things thee might think, but they grew. He very rarely takes me anywhere, just makes excuses. He misses meals. On one occasion he went to France on business but told me he was going to London. I only found out he'd been to France by a slip of the tongue. When I asked him if he had had a good journey he said, yes, apart from the Channel crossing. When I showed surprise he said it was something that had come up when he was in London, but I could tell he was lying. It had been planned before he left here. When I asked him why he had gone to France he told me nothing, saying his business wouldn't interest me. But it would! I want to know what he does apart from running the estate, but he doesn't seem to want to share it with me. And there have been a couple of occasions when he hasn't come home until the next day, telling me business kept him in Whitby, but again he wouldn't tell me what.'

'The weather has been bad,' put in Emma lamely.

'Thee may have had it bad at Beck Farm but it has never been bad enough down here to prevent him getting home,' Meg pointed out.

'Is it like this all the time?'

'No. There are times when he's kindness itself.'

'Is thee happy here? Does the house upset thee? It is a bit oppressive.'

'I found it so when I first came but that was countered by Edward's love and his father's kindness. I'm used to it now. Though I don't think I'll ever get used to the garden.'

'The garden?' Emma was puzzled.

'Don't misunderstand me. It's beautifully laid out and I can enjoy it, but there are times when it scares me. It's as if it was meant for tragedy.'

'What do thee mean?'

'Thee can see it better from my bedroom window. Come, I'll show thee.'

They went upstairs and, on entering the bedroom, Meg made straight for the window. Emma joined her and found herself looking down on what appeared to be a maze formed by high hedges. Even on this bright day there were corners where the light failed to pierce. In the darkness of the hedges she could make out statues, their mute, unmoving appearance casting an air of mystery around the garden which at times seemed to permeate the house itself.

She shivered.

Meg noticed. 'That's just it,' she exclaimed. 'At times it gives me the shivers.' She inclined her head thoughtfully.

'At others, it's a beautiful place. I think it's this switch of moods which brings menace to it.'

'But it's only a garden,' said Emma, trying to sound reassuring.

'I know. But thee felt it too.'

She had to agree.

They turned away from the window. Meg saw Emma glance at the bed and knew she had noticed only one set of pillows. She glanced shyly at her cousin.

'He doesn't sleep with me any more. Says it's better until after the baby arrives. But, Emma, I'm not at that stage yet.'

'Something troubling you?' Mark asked as he and Emma walked beside the ruined abbey. The day was fine with a gentle sea lapping the bottom of the cliffs. It was a day for lovers to share away from the bustle of the busy seaport. Satisfied that he had dealt with all the important matters Mark had seized the opportunity to be with Emma but had become disconcerted by her demeanour as they crossed the river and climbed the Church Stairs. 'You've been quiet since we left Bagdale. I hope you aren't having second thoughts about us?'

'No, Mark. No! Never about us,' she cried. Her expression held a plea for him not to misunderstand. 'I'm worried about Meg.'

'Why?'

'She was different. Oh, when I arrived she was her old bubbling self, but as the day passed a lot of the Meg I knew had disappeared.'

'In what way?'

'She's become more withdrawn, less lively, and at times I could tell she was only pretending to be happy.'

'Maybe it's adjusting to marriage,' he suggested. 'Becoming mistress of Thorpe Hall was a big step for her.'

'I realise all those things but the Meg I knew would have coped. I was troubled because there was real sadness about her. She was so happy before and so in love with Edward. She confessed that at times he neglects her, isn't always at home at nights. There was one occasion when he told her he was going to London but he actually went to France. When she asked him about it he brushed her questions aside and said it was business which needn't concern her.'

'That could be from consideration for her,' Mark pointed out.

'Wouldn't thee want me to be interested in your business?'

'I would, but Edward isn't the same temperament as me.' He added lightly, 'It could be just a passing phase, one of the unsteady patches that all marriages go through. I'm sure it will all blow over. Maybe it's brought on by Meg's condition.'

'Maybe thee's right. I hope so.'

'Visit her when you can. I'm sure you can be a comfort to her. She may be missing her family and friends.'

Emma nodded but in her heart she was not convinced.

Mark stopped and turned her to him. 'Enough of your worries.' He brushed his hand gently across her forehead. 'Forget them. There's just us today.' He looked deep into her eyes, claiming her love. 'I love you, Emma Dugdale, always have and always will.'

'And I love thee, now and forever,' she whispered. Her words faded into a tender kiss, held until it soared into overwhelming passion.

It was not until he had left Emma, with her promise to dine with him that evening, that the information which had been niggling at the back of Mark's mind came clearly to him. She had said Edward Beaumont had been to France. Mark wondered why? Not only that, he had said that he had gone to London and it was only a slip of the tongue which had betrayed him. Why attempt to hide his actual destination from his wife? What didn't he want her to know? What had he to hide?

Edward had mentioned business. What business had he in France? Could it possibly be to do with smuggling? Could Beaumont be The Fox?

Mark had much to occupy his mind and this line of thought was only interrupted when he made arrangements with his housekeeper for the dinner with Emma.

'I've been thinking about what you told me about Meg and Edward,' said Mark during the meal in the cosy dining room of his house in Bagdale. 'I don't really know him. Only met him at the party your aunt gave, and I've run into him a couple of times since.'

His query drew the information from Emma.

'Most eligible bachelor around here until Meg married him. A lot of young women set their hats at him. Mistress of Thorpe Hall had its attractions apart from getting a handsome man. But he was a bit of a wild one. His father spoilt him after his mother died and Edward came to expect to receive whatever he wanted. Mind thee, he proved himself capable when his father handed over the running of the estate to him. I think he did it to give him responsibility and try to curb his wild ways.'

'And did it?'

'To some extent. I hear that his father kept a tight rein on money, only made Edward a moderate allowance.'

'That would restrict him.'

'I'm not sure that it did. He always seemed to have plenty.'

'How was that? Does he have business ventures outside the estate?'

'I don't know.'

'What about this trip to France you mentioned?'

'I've no idea what that could be. Meg didn't know. Why this interest?'

'Just curiosity after what you told me, and also because at your aunt's there was talk of interest in investing if ever I should be looking for more money.'

'And are thee?'

'Not sure. I'd rather be independent but I just might need some backing with this ship I'm having built.'

Mark was satisfied. He had learned something which he thought might be of importance. Restricted by an allowance from his father, Edward could well have sought to increase his income by organising a gang of so-called free traders.

'And this other job?' prompted Emma as she sat down on the sofa drawn up in front of a blazing fire in the withdrawing room. 'Do thee really think Zac Denby will lead thee to the person behind the smuggling?'

'I'm hoping so,' replied Mark, turning from the sideboard with two glasses of Madeira in his hands. He placed one on a small table beside Emma and the other on a second table where he could easily reach it. He sat down beside her.

'Have thee any idea who it might be?' she queried with a certain eagerness.

'I have two suspects in mind.'

'Who?' she broke in sharply.

'I don't want to say at this moment. I might be entirely wrong.'

'But I might be able to help,' she pressed. 'After all, I'm keen to see whoever it is brought to justice. He must have ordered my father to be killed, or at least agreed to Zac's suggestion.'

Mark shook his head. 'No, my dear. If I told you your life could be in danger. What you don't know can't hurt you.'

'Please, Mark?' she pleaded.

'No, not yet, but I will if ever it looks as though you can help. In the meantime you can keep me informed as to what happens to the contraband at Beck Farm, and if you get any word from Sue.'

'Certainly I will.' She looked at him with a loving concern. 'And thee be careful, darling, thee's very precious to

me. Having found thee again, I don't want to lose thee.'
She leaned towards him and kissed him seductively.

He responded with a fire which would not be denied.
The understanding of lovers needed no words as he took
her hand and led her from the room to the stairs.

Chapter Twenty-Four

The following day, Emma left her aunt's early, still enraptured by the time spent in Mark's arms last evening. Their loving had been tender and gentle in its first exploration, bursting later into the fire of passion which swamped them in an ecstasy of love.

Reluctantly she had torn herself away when she thought it wise to return to her aunt's. She had done so with a promise to return to Whitby as soon as possible. Now, as she rode to Thorpe Hall, she knew that time could not come quickly enough and that the days between would be spent dreaming of the loving she had experienced with Mark.

When the maid ushered her in to see Meg she found Edward there. He jumped to his feet to greet her with a friendly smile and warm kisses on both cheeks.

'I'm so glad to see you, Emma. Meg told me you were here yesterday, I'm sorry I missed you.' He ordered the maid to bring some tea for them all and escorted Emma to make her greetings to Meg. 'Don't you think she is looking well?' he asked brightly as he cast a loving smile at his wife.

'Remarkably well,' replied Emma. As she bent and kissed her cousin, Meg responded with a hug which indicated her pleasure at seeing her again.

Edward was charm itself and fussed over them when the maid brought the tea. He was particularly attentive to his wife and Emma began to think that Meg's suspicions were exaggerated. He asked after Emma's family and offered help if they were unable to cope with any of the heavy chores, expressing his condemnation of the dragoons once again.

Emma thanked him and kept her own counsel on the shooting. She had no wish to reveal Lieutenant Boston's theory.

After half an hour's pleasant conversation Edward jumped to his feet, saying, 'Now I must be off. All sorts of things to see to. It's been good to see you again, Emma. I hope you'll call as often as you can. Meg enjoys your company and it will be good for her during the coming months.' He kissed Meg dutifully and hurried from the room.

Meg glanced at her cousin when the door closed. 'I expect thee's thinking no one could be more charming?'

'Well, after what thee said . . .'

'I know,' broke in Meg. 'He can be like that, but most times it seems forced and at others he is downright rude to me. Sometimes I think he wishes he'd never married me.' She swallowed hard and Emma saw she was making an effort to hold back the tears.

'Oh, I'm sure he doesn't feel that,' she put in, trying to smooth over the situation.

'I'm not so sure,' said Meg hastily. 'Last evening, about dusk, he took me for a walk in the garden. Why he chose that time I don't know. Why couldn't he have chosen a bright sunny day? Unless he was trying to scare me.'

'Why should he want to do that?' Emma gave a half laugh of protest.

'I don't know. But it was scary. It was so gloomy with those high hedges. And the statues . . .' She shuddered at the memory. 'I had a feeling there was evil in the place. Edward just laughed at my concern. And when I said I wanted to return to the house, he said I could if I could find my own way along the maze of paths, but he was staying.'

'Thy imagination was running away with thee,' Emma offered by way of explanation.

'Thee saw it from my window,' Meg pointed out.

Emma nodded. 'I know, but surely Edward wouldn't deliberately frighten thee.'

Meg held her face in her hands then looked up wearily. 'I don't know what to think. He's so changeable. I've seen sides to him I never suspected before I married him, and yet as thee's just seen he can be so charming. And that makes the times when he isn't all the harder to bear.'

'Is there anything troubling him?'

'Not that I know of, but he doesn't tell me everything. Maybe some business venture has failed, bringing money problems. I just don't know.' She shrugged her shoulders resignedly then brightened. 'But let's talk about thee. When's that wedding going to take place?'

Emma laughed. 'I don't know. We won't discuss that until Ma knows. Mark's riding out with me when I return home this afternoon.'

'Thy ma will be pleased.'

By the time she left, Emma was pleased that Meg was her old self again, chatting and laughing brightly.

'Come again soon,' she said as they made their goodbyes.

'I will,' promised Emma.

'Ma, Emma's here!' Amy's shout filled the house.

Grace and Jay came hurrying into the kitchen and to the door which Amy had already opened.

'Mark's with her,' she added when they joined her.

As the horses came to a halt at the gate the family hurried out.

Mark swung easily from the saddle and came to help Emma to the ground. Her greetings were warm and affectionate as she kissed and hugged everyone in turn.

Intuition told Grace that something special had pleased her daughter for she exuded happiness.

'Ma, we've something exciting to tell thee.'

'What, even before we get inside?' Grace's lips twitched with amusement.

'Even before we get inside,' Emma confirmed with a laugh. She glanced at Mark.

He turned to Grace. 'I've asked Emma again to marry me and she's said yes. I hope you agree?'

Grace smiled as she looked from one to the other and saw them waiting anxiously for her approval. 'If that is what she wants then I am happy to say yes.'

'Oh, Ma, thanks.' Emma flung herself into her mother's arms and hugged her with all the joy she felt.

'Mark.' Grace turned to him and held out her arms, a gesture of welcome to the family.

He came and kissed her lightly on the cheek. 'Thank you,' he said softly, the two words full of meaning. Grace read into them an assurance that he loved Emma deeply.

Amy showered her sister with questions while Jay, after dutiful kisses and handshakes, thought of more practical things by offering to take care of the horses.

'Have thee any date in mind?' asked Grace as they went into the house.

'We haven't discussed it yet, Mrs Dugdale,' replied Mark. 'Probably early-summer. I have some business I would like to get sorted out first and I will have to go to London to see my parents. I hope you will allow Emma to accompany me when I go to see them?'

Only she knew the nature of the business he wanted to complete.

Two days later a note delivered to his office and marked for his personal attention took Mark to Armstrong's Farm. When he went into the cottage he found Zac Denby already there.

Mark's jaw tightened with the effort of controlling his feelings, faced as he was by the man whom he felt sure had killed Emma's father. 'Well?' he demanded coldly.

Zac looked up at him. He realised there was to be no parrying of words. 'Is thee still interested?' The question was almost casual, but Mark detected a close scrutiny from the one good eye as if Zac had been wondering how genuine he was. Was the smuggler harbouring suspicions or was this a routine check? Mark knew he would have to be wary.

'Of course,' he answered curtly.

'Still think thee can get rid of the quantity thee mentioned?'

'I wouldn't have quoted it if I couldn't.' Mark's tone poured scorn on Zac's doubt.

'Good,' rapped the smuggler. 'Thy brandy and lace will be coming on the next consignment from France on the second of March.'

Surprised that he had been given this detailed information, Mark's mind reeled under its impact. The goods were coming from France. Someone must have arranged for their despatch, maybe even been there. Edward had been to France! Could he possibly be The Fox?

'I swear thee to secrecy on this information. Divulge it to anyone and thee's a dead man.' Zac's words were cold and threatening, precisely uttered so that there could be no misunderstanding. 'I'm only telling thee this because it means a change of plan when the contraband is run ashore.'

Mark nodded and waited for Zac to go on.

'Thy order is extra to our normal quantity. I haven't the room to hide it so I want it to be delivered straight to thy warehouses in Whitby.'

'Won't that be risky?' protested Mark.

'Aye, but all smuggling carries risks. I'll arrange for thy goods to be loaded on to pack-horses and taken by a circuitous route to the Pickering–Whitby road. Then, when it comes into Whitby, it will appear as if it is a consignment coming from Pickering. How thee deals with it in Whitby is up to thee.'

'So I've got to know when I can expect it,' prompted Mark.

'This lugger will be off Baytown at seven in the evening. Give us two to three hours.'

'Right. What about the dragoons? They could be around when the pack-horses come into Whitby.'

Zac chuckled. 'They won't. I'm ganning to lay a false trail.'

Mark took precautions when he left Armstrong's Farm. Time and again he checked to make sure he was not followed. On reaching Whitby, and after stabling his horse, he was even more cautious as he made his way to Boston's office.

'We've got the break we need,' Mark informed him. 'Contraband is being run ashore on the second of March. The lugger will be in the bay off Baytown at seven in the evening.'

Boston slapped his thigh with delight. 'Got him! We've got him! Good work, Roper.' His face took on a momentary seriousness as the unlikelihood of the smugglers divulging their plans struck him. 'How did you get that information?'

Mark smiled at the doubt he detected. 'It's genuine. Because my order for contraband was big, Denby wants it to be delivered straight to my warehouses so he had to tell me when it would arrive.'

Boston grinned. 'A big order on purpose, good idea. Well, I'll have a nice reception party waiting for him.'

'Two things,' went on Mark. 'I questioned the likelihood of dragoons being about when they brought my goods into Whitby by pack-horses. Zac is going to see that you are out of the town.'

'We will be, but not where he'll think.' Boston grinned at the thought of surprising Denby.

'The other thing is, I don't want Denby taken prisoner.'

Boston stared incredulously at him. 'But this is our chance to smash the gang once and for all.'

'You can do that but I want Denby free. When your

405

victory is assured I'm banking on his having to warn The Fox. I'm hoping he'll lead me to him.'

'So you'll be with us that evening?'

'I will,' Mark confirmed, and the two men laid their plans.

It was late-afternoon when the pedlar sold the last of his wares in Baytown. His first journey of the year had been highly lucrative. He had beaten other pedlars here, to a place starved of goods throughout the winter, and it had proved successful.

'Ale and some pie before I leave,' he ordered from Nell.

'Ganning all the way, Toby?'

'Aye.'

'It'll be dark before thee gets across the moors,' Nell pointed out.

'Aye, doesn't trouble me. I can take care of myself.' He tapped the knife in his belt. 'No one's ganning to relieve me of my brass.'

When Nell returned to the kitchen, she informed Zac, 'Toby Mills is in there, says he's ganning to Pickering as soon as he's had his ale and pie.'

Zac was immediately alert. 'And Toby Mills likes his money. Fetch him through here, Sue.'

'Wait a minute, Zac. If I gan to Pickering first thing in the morning I can check that Toby has delivered the contraband, so we'll get to know before The Fox. And it'll give me a chance to see if there's been any word about Ben during the winter.'

'Good idea,' agreed Zac. He liked the thought of knowing about the arrival of the pedlar before The Fox. 'Let's see Toby.'

'Nell had better fetch him,' said Sue. 'He knows me so I'll get out of the way.'

Zac soon had Toby interested in taking contraband from Beck Farm to Pickering. The pedlar saw no reason to be taking empty panniers when they could be stuffed with goods which would bring him some extra money. Zac issued his instructions and gave him the coloured ribbons to tie on his lead pony.

Emma was surprised when the pedlar called asking for a drink before he went on his way, but then she noticed the ribbons.

She drew her mother to one side as Toby enjoyed his ale. 'The signs are there. He's from Zac to pick up contraband.'

'Good, the sooner we have rid of it all the better,' said Grace. 'Take Jay with thee.'

'Know Ben Thrower?' Emma asked as the three of them headed for Black Wood.

'Aye. Haven't seen him lately. Last time was on the Helmsley route. Know him?'

'He's called on us,' replied Emma, her hopes dashed that she might learn something of value to Sue.

There were still some remnants of daylight coming from the west when Toby left Emma and Jay, who had insisted that he remain in Black Wood until he received their signal that all was ready for him.

Emma was coming from the cow byre with a pail of milk when she saw Sue approaching in the early-morning light. After exchanging greetings, Sue informed her that she was on her way to Pickering and hoped to return in two days' time. She gave no reason for her journey until she and Emma were leaving Beck Farm together, after Grace had suggested that her daughter accompany Sue part of the way.

'Checking on the pedlar? Do be careful, Sue,' said Emma, concern for her friend etched on her face.

'I'll be all right,' laughed Sue. 'I've survived these months in the heart of the smuggling fraternity, I'll be all right in Pickering. And hopefully I might find out about Ben.'

'If ever thee's in trouble or need help, try to see or get word to Mark Roper. Thee'll find him at Roper and Sons, merchants in Whitby, offices on the west bank, or at his house in Bagdale, number twelve.' Emma went on to relate the story of her love for Mark and of his role in Whitby for Sir William Bailey, keeping to herself the theory he held about her father's death. Imparting that knowledge might put Sue in danger. 'I must swear thee to secrecy on all I have told thee,' concluded Emma.

'It's safe with me,' replied Sue. Once she might have used some of it to help Zac should the law close in on him. She had had a liking for him until she realised that Nell was his woman, and all respect for him had finally evaporated with his threat to kill John Dugdale. Though the dragoons had accepted blame, she knew now that Zac could be a ruthless murderer, and realised that she must keep a hold on her feelings, for Zac was ever watchful, even of his friends.

Sue was startled when her enquiries in Pickering later that day elicited no news of Toby Mills. She busied herself the following morning removing signs of neglect from her house, all the time finding herself having to stand firm against the memories of Ben which were all around her. She shed a few tears, especially in the silence of the night when she recalled their tender and passionate loving.

She learned nothing the next day. Ben had disappeared from the face of the earth. Where had he gone? Why? And now Toby Mills. What curse haunted these pedlars who touched contraband? But not all of them. Why only some of them? Only some . . . The words dwelt in her mind. Who? She went through them in her mind. Suddenly it struck her. They had all chosen to travel at night! So had they lost their way? The moors could be death-traps at night for the unwary. Surely there must be more to it than that. Why should all the night travellers go missing? Maybe Zac could figure an answer.

When she returned to Baytown, he was stunned to learn that Toby had not reached Pickering, that he too had disappeared.

'Zac, I've had time to think things out,' Sue concluded. 'The contraband that hasn't got through has been carried by pedlars travelling at night. Could there be something significant in that?'

Zac looked thoughtful for a moment and then nodded. 'There could be. It's something that had entered my mind. This disappearance of Toby Mills seems to confirm it.' His face took on a troubled expression. 'I blamed John Dugdale for their disappearance, but he couldn't have had anything to do with Toby. Damn The Fox for ordering me to kill an innocent man!' He spat the words with venom.

Sue's mind reeled under the impact of these words. Zac had threatened, now he had admitted the killing. She stared at him almost disbelievingly. 'But I thought the dragoons said they were to blame?'

'Aye, they have,' he replied, 'and that's convenient for me, but I killed him. I took advantage of their presence.'

Sue was horrified. She faced the man who had killed Emma's father. She had the power to turn him over to the authorities. She was witness to his admission of guilt. So was Nell. She glanced across at her but Nell was attending to a pan on the fire as if nothing had happened, as if Zac had never made his statement. Sue realised if she tried to bring him to justice they would both deny that he had ever spoken of John Dugdale's death. The realisation brought cool reasoning back to Sue. If she turned him in she would lose the one person who might help her discover what had happened to Ben, for already a plan had begun to form in her mind.

Though she was revolted by his confession, Sue put forward her idea calmly. 'Too many pedlars have gone missing for there to be any question of collusion to dispose of contraband for their own advantage. I believe something has happened to them between Beck Farm and Pickering.'

'Lost their way, strayed into a bog?' said Zac.

'One maybe, but not all of them. And it would mean

the bogs had swallowed the ponies as well. Too many. Surely some would have escaped and been found wandering on the moor.'

'So what do thee think?'

Sue shrugged her shoulders. 'Who knows? Robbers? Thieves? I'm willing to test it out. Let me, disguised as a pedlar, take a consignment to Pickering at night.'

Zac stiffened. His one eye glistened with admiration and caution. Sue's idea was admirable but it was filled with danger. 'Nay, lass, I can't let thee do it.' Objections started to her lips but he halted them by raising a hand. 'I'll do it.'

'No!' Nell's crisp reaction startled them. 'If thee goes missing, what'll happen here? We need thee. I need thee.'

Zac gave her a wry smile, appreciating her concern. 'It's probably the only way we'll find out. I'll be all right.' His voice strengthened. 'I'm going.'

Nell knew his word was final. It was no use arguing or pleading.

Zac glanced at Sue. 'Me, not thee, and that's an order.'

She looked at him defiantly. 'All right, but I'm coming with thee. I need to be there if thee finds out what happened to Ben. And I'm not taking no for an answer.' She was equally adamant in her attitude.

The momentary silence between them was charged with a clash of wills. Sue did not turn her gaze away from the one eye which for a moment gleamed hostility at her.

Zac relaxed finally. 'All right, we'll go together.'

'Good.' Tension drained from her. 'When?' She was keen to get the plans made, eager for them to solve the mystery of Ben's disappearance.

'Tomorrow night.'

'But that's when the lugger will be here with the contraband,' put in Nell.

'Aye. Everything's organised. Everyone knows what they

have to do and Pete Bray can take charge. Sue and I can take advantage of the fact that there will be no dragoons about. I've made sure rumours of a big contraband run at Staithes have reached Boston's ears. The dragoons will be well out of our way.'

Chapter Twenty-Five

Lieutenant Boston, knowing that the movement of his troop out of Whitby would be watched, did not attempt to conceal his actions until he neared Staithes. After making pretence of taking up position, he let his men filter away in three small groups on a circuitous route which would bring them to a prearranged vantage point overlooking Robin Hood's Bay.

There, with the light fading, they were joined by Mark who had hopes that before the night was out Zac would have led him to The Fox.

Boston issued last-minute instructions and reminded his men that Zac Denby must be allowed to get away and that pursuit of him would only be undertaken by Mark Roper.

The evening was still. Hardly a ripple marred the sea which seemed too lazy to lap the beach. A high, thin haze of cloud masked the sky, seeming to add a mysterious aspect to the coming night. Each member of the dragoons tried to hide his nervousness as he checked his weapons for the tenth time. Tension filled the air as they waited, anticipating that this encounter with the smugglers would be bloody. They drew confidence from the fact that they held the element of surprise; that the smugglers, expecting them to be at Staithes, would not have the advantage of a supporting force.

They waited, uneasy but full of determination. This time the smugglers would not get the better of them. But Mark would have been dismayed had he known that at that moment Zac was approaching Beck Farm.

*   *   *

'Pedlars, Ma,' announced Amy as she came into the house after checking some ewes which were nearing lambing.

'Which way?' asked Grace.

'From the coast, saw them just start down the hill.'

Grace went to the door where she was joined by Emma who had been laying the table for the evening meal.

'Late to be setting out for Pickering,' she commented.

'Aye,' agreed her mother. 'Hope they know the moors. Expect they do.'

'Not a bad night for them.'

'My God, it's Zac Denby,' whispered Amy when she recognised him.

'Thee sure?' gasped Grace, though she did not doubt her younger daughter's exceptional eyesight.

'Certain,' returned Amy.

Grace started to shake. She would be facing the man who had killed her husband. How could she do so? She felt Emma's comforting arm on hers.

'Who's with him?' she asked.

'Not sure,' said Amy. She hesitated a few moments, trying to identify the figure who walked beside Zac leading two ponies. 'Sue Thrower.' She said it almost disbelievingly.

'Can't be,' doubted Emma.

'It is.'

'What on earth is she doing with Zac Denby in pedlar's garb?' Emma was not only puzzled but alarmed. Something strange was going on. She felt her mother tremble.

'How can I face him?' Her words were hoarse, full of trepidation.

'Be strong, Ma. We don't know for certain if he did it. We'll be in danger if we accuse him.'

Grace, knowing the truth of Emma's statement, drew a deep breath, took a grip on herself and waited.

'Evening, ladies,' called Zac as he and Sue reached the gate.

'Evening, Zac Denby, and thee, Sue Thrower.' Emma spoke for them all. 'What brings thee here as pedlars?'

'We're ganning to take some goods to Pickering. But first a word if we may?'

Emma nodded. 'What is it?'

Grace stood silently by, making no move to invite them into the house.

'Thee gave the goods to Toby?'

'Aye.'

'Nothing passed between thee?'

'What does thee mean by that?' snapped Emma indignantly.

'Did he say anything which might make thee think he was not going to Pickering?'

'No. He was eager to get home. Why?'

'He never got there.'

'What?' She glanced at Sue whose shake of the head told her that her journey to Pickering had been fruitless.

Emma's genuine surprise satisfied Zac. 'Thanks, ladies, we'll be on our way. Thee needn't come, Miss Dugdale, I can get what I want.'

'Very well,' replied Emma. She looked at Sue. If only she could get a word with her to find out what was going on, but it was not possible. Puzzled, she watched them leave, hoping that Sue would be all right.

Mark stiffened. A movement where Baytown's main street ran on to the beach. He trained his spyglass. Figures moving towards the cobles close to the water's edge. He tapped Boston's arm and drew his attention towards the beach.

The lieutenant studied it for a moment and then swung his glass towards the great headland at Ravenscar. Mark followed suit and both men directed their gaze to the sea just beyond the cliff.

A few minutes passed then they saw the darker mass of a ship come into view. It swung into the bay and hove to.

The cobles were already halfway across the bay and on the beach men waited for their return. The first consignment was run ashore but Boston waited. By the time the second load had been brought from the lugger a pony-train had been assembled on the beach. Tubs were being loaded into panniers when the third consignment was nearing the sand.

'My brandy,' chuckled Mark, thinking how that very batch had been the undoing of the smugglers.

'Now,' whispered Boston.

As one, his men began to move down the slope towards the beach. They moved carefully, silently, aware that the slightest sound could betray their presence. They reached the beach and stopped, moulded against the low cliffside. Boston, tensed for action, looked around, weighing up the situation, needing to judge the moment just right.

The cobles were there, swinging round, men in the water, hauling at them, bringing them on to the sand, ready for a quick unloading and then away to the lugger again. Men were fully occupied.

'Now!' Boston's low voice reached every dragoon.

A volley of shots rang out, the suddenness of the unexpected sending alarm among the smugglers. Two men dropped. Most of them, unarmed, started to run. Others, some with cutlasses, some with knives, met the sudden onslaught of sword and rapier. Steel clashed against steel, hand against hand. Four men, trying to refloat a coble and escape were cut down. Blood flowed and stained the sea red.

Three dragoons who had been stationed nearer Baytown were on the beach, cutting off any escape. Fleeing smugglers turned, panicking, to find some means of evading capture.

Boston was in the thick of the fighting. As he pinned a man against a coble, the point of his sword at his throat, he was aware of a scuffle behind him. In a quick glance sideways he saw a man tumble beside him, his eyes wide with disbelief. He hit the side of the coble and slid into the water, not feeling the cold which closed over him.

'Thanks,' he shouted to Mark who swung round with his back to the boat, his rapier dripping blood.

'Seen Zac?' he asked.

'No.' Boston turned his attention back to the man he had at his mercy. 'Where's Zac Denby?' he demanded. He pricked the man's throat with his sword, urging an answer from him.

'He ain't here,' gurgled the man, pressing himself back against the coble.

Mark, alert for another attack, rapped, 'Where is he?'

'Don't know.' Boston gave him another slight touch with his sword. The man's eyes widened. 'Honest I don't.'

'Who's leader tonight?' hissed Boston.

'Me, Pete Bray.'

'Ah, seems as though we've captured a prize here, Mark.' Boston's eyes gleamed with triumph as he glared at Pete. 'Right, call on your men to surrender.'

Pete realised that the surprise attack had given the dragoons the upper hand; his own men could not win. He nodded. Boston eased back a little, allowing Bray to stand upright. 'Get on with it!' he rapped.

'Throw down any weapons.' Pete's voice rang clear on the night air.

As men surrendered Pete realised that they had been betrayed and only one man could have done so. The one here beside him, Mark Roper, who should have been in Whitby ready to accept the consignment of brandy which was on the pack-horses. Only he outside the community of Baytown knew of the time of arrival of the lugger. Pete's lips tightened. Hate filled his eyes as he glared at Mark. 'Thee bloody bastard! Thee betrayed us, set this up.'

Mark ignored him. He was too preoccupied with Zac's whereabouts. Where could he be? What had been so important as to take him away when a big consignment was being run ashore? Was Mark going to lose his chance of

416

finding The Fox? He needed to know where Zac was but realised that Baytown folk would draw in on themselves to protect their own. There was little chance of finding out here. Maybe his best chance would be to accompany Boston and the prisoners back to Whitby. Maybe there one of them would break down under interrogation. That is, if they knew where Zac was.

With contraband loaded, the hiding place made secure and Sue sworn to secrecy, Zac led the way on to the moors. The night was fair but dark. As they made steady progress to the moorland tops both Zac and Sue were alert for any possible clue which might help them to discover the truth about the missing pedlars.

'We may not even be on the right track,' complained Zac.

'I'm sure we are. Ben, not really knowing these moors, would take the obvious route: Beck Farm to the main track to Pickering. I think the others would do the same at night.'

Zac grunted and kept his steady pace.

When they ceased to climb, the wild moorland stretched before them. Sue shivered. It looked dark and sinister and a sense of foreboding hung over her. If it hadn't been for the prospect of finding out what had happened to Ben she would have turned back. She tried to get a grip on herself but could not throw off the uneasy feeling. Had Ben felt like this? Why hadn't he turned back and waited until daylight? She was glad she was with Zac even though she knew he was a murderer. But she had nothing to fear from him. The uneasiness which haunted her mind came from beyond him, came from out there on the moors. But what? And was it the cause of Ben's disappearance?

They had been walking almost an hour when Zac stopped. Sue sensed him stiffen.

'Something wrong?' she asked, keeping her voice to a whisper, as if any strength to it might disturb some evil spirit.

Zac inclined his head, listening. He shook his head. 'Thought I heard something.'

'What?'

'A call. Thee hear anything?'

'No.' Sue shook her head, but when they started off again her ears were alert for any sound which might fit Zac's description.

Ten minutes later, she froze. 'Zac!' her whisper carried alarm.

'What?'

'Someone called.'

'I didn't hear anything.'

'It was like a distant voice saying, "Come, come."'

'Thee's imagining it. It's the breeze,' he offered.

'There isn't one.'

Zac was startled. He hadn't noticed that the light breeze, which always seemed to haunt the moors even on the stillest of days, had vanished. He felt ill-at-ease then chided himself for being susceptible to such fears. He started off again. Sue kept close.

They had only gone a hundred yards and had topped a slight rise when they both stopped together. A light across the moor held their attention.

'A cottage?' queried Sue.

'Could be,' replied Zac.

'Do thee think Ben and the others . . .'

'Maybe we should investigate.' Throwing off his uneasiness, Zac was now alert to the possibility of finding out what had happened to the missing pedlars, but he was not prepared for the voice behind them which said, 'Ma's expecting thee.'

Startled, both swung round and gasped at the sight of the huge figure which stood on the path.

'Ma's been expecting thee.' The man gave a deep-throated chuckle as if he had enjoyed startling them and was enjoying even more creating the sense of mystery. 'Did thee not hear her call?'

Sue shot Zac a glance but his attention was riveted on the man. The hairs on her neck bristled. How had anyone known they were on the moor? Were they walking into the realms of witchcraft, of the all-seeing eye? She felt a little relief when she heard Zac speaking.

He drew on all his strength to combat the unexpected for he felt like a dwarf beside this hulk of a man. 'And who might thee be?' he demanded.

'Dick Petch. Ma's Eliza Petch, sister's Phoebe. We've been expecting thee ever since Ma sensed thee was on the moor. Sent me out to bring thee to our cottage on Dead-man's Howe.'

The name sent a shiver down Sue's spine.

'Thee'll be wanting a bed for the night.' It was more of a statement than a question.

'Supposing we don't, supposing we want to be on our way to Pickering?' said Zac, putting a little defiance into his voice for Sue's sake.

Dick guffawed. 'Thee will.' As if to confirm his statement lightning flashed and thunder rolled in the west.

Sue trembled. What witchcraft had they come to? Had Ben experienced this? Was his fate tied up with this weird family living in isolation on Deadman's Howe? The thought of him gave her strength. If they were on the verge of finding out what had happened to him, she wanted to go on.

'I think we'd better find shelter, Zac. If that storm comes it'll be hell on these moors.'

He deduced her thoughts from the strength she had put in her voice. He was glad for he too felt the mystery of the missing pedlars could be held on Deadman's Howe.

'Then follow me,' said Dick.

He led the way unerringly across the moor. His famili-arity was uncanny, especially when there was bog on either side.

As they neared the cottage the door opened, sending a pool of light along the path, and silhouetting the tall shapely figure of a young woman in the doorway.

419

'Welcome,' she called loudly, 'welcome to Deadman's Howe. Especially to the young lady.' There was a hint of mystery in the low thin cackle which cut through the still air.

Sue shivered. How had this person known she was a woman when she was disguised as a man? There was something uncanny about the whole business.

She felt even more uneasy when they went into the house and she saw the old crone sat in a chair to one side of the fireplace.

'Welcome to Eliza Petch's humble home,' she croaked, the words coming from deep in her throat. 'Thee's met my son Dick and this is my daughter Phoebe. We're all here to serve thee before thee continues thy journey.' All the time she was rubbing her long bony fingers together as if anticipating with great delight some future pleasure of which they were a part. 'Dick taking care of the ponies?' She glanced at Phoebe.

'Yes, Ma.'

'Good, good,' Eliza chuckled. 'Show them the room, Phoebe.'

'Thee have to share the bed,' she said as she held the door open for Sue and Zac. She gave a little knowing smile. 'I'll get thee something to eat.'

As she closed the door, Sue looked at Zac with worried eyes touched with fear. 'It's weird, almost as if they were expecting us. Witches?'

'Aye, more than like,' he whispered. 'Don't eat or drink anything. The pedlars disappeared here, I feel it in my bones.'

'What are we going to do?' asked Sue, her mind confused.

'We'll have to take it as it comes. Be alert and take thy lead from me. Thee's armed?'

Sue's face clouded with confusion. 'My knife's in a bag on one of the ponies.'

'I told thee to wear it in thy belt,' snapped Zac with exasperation.

'I didn't think I'd need it,' replied a repentant Sue. 'I'll get it.' With that she was gone before he could stop her.

She was across the room without a glance at Eliza and out into the darkness. She paused for a moment, orientating herself while she recalled that Dick had taken the ponies to the left. She moved down the path to the gate and followed the low wall, aware of the darker mass of a building ahead. By the time she reached it she had become more accustomed to the dark. She could hear the scraping sound of horses' hooves, and moving alongside the building soon found a door. She pulled it open and by the light of a lantern hanging from a beam gained the impression that Dick was examining a pannier strapped to one of their ponies.

His gleeful smile vanished as he looked up and saw Sue.

She kept a grip on her reactions, appearing not to notice what he was doing, and said, 'Forgotten a bag.' With hesitation she moved to her pony and pulled a small bag from the pannier.

Dick grunted, his face darkening with annoyance at being disturbed. His eyes narrowed. He made no move towards her but his eyes watched her every movement.

Feeling his eyes on her sent a shiver down her spine as she turned to leave the stable. She almost stopped in her tracks and it was only with the utmost willpower that she kept moving for there in one of the stalls was Ben's favourite Galloway. She would have known the markings anywhere.

She felt herself trembling, her legs threatening to collapse under her. She forced enough strength into them to carry her outside. She pushed the door closed and breathed deeply. She dared not stop, must get back to Zac. The whole weight of the discovery seemed to be trying to prevent her from reaching the cottage.

She burst through the door, almost oblivious to Phoebe setting the table and Eliza rocking in her chair.

Zac, sitting on the bed, awaiting her return, jumped to

his feet when he saw the expression on her face as she closed the bedroom door behind her.

'What is it?' he asked, his eye trying to put meaning to her agitated expression.

'Ben was here. One of his Galloways is in the stable.'

'Thee sure?' His hands gripped her arms, trying to calm her.

'Certain.' Her eyes, wild with the discovery, held no doubt. Tears welled in them at the thought that it was unlikely she would ever see Ben alive again. These evil people must have murdered him and probably the other pedlars lured here as they had been tonight. Dick knew what they were carrying. He would be back in the cottage at any moment, no doubt intending to kill them, and get rid of their bodies in the bog.

The shock generated by her wild thoughts was replaced by cold calculation. She wanted vengeance on this household.

'Thee all right?' Zac asked, concerned at the sudden change in her.

Her lips tightened. 'Aye. I want revenge for Ben.' The firmness in her voice and the steady look in her eyes convinced him. She felt in her bag, drew out a knife and stuck it in her belt, making sure that the folds of her jerkin hid it from sight.

She had only just done so when the bedroom door burst open and in its place stood Dick, filling the room with menace. His intentions were obvious as he stepped forward, his eyes fixed on Zac.

Drawing his knife, Zac backed away, encouraging Dick to come forward. He circled to his left, knowing that he must not let himself come within reach of this huge man. Dick struck out with a blow which would have felled Zac had he not ducked under it. In the same movement he slashed at Dick, drawing blood from a long gash in the arm. It raised him to an overpowering fury.

A deep roar came from his chest. He moved fast for such

a big man and this time the blow sent Zac crashing against a wall. The breath was driven from his body. He tried to move but Dick was on him with a cry of triumph. A huge hand closed round Zac's throat, pressing him hard against the wall, choking the life out of him.

Zac struggled. He found strength to drive his right hand upwards. The knife struck; he knew not where but felt the grip relax. He dragged the hand away from his throat and slid away from Dick. He saw the big man staggering, holding his side, trying to swing round at Sue who was driving her knife time and again into his side. His fist came up but before it had time to wreak havoc, Zac's knife was at his throat, making sure that he would never see another day.

As Dick collapsed, Zac, breathing deeply, trying to draw back the strength which had nearly been choked from his body, was unaware that Phoebe was in the doorway, a kitchen knife in her hand. She lunged forward. Sue's scream was too late. The knife plunged deep into Zac's stomach. He gasped, doubled up and fell to his knees. Wild triumph blazed in Phoebe's eyes as she prepared to inflict the final blow. But triumph turned to disbelief as Sue buried her knife to the hilt in Phoebe's side. She pitched to the floor and lay still.

Sue stared at the lifeless form, almost in disbelief at what she had done when driven to it. She shook herself out of her momentary stupor when she heard Zac groan. In an instant she was on her knees beside him.

'Zac, what can I do?' she cried desperately.

'Help me up,' he spluttered.

As she took his weight he felt an excruciating pain shoot through his body. He knew he was dying but had one more thing to do. 'Get me to the doorway.'

He propped himself against the doorpost. They both stared at Eliza. Her back was to them. She was still rocking. A triumphant chuckle rose from her throat and they heard her words coming as a whisper: 'Finish them off, Dick, finish them off. Then pitch 'em in t' bog with the others.'

Sue stared at Zac. He patted her arm comfortingly and whispered, 'Get the Galloway.' Sue hesitated, looking at him with concern. 'Go on,' he urged. 'Don't bother about me.'

Sue crossed the room and slipped outside. She hurried to the stable, strangely aware of the thought that had entered her head – there had been no more thunder and lightning since the moment when Dick had lured them to the cottage. As she led the horse from the building she became aware that the whole atmosphere had suddenly changed. It was as if an evil cloak had been lifted. There was a faint breeze which had not been there before. The haze in the sky had vanished and, though there was no moon, a scattering of stars bathed the night with a gentle light.

Sue entered the cottage. Zac lay on the floor beside the chair in which the old woman lolled, her throat slit from ear to ear. Sue knew precisely the moment she had died.

'Zac.' She knelt beside him, cradling his head.

He gave a half smile as if enjoying the feel of her hands. 'Ben has been revenged. The evil has gone.'

'Let me get thee to the Gall.' She started to try to raise him.

'No, Sue, I'm done. Thee get . . .' He coughed, the rasping hurting his body. His face creased with agony.

Though she knew it was no good she had to make the effort of persuasion. 'Thee can do it.'

He gave a little shake of his head. 'No. I wouldn't even reach the door.' His glazed eyes stared at Sue as if he wanted to impress something on her. 'Give my . . .' His words started to come in gasps '. . . love to . . . Nell. It was always her.' He coughed then swallowed hard. 'I regret . . . killing Dugdale . . . tell them.'

'I promise.' The words caught in her throat. Tears came to her eyes. This man may have been a murderer, a conniving ruthless smuggler, but now he was filled with genuine remorse.

He grasped Sue's arm trying to find strength. 'Get . . . get word . . . Fox.'

'Fox? Thee wants me to get word to The Fox?'

Zac nodded. 'Tell him . . . what's happened.'

'I don't know him. Who is he?'

Zac stared at her as if he did not comprehend.

'Who is he?' she pressed firmly.

Zac blinked. He had heard.

'Who is The Fox?' she asked gently, encouraging the answer from him.

'Ed . . . Edward.'

She stared at him. He seemed to be slipping away. She needed another name. 'Who?'

'Beau . . .' The word was hardly a whisper. She leaned closer, trying to catch the intonation. 'Beaumont.' The word faded on the dying lips and Zac was gone.

Chapter Twenty-Six

Sue set her horse for Beck Farm. Emma must be told as soon as possible.

The events at the cottage on Deadman's Howe crowded her mind. Her dearest Ben dead, somewhere in that detestable bog, murdered for a few smuggled goods.

Oh, Ben, why did thee get involved with the smugglers? her heart cried out. Money. Because thee wanted a better life for me. But I was happy, Ben, I was happy as we were. I wanted nothing more than thee. She let the tears flow. Thee'll still be in my heart and we'll still be close in our house in Pickering.

'Someone's coming.' Amy glanced up from the game of merrels she was playing with Jay.

Grace and Emma looked queryingly at each other. They had heard nothing but they did not doubt Amy's acute hearing. Who could it be at this time of night?

'A horse,' she added.

Emma inclined her ear, trying to catch the sound. Then into the silence of the room, marked only by the crackling of the fire in the grate, came the drumming of hooves pounding out their message of urgency.

Grace, followed by her family, went to the door. In the pale wash from the moonlit sky they saw the rider haul the animal to a halt, swing to the ground and stagger to them.

Emma rushed forward. 'Sue!' she cried, catching hold of her. 'What on earth are thee doing here?'

As Sue tried to gather her breath they ushered her into the house, anxious to know what had brought her back alone, dishevelled, her face drawn as if she had witnessed the devils of hell.

She flopped wearily on to a chair. 'Zac's dead,' she gulped.

'What? Zac dead?' gasped Emma. He had always seemed indestructible.

'Thank God for that. He had it coming to him,' snapped Grace. 'Quick, some brandy for Sue.' She saw the shock, that had been held back by Sue's urgent ride, starting to take effect.

Amy took a bottle from a cupboard, poured a measure and passed the glass to Sue. She drank and shuddered as the liquid bit into her throat and jolted her mind.

'What happened?' urged Emma.

Amy recharged the glass and Sue, between sips, told them what had happened at Deadman's Howe. She trembled as she relived the moments of discovery and murder, her vivid words charging the atmosphere with witchcraft and brutal killing.

'So thee knows what happened to Ben?' said Emma sadly. 'I'm so sorry.'

'I dread to think of him in that horrible place.' Sue shuddered. She almost broke down but caught the tremor in her own voice, drew on an inner strength and went on, 'Before Zac died he asked me to get a message to The Fox.'

'The Fox! Thee knows who it is?' There was eagerness in Emma's voice. In a moment she would have the information Mark wanted. She could inform him and he could have the notorious head of the smugglers, the man who had ordered her father's death, brought to justice.

Sue nodded. 'Edward Beaumont.'

Emma's eagerness was shattered. Grace and Amy exchanged shocked glances, each realising how devastating this information must be to Emma. Jay moved closer to his sister as if to offer support. She stared disbelievingly at Sue. This couldn't be true. Not Meg's husband. The information bewildered her. Lies, all lies! But Sue's tone was serious and spoke of the truth. Besides, Zac would not lie when, on the point of death, he needed to get information to The Fox. Emma stiffened herself against the dilemma in which she found herself.

To reveal The Fox's identity would break up her cousin's marriage, yet Emma burned with revenge against the man who had needlessly ordered her father's death. Zac had done the actual killing but Edward had been the instigator. Left free he could condemn others whom he thought against him, innocent folk, given no chance of redress. His role must be exposed. She could do nothing but condemn him. As much as she wanted to spare Meg, she hadn't the right to ask Sue to withhold the information.

Emma had a sudden overwhelming desire to be with Meg, to warn her and ease the shock.

'Ma, I've got to go to Meg,' she cried passionately.

Grace, seeing how the shock had affected her daughter, nodded sympathetically. 'Get the horse ready, Jay, she must go straight away.'

He lit a lantern and ran to the stable while Emma prepared for the ride.

'Be careful, both of thee, The Fox could be dangerous,' warned Grace as the two friends hurried to their horses. Dazed by shock, she was still unable to grasp that The Fox was Beaumont, her niece's husband.

The winding ribbon of the track to Whitby was clear in the soft light from a moonlit sky. A mist, held low in the Esk valley, twisted with the river as if seeking direction.

The riders pulled to a halt close by and involuntarily shivered in the thin clinging dampness. The mist wreathed and swirled, revealing the moon one moment and blotting it out the next.

'Sue, ride into Whitby and tell Mark. I'll go to Thorpe Hall. I must be with Meg, I must warn her of what might happen.'

Emma turned her horse and galloped off into the mist,

expecting Mark to be on his way before she reached the hall.

Sue rode quickly to Whitby. It was imperative to reach Mark without delay, but when she found that he was not at home, and neither the maid nor the housekeeper knew where he was, she was desperate. Every wasted minute might put Emma in a more perilous position. To search might be futile. Maybe Boston would be easier to find. Going into town, she was aware of commotion and soon learned that the dragoons had been active that evening in smashing the smuggling ring in Baytown and that prisoners were being interrogated at Boston's office.

She forced her way through the throng of people outside the building, buzzing with speculation and rumour. Sue stood no nonsense from the dragoon on duty at the door when he tried to stop her. She burst into the packed room where Mark and Boston were trying to find out the where-abouts of Zac from Pete Bray, standing between two armed guards. Anger at the unexpected intrusion darkened Boston's face. He had ordered that no one be admitted.

'Zac Denby's dead,' announced Sue, 'and before he died he asked me to get a message to The Fox.'

A stunned silence settled on the room and all eyes turned to her. Tension mounted as everyone waited for a name.

Suddenly it was broken by a vicious snarl from Pete. 'Thee damned traitor! Thee bloody bitch! Keep thy bloody mouth shut!'

'Get him out of here,' snapped Boston.

As the two guards hustled the prisoner away, Bray hurled abuse and threats at Sue.

Boston turned to her and said quietly. 'Now, who is The Fox?'

'Edward Beaumont.' She leaned wearily against the desk and glanced at Mark. 'Emma knows and has gone to Thorpe Hall to be with Meg.'

Her voice trailed away and she collapsed from complete

exhaustion and emotional fatigue as gasps of disbelief echoed round the room.

Realising the implication of her words, Mark was filled with alarm. 'Oh, no! Doesn't she know the danger she'll be in if she reveals what she knows?' He sprang to the door and was out of the office quickly, pushing his way through the crowd.

'Sergeant, take charge and look after her,' yelled Boston, and left sharp on his heels.

'Come, my love, a walk in the garden.'

Edward's voice was too smooth for Meg's liking. Of late she had come to know that this mood inevitably heralded a bid to frighten her. He seemed to derive pleasure from it, demanding it as once he had found pleasure in demanding her body.

'It's late, Edward.'

'Not too late for a peaceful stroll.'

'But it's dark.'

'No, it's a beautiful moonlit night. You'll like the atmosphere of the garden. Come, my dear.'

Meg knew there was no refusing him. Besides, better to go and get it over with.

Reluctantly she threw a shawl round her shoulders, but when they stepped outside she had to admit that it was a beautiful night. The thin haze of earlier had gone, leaving the heavens adorned with pin-pricks of light. She hoped they would just stroll on the lawn in front of the house but knew in her heart that Edward would make for the maze of hedges.

She shivered as they approached the first opening. They passed from one small open lawn, surrounded by high hedges, to another, moving through patterns of light and shadow in which the unknown seemed to be lurking menacingly. Meg shivered and drew her shawl closer around her as if seeking protection. The life-size statues standing in corners or resting in alcoves cut in the hedges, always startled her, even in daylight. Now, in the silver light from the moon, they seemed to carry a sinister aura, casting eerie shadows over the grass and putting this whole maze of paths and hedges under a strange spell.

'Let's go back, Edward,' she said with a tremor in her voice.

'Not yet, my dear,' he replied, a hint of amusement in his attitude, as if relishing her nervousness. 'We must go and look at the statue of the boar and I'll tell you its story.'

'Thee's told me before. It's horrid and I don't like it.' She shivered at the recollection.

'I enjoy it.' His strange laugh revealed the pleasure he found in frightening her. 'Come.' He took her arm so that she could not escape, even if she wanted to try to find her way through the maze back to the house.

They had only gone a few steps when the sound of a galloping horse drew their attention.

'Who can that be?' snapped Edward, irritated at being denied his morbid pleasure.

He turned and, still keeping his grip on her arm while twisting his way through the maze of hedges, led her unerringly to the nearest opening on to the main pathway to the house.

He stopped in the shadow of the hedge and waited for the rider. The horse thundered nearer. When it was almost upon them he stepped out, waving his arms and yelling, 'Hold on there! Hold!' He drew the last word out in command.

Frightened by the sudden apparition, the horse pulled up sharply and reared, stabbing at the air with its forelegs, almost unseating its rider.

'Fool!' the rider snapped, bringing the animal under control and soothing it with a quick, gentle word.

'Ah, a female,' he cried with surprise. 'Who rides alone this night?'

Her hood fell back.

'Emma!' gasped Meg. 'What brings thee here at this time?'

As her eyes swept from Meg to Edward, Emma's expression changed from pity to contempt. She swung from the saddle.

'*He* did.' Her voice was terse and her look towards Edward full of loathing.

Meg was at a loss to understand Emma. She had never seen her like this before.

'What do thee mean?'

'He ordered the death of my father.'

Meg looked bewildered. What was her cousin saying? Had she taken leave of her senses? 'I don't understand.' She glanced at Edward. 'What does she mean?' She looked back to Emma, wanting an explanation.

Edward's mind was coolly assessing the situation. What had brought Emma here with this accusation? What did she know? He laughed. 'What on earth are you talking about, Emma?' His voice was filled with contempt. 'Are you out of your mind? The dragoons admitted to killing your father.'

'They were wrong and thee knows it,' she lashed. 'Zac Denby shot my father on thy orders.'

'Emma, please,' put in Meg, her eyes begging her cousin to stop making such wild statements and accusations.

Emma ignored her and went on, 'Zac's dead, killed trying to solve the mystery of the missing pedlars. He asked the person he was with to get a message delivered to The Fox – and named thee, Edward.'

His eyes narrowed.

'The Fox, head of the smugglers!' Meg stared at her husband in disbelief. Her mind was floundering, trying to grasp the significance of this. 'Edward, say it isn't true?'

'But it is, Meg,' insisted Emma.

'You'd destroy your cousin's marriage and her happiness?' stated Edward coldly.

'Not me. *Thee's* done that.'

Meg gazed at her husband and did not need him to voice the truth; it was there in the malevolent look in his eyes. The implications were terrifying. She stared at him with horror. The man she loved, the man whose child she carried, was the notorious Fox, the person who had condemned her uncle to death. The garden spun before her, hedges whirled faster and faster, statues reared up, moving closer and closer, grinning, laughing louder and louder until it seemed her head would burst. 'Edward!' Her cry faded. Everything swam before her in an enveloping mist as she fell to the ground.

'Meg!' Emma's anguished cry rang sharply. She dropped on one knee beside her cousin, hoping it was nothing more than a faint.

With her thoughts only on Meg she was unaware of Edward's movement until she felt firm hands grip her by the shoulders. The fingers dug into her flesh, the pain sending warning signals. She had been careless in taking her attention from him. She tried to twist away but the grip tightened.

He dragged her upright and jerked her round to face him. She recoiled. Even in the moonlight she could see the madness in his eyes. 'You bitch, you'll not ruin everything.'

She glared at him defiantly. 'Killing me will do thee no good, there are others who know.'

'I'll deal with them.' His eyes blazed with the belief that he was invincible. His hands came towards her throat but Emma seized her moment. She pushed at his chest and, as Edward staggered backwards, took her chance to escape into the maze of paths. She must get away from him. Surely Mark must be coming. Sue must have seen him by now.

The chase became one of stealth and cunning. The moonlight played tricks as Emma moved quietly through the maze of paths, ears attuned to Edward's movements. Her heart was pounding so hard she felt sure he must hear it. She kept to the shadows, her attention directed ahead for Edward's appearance, or behind in case he should be there.

More than once the life-sized statues sent shivers of terror coursing through her veins as in her mind they momentarily took on the appearance of her pursuer, blocking her path to freedom. She ran fearfully to escape the grasping hands she imagined reaching out for her. Edward's deranged laughter shattered the silence as if he knew he would eventually win this game which had death as its prize.

Where was Mark? Would he never turn up? What if Sue had been unable to find him? Or what if she had happened on an accident and was now lying dead in some ditch? Her mind weaved through crazy suppositions while she tried to bring her reasoning under control. She must stay calm, must outwit Edward. Help must come soon.

How long she held her freedom she never knew. It seemed eternity. The tension was exhausting. She felt weary and shrank into a corner. She heard breathing just the other side of the hedge. Panic gripped her. Then she heard the sound of galloping horses. Mark! If only she could keep away from Edward a little longer. She slipped out of her corner quietly. The pounding of hooves drew nearer.

She heard a shout and recognised the voice as Edward's father's. He must have been drawn from the house by the horses. 'Edward where are you? Meg's hurt. Edward!'

A small measure of relief touched her. Meg had been found.

The noise from the horses was close. They stopped. She heard voices.

'Mark! Mark!' she yelled.

'Emma!'

Relief swept over her. Mark was here.

She kept shouting, risking the appearance of Edward for the safety of Mark's arms. Then he was there, his arms enfolding her, holding her tight. 'My love,' he whispered. She felt safe. Edward could not harm her now.

'Thank goodness Sue found thee. How is she?'

'The shock has taken its toll, but she'll be well enough

434

to go home in a few days.' He glanced around. 'Where's Edward?'

'Somewhere in here. He was trying to kill me.'

'Let's get back to Boston, he's with Meg.'

'Is she all right?'

'Yes, and Mr Beaumont's with her.'

They made their way back, getting on to two false paths before they found the correct one.

On seeing her cousin, Emma rushed forward and hugged her. 'Is thee all right?' She stepped back, her eyes searching, trying to read Meg's feelings.

Meg sensed the anguish in Emma and patted her comfortingly on the shoulder. 'Yes, but what about thee? Did Edward harm thee?'

Emma shook her head. 'No.'

'Thank goodness,' sighed Meg. She seemed to draw strength from that knowledge and looked at her cousin steadfastly. 'Don't worry that thee were the one to tell me. It would all have had to come out eventually. Lieutenant Boston has told us everything.'

Cornelius Beaumont shook his head slowly, the truth barely penetrating the shock. 'I can't believe it,' he muttered half to himself. 'Edward, how could you?'

Meg's haunted eyes searched the moonlit shadows. 'Where is he now?' she asked with frightened concern.

'We must find him, Lieutenant,' said Mark. 'Mr Beaumont, please take the ladies inside. We'll search . . .'

His words were halted by a movement along the hedge close to the horses. A figure moved swiftly into the open, grabbed a horse's reins and swung into the saddle, turning the animal at the same time.

Mark spun round, raising his pistol.

'He's mine!' yelled Boston.

'Don't!' shouted Cornelius and flung himself at the lieutenant, but he was too late.

Boston fired and Edward jerked in the saddle, lost his hold and fell to the ground.

'Oh, no!' The cry of anguish burst from Meg.

Cornelius stepped forward and looked down at his dying son. Edward's eyes flickered open.

'Why Edward, why did you do it?'

He stared wonderingly at the tears streaming down his father's cheeks. 'For money. You always kept it from me.' His voice was hoarse. His gaze moved to Meg, on her knees beside him. Her fair hair shone in the moonlight and her eyes held a love which would not be quenched. 'Forgive me, Meg, I didn't deserve you.'

As she leaned forward she knew he could not feel her kiss on his cheek. She still loved him for his debonair charm, his handsome face, and reckless attitude which ran against convention, but in the cold light of a new day would she be able to forgive him for what he had done?

Sadness filled her heart at the thought of the corrupt side to his character which had led him to a life of ruthless crime.

She glanced up at the man who had killed her husband. She wanted to condemn him but knew he had just been doing his duty. He met her cold gaze, read her feelings and turned away, hoping that with his mission completed he could leave this Godforsaken north country and return south.

Meg felt a consoling arm come round her shoulders as Cornelius helped her to her feet. She saw the pain on his face and wanted to comfort him. Remembering his kindness and feeling it in his touch, she knew that the future for her and her child was still at Thorpe Hall when he said gently, 'Come, let us go home.'

Emma watched them, thankful that Meg was not alone. Still wanting to be near her cousin, to help her in this devastating hour, she touched her arm.

Meg turned understanding eyes on her and said, 'No, Emma. Go with Mark. I'll be all right. I must be here with Cornelius. Thorpe Hall is my home and the home of my child.' Her gaze turned to the garden of hedges and paths.

'Those will be torn out,' she said venomously. 'The statues smashed, the whole area flattened. Maybe then the bad memories will vanish for ever.' She looked back at Emma, came to her and hugged her. 'Be happy with Mark. Visit me soon.'

'I will,' whispered Emma. As sorry as she felt for her cousin, she was satisfied that her father's murder had been avenged with the death of The Fox. There would be no trial, her father's good name would not be muddied in public, and for that she was thankful.

As Meg walked towards the hall with Cornelius, Emma turned back to Mark. 'Oh, Mark, I'm so sorry that I ever doubted thee.' Her eyes pleaded forgiveness for almost destroying the love which had brought them together.

He took her in his arms. 'There's nothing to forgive, my love.' His voice was soft and gentle. 'The bad memories will fade, leaving the good times remembered. Our love will endure. Come, I'll take you home.'

A Distant Harbour
Jessica Blair

When the boats came in . . .

After a shipwreck robs Captain David Fernley of his wife, he can see no future for himself in Whitby, the whaling port where he has made, and lost, his fortune. But whaling is the only life he knows. Determined to change his bad luck, he starts anew in London, where he is offered command of the *Hind*. And where he meets Lydia, a woman who can understand the call of the sea.

Thus begin his voyages, which will take him to the Arctic, through treacherous icefields, to America and the fatal calms of the Pacific. But these adventures are as nothing compared to events in Nova Scotia and New Bedford – in which distant harbour David finds the one danger he'd long since forgotten . . .

Acclaim for Jessica Blair's *The Red Shawl*:
'A brilliantly researched book about Whitby, whaling and the havoc one woman could wreak on those touched by her ruthless ambition'   Elizabeth Elgin

ISBN 0 00 647912 X

Other paperback titles by HarperCollins include: